W9-ALJ-101

THE COURT DANCER

THE COURT DANCER

KYUNG-SOOK SHIN

Translated by Anton Hur

PEGASUS BOOKS
NEW YORK LONDON

THE COURT DANCER

Pegasus Books Ltd.
148 W. 37th Street, 13th Floor
New York, NY 10018

First Pegasus Books edition August 2018

Interior design by Maria Fernandez

Library of Congress Cataloging-in-Publication Data is available.

ISBN: 978-1-68177-787-0

10 9 8 7 6 5 4 3 2 1

Printed in the United States of America
Distributed by W. W. Norton & Company

PART ONE

1
Two People

It took four whole days to reach the harbor.

The winding mountain road led to a new highway covered with dust, which carried them to a gravel path that overlooked a river dotted with ships. They passed the occasional rice paddy where rows of sprouts swayed in the breeze. They passed sumac trees, cherry trees, and zelkova trees, and marigolds, irises, dandelions, and guelder roses. They came upon a wild peony tree, which made them linger for a while. She captured every view outside her palanquin's window by heart, thinking that she might never see such sights again.

Then, for the first time in her life, she took in the endless spread of the ash-colored tideland.

There wasn't a hint of a cloud in the sky and the wind had quieted down. Casting her gaze farther, she could just make out the shapes of islands floating on the blue sea as in a dream, seemingly oblivious to the precarious status of the Joseon Dynasty. Ships carrying kindling and other cargo undulated with the waves as if being tugged to and from the shore. The smell rising from the stockfish yard permeated the entire harbor. Freshly caught fish were laid out on boards. A straw-shoe seller hurried by, carrying a rack full of wares on his back. Early summer sunlight, untouched by heat, shone upon the busy people going about their livelihoods.

Her companion was a diplomat who was used to spending two months of the year on a ship, but she had been a dancer in the royal court and was about to board a boat for the first time.

The companion, a tall Frenchman, his pale face covered in a mustache, wore a short vest and a pair of wide, loose trousers that came down to his ankles under a traveling coat fastened with a belt. The woman, a Korean who held a hat embroidered with roses and a coat to wear later when the wind blew, had on a light blue dress that rustled like lapping waves. They both caught the eye. An old man with a long pipe in his mouth, the man selling clogs, the loitering youth, not to mention the dusty children at play, and even foreigners—like the Chinese who had come on their rafts to sell their tea and kindling, or the Japanese who were selling rice at the docks—stared at the two as if a door had opened into a strange world, and they were looking in.

Especially at the woman.

Her thick, lustrous black hair was combed and arranged into piles of ebony atop her head, her eyes like dark indigo marbles set in her smooth-complexioned face. It was inevitable that she would stand out, as Western hairstyles were still a rare sight.

Her light blue dress flowed down from her shoulders past her waist to her ankles in the shape of an S. She was clearly distinct from the women by the docks in their linen tunics. Each step she took made the gawkers approach from behind and retreat before her. They looked at her as if thinking, *Is she a foreign woman? Ah, a Korean one.* Their curious gazes lingered on her face, then moved to Victor's arrogant nose and white skin, and to his brown curls. Some couldn't take their eyes away from the brilliant white lace framing the woman's décolletage. They kept at a distance as if afraid to tread on her hem, but their looks were frosted with suspicion. *Why is a Korean woman going about in Western clothes?* Some, disapproving, openly frowned at her.

Her mystique wasn't merely due to her exotic clothes. Nor was the reason she caught the eye, despite being among countless other women, because of the dazzling nape of her neck or the depth of her gaze. But her bared nape truly was pleasing when she lowered her head, resolute when she stood tall and centered, and magnetic when softly bending and twisting, drawing the touch of the hand.

And how sparkling her eyes were underneath her perfectly symmetrical eyebrows. Her eyes seemed ready to sympathize with the most heartbreaking of sights and were as dark as the undiscovered ocean deep. Her skin from below her ear to her cheek was pink, which made her seem shy, but the straight and narrow nose between her eyes helped overcome that impression by giving her face an air of intelligence. It was a striking combination. Around her lips, which were neither thin nor plump, were soft, white hairs, finer than a hint of sprouts in spring, a mouth so lovely that no amount of silliness could make her anything less than embraceable. And yet that loveliness was not the only reason she exuded charm. It flowed from how she maintained the character of her neat and measured walk, conveying a sense of confidence despite the crush of attention. She made no sign of acknowledging the people's leers and stares. Her walk was clearly distinct from the walk of normal Korean women, who went about in a slight bow with their faces peeking out from the long coats modestly covering their heads. The woman's walk never wavered in its perfect balance, even for a moment. She didn't bother with such conceits as pretending to stare out at the ocean to avoid the gazes that were full of suspicion. Her shoulders were spread wide, and the way in which she advanced gave a sense of her being strong enough to walk through any situation that met her way. The provocative quality of this walk was softened by the depths of her gaze, the beauty of the nape of her neck, and the loveliness that flowed from her face.

If anything, her steady poise in the face of their scrutiny made them sigh and turn away toward the ocean.

This lovely woman taking in the view was not aware that only ten years ago, before the signing of the Jaemulpo Treaty, the harbor surrounded by low-lying hills had been nothing more than a quiet village of ten or so thatched-roof houses. As is often the case in life, change came only when forced. The tiny fishing village, surrounded by water on almost every side, changed rapidly after the signing of the treaty. A Japanese concession was established, followed by that of China and other nations, with their businesses popping up everywhere in the once sleepy environs. Soon, one out of every ten persons in Jaemulpo were either Japanese or Chinese. And at this point in time, no one knew for sure, yet, whether they would breathe life or sadness into this small seaside town.

∞

She thought to herself that it was good weather to set sail in but quickly dismissed the thought. A district official, tasked by the Board for Diplomacy and Trade's Cho Byungsik with seeing off Victor, had greeted them with the advice that it was unlucky to say, "good weather for sailing" when about to board a ship. Commenting on good weather foreshadowed storms in the voyage ahead. Among the people seeing them off were harbor officials and French missionaries. There were also French nuns who had settled in Korea.

There wasn't a single tall building or large ship in sight. The harbor was an international port but looked no different from any local pier. The waves near the shore were as calm as those farther out. Among the low roofs were the occasional white, European-style habitations. The eaves of the thatched-roof houses seemed to overlap in the absence of tall buildings. Sunlight seeped between them. The woman, who had once danced for the King and embroidered tortoise patterns in the palace, was now soaking herself in the warm light of the harbor. The eaves of the palace buildings had been high and wide, almost touching each other, allowing only shade underneath. The journey to the harbor had been a constant meeting of and parting from things she had never before seen, land never before stepped on, and people never before met.

Where was it that he'd said those words?

The day they left the capital, the company had spent a night at an inn in the country. The inn, which was surrounded by a driftwood fence, had twelve ponies. The ponies puffed, their nostrils quivering, as if impatient to run the fields, but they too were enclosed by the fence. When darkness fell, the cries of the mountain creatures carried into the windowless rooms.

Sometimes a kind word can encapsulate love like a seed buried in the soil.

In that mountain inn, the former palace dancer Yi Jin heard the French legate Victor call out to her in Korean, "My angel." She was more surprised by his unaccented pronunciation than by his calling her an angel. Victor practiced his Korean when he could, but there had always been something missing in it, his words scattering in the air.

Crossing the ocean to his country meant living with a people who spoke an utterly different language. Perhaps he had sensed her hidden anxiety. It was unmistakable that Victor had called her an angel, for the first time in perfect Korean, at this traveler's inn nestled in the mountains of her own country.

The Korean words flowing smoothly from his lips made her experience a moment when language changed her very emotions. Victor, who still found it difficult to pronounce her name, had made her placid heart tremble. She was flooded with a longing that felt as if her feet were dipped in warm water, a feeling that washed away the fatigue of being shaken all day in a palanquin. That older feeling of needing to keep her distance, a feeling she had felt since the day she met Victor and persisted over his efforts to be closer to her, disappeared in that single moment.

She let her black hair fall down the nape of her neck and held out her hairbrush.

—*Peignez-moi.*

Victor's eyes grew wide.

He had yearned to brush her hair. The first thing he had gifted her after her engagement ring was a hairbrush he had brought from his country. Unfortunately for him, Jin did not like other people touching her hair, apart from Dowager Consort Cheolin when Jin was a child at court, or Lady Suh. Even as the other young court ladies would chatter and laugh as they combed each other's hair, artfully knotting the two braids and pinning them up with a violet ribbon, Jin would sit alone at a distance, her fingers struggling to re-create the weeping-willow style. And later, whenever she let down her hair to brush it, she would ignore Victor as he passed her an imploring look. But here she was now, her hair down and her hand offering him her hairbrush, asking him in his own language to brush her hair for her.

Victor took the brush and sat behind her. Never having imagined she would ask him to brush her hair, he took a moment to bury his face in the lustrous blackness of it. A smile was about to break through his face. It was the same expression Jin made whenever Victor awkwardly pronounced her name, Yi Jin. Victor began brushing her hair, and in the middle of it, he put his face next to hers and said, "*Peignez-moi?*" in a playful imitation of her accent earlier.

Jin's hair swirled like eddying waves as she turned to face Victor. The brush still in Victor's hand, she held his smiling face in her hands and brought her lips to his. His beard touched her heated cheek. She softly prodded his hand. He dropped the brush on the floor. They heard the horse that Victor had ridden all day exhale outside. They had rented three horses from the city along with the palanquin. Two of these carried their baggage, costing a hundred *nyang* for every twenty *li*. One of the three horses sported a wound on its abdomen. It probably had its oats with the ponies kept at the inn and was now fast asleep. Listening to the burbling sound the horses made in their slumber, Jin undid the buttons on the shirt Victor wore. His revealed chest was flushed red.

She had him lie on his stomach.

Her fingers entered the thicket of hair on the back of his head and grasped it gently. She pressed her fingers down on his scalp. Her hands followed the contours of his body from his neck down his spine. Every spot where her fingers touched released its tension and turned supple. Jin's hands would spread as wide as a coltsfoot leaf and then scrunch as tight as a block of quartz. She would use the edges of her hands, round them into fists, and spread them again. These changes in the strength of her grip made a pleasant heat bloom across his body. The heat flowed to the soles of his feet and rekindled the desire that had been extinguished by the long ride on horseback and his fatigue.

Before her hands could travel any farther down, Victor turned to lie on his back.

He pulled her face toward him and kissed her, caressing her breasts over the thin material of her nightdress. Her soft tongue curled. He removed the clothing that covered her body, and his bare hand touched the mound of her shy breast. He felt a hot wave wash over him from below. He grasped her close against him and soon they were entangled, their hands searching each other's bodies in the dark. Victor caressed Jin's face, buried his nose in her breasts and hugged her close to him as Jin arched her back. Victor's lips grazed her neck and bit her earlobe. Jin blushed, the earlier frosty melancholy of her eyes melted away, her lips red. Their knees, as each lover tried to cover the other, bumped into each other. Not a single shade of dark thought existed between them in that moment.

The four hooves of a swiftly running horse barely touch the ground.

They were both sensitively responsive to each other's passionate lovemaking, bringing forth waves of mutual pleasure. Dew drops of perspiration beaded on their foreheads and the slightest tremor in one carried to the other. It was difficult to tell whether the heated body of the woman had enveloped the man, or whether the man's hardened body had entered the woman. All at once, sparks burst inside of both lovers. As her back arched into her climax, she covered her face with her hands. She didn't want him to see the teardrops gathered in her eyes.

—Jin!

She gave no answer.

—I love you!

He gently stroked away her tears with the tip of his tongue.

A deer. A falcon. Or perhaps it was an otter. They heard an animal chirping from a place not far away.

Jin closed her moist eyes and listened again for the sound. It wasn't the breathing of the horses. The two lovers lay drenched in sweat as they fell asleep to the sound of a lost pup of some mountain beast crying for its mother as it crawled into the courtyard of the sleeping inn, somewhere in the mountains of Korea.

On her last night, Jin shared a bed with Soa at the Japanese-run Daibutsu Hotel at the harbor. This was a special concession given by Victor for Jin to say her good-byes. Soa had roomed with her at the palace since they entered at the age of six. The two made the appropriate ritual greetings and danced together. Soa was posted to the Refreshments Chamber and Jin to the Embroidery Chamber, but they shared the same futon in the palace. There was a time when one would feel anxious if the other were not in sight. They had to know where the other was and what she was doing if they were to dance the Dance of the Great Peace, the Dance of the Dragon King's Son, or the Dance of the Mountain Scent, else the turn of their hands or the steps of their feet would not create the right, felicitous movement. Jin had to know what Soa was doing for her handiwork to be flawless on the tortoise and peony embroidery of the palace's many silk pouches and quilted socks. Soa had to know what Jin was doing if she wanted her hands to be calm and steady as she prepared fruit to place on the King's table.

That night, Soa gave her a bit of earth, flower seeds, and a jar with a lady's slipper orchid planted inside. It was the same orchid they had planted together in the Embroidery Chamber. Jin had to close her eyes upon seeing the deep greens of the tapered blades. Soa said that once Jin crossed the ocean and reached Victor's country, she would have to change the soil. The carefully wrapped earth was for this purpose. She had also prepared seeds from flowers that bloomed in the palace for Jin to plant in that unfamiliar land. Soa said, "Do think of me when the seeds burst and the flowers bloom." Her eyes began to tremble as she said the earth she had brought was from the courtyard of the Embroidery Chamber. Her eyes conveyed the good-bye that her voice couldn't bear to express.

When Jin had her luggage loaded onto the ship, she took the orchid, earth, and flower seeds on board to keep in her cabin. She sensed this talisman from Soa was something she would need during her long voyage over the ocean.

Soa, who had assured Jin that she would return to the palace at daybreak, was, in fact, standing among the crowds at the harbor even after Jin had boarded, waving her hand. And it was at that moment, as Jin stood on the deck of the ship and Soa stood on the pier, that her departure from Korea finally felt real. The busy harbor became invisible. All that filled her sight now was Soa waving to her from the pier. But then she noticed a man standing still beside a white building near the entrance of the harbor. Everything else moved, especially Soa's hand as she waved good-bye, but the man stood there, frozen. Only when the boat announced its departure did the man take a few steps onto the white sands of the shore. Jin had just noticed him, but he had been out in the harbor since dawn. He was there when the sun rose and Jin had drawn the attention of everyone gathered at the harbor. He was there when she had stood next to Victor as they bade farewell to the French missionaries when the nuns by the rickshaw approached her and genuflected. He was there now, standing in that same spot, never taking his eyes off her.

Could it be Yeon?

Her eyes, once calm as if they hid the bottom of the ocean, suddenly trembled like the waves. Had he come here? She tried to lean out, but Victor placed his hand on the nape of her neck. She briefly lost her balance, but in a moment that white nape of her neck was upright again, having recovered her center and natural tension.

Her eyes searched the harbor for Yeon.

—Jin.

Victor called her name, but she did not hear.

Yeon, with whom she had watched over the apricot tree that she planted when she was five grow thick as a hug. Her gaze rapidly swept through the people coming and going at the harbor, lingering between the endless stretch of tideland and the buildings in the bright sunlight. She couldn't find him, and she sank into bitter acceptance. Soa had just barely managed to see her off, thanks to a special dispensation from Lady Suh. *I must be mistaken*, Jin thought as she bit her lip. How could Yeon have freed up the time to come all the way to the harbor, which was four days of travel from the capital? And he had avoided her since a few days before she left the city, as if refusing to hear her good-byes. *I must be seeing things*, she thought as she closed her eyes.

When she opened them again, she was calm.

—I love you . . .

She placed her hand on Victor's.

How different this man who stood beside her was, even more so than the Japanese or Chinese men one met at the harbor.

He did not have the prominent cheekbones of Korean men, nor did he have the wild look of men from the north, and his eyes were not so narrow, his complexion not so heated, his manner not so energetic. More than anything else, he spoke of love more frequently than any Korean man. These differences were as distinct as the Western suit he wore.

Jin and Victor seemed different from the other passengers despite their having boarded with everyone else. Though they faced the same long voyage as the many other people on the ship, they gave off an air of being on their own private journey. Her Eastern eyes, with their sparkle and discretion, and his Western eyes, underneath their creased eyelids and thick eyebrows, met each other's gaze in the air between them. Her gaze was deep with melancholy, while his was filled with bright joy.

—Jin.

The ship began moving in earnest toward the ocean.

—You cannot imagine what a shining soul you possess. As beautiful as you are in Korea, once we cross the sea and you are in my country, you will have the beauty of freedom. The people of my country will fall deeply in love with you.

—. . .

—When we reach my country, we shall hold a proper wedding ceremony. We shall invite many people and show them just how lovely my bride is.

Jin's heart sank. To a court lady, the Ceremony of Initiation was no different from a wedding ceremony. And she had gone through her initiation a long time ago at the palace. She had worn a glittering light green wedding tunic, given to her by Lady Suh, resplendent with the two phoenixes embroidered on the chest and back, on which her roommate Soa hung a scented ornamental pouch made of green satin, adorned with lotus-bud knots and strawberry tassels. She placed a ceremonial crown of embroidered flowers upon the carefully plaited braid wrapped around her head and paid her tributes. She made flower-shaped rice cakes as if for a banquet and sent them up to the court lady in charge and procured a mountain pheasant from the poultry store to serve to her roommates. Because she had undertaken such a ceremony, she was, in the strictest terms, one of the King's women. But the King had sent her away to this man.

—This I promise you.

She felt uncertain of her feelings. An emotion, whether of sadness or happiness she couldn't tell, came upon her in waves. She tried to imagine this country that he called his and failed. Whenever she could find the time, she had memorized the names of the famous streets of his country and tried to understand its people through books, but the only thing she remembered in that moment was that their president was named Sadi Carnot. Where at the end of this ocean could this country be, a land with a president instead of a king? It could only be reached after a two-month ocean voyage. What sights were its streets, what mountains and rivers appeared in its scenery, what shoes did its people wear as they walked its land? Her pupils trembled with the unexpected onslaught of hopes and fears for the future.

When Victor, who served as the resident French legate in her country, gave notice of his orders to return to France, the King had given him his blessing. His Majesty entreated, "Do not forget Korea when you have returned to France." The King had turned to Jin, who stood before him next to Victor, and closed his eyes. The King was pale and fatigued. He looked lonely and sorrowful, and more drained by the day in the various conflicts between China and Japan, the people and his advisors, and his father and his wife. Presently, the King half-opened his eyes and asked Jin to raise her head. She did, facing the imperial robe where the golden dragon writhed in a sky of red velvet. A silence passed between them before the King spoke to issue an unexpected decree.

—We hereby grant you a name. Henceforth, your surname shall be Yi. Your given name, Jin.

Jin, standing by the man who was going to take her over the ocean, felt a tremor pass through her body. Countless emotions intermingled and surged, but the only words that barely managed to seep through her parched lips were, "I am greatly honored by Your Majesty."

The King spoke to Victor, the French legate appointed as the first envoy from France during this time when Korea was besieged by foreign powers.

—That young woman and I now share the same surname. This decision is done in the hope that she is properly received as your wife when you return to France.

Through one's name, we see into one's being. Victor unhesitatingly accepted this name that the King had given her, and immediately called her by it. She, once known as Suh Yuhryung when she danced, Lady Attendant Suh when she embroidered, Jinjin to Soa, and Silverbell to Yeon, was now Yi Jin.

On that same night, Jin was summoned to the Queen's quarters. Three years had passed since taking leave of the Queen to live with the French legate. Coffee and cake were placed between them. The Queen said, "Come closer." Upon the Queen's tunic hung a glittering green pendant tied in chrysanthemum knots. It had been a long time since she had sat close enough to the Queen to observe the waving of the soft tassels of the ornament.

The Queen said that the King's granting Jin his own surname meant he considered her a daughter. Because it was not allowed to look directly upon the pale face of the Queen, whose hair was neatly wound in a bun and fastened with a jade pin, Jin could only keep her head bowed.

—Indeed, if this were an ordinary family, my own heart would be that of a mother sending away her daughter in marriage.

Jin bowed her head yet lower.

—The sense of a person's name is created by the way the name's bearer conducts her life. Take care to live beautifully, so your name inspires a feeling of grace in the people who speak it.

Jin could clearly sense the thoughtfulness in the Queen's own name.

—Is there nothing you would like to say to me?

Jin's heart was fit to burst with all the words she had wanted to say to the Queen since her life in the palace had abruptly ended three years ago. Words of resentment and love and concern and sadness . . .

She pressed down on them and raised her head.

—I wish to dance for you the Dance of the Spring Oriole.

The Queen's exquisite face took on a thoughtful expression. She was likely the person in the palace who had enjoyed Jin's dancing the most. The Queen once praised her by declaring that, out of all the dancers in court, Suh Yuhryung was the best performer of the Dance of the Spring Oriole.

—Do so.

Jin carefully backed out of the Queen's presence and stepped lightly onto the flower-patterned mat. The Dance of the Spring Oriole was invariably the most popular solo dance during spring banquets. The flying step, the stone tower, the falling flower and flowing water, the before-the-bloom . . . every step of the palace dances featured in it. There was no music and she wore no crown of flowers on her head, but Jin's movements were graceful in their restraint and care. After all, it might be the last dance she would get to perform for the Queen.

—As one who dreams of the new enlightened world but could not step one foot outside of this palace, I envy you.

The Queen's voice hovered like a cloud by Jin's ear where perspiration began to gather.

—And you are going forth into this world because of love. So do not feel regret.

As she danced, Jin became a tree, and became fire.

—Go to this new world and release yourself from your bonds, learn as many new things as possible, and live a new life.

Jin danced to transform herself into the earth, into steel.

—You are likely the first Korean woman to voyage this far.

At last, she became water.

—Do not forget this fragile country that you leave behind.

She would not. She could never, moreover, forget the Queen, who was once treated as if she were deceased, and given a national burial. Like an oriole singing on a tree branch in spring, Jin prayed with every light step of her feet for the Queen's days to be full of peace.

Drenched in sweat, Jin lowered her head once more before the Queen.

—Would you write down what you see and hear and feel in that strange land, and send it to me?

The dragon engraving of the white jade hairpin pierced through the Queen's hair seemed to float before Jin's eyes. The Queen was always curious as to how people in foreign countries lived, what laws they followed, what treatment they sought when sick, and what they ate, wore, and learned.

—Would you do this for me?

Jin answered yes.

—It will take two months for the letters to reach here, but I already look forward to them.

The Queen bestowed a peony painting to Jin, whose perspiration had still not cooled on her apricot-colored face. This was in keeping with her practice of rewarding the best dancer at every banquet.

—When you reach that country, hang this on your wall and look at it from time to time.

The Queen rolled the scroll herself and placed it in Jin's hands.

—Farewell.

The Queen removed her cupronickel ring and slipped it onto Jin's finger.

Where could they be?

Her eyelids fluttered open, her body rocking in space. Crushed underneath a strange and confusing dream, her forehead and her loose black hair were damp with sweat. Jin wiped her face with her palm. She felt the Queen's ring on her finger graze her face. She spread open her hand and gazed up at the ring with an expression of deep melancholy.

She sat up. Moonlight seeped through the portal of the cabin as the vessel sailed out toward the great ocean from the rough waters of Korea's long-secluded ocean territory. On the wall before her hung Victor's dress uniform with its round golden buttons and Roman collar. Gold braids were sewn on the chest, sleeves, and epaulets. Victor took care to hang up his uniform despite his never having an occasion to wear it on board the ship. At the legation, he had also hung his uniform on days when he did not wear it. Jin stared at it and at her light blue Art Nouveau–style dress hanging by its side, the same dress that had attracted so much attention at the harbor. A black woolen suit jacket, a striped vest with a small feather on the lapel, a pair of slightly narrow trousers, and a traveler's coat that came down to the knees were hung in layers on a single coat hanger next to the other two garments. Next to that were his black cap with the thin visor and her hat with the rose embroidery.

Jin's hand moved in the dim moonlight.

Her fingers slid over Victor's forehead, the man who was so eager to promise things to her. He seemed preoccupied or businesslike during the day, but at night when he was asleep, he was like a vulnerable, innocent animal.

On the night in Shanghai where they transferred on board the steamship *Villa*, he tried, once again, to promise her something before he fell asleep.

—Yi Jin.

When darkness fell, the ocean turned from blue to black. Jin bit down on her lip to suppress the laughter that threatened to explode from her mouth. Whenever he called her by her name, his throat constricted because of the unfamiliar syllables. She had to keep her laughter from pushing its way out. Because if she laughed, he might never look into her eyes and call her Yi Jin again.

—Victor . . .

She was the first Korean woman to be on a ship sailing to France, and in trying to banish her fear that came from the thought that she was floating atop the ocean, she quietly uttered the name of the sleeping man next to her.

Victor Collin de Plancy.

The exotic name belonging to the man whose forehead she stroked. In each name lives the character of the person who owns that name. In the land they left behind, Victor repeated his long name to her many times, wishing her to say it. But she did not. The more Victor wanted it, the more she was unable to because she felt saying his name would make an unforeseen side of him materialize before her and irrevocably change what was between them. Since leaving Korea, Jin sometimes murmured her own name to herself, so quietly that even Victor, who stood next to her, could not hear. "Yi Jin . . ." This name, Yi Jin, was still far from real to its owner.

Jin turned her head to look at the peony painting that hung over the headboard of the bed. These traces of the people she had left behind always calmed her anxious heart. The peony was unquestionably spectacular, even in the dim light. Below it was Soa's white porcelain jar, and next to it, the pot with the planted orchid. The box, with the earth and flower seeds, was securely wrapped in a black linen square, and beside it, inside an even more tightly knotted white linen wrap, was the French-Korean dictionary transcribed by the late Bishop Blanc. As she wrapped this well-worn volume in linen for safekeeping, Jin had the feeling that she would be looking in this dictionary far more than anything else she had ever looked at in her life.

She raised herself out of bed, careful not to wake Victor. She threw on the thin, cylindrical coat she had worn over the blue dress, opened the cabin door, and walked out onto the oval deck of the *Villa*. The ship sailed forth into the wide ocean. The ocean never overflowed, even when all the waters of the world flowed into it. The *Villa* weighed seven hundred tons and sailed on rough waters. It had a wide hull and a deep draft, enabling it to carry large cargo. When she expressed her fascination with the steamship, Victor told her that not even the president could sit in the captain's chair. But what about a king? The crew never whistled once they were on board the ship. They believed that whistling brought bad winds.

The dull clanging from the engine room was audible over the sound of the waves crashing against the ship. The sea wind whirled about the bow and the large sails of the ship, whipping her clothing about her. Jin gripped her coat, determined not to be dictated by the wind. Her knees felt weak. The rough waves were relentless. They smashed against the ship before flowing outward again.

Keep coming to me, O black and blue ocean.

Jin stood on deck and leaned her body out toward the water. A round, full moon rose above the black eaves of the endless ocean. All the world was the sea and the moon. She looked down at the foam of the waves that shattered like shards of white ice. It looked as if hundreds of white horses were being whipped into a run before sinking into the water. A strong wind managed to blow the coat off her, and she instinctively reached out her arms before it flapped away over the black and indigo ocean. The gesture was futile. The coat left her behind to soar freely, swooping upward with the wind almost dipping into the ocean, then flying out again until it was too far away for her to see its silhouette.

Jin pushed against the wind and stood herself upright. She raised her arms to above shoulder level and slightly lifted one foot. The movements of her body became lighter, as if she wore a dancer's robe embroidered with butterfly pairings. The waves crashed. The winds crashed. The moonlight, shining down upon the ocean from above, crashed into the water. Her body became supple. Pushing against the things that crashed against her, she let her body fall into a rhythm. A smile spread on her face.

Victor, who had woken at dawn and come out on the deck in search of her, found Jin dancing as if she were possessed by the spirit of the ocean. The longer one wants to stay together with someone, the less they should try to change them. Even if he hadn't been Victor, or precisely because he was, he did not call out to the dancer lost in movement beside the moonlit waves. Dewy beads of sweat covered her despite the cold and violent ocean winds. An intense heat enveloped her face, neck, chest, hips, and legs. A weight lifted from her heart and she was no longer afraid of the ocean. She became as light as the waves, the wind, and the moonlight. She became a butterfly.

The steamship *Villa* was about to carry this court dancer of Joseon past Saigon, Singapore, Colombo, and the Suez Canal, and onward to France, Victor's home. She ended in a pose that stretched her body toward the ocean. She exhaled. Victor, who had watched her with bated breath, came up to her and placed his hand once more upon the nape of her neck. Breathing slow, Jin leaned against the railing and gazed out at the boundless ocean.

∞

The year was 1891.

Yi Jin was twenty-two.

2
The Pear Blossom Child

A horse born in the north will run against the northern winds. A bird that has flown from the south will perch on a southern branch.

Yi Jin was born in Banchon, its name meaning "half-village."

Banchon lay at the northern end of Eunglan Bridge, which spanned a ditch near Gyeongmogung Palace to the right of Changgyeonggung Palace. The Sungkyunkwan School of Confucian Thought at Banchon was nicknamed Bangung, or "half-palace," after a famed school called Biyong from China's Zhou Dynasty. The original Biyong was built in the middle of a pond, surrounded by flowing water all year round, with a bridge built in each of the four directions. But unlike Biyong, the waters of Bangung flowed only to the east and west, in the shape of a half-moon. This was half the water of Biyong, which was why Sungkyunkwan came to be called the half-palace. Its waters were called Bansu, or "half-water," and its surrounding village became the half-village of Banchon. And the people who lived in Banchon were called Banin, the "half-people."

No one knew how Yi Jin's family had found themselves living among the Banin.

What Jin remembered were the pear trees that bore blinding-white pear blossoms every spring, a white as pure as her memory of biting into her first pear.

Spring found its way into Korea every year despite the peninsula's tight seclusion on the edge of the world. The soft winds blew into the thatched-roof hovels on the eastern banks of Banchon's waters. Sunlight entered the house from the early hours in the spring. Across the banks stretched the pear orchards. Perhaps the stomachs that had been empty all winter craved a bit of fat, for in the spring there would be several cow heads on display before the butcher shop. Five hundred cows were slaughtered in the spring, amidst the blooming of dogwood, apricot, azaleas, and camellias. White pear blossoms followed, floating into the air at the slightest breeze and piling up on the ground like snow, only to be washed away with the rain.

Had Yi Jin's mother been waiting for the pear blossoms?

As if wanting to see the flowers before she died, her mother, who coughed up phlegm mixed with blood all winter, breathed her last only when the winds changed, the sunlight brightened, and the pear blossoms crowded their branches. To the last, she held her precious little Jin tightly by the hand.

Jin's mother was put into the earth wearing the same clothes she wore on her deathbed. Her lonely death left not a word in terms of a will. The woman Suh, who also lived in Banchon and took in sewing with Jin's mother, witnessed her passing in mournful silence. Suh was the daughter of an interpreter official and was once married into the nobility, but when she bore no children four years into the match, she left that home on her own two feet. Suh's father was wealthy enough to have her ride out in a palanquin at her wedding, a privilege observed only in the households of high officials. When Suh left her husband's home, her father bought her a house on the water bank in Banchon. He then told her she was never to step foot in his household again. Suh, who had unsurpassed skill when it came to her needle, spent her days in that house working as a seamstress. Her younger sister, Lady Suh, a court lady, sent her extra work that the palace's Embroidery Chamber could not manage. Suh had just begun to rent out room and board to scholars studying at Sungkyunkwan when the *General Sherman*, an American merchant ship, sailed up the Daedong River into Pyongyang. Korea's military and militias, rallying around Governor Park Gyusu of Pyongan Province, burned the ship down. Determined to receive a formal apology and sign a trade deal, President Ulysses S. Grant retaliated by sending a new ironclad warship to Korea. Jin's father, who hid his real name and lived in Banchon as a manual laborer, volunteered for the militia and left for Ganghwa Island. Jin was a baby in her mother's womb at the time.

But death is sometimes a weapon that could never be defended against.

The Korean military used mostly rocks and spears to fight against the guns of the Americans. The civilian militia, when they ran out of even that, went against the invaders with their fists. Scores were shot at a time by the guns, their bodies falling into the ocean. Some, in despair, chose to take their own lives rather than die at the hands of foreigners, throwing themselves in great numbers into the water. But they never retreated. America was unable to initiate any kind of trade negotiation in the face of such determined resistance. The ironclad ship sent by President Grant filled itself with the spoils of war and left for China after forty days.

But Jin's father did not return to Banchon.

Jin's mother gave birth to her child alone.

While Korea locked its doors to the world and declared a ban of all foreigners from Korean soil, the Qing Dynasty of China, under its *zhongtixiyong* policy of "Chinese spirit, Western technology," was already sending students to England and France. China, which once gave the West such technologies as the compass and block printing, was sending emissaries to learn foreign ways, a thing unheard of until then.

Japan also sent about fifty of its own students in a group bound for America. Among them was an eight-year-old girl who declared to the people who came to the harbor to see them off that her dream was to establish an institution of higher learning for future female leaders of modern reform. Meanwhile, in France, a few young artists including Cezanne, Monet, Renoir, and Degas broke off from the *salon* system and mounted their own exhibition, sending shockwaves across the traditional art world.

Jin's mother used to carry Jin on her back to the woman Suh's house during the day and to help her with her sewing work. Suh thought things would always be this way, with Jin's mother and herself keeping each other company. When Suh found herself with the abruptly orphaned Jin in her arms, she could only stare into the little one's eyes with a feeling of deep loss.

—How pretty you are.

The child, who hadn't an inkling that she had no family left to her in this world, possessed the clearest eyes. All she could do, this little one Suh had known only as Baby, was blink at Suh's words.

—How heartless your mother was. If she was going to leave you all by yourself, she should've told me something about you. She should've given you a name. What could your family name be? What was she so afraid of that she couldn't even tell me that?

There were people who went into Banchon to hide, those who had broken the country's law by illegally cutting pine or brewing and selling wheat beer. The constables dared not enter Banchon, for a number of the nobility lived there. Even when illegal woodcutters managed to scramble into Banchon, there was no way of arresting them without a special warrant. And those who concealed themselves in Banchon never left it. They harvested cows and pigs for the Sungkyunkwan scholars or borrowed land to farm on, with young girls becoming servants attached to Sungkyunkwan while the boys worked as butchers at the slaughterhouse.

The crowing of roosters and barking of dogs was constant in Banchon.

On summer nights, the cries of the frogs penetrated every room of every house. In this village where no one put locks on their doors, Jin had lost her mother at the tender age of five and was left all alone in the world.

Around that time, Lady Suh, the woman Suh's sister, was appointed to the Queen's Chambers. She had previously served under a childless dowager consort who was widowed at a young age.

A lush bamboo forest grew behind the woman Suh's house in Banchon. It made anyone who harbored love in their heart, whether for a person or the birds or the trees, send up a prayer to the heavens. Since bringing Jin into her home, Suh started her days in prayer before the bamboo forest over an offering of a bowl of clear water. Jin, who fell asleep to the sound of the bamboo leaves rustling, often dreamt of pear blossoms. Even when listening to the splattering of rain on leaves, a vision of a sea of pear blossoms spread before her. She repeatedly dreamed of walking among trees laden with pear blossoms, coming upon a lily pond of fathomless depths, and jumping headlong into the water.

She was dreaming it again during her nap the day Lady Suh brought more sewing to the woman Suh's house in Banchon. Lady Suh's steps were swift in her desire to give her older sister some black pepper, which was precious even in the palace. The welcome sight of her younger sister, whom she hadn't seen in a while, made the woman Suh step down into the courtyard without even pausing for her shoes. Despite being the older sibling, the woman Suh never failed to call her sister "my lady." Lady Suh had entered the palace at the age of eight and risen steadily to the ranks of the higher court ladies. She exuded an elegance befitting her station. As she dropped the outer coat that covered her head during out-of-palace excursions, the first thing she noticed was the child lying in Suh's room.

—Who might this child be?

Suh hesitated, uncertain as to how to explain Jin's presence.

—Sister! Who is this child?

—Do you remember the woman who used to come to this house and take on my extra work? She used to live on the banks . . . She's left this child and gone on to the next world. The child has no other place to go . . ."

—How old is she?

—She's five now.

—Her name?

—She has no name yet.

—Has no name? Then what have you been calling her?

—I just say, "Hello, Baby" . . . Sometimes I call her Ewha.

—Ewha?

—After the pear blossoms. Her house is by a large grove of pear trees . . .

Lady Suh stared down at the sleeping child. The woman Suh spoke.

—We could give her a name, but she has no family name . . .

—How is it that you do not know her family name?

—Her mother and I were neighbors, but she never talked about her life.

—Perhaps they were running from something?

—Well . . . maybe they were Catholic? I think she mentioned her family going to ruin in the Year of the Red Tiger. That's the year the Catholics had to run for the hills. If they came here then, it must be so. Maybe that's why the child's father volunteered for that mess at Ganghwa Island. They were told they would be pardoned if they fought well, but he left and never came back.

—And as for this child, will you be the one raising her?

—I see no other way, my lady.

Lady Suh gently placed a hand on the sleeping child's forehead.

—How pretty you are. Was that why you lost your parents so early?

Little Jin, who was dreaming of walking through clouds of pear blossoms, seemed like a young seagull trapped in a landlocked country.

—This child . . . shall I take her into the palace, sister?

And so, on a day when the early summer rain pattered upon the bamboo leaves, Jin entered the palace on the back of the young Lady Attendant Lee sent by Lady Suh. Love cannot happen without attachment, and Suh was distraught, questioning her choice of sending the girl away into the palace. Her desire to keep Jin close bubbled up from inside her. Lady Suh herself had said that bringing the girl into the palace now did not guarantee she would be made a court lady in the future.

In the palace were three dowager consorts who were childless and spending the rest of their days in loneliness. Dowager Consort Cheolin, whom Lady Suh had once served, was one of these three. Lady Suh hoped that the presence of a child would bring warmth to her former mistress, that Jin's playful and pretty nature would lessen the old woman's solitude. They agreed to try this arrangement for a few years before deciding the little girl's future.

Every morning, Jin left for the palace on the back of Lady Attendant Lee, escorted to Banchon's entrance by the woman Suh. She was brought home upon sundown, again on the back of Lady Attendant Lee, to the house in Banchon.

A pear blossom, a pear blossom, my baby's face is a pear blossom . . .

Jin played with the woman Suh's sewing basket as Suh did her work and drifted to sleep to the sound of Suh singing these words. Suh always said, as Jin was carried into the palace, "Have a good day today, Baby, don't forget to smile, Baby."

Jin had to be carried home every evening because she was very young, but also because she would wake around midnight and cry until she was breathless, her legs stretched out like planks. That was the hour when Jin's mother had died.

Jin must have danced and sung for the dowager consort across from her gloomy royal meal table. She must have massaged with her little hands the dowager consort's back that had grown crooked under the weight of the elaborate royal hair ornament. She must have fallen asleep in the presence of the dowager consort, who was not much for words and allowed silence to settle. Jin might have naively reached for the jeweled bits that dangled like water droplets in the hair ornament of the woman condemned to become a dowager consort at a young age. She might have walked behind the dowager consort across the

Golden Flower Bridge as they took a stroll in the gardens during an appointed time.

All memory of this was gone. Only one scene remained.

For some forgotten reason, Jin was wandering the wide palace alone that day. She must have tiptoed out of the dowager consort's chambers in search of a latrine. The dark tones of the palace scared her. She felt the beasts carved into the stones of the pillars were peering at her. The earth underneath her feet was sticky and black. Even the trees took on a deep blue hue. The moss growing on the granite was damp to the touch. Sunlight shone through the branches, but the blue, yellow, and orange of the leaves lost their usual coloring in the shade. The vast gardens of the palace were too wide for a five-year-old to spread out and play on her own. Even the green grass that carpeted the grounds seemed shady and dark. The large trees and flowers with names she didn't know seemed to follow her. Jin looked up at an umbrella pine that a magpie had alighted upon. She followed a clear stream that babbled past her in a clearing. She skipped over a dry streambed. She stood on the edge of the flowing stream and looked at an arch built over it. The faces of the ferocious *dokkaebi* carved into the stone gave her a fright. Four beasts in the stone wore four different expressions, one of whom seemed to beg to be played with. It happened then, when Jin crouched down to look at that one animal.

—Who is this child?

The bright voice made Jin look up, and she had to close her doe-like eyes.

Just a moment earlier she had thought the palace was dark, but now it seemed that all the light of the world shimmered before her. The scent of flowers floated over to where Jin was. When the owner of the bright voice moved, a rustling issued from her beautiful green robes that looked as if they would carry her into the air.

—You are in the presence of the Queen.

Was it a dream?

Jin could only look up at her. The Queen was the first person who had ever asked her who she was. All she could see of her were her eyes.

Her face quietly shone with good health, but her gaze was especially clear and present. They contained an emotion not as simple as joy or sadness but something too subtle to be spoken of. Underneath these eyes were a pair of slender lips, which were smiling.

—Who are you?

Jin could only gaze up at her from below.

—Why are you alone?

—. . .

—What were you looking at?

Jin was too young to say who she was, why she was alone, or what she was looking at. From behind the Queen, one of the many lady attendants, who all had their heads bowed, explained, "This is a child from the Dowager Consort Cheolin's chambers." From the band of white at the end of the Queen's wide green sleeve emerged a pale, thin hand, which reached for Jin's and held it.

—How clever you look, little one.

—. . .

—Would you like to come with me?

Jin's tiny hand was wrapped in the soft hand of the Queen. The Queen's touch was so warm and lovely that Jin kept wriggling her fingers in it. Together, the two went down the wide path of thinly spread pebbles. They walked among the pine trees that threw shadows on the ground. Lady Suh, who had just heard what had happened, her face as white as a sheet, came hurrying before the Queen as she repeatedly bowed and said, "Forgive me, Your Majesty, forgive me." But the Queen did not let go of Jin's hand.

A kind of affinity appears between two people who hold hands. The woman and the child didn't let go as they watched the sun go down over the faraway mountains and as they walked by the pond that contained the moon. They passed Amisan Hill, made from the earth dug up during the construction of the Pavilion of Festivities, and the gardens that were their own world of flowers and grass and decorative rocks.

They reached the Queen's Chambers deep in the palace, a building distinguished by its lack of a dragon ridge along the apex of its roof. Only then did the Queen stop to speak to one of the many lady attendants following her with their heads bowed.

—Are there pears in the Refreshments Chamber?

The Queen's voice wasn't loud, but it was clear.

—Bring one, and a fruit knife and spoon.

Jin's heart was stolen by the beautiful flowered wall that she could see behind the Queen. She was fascinated by the chimney that was built by stacking red bricks into a hexagonal tower and crowned with black roof tile and a flue cover. There were engravings all over it, of demons, phoenixes, fantastic deer, the Ten Immortal Elements, and the Four Gentlemen.

As they passed through the Gate of Dualities, the doors of the Queen's Chambers were slid open.

Avid as a seagull spotting dry land, pure as a drop of dew on a pear blossom, Jin was seated next to the Queen.

A lady attendant placed a tray containing a glistening pear, a fruit knife, and a small spoon between Jin and the Queen. The Queen spread Jin's hand and placed the pear upon Jin's tiny palm.

—Are you lonely like me?

The rough wet skin of the pear pressed into Jin's palm. The moment its coolness touched her skin, Jin remembered her mother's face.

The face unseen since the day the thousands of pear blossoms opened and fluttered in the wind.

—Shall I feed you?

The Queen's eyes still shone, but unlike in the gardens, her voice was infused with sadness. Taking the fruit knife, the Queen sliced off the top of the pear, exposing the moist, white flesh. The Queen gently scraped the white insides of the pear with the spoon. Once the bowl of the spoon was filled, she fed the spoon into Jin's mouth.

—Is it good?

The child nodded.

The Queen smiled and scraped at the white pear flesh again. Pear juice dribbled on her sleeve, to which the Queen was oblivious. When the spoon filled with pear again, she fed it to Jin and smiled once more. The lady attendant from the Refreshments Chamber, standing at a distance, was so disconcerted that she blushed.

—Do you like it?

The child nodded again.

It was something the girl's mother used to do for her when they lived by the pear orchard. Her mother would scrape the insides of a pear earned from doing some sewing and feed it to Jin, asking, "Is it good?" Jin, her mouth full, would only be able to nod. The mother waited until the child swallowed all the pear before scraping another spoonful of pear and asking again, "Is it good?"

Watching Jin's cheeks puff, her mouth full of pear juice, her mother would say, "You're a pear tree, you are.

"How strange it was, to see a lone pear tree growing by the sea. A pear tree on the beach? It's the last place you would expect one. Would its flowers bloom in the ocean storms? Would it bear fruit? I kept worrying about it, so I brought that pear tree home. Then I had you, so you must be a pear tree."

It was the Queen who sat before her, but Jin thought she heard her mother's voice and looked about the chamber, tears trembling in her eyes.

—Why are you crying when you're eating something delicious?

The Queen reached over to wipe the child's eyes.

Jin, in a vague wave of longing, kept eating from the Queen's spoon like a baby seagull as the Queen scraped together the watery flesh. The sweetness pooled in her mouth and droplets dewed in her eyes. Jin was on the verge of realizing that she could never go back to that time when she was with her mother, to that place where all the pear blossoms of the world had floated and scattered in the wind.

3
The Boy from the Pond

To the lonely, the presence of a young child is like a breeze blowing in from a warm climate.

The Dowager Consort Cheolin began looking forward every morning to the arrival of Jin, who was as dainty as a leaflet of a crabapple tree. Ever since having young Jin's vigor, speech, and childish mannerisms by her side, the dowager consort nitpicked on the young lady attendants less. She wrinkled her brow less, answered the greetings of the lady attendants cordially, and accepted her meals without complaint.

"*Chun, gwi, man, su, nak* . . ." Whenever she felt gloomy, the dowager consort taught Jin the characters engraved on the Dowagers' Chambers' patterned wall. "*Gang, man, nyun, jang, chun* . . ." Clever enough to hear them once and immediately commit them to heart, Jin read the characters back with no mistakes. Whenever her tiny mouth recited each character's meaning and sound, the dowager consort smiled broadly. She never reprimanded her, even when Jin ate the dishes on the dowager consort's meal table that the dowager consort hadn't touched yet, or when Jin made childish scrawls on the patterned wall.

Jin received the love of the Dowager Consort Cheolin during the day and the care of the woman Suh of Banchon at night, and her cheeks grew round and pink with good health. No trace remained of the listless girl who had just lost her mother. Her black hair shone, and her arms and neck became plump. Even when the woman Suh prepared Jin's hair before Jin set out for the palace, Dowager Consort Cheolin would insist on sitting the girl before her and lovingly comb her hair again herself. When Jin napped, the dowager consort would place the back of her hand on Jin's forehead. Sometimes she would sigh deeply and gaze into the child's face for a long time.

The dowager consort was loath to part with Jin, and Jin was returned to Banchon later and later.

Meanwhile, after a decade or so of regency rule, Heungseon Daewongun, or the Regent, stepped down from the throne as the Enlightenment reformists came into power. Japan managed to force Korea into opening its harbors. Western powers such as France and America, which had failed to forge trade relations in the face of resistance from the Korean people, cheered in unison as this secluded kingdom on the eastern edge of the Eurasian continent opened its gates. Jin turned seven the year the other powers rushed to enter Korea before Japan could establish a monopoly. She was in her second year as the child companion of Dowager Consort Cheolin. This was also around the time when Korea sent seventy-six emissaries to Japan on a twenty-day trip to experience the fruits of Japan's modernization.

It was an evening when Jin was returning as usual to the woman Suh's house in Banchon.

On the back of Lady Attendant Lee, Jin was the first to spot an unfamiliar person standing next to the apricot tree in the courtyard. Jin's eyes grew wide with surprise. His face and clothes resembled that of no one else she had seen before. The stranger wore a black robe that came down to his knees. He was tall, with a curly brown beard that reached below his chin and down to his neck. His face was white, and his eyes were blue.

Lady Attendant Lee was just as surprised as Jin. Still carrying Jin on her back, she fell backward, causing Jin to bite her own lip. It swelled and began to bleed. Lady Attendant Lee put Jin down in front of the woman Suh and gazed at the strange man.

—*Oh, mon Dieu!*

Strange words came out of the man's mouth as Jin's lip bled.

Suh hurried into the house and brought out a towel to wipe Jin's lip. Despite having injured Jin, Lady Attendant Lee fearfully vacated the premises through the courtyard gate without a hint of apology.

Next to the blue-eyed stranger stood a boy wearing a linen jacket so soiled it was gray. He looked like an untamed seagull.

His sun-darkened face indicated poverty and loneliness, but at the same time hinted of an ambitious force that could break old fetters. He wore nothing inside the linen jacket, and his shoulders and arms were half-bare. He had walked for so long in his straw sandals that they were misshapen beyond recognition, with some of his toes peeking through.

The boy with the skinny shoulders met Jin's gaze. He shyly prodded the apricot tree with a sandaled foot.

—This is Father Blanc.

—Blanc . . .

Just as she had done when Dowager Consort Cheolin had patiently recited *chun, gwi, man, su, nak* to her, Jin imitated the shape of Suh's mouth and said, "Blanc." Blanc smiled as Jin said his name despite the injury to her lip, its bleeding stanched but still clearly swollen. Blanc extended a hand to little Jin.

—Yes, my name is Blanc. Jean Blanc!

This time it was the Korean language that issued forth from the priest's lips.

When Jin hid her hand behind her, Blanc smiled and patted her on the head instead. Jin looked up at the priest's dangling cross hanging from a chain over his black robes.

—You should stay in my house for now. I don't think there is any other way.

Jin could only cling to Suh's skirts and look up at Blanc. The more Suh tried to get Jin to greet him properly, the more she tried to hide behind Suh's skirt.

—I think she's shy.

At Suh's observation, Blanc smiled again and looked down at Jin.

—She must be surprised as well. Is this the child you spoke of earlier?

—She is.

—She must be returning from the palace?

—Yes.

Jin pulled tighter at Suh's skirts as she heard the accented Korean coming from Blanc's mouth. She looked as if she were about to cry.

—Don't be afraid of him.

Suh gripped Jin's hand. With her other, she pointed to the boy standing by the apricot tree.

—How old is the boy?

—They say he's seven. Some say he's six. I don't know for sure.

—They're both shy. I'm sure they'll be friends.

—Do you think so?

—They're children after all.

Jin kept trying to hide behind Suh's skirt, and the boy continued to stand by Blanc. They looked at each other.

There were people who leaped into the waves of mountains to hide. They melted into the valleys where rocks and pine and other trees lived out centuries as if they were a day and became part of primordial nature itself.

On the hill where the Sobaek and Noryeong mountain ranges split, along the path between Namwon to Jangsu, was an incline wide enough to clear for farming. The clearing was concave and surrounded by mountains, making it difficult for travelers to spot. This hidden clearing was a paradise to those fleeing the persecution of the Catholics years before. They managed to settle and grow crops, aided by a spring that flowed all year round. This was the beginning of the Subunli village at the split between the Geum and Seonjin rivers.

Blanc searched for Subunli as soon as he set foot in Korea.

He was looking for Father Ridel, who was said to be fulfilling his missionary work and living in a nearby cave. Blanc's party had met the boy in a village along the way to Subunli. The boy was an orphan who slept in the kitchen next to the earthen stove of whatever household would have him and lived off of their leftovers.

—Whenever I ask him where he lives, he always points to a pond.

Blanc patted the boy's head as he told the boy's story to the woman Suh. After Father Blanc's group spent a night in Subunli, the boy insisted on following them. The boy wore rags at the time, so Blanc had cut out the lining of his clerical robe and covered the boy's shoulders with it, a kindness the boy apparently had not forgotten.

—What do you call him?

—Yeon, as in pond. We gave him the surname of Kang. He points to a pond whenever we ask him where he's from, so there must be a pond near his home. The people of the village called him Sobaek. Only because the village was close to the Sobaek Mountains.

—Kang Yeon . . .

Little Jin murmured Yeon's name, just as she had done with Blanc's a moment before. Suh and Blanc both smiled at her. Despite his being the topic of conversation, Yeon continued to silently tap the apricot tree with his foot. His hungry belly protruded like a tadpole's. His kicks could hardly do any harm to the apricot tree.

Suh took Blanc and the boy to a room recently vacated by a Sungkyunkwan scholar who was off taking his first exams for officialdom. She opened the door and showed it to them. There was a neat pile of folded futons and linens in one corner, but the room was otherwise empty. Blanc was still examining the room from the outside when the boy simply slipped in.

—He must be very tired. We walked a great deal today.

Blanc closed the door with the boy lying inside and left the house saying he had some people to meet. Suh stood outside the room for a moment, looking down at the tattered straw sandals the boy had left on the stepping-stone in front of the porch and sliding door. They wordlessly conveyed the boy's vagabond days of begging on the streets.

Suh drew water from the well and poured it into the iron cauldron built into the stone oven.

Water can be carried or poured in any shape. It can fill up any contained space and flow in any direction. Its basic nature is immutable, which is what gives water its power.

Little Jin followed Suh as she went back and forth between the well and the cauldron. Once it was full, Suh opened the furnace door underneath the cauldron, placed some firewood inside, and lit the fire.

—To think you can walk around in broad daylight wearing a Christian cross now . . . Even being caught with rosary beads used to earn you a death sentence.

Such deaths were never suffered alone. Entire households with only a single Catholic member were extinguished as a group. Suh went on.

—They say that forty people at a time would starve in the snow when they ran for the hills. The little ones would be dead with their eyes closed, as if they had been too weak from hunger to open them. Even the beasts of the house were killed, just because of one believer in the family. Such were the times.

But for those who survived, their faith laid even deeper roots. The more it was suppressed, the more Catholicism spread into the daily lives of the Koreans.

Suh fell silent as she thought of Jin's mother. A woman whose eyes were always filled with fear, eyes that seemed to have seen things they should not have seen. Jin's mother was so careful with her words and actions that Suh had felt sorry for her. How could anyone be expected to live out their years in such constant vigilance? She wondered if that was how Jin's mother fell ill.

And how could she have breathed her last with this little one on her mind? Suh gave Jin a consoling pat on the back.

—I wonder if they ever thought that the Lord they believed in was unfeeling?

—. . .

—Listen to me go on . . . How would you know of such things, little one?

Suh paused in shoving more kindling into the oven and looked at Jin.

—That child in the room. He has nowhere to go. Shall we ask him to live with us?

Jin shook her head.

—You don't like him?

—. . . He's dirty.

Jin watched the fire dance. Her cheeks took on the red of the flames. She didn't hate the boy. But she shook her head anyway. She tilted her head, confused by her own feelings.

—Dirt can be washed off.

—. . .

—Anything that can be washed clean is not really dirty. Just unwashed. You mustn't think a person in rags is a dirty person. They're poor, not dirty. There's no fault in being poor.

—. . .

—But if a person's heart were dirty, that can't be washed clean. That is sin.

She patted Jin's back again, thinking she had spoken too much to the child, when from somewhere they heard the faint strains of a bamboo flute. Suh and Jin both turned in the direction of the music. It was the room where the boy was. Where in those rags had the boy hidden a bamboo flute?

A sound that moves the heart makes one listen even amid chaos. It makes one close one's eyes.

The two listened to the boy's music as little Jin snapped kindling in half and Suh pushed it into the oven. Crouched in the light of the oven, Jin buried her face in her arms and closed her eyes.

—They do say playing the flute at night attracts snakes . . . but how sad a child's music can be.

Suh kept murmuring to herself. Once the water in the cauldron was hot enough, she had Jin stand back. She transferred the water into a large earthen jar in the backyard. She did this for Jin whenever she bathed her. Carrying the water made Suh's forehead bead with sweat. The bamboo leaves whispered. Once she had poured the hot water with some cold and tested the temperature, a satisfied smile spread across Suh's face.

—Get Sobaek.

Jin looked at Suh with a quizzical expression, as if to ask, *Who is Sobaek?* Suh replied, "You know, Kang Yeon," then laughed.

—I wonder if you're older than him?

—. . .

—Don't you want to be a *nuna* to him?

Little Jin narrowed her eyes at the mention of being an older sister.

—Wouldn't you like a little brother like Sobaek? Well, maybe he's your *oppa* instead.

Instead of fetching the boy, Jin shook her head and crouched down again in front of the stove.

Smiling, Suh fetched the boy herself. "Sobaek-ah!" Jin could hear Suh calling for the boy. Just as Suh had done, Jin tried calling his name softly from her solitude before the oven. "Sobaek-ah." The music of the bamboo flute ceased.

The boy, who followed Suh to the kitchen, stopped when he saw Jin and took a step back. When Suh left through the door that led to the back and instructed the boy to undress, he only gripped his clothes tighter and stared at Jin. Suh said, "Baby, go to our room." Jin made a sour face and ran out of the kitchen.

—Come here, Sobaek.

The boy fidgeted as he approached her. Suh regarded the child who looked as if he did not want to give up his rags.

—Don't you want to be clean?

The boy kept grasping at his clothes.

—Do you like going around in such a dirty state?

—. . .

—Let's clean your body and wash your hair. Once you're cleaned up and wearing new clothes, Father Blanc will have a nice surprise. "What a handsome boy you are," he'll say. Maybe he won't even recognize you.

At the mention of Father Blanc, the boy loosened his grip on his clothes.

—Do you like the priest?

The boy nodded.

—I see . . . Well, good. When you like someone, life gets a bit easier. Hardship from helping someone you like is a happy price to pay. You are rich. You have the priest in your heart. It's only those who have no one who are truly poor.

The boy undressed and climbed into the earthen jar filled with heated water. She gently pressed him deeper into the water by his shoulders.

The boy, still shy, kept his gaze fixed on the bamboo forest where darkness had descended. Suh began to softly sing the "Ode to the Five Friends."

You that is not tree nor grass, who taught thee to be so straight, why must your insides be hollow? You who are so green in all seasons, that is why I love thee.

As she dipped from the hot water in the jar and poured it over the boy's shoulders, Suh stopped singing. She could feel the sharp bones of the boy's body bumping against the palm of her hand. How would such a scrawny boy ever manage to grow? She thought he might already be eight or nine. As skinny as he was, the length of his bones suggested he was older than they thought.

—You're very good with the bamboo flute.

The boy looked her in the eye for the first time. The heat of the bath drew color to his face, which was studded with water droplets.

—Who taught you?

—. . .

The child didn't answer.

—Did you learn on your own?

As she asked this, Suh suddenly realized something, and she felt her heart break in two. She had never heard the boy speak.

—Oh, Sobaek!

She could see the boy's eyes, like little dark grapes, blinking up at her from the jar, beads of water hanging over his cheeks.

—. . . You can't speak, can you?

The boy broke his gaze. His hands grasped each other underwater and his skinny neck bowed in shame. The two were silent. Blanc had never told her the boy couldn't talk. Perhaps he thought he was only quiet. Suh poured another gourd of water over his back and cleared her throat. What could be done for such a child? Sympathy welled in her heart.

—Close your eyes.

While waiting for the hot water to soften his skin, Suh combed through the boy's tangled hair with her fingers. She scrubbed the dirt and dead skin from his back with a handful of mung bean powder and rubbed his scalp with her fingertips. The boy put up no resistance as he submitted to her handiwork. He was so solemn that Suh tried tickling his armpit, but the boy didn't so much as smile and only twisted his body away from her.

Suh wrung the water from his washed hair and fastened it into a knot so it wouldn't get in the way, then scrubbed the dirt and dead skin from his neck, arms, and back. Her hands kept feeling hard knobs of bone as he had not an ounce of excess flesh. A bamboo shoot grows quickly once it breaks through the earth, and a bamboo shoot after rain makes those who see it wonder if it is the same shoot they saw the day before. As Suh rinsed the boy with more hot water from the cauldron mixed with cold water from the well, she wished for him to grow like a bamboo shoot into a pristine bamboo tree. The boy who had refused to smile was now beginning to open up. Seeing his shy hint of a smile, Suh gave the boy a playful slap on his reddening back.

To her surprise, the boy grabbed her hand and pulled it toward him, spreading the palm wide. Suh's hand was more used to giving than taking. It was the hand of someone who knew nothing of idleness, a hand that was constantly making things. The boy gazed at Suh's rough hand as if it were an icon of worship, and then used an index finger to trace letters on her palm.

When my father played the flute, the people gathered.

Despite the overlapping letters, Suh had no trouble putting together the sentence in her head.

—He must've been very good at it!

There were people who cried.

The more he wrote, the closer he pulled her palm to his chest, as if he was determined to never let her go.

—Did you learn to play from your father?

The boy nodded. What had become of his father? Suh sighed deeply and wiped the face of the boy who pointed to a pond whenever he was asked where he lived. She held his nose and had him blow out of it to clear it. Then she guided him out of the jar and dried his chest, thighs, and calves, underneath his arms and between his fingers and toes.

A cool breeze blew in from the bamboo grove. The leaves whispered as they trembled. Suh gave the boy a new linen jacket. She had sewn it on order from the mother of Jikdong, a Sungkyunkwan scholar, and it hadn't been collected yet. Banchon was crowded with onlookers whenever the King visited Sungkyunkwan to converse with the students. Jikdong was taller than Yeon, making the latter look as if he were wearing his older brother's clothes. Suh had to fold back the sleeves and the hem of some old trousers to make them fit.

—Oh my, we do wear grand ceremonial robes to impress others, but this is too big.

The boy grinned.

—I'll make you some new clothes later. I'll even add an inner pocket for your bamboo flute.

Having known only neglect during his short life, Yeon simply stared at the floor in response to Suh's kind words. Suh dried his still-damp hair. Jin, who had been in their room while Suh was bathing Yeon, opened the door.

—Look, look how handsome Sobaek is!

Jin's gaze lingered on the freshly bathed and clothed Yeon and seemed to hold back a smile of surprise.

—Could you help me? Go pick some lettuce and perilla leaves from the garden. Some leeks, too. We'll have dinner when the priest returns.

Jin, carrying the basket Suh had given her, went out to the vegetable patch with Yeon following her. Suh smiled as she saw the two children walking away together. White smoke rose from the chimneys of the Banchon houses, and lanterns were being lit. There was the occasional sound of dogs barking. A man wearing a formal *gat* hat walked by on the road visible from the vegetable patch. A horse and its rider plodded by. Sunset marks the women's hour. A wife of the nobility class walked along the bank, wearing a silk dress and a long coat that was thrown about her head as a veil, her servant girl leading the way. When the night deepened, the female servants wedged letters into the doorframes of those whom they were in love with. Young ladies of the nobility, trapped all day in their compounds, had their nurses light the way with lanterns for walks by the fortress walls of the city.

The two children crouched down in the patch surrounded by an arborvitae-wood fence and picked lettuce leaves. Their hands bumped into each other's as they gathered leeks. They looked up at the same time at geese flying over them in formation. The scent of *dwenjang* floated through the vegetable patch. Suh must have been preparing a *dwenjang*, fermented-soybean stew.

Yeon's stomach growled at the scent. The shy boy held a hand to his stomach. Jin would have laughed if it had been any other day, but she only pretended not to have heard as she continued to pick perilla leaves in her corner of the patch.

Coming back from having met a member of the faith who kept a poultry farm in the western part of Banchon, Blanc stopped in his tracks when he saw the two children. The boy jumped up at the sight of the priest and ran to greet him. The scent of mung beans that lingered on Yeon's body wafted ahead of him on the breeze. In the hug that followed, Yeon smiled at Blanc's surprise at his washed and newly clothed appearance.

Suh, who usually had only Jin to accompany her at dinner, placed four sets of spoons and chopsticks on the low dining table for the first time in a long time. The only side dishes were garden vegetables gently stir-fried in green onions, some garlic and soy sauce, acorn jelly, and pickled leeks with *dwenjang* stew, but no food would taste bad in such an atmosphere of happy simplicity. A pot of rice, cooked with slices of turnip, took the central place of honor at the feast.

The large pot of rice made Blanc smile. When he first came to Korea, he was surprised by three things. One was how this small and isolated country had its own language and letters. Aside from the ideograms used mostly by the *yangban* class, the common people had use of their own unique alphabet. The second was the number of books. There seemed to be books under every modest thatched roof, and even the lowliest girl servants would copy books of stories by hand to share with each other. The third surprising thing was how much Koreans ate. His jaw would drop at how little children swiftly emptied large bowls of rice. Those without side dishes would simply pour water into a bowl filled with rice and fill up on that. The many kinds of rice—potato rice, bean rice, mixed rice, barley rice, sticky rice, bean-broth rice—made Blanc conclude that rice was responsible for the strong bodies of the Koreans. Of course, they could not always eat their fill. Perhaps that was why they ate so much whenever they had the chance.

The four people under the light of the candle lamp seemed like a family.

"Give us this day our daily bread . . ." Blanc's blessing before they lifted their spoons was the first time Jin had heard a prayer. "Forgive us our trespasses as we forgive those who trespass against us . . ." Jin's eyes widened, and she childishly mimicked Blanc's pose.

Blanc, still unused to chopsticks, made Jin giggle whenever he dropped a slippery piece of acorn jelly. Of the four, it was Yeon who ate the fastest, having suffered from the most hunger. Suh piled his bowl with more rice. *Where does he put all of it in that scrawny body of his?* Blanc wondered as he began to speak.

—After we sign a trade agreement with Korea, I hope to establish an orphanage here. It's surprising that Korea has no such institutions.

Suh gently pulled back Jin's bowl, which was on the verge of falling off the table, and turned to Blanc.

—I've seen so many children who have lost their parents wandering this land. We need a place that will take children in off the streets. I don't understand why a people who are as caring as ours could be so unfeeling toward orphans. No one thinks of adoption.

Suh, as the daughter of a successful interpreter official, rode out on a palanquin on her wedding day, a privilege reserved only for daughters of the nobility. She could speak the language of the Qing and enjoyed reading their books thanks to her father's influence, but her inability to have children was her undoing. She had forsaken books since coming into Banchon to become a seamstress. Her face darkened. It would be impossible to explain to this foreign priest the importance Koreans placed on bloodlines. It was a mentality that did not spring overnight but was built over centuries. Suh gazed at Yeon, who was busy emptying his bowl, a few grains of rice stuck around his mouth.

Sitting at this simple Korean dinner, Blanc thought about Japan, where he had briefly dropped by before entering Korea.

It had been a world away from the Japan he had known only three years earlier, enough for him to doubt his own senses. He privately wished that a people's clothing wouldn't change despite reforms in their lifestyles. The clothing of East Asia, so different from that of the West, was particularly charming as it reflected the character of its people. There was a variety of shapes and colors, each beautiful. Yet the modernized Japanese on the streets had cut their hair short and used pomade. Convenience was a virtue that conquered all else, and it was becoming difficult to spot people wearing traditional clothes. Men walked about in suits and leather shoes, and even before the telegraph caught on, the telephone was already making headway in spreading news far and wide. A steam train ran in Yokohama.

Blanc wondered what Korea thought of these changes in their southern neighbor.

—In France, there is an order of nuns called the St. Paul Sisters of Chartres. They have branches throughout the world and provide education and nursing along with their religious work. If they could only come to Korea . . . they could help Yeon and others like him. They are already in Japan.

Suh could only answer, "Yes," and listen to the priest's words. She was not a follower of the Catholic faith. She knew, vaguely, that Banchon had its share of Catholics, some of whom were Confucian scholars. There were also *giseng* women artisans, certain officials, and that man who did errands for the butcher by Supo Bridge. Hearing there were also believers at court made Suh think the religion truly embraced rich and poor. She heard that during mass the congregants mingled instead of sitting according to social rank.

Suh was ashamed that it took a blue-eyed foreigner to worry over the wandering beggar children who had lost their parents to disease and war, most of whom weren't even from Catholic families.

—Father Blanc . . .

Blanc looked at Suh.

—That child, Sobaek . . . I mean, Yeon. Why don't you leave him here with us? We aren't well off, but I shall try to keep him clothed and fed.

A brief silence flowed between Suh and Blanc.

—But are you aware, madam? The child cannot speak.

He went on to say that Yeon's silence was perhaps not because he could not speak, but because he wouldn't.

—I am aware.

—How surprising. It took me four days to realize it. At first, I thought he wouldn't speak to me because I was a foreigner. I didn't tell you, because I thought you might not notice before we left . . .

Jin's face was sad as she stared at Yeon.

—He knows how to write. I think he was born that way, which is why he was taught his letters at such an early age.

Suh did not add, *His father who taught him the flute probably taught him to read.*

—Leave him with us.

—But he must have his own thoughts on the matter.

Blanc turned to Yeon. The child backed away from the table. The lamplight threw shadows across his face.

—That child thinks he owes you his life. He won't wish to part with you.

Suh spoke to Yeon.

—Stay with us just until Father Blanc gets settled. He doesn't have a home right now . . .

Jin stood up and approached Yeon.

Her delicate nature brought to mind a deer that would cry together with a child who was lost in the forest.

—Live here with us. We can go to the forest together . . . There are deer in the forest across the bridge.

Yeon hung his head. Jin thrust her face underneath Yeon's, determined to get an answer. How lonely the little one must have been all this time. Suh watched in silence at this change in Jin, so different from when she had first asked the girl if it would be all right if Yeon stayed with them. When Yeon didn't answer, Jin pulled his hand toward her and wrote on his palm with her finger.

Live here with us.

Suh, who had been watching them, spoke up.

—A person could get sick living all alone. Wouldn't you like to be with someone?

Yeon went up to Blanc and spread his palm. Jin took in the contrast of Yeon's bony hand on Blanc's hairy arm.

Where would you go, Father?

—Wherever I am, the Lord and I shall be near you.

Will you come to see me?

—*Bien sûr!*

"*Bien sûr.*" Jin imitated Blanc's French. The other three people burst out laughing, lifting the serious mood. Only then was the boy reassured. He nodded.

—Good thinking. You can always go back to Father Blanc once he is settled. Look, our dinner will get cold. Let's eat.

The four rallied around the food again. They were more comfortable than four strangers would usually be at their first meal together. As Blanc dipped his spoon into the *dwenjang* stew, it clanged against Jin's spoon. The other thing that had surprised Blanc aside from the amount of rice Koreans ate was how they casually shared from one pot of stew. But he got used to it, and the food did seem tastier when shared.

—What is the girl's name?

—We call her Baby.

—She has no name?

—It just happened that way. At court, they call her the Dowager Consort's baby companion . . . I suppose we ought to give her a proper name.

Yeon moved aside his rice bowl and wrote the Hangul letters for *eunbangwul*—silver bell—on the space where it had been.

—Silverbell!

Suh and Blanc said out loud together.

—She must seem as pretty as a silver bell flower to him. All right, why don't we call you Silverbell from now on?

As Suh said this, the thought that Yeon wouldn't be able to call her that himself made her sad.

—How clever she is at mimicking French.

—She learns quickly. Once, she watched a court dancer perform, and danced the steps herself as perfectly as you please from memory, right there in that courtyard. People gathered to watch. Teach her something once and she never forgets it. She learned how to read at the dowager consort's court, she can read and write anything. Her handiwork is excellent. She would look over my shoulder as I worked, and now she can embroider so prettily . . . my father was an interpreter, so I learned some Chinese from him. I taught it to her and she picked it up immediately. A Chinese student who stayed here some time ago conversed with her in his language. She's terribly clever. I don't know what to do with her now.

Blanc was about to take a sip of the hot rice water Suh had poured into his bowl when he put it down.

—Shall we try teaching her French?

—French?

Suh looked at Jin, and then Blanc. *What use would a Korean girl find in French?* As if he'd read her mind, Blanc spoke again.

—Korea is changing rapidly. It's a unique skill that may be useful someday. Since the only thing I can do better than any Korean is to speak French, I might as well share that with her.

Feelings of love naturally lead to a desire to teach the beloved something, anything that would aid the beloved in their hour of need.

—She seems like a clever child. I say that I will teach her French, but in truth, I will end up learning Korean from her.

Blanc continued in this modest vein, adding that he happened to have copied by hand a French-Korean dictionary written by Father Feron of France, which would serve as a textbook.

—You copied an entire dictionary?

—Yes, from the handwritten original written by Father Feron himself. That is how I learned my Korean.

It is unknowable whether a unique talent will prove to be a strength or a stumbling block in one's life. The only way to find out is to live.

If only she were a boy, thought Suh as she stroked Jin's hair, who looked at Blanc with wide, happy eyes at the prospect of learning French from him. Suh had known for a while that Jin's ability to absorb words and writing was extraordinary. If Jin were a boy, she would have been praised for enjoying books and for being able to write and speak so well.

She sighed.

What kind of life could such a clever Korean girl look forward to? She was even good at drawing and dancing. Suh, who had hardly been a noble lady in her youth, had often felt harshly judged for her fondness for reading. Her father used to exclaim, "Why does a common girl need all these books?" But he nonetheless enjoyed finding books to bring home for her. Suh had liked to read before she was wed and reading through the night was a source of consolation during the years of childlessness. But her in-laws found her joy of reading unacceptable. Even when she would read in the brief recesses of time that came after finishing her housework, they resented her for having a book in her hands instead of concentrating on having a child. Her husband was indifferent and did not come to her defense.

As the years passed, she could no longer silently endure the indignities visited upon her for their childlessness. With all the accusatory stares and point-blank insults, she was getting swept up in a dangerously explosive feeling that became more intense with time. In the end, she left that house. What had made her rebellion possible were the books.

Suh's face darkened at the thought that learning would someday bring Jin as much hardship as it had to her.

Blanc returned to his room after dinner. With the lamp glowing between them, Blanc had Jin repeat the French words for *I*, *you*, *he*, and *she*. Yeon sat beside her, and Suh did the dishes as she listened to Jin repeat the words. Jin had been dutifully following Blanc's instructions when she suddenly asked what the French word for *flower* was.

—*La fleur.*

Jin used her tongue, the roof of her mouth, and the insides of her nose and throat, parts she had never used for speech before in her life, to say, "*La fleur.*"

Once she had stacked the dishes to drain, Suh cracked open the guest room door to glimpse inside.

It is not only a great joy to teach a child. It is also joyful to watch a child learn, a feeling akin to seeing lilies planted the year before sprouting from the earth.

This is how Suh felt, watching Jin's eyes sparkle in the lamplight as the little one repeated the foreign sounds Blanc taught her. Suh was moved. *She shouldn't stop at just memorizing.* She was worried that learning might hurt the child, but a new desire had already sprung in her heart. Since she's so keen on learning, she thought, it would be good if we discovered what her talents were and helped her realize them. Blanc turned to Suh, who sat on the porch outside the sliding door, and said, "Look how good she is!" He grinned widely. When Blanc taught Jin the word for *we*, or *nous*, Jin gave Suh, Yeon, and Blanc each a look and said "*nous*," as if pulling them together into one word. To those who truly feel music, a song can give them a look of solitude, even when they are sitting with many others. This is because music is not of the outer body but the inner soul. Jin's face grew flushed in her efforts to roll her tongue and pronounce the words properly, but Yeon was listening to the sounds coming from Jin's rounded mouth, his head tilted. He seemed as if he were all alone.

Suh quietly closed the door. She heard Blanc say that Jin must not keep her language inside of her but practice out loud as much as possible.

Jin, who had learned strange new words long into the night, overslept the next morning.

She was reluctant to rise despite Suh's reminder that she needed to be ready before the lady attendant came for her from the palace. She thought of the faces of Yeon and Blanc, which made her blush. Leaving her bedding, she quietly slid open the door and looked out into the courtyard. Yeon was out there sweeping it, every so often hiking up his oversized linen trousers. Blanc was mending the old arborvitae fence. Yeon finished sweeping, tapped the dust off the broom, and leaned it against the fence. Jin quickly went back to her room before she caught his eye. When she peeked out again, Yeon was walking toward the well. He must have wanted to wash his hands and face. Jin closed the door, a smile playing on her lips. The courtyard was usually empty at dawn, but this morning there was someone sweeping it and another someone mending the fence. It felt like any other house where parents were raising their children. She felt wonderful, and smiled as she folded her bedding, the French words she had learned the night before fluttering like butterflies in her mind.

Lady Attendant Lee came for Jin before she had time for breakfast.

Despite her weary dodging of Father Blanc the night before, Lady Attendant Lee's expression had warmed up somewhat. She did not scold Jin or rush her as she would on other days when Jin dawdled over breakfast. Instead, she seemed to have something to say as she took in the presence of Yeon and Father Blanc.

—Have you decided to stay here?

Blanc, at the lady attendant's unexpected question, stopped his work. Suh answered the question for him, her face suddenly tense.

—They plan to stay here for the time being. Why do you ask, my lady?

—Will you be holding mass here?

Suh, uncertain, glanced at Blanc, who stood still next to the fence.

—What could you mean by that?

Lady Attendant Lee hesitated. Then, as if having decided something, she pulled out a gourd case from her sleeve, the kind made with a removable lid. She handed it to Blanc. When he opened it, he saw a cross, rosary beads, and a handwritten copy of the Lord's Prayer.

Secrets cannot stay secret unless, perhaps, the one who is passed the secret dies. Lady Attendant Lee, looking as if her heart were heavy with secrets, began to speak.

—They belonged to my mother. Please do not ask me about them. That is all she left me in this world, which is the only reason I've kept them. I was always fearful of having them with me, and I am still fearful. But as she left them to me, I could not bear to throw them away.

—. . .

—Please take them for me, Father. That way, even if they're not in my hands, my mother will not be disappointed.

Caught in the moment of Lady Attendant Lee's wish, Blanc was unable to hand back the gourd case filled with the holy relics. He could only stare at the case. It was familiar, much like those that hung from the rafters at the houses in Subunli where he had visited Father Ridel. The persecution that had left so many without home or family had ended, but they were still unable to bring themselves to openly display their instruments of faith.

—Please keep them for me.

He could not imagine how her mother must have suffered for the young woman to fear to keep her rosary beads with her. Lady Attendant Lee's situation seemed to foreshadow how difficult his mission in Korea would be.

—I shall, my lady.

Lady Attendant Lee found calm again, but Blanc's expression had darkened.

Yeon and Blanc stood beside Suh as they watched Jin leave hand in hand with Lady Attendant Lee. Whenever Jin glanced back, Yeon waved. During the day while Jin was at the palace, Blanc, with Yeon in tow, went around Banchon's mud-wall houses among the alder and chestnut trees. Yeon gazed at the cuts of meat hanging at the butcher's and into the woods where Jin had said there were deer. An ox laden with vegetables and kindling eyed Blanc as it passed. Blanc approached people with a kind expression, but the people moved quickly away from him. The women by the well scampered off, the buckets perched on their heads only half-full, and the straw-sandal seller and other merchants with their bundles avoided him as he passed. If he happened to visit any homes, they hurriedly left by their low, thatched gates or shut their doors to him. This didn't bother Blanc, who simply stood outside some other gate of a house where mugwort, thistle, and silver grass grew.

When the sun set, Yeon leaned against the bridge over the water and waited for Jin.

As soon as he spotted Lady Attendant Lee and Jin, his eyes filled with happiness. Normally a calm child, Yeon always broke into a run when he saw Jin. He would run and stand behind her, then next to her. Each time, Lady Attendant Lee turned back for the palace instead of seeing Jin all the way to Suh's yard. The fear she had showed when she first saw Father Blanc eventually melted away. *Yea, though I walk through the valley of the shadow of death, I will fear no evil, for thou art with me, thy rod and thy staff they comfort me. Thou preparest a table before me in the presence of mine enemies, thou anointest my head with oil, my cup runneth over* . . . Sometimes, she remained silently standing in the courtyard, listening to Blanc as he read aloud a psalm.

Neither Jin nor Yeon could remember who had reached for the other's hand first, but they were soon walking home hand in hand. Summer was passing. They would come through the thatched gate with their linked hands swinging in the air, and Suh would smile at them from the kitchen. As autumn approached, Yeon would play his flute nearby while Jin learned French from Blanc. Whenever the lesson ran late, Yeon used Blanc's lap as a pillow and fell asleep. Autumn deepened.

It was the middle of the night in November. Gyeongbokgung Palace, which the Regent had spent seven years restoring to promote the authority of the throne, was on fire. Black smoke filled the air. Jin had been held back by the Dowager Consort Cheolin, who was particularly reluctant to send her home that evening, and so she was spending the night at court for the first time.

The once silent palace was swept up in chaos. Rank was thrown into disarray, doors slid open and shut without permission. Jin had followed the dowager consort's attendants as they fled the flames, but at one point fell back and stood alone in the flickering chaos. Sparks flew as the flames seem to creep toward the Dowagers' Chambers. Jin ran toward the Queen's Chambers, remembering the comfort of the Queen who had fed her the pear. Later it was said that it was the Queen's Chambers where the fire had started.

Already the building was unrecognizable. Countless people had been called to tame the fire, but the flames only reached more boldly for the sky. Jin finally found whom she was looking for, the Queen standing near the Gate of Dualities. The Queen was illuminated by the light of the flames that flickered like the tongues of demons. A court lady repeatedly urged her to flee, but the Queen stood her ground. Jin managed to slip through the crowd toward the Queen, the retinue of lady attendants too dumbstruck by the fire to notice her approach. She tugged at the Queen's sleeve. Before the senior court lady could stop Jin, the Queen, who had been staring into the flames of her chambers, was already looking down at the little girl. The Queen spoke to her.

—Look at this. They tried to kill me.

The Queen gripped Jin's hand. She gripped it so hard it felt about to break.

—But I do not die.

Until the moment the Queen's Chambers finally collapsed, the Queen stood where she was, holding on to Jin's hand. Her grip, following the ebb and flow of the feelings in her heart, was strong as a vise one moment and weak enough to slip away from the next. She seemed unaware of whose hand she was holding. The senior court lady continued to urge the Queen to move to a place of safety, but the Queen held her ground. She watched her chambers burning into a handful of ash.

Even when the King came to her, she looked only at the flames and not at him.

—We must move to Changgyungung Palace.

The King's words were also futile. When his words refused to move her, the King looked down at Jin, whose hand the Queen was holding so tightly. Jin looked back at the King's face which reflected the undulating light of the flames. The dragon on his tunic danced in the firelight.

—Who is this child?

Only then did the Queen look down at Jin. Her eyes were full of the fire before them.

—A child who will keep me safe.

This was the first thing the Queen had said to the King.

—But who is she?

—Whoever she may be, can I be any less safe than in the hands of your father at Unhyeongung Palace?

Her voice was cold.

—Do you think the Regent is responsible for this fire?

—Do you disagree, Your Majesty?

—. . .

—Do you? Is there anyone else in Korea who could start such a fire so deep in the palace?

—. . .

—He was trying to kill me.

—If you are injured standing here, no one will take care of the prince. You must think of the prince.

—I might already be dead!

The King's face hardened. Heavy with concern, he left the Queen as she was. The flames, having consumed the Queen's Chambers, went on to the Dowagers' Chambers and burned down eighty sections of the palace compound before dying down at dawn. The chrysanthemums, pomegranate, and peonies of the flower wall, the pattern upon it with the bird sleeping on an apricot branch, had also burnt and crumbled. The Queen, who stood there until dawn, suddenly seemed to come to and look down at what she had gripped so tightly.

Jin could see the fine capillaries of the Queen's bloodshot eyes. Tension slid out of the Queen's body and her arm went limp, finally dropping Jin's hand.

—I am grateful you were here with me.

The Queen turned her red eyes away and began to walk, her back straight. This, despite spending the whole night on her feet. The Queen could not have walked with such a straight posture if she weren't determined to show she was undefeated.

Jin tried to follow her but was held back by the junior lady attendants.

Jin made her way out of the palace alone. Light dawned, and small tongues of fire still flickered in the ruin. She passed the King's Chambers and the Hall of Thoughtful Rule and came out the Gate of Greeting Autumn. A crowd had gathered along the palace wall. She heard a voice call out, "Silverbell!" Someone was running toward her. Jin, covered in flecks of ash, stared as she saw Yeon running toward her and shouting his name for her. She had never heard his voice before. Yeon ran along the palace wall and did not stop until he stood practically nose to nose with Jin. He seemed to have waited for Jin all night outside the palace as his linen clothes were damp from dew.

—Did you call my name?

—. . .

—You can speak?

Yeon could only stare back at Jin, eyes wide.

—Did you not just call me Silverbell?

Yeon seemed more surprised than she was. He had spent the night watching the flames tower over the palace. The strength in his knees had left him when he thought of how Jin may have perished in the fire. The fear that filled his heart made him breathe faster, and when he saw Jin emerge from the Gate of Greeting Autumn in the light of dawn, he thought he would stop breathing. And that was all he knew.

Jin gazed at Yeon, who seemed to have retreated once more into silence, and started walking again. This was the first time she was returning to Suh's house alone. Unlike when Lady Attendant Lee led the way as Jin took in the scenery, she was mindful of where she was going.

—You know how to talk.

—. . .

—I heard you clearly.

Yeon hadn't been afraid at first that Jin may never return. He had stood waiting on the bridge until late at night. Even when the woman Suh suggested Jin was spending the night at the palace, he went back to the bridge after dinner to keep waiting for her. It was then when he saw the orange flames in the night. Not thinking it was the palace at first, he only wondered about the fire from afar. He realized it might be the palace when the orange flames persisted. Imagining Jin caught in the smoke, he ran, darting through thickets of reeds and pine groves, and jumping across the river when the footpath didn't seem fast enough. But once the palace was in sight, he was forbidden to enter. His eyes became as bloodshot as the Queen's as he stood outside the walls, staring at the flames.

They could see the woman Suh's house in the distance.

Jin felt tired and hollow, but she quickened her pace. No one looked out when she stepped into the courtyard. A house without anyone waiting in it, no matter how small the abode may be, is larger than the empty sky. Suh, no matter what errands she needed to run, would always be home around the time Jin returned from the palace. Feeling out of place in the emptiness, Jin forcefully slid open the door to the room she shared with Suh. Suh's sewing things were messily laid about. The guest room where Blanc had taught her French every night was also empty. Even the furnace door was shut tight. She pushed open the door to the backyard. Suh wasn't in the bamboo grove or by the large earthen jars of preserved sauces. Yeon sat on the porch surrounding the courtyard and watched Jin go in and out of the house looking for Suh and Blanc. Presently, Jin sat down next to him.

—Where did they go?

Yeon pulled Jin's hand toward him and tried to write on it. Jin whipped her hand back.

—Say it out loud.

Yeon hung his head. Silence fell between them. Jin held out her palm for Yeon.

The priest left.

Jin felt her mind go blank.

—Where did he go?

Instead of answering, Yeon got up and went to the guest room. He returned with Blanc's old French-Korean dictionary. Inside this well-thumbed, dog-eared volume was a letter written in both Korean and French.

I am very happy to have come to Korea and met you. Keep thinking and keep learning.

But it was Yeon who had always hung on Blanc's every word, even as Blanc turned the pages of the dictionary and taught Jin his strange language every night.

—Why didn't you follow him?

—. . .

—Are you all right?

Yeon entwined his fingers together and hung his head again. The thought of Father Blanc having left made Jin feel empty inside. The happiness she had felt when the four of them sat around the small dinner table, their utensils clinking against each other's, already seemed like a distant memory.

Suh, who had learned late that Gyeongbokgung Palace was burning and had rushed to the site, was returning, bereft, when she glimpsed Yeon and Jin sitting on the porch. She broke into a run. The moment Jin spotted Suh, her face broke into tears. She hadn't cried at the fire, with the Queen, or with Yeon, but now she started to cry. The sight of Suh made all the fear she had kept at bay wash over her. Jin hugged the French dictionary to her chest.

If you die, I'll die too.

Yeon took her palm in his and wrote again. *If you die, I'll die too.*

—I'm not going to die!

She shouted this at Yeon but then fell silent. The memory came to her of the Queen's chilling voice, "But I do not die," as she gazed at the red flames that engulfed her chambers. The sight of the Queen's cold face, filled with isolation and rage, was not the same as that of the Queen who had scraped the white insides of a pear as she fed it to Jin. Jin echoed the words to Yeon.

—I do not die.

It was a time when France was promoting the metric system, an achievement of the French Revolution, as an international standard of measurement. Germany was bringing out the internal combustion engine, which converted the explosive energy of fuel into movement. And in Korea, a young girl, who had witnessed the burning of the palace of her country that had just begun to open its doors to the world, was clutching a French-Korean dictionary to her chest and crying.

PART TWO

1
First Sight

Your Excellency,

It is my honor to inform you that I have entered Seoul on June 6 after appropriate preparations since arriving in Jaemulpo on the third of this month. On the very next day, I submitted your request to the proper authority at the Board for Diplomacy and Trade as a representative of the French Republic.

I remain your honored and obedient servant in the capacities you have invested in my humble person.

Victor Collin de Plancy
June 10, 1888, Seoul

There are encounters that are as brief as the clear dew evaporating from a grove of trees but still last a lifetime in the mind.

It was a June morning in 1888.

Victor Collin de Plancy was putting on his dress uniform before a mirror in his quarters at the French legation near Seoul's Seosomun Gate. A glass window was installed in the room of this house, which was otherwise in the traditional Korean style, and the scene outside showed a courtyard full of flowers and trees. Among the hydrangeas, peonies, and touch-me-nots grew Chinese quince and persimmon trees, and farther back, bush clovers and briers crowded behind crape myrtle trees with branches luxuriously entwined with trumpet creepers.

Whenever Victor felt tense as he made his preparations before the mirror, he turned his gaze outside to the large, green leaves of the phoenix tree swaying in the early summer wind. He had the feeling that Asians loved these trees. There was a phoenix tree in the lawn of the French legation in China as well. When he recognized it here, the Korean interpreter official had told him the phoenix ate only bamboo fruit and nested only upon the phoenix tree. A Chinese official had told him the same. Victor asked the Korean official whether he had ever seen a phoenix. The official replied that seeing a phoenix meant he would live forever, and he hoped Victor would see one while he was in Korea. Victor had received the same answer in China. He mused aloud that China and Korea both planted this tree, but no one seemed to have witnessed the fabulous bird in either country. The Korean official responded that if no one could see one, then it was as good as if he had already seen one. Victor was fascinated by this Eastern way of talking, as if one thing could naturally be another at the same time. It contained the power to make sharp edges round.

Victor turned from the tree to the mirror again.

He had heard the following story as soon as he landed in Korea. Thomas Watters, at the end of his long tenure in Korea as the British acting consul-general, had gone to the palace, wearing evening attire instead of his dress uniform, to bid farewell to the King. After being made to wait for two hours, Watters was informed that he was not properly dressed to be presented before His Majesty.

Watters had requested an audience several times to formally make his farewell, but the palace had complied only two days before he was to set sail. He had already sent his dress uniform off with his other luggage, thinking the palace was never going to answer him. He had only his evening tails with him, but he had assumed he would have the opportunity to explain once he was in the King's presence. But he was forced to leave without having introduced his successor to the King.

Victor, who considered it his duty to avoid mistakes and leave a good impression, polished his already polished silver and gold stars and epaulets one more time. He combed the tassels on his chest and pulled at the sash on his shoulder so that it lay flat. He palmed a few drops of oil and smoothed down his hair and beard. He paused to think after taking a long look up and down at his reflection and, gathering up his courage, took his new camera and slipped it into its hiding place inside his vest. The camera's forty-millimeter lens fit neatly into a buttonhole. Surreptitiously pulling on a wire in his pocket would enable him to take photos. Victor liked the fact that he could also mount the camera on a tripod when he needed to. Having become a fan of photography five years ago, he was intrigued by this camera built for secret photography.

The King was to receive him at eleven in the morning, but he set out an hour beforehand, so he would arrive with time to spare.

The ground was muddied from the rains in the night.

But the vegetable patch in front of the legation building looked beautifully fresh in its cover of rainwater droplets. Victor could see the outlines of the Russian legation building beyond. The sight of this building made him think that France had come too late. Two years had already passed since Korea petitioned France to send a legation. Victor was the first French legate to enter Korea with a letter of credence from the French Ministry of Foreign Affairs. When Victor arrived in Jaemulpo Harbor via China, an official from the Board for Diplomacy and Trade came all the way from Seoul to escort him. Once he had made sure that Victor had the necessary authority as the French legate to Korea, he joyfully declared that the King would be informed immediately of Victor's arrival.

What made the most lasting impression of Korea on Victor's way from Jaemulpo to Seoul was the ubiquitous presence of burial mounds, whether on low hills or between the mountain pines. He had wondered aloud what these round, grassy mounds were that not only dotted the mountains but also the embankments that bordered the fields or any sunny side of a hill near the villages. Burial mounds, he was told. The sight inspired the same strange feeling of witnessing a heat shimmer in the distance. Such a round, cozy, and green home for the dead. The thought of living in this country where the living and the dead lived together made him feel nervous and excited at the same time.

Victor wanted to walk the Path of the Four Symbols and the Road of the Six Offices that stretched from the main gate of the palace that was in turn tucked into the arms of Inwangsan Mountain, but the interpreter official informed him that walking before the main gate was forbidden. Victor had no choice but to ride in the palanquin. He was thrown about inside whenever the carriers jumped to avoid puddles, which made him take special care with his uniform. When he was let off before the main gate where the great stone tigers stood guard, a Chinese-speaking official approached to help guide him into the palace. Victor aimed at the stone tigers and pulled the cord in his pocket. He also took photos of the dragons carved into the three headstones of the main gate without the official noticing. Once in the palace, they had to make their way to the reception hall across streams and bridges to meet the King.

They were passing a pond surrounded by granite stones.

Young palace girls in yellow jackets and pink skirts, smiling and teasing one another, were surprised by Victor's appearance. They stared at his hair, brown not black, and the paleness of his skin. The fancy dress uniform also must have been a sight. When Victor stopped in his tracks, the palace girls immediately broke into a run, bursting into laughter as they did so. One of the young girls looked as if she'd seen a ghost. Victor pulled the wire at the girls running spiritedly away. As he watched them disappear, the official told him they were the youngest of the court ladies training to be official attendants.

—Do they live in the palace from a young age?

—Yes, so they can acquire the virtues of court ladies.

—What do they learn?

—The ways and traditions of the palace, singing and dancing, the healing arts, classical literature, and Korean writing.

The clear waters of the Silk Stream ran underneath one of the bridges leading to where the King resided. Having stopped to take in the sight of the stream, Victor spotted a senior court lady attendant and a junior one walking over the curve of the bridge toward them. The older court lady wore blue slippers and her step was confident, a walk that spoke of pride in her position. Victor aimed his camera toward the younger court lady behind her, the one in red slippers who was following her superior.

Some eyes contain destinies.

The official felt something was amiss and looked back at Victor. Victor and the younger court lady were also looking back at each other. In the moment their eyes met, Victor felt nailed to the spot. It was because the court lady's deep, dark gaze was one of friendliness. It was the first time that Victor had met a Korean gaze that wasn't teasing, surprised, or curious but simply kind. But it wasn't just this friendliness that made him stop in his tracks. It was because he was faced with a sudden memory, a face he had thought forgotten coming back to him through the sparkling dark eyes of this young court lady. He felt as if his feelings were riding on rapid waters.

Without even realizing it, Victor greeted the woman, who had her hands gently clasped before her, in French.

—*Bonjour.*

To his surprise, she responded in kind.

—*Bonjour.*

Victor couldn't believe his ears. A woman in court lady attire in a Korean palace had just spoken French. Overwhelmed and confused, Victor instinctively pulled the wire again, capturing the dark eyes of the young woman. The court lady drew in her slight smile, dropped her gaze downward, and lightly turned away. It was like seeing a butterfly sitting on a trumpet vine fold its wings. He quickly pulled the wire again and caught the profile of the woman as she turned back toward her superior.

Her jade-green tunic and indigo skirt, and the silk jacket she had thrown over it, all fluttered in the early summer breeze.

Victor pondered what had just happened as he followed the official again along the stream toward the reception hall. *Bonjour.* The court lady had clearly answered him in French. He suppressed the urge to ask the official if he had also heard her say it.

He forgot about his plan to photograph the things that caught his fancy as the memory of the girl's dark eyes filled his mind. They reminded him of his birthplace, which he had not thought of in a long while. The village of Plancy, in the northeast of France. His novelist father, an Irish immigrant. His mother, who loved to write and recite her own poetry. Victor sighed deeply. And Marie, the only girl in Plancy with black hair and dark eyes. The village of Plancy had humiliated Victor's family as well as bestowing upon him the ambition to leave it. Once the family moved to Paris, the Collin de Plancys forgot about the village they had once called home. Victor had not been back since. Thinking about it only brought him pain. It was even more unexpected that he would be thinking about it in a royal palace in a faraway land in the East.

—What could her name be?

The official walking in front of him turned around and gave him a look as if to ask, What could *whose* name be?

—The court lady we just saw.

—Lady Attendant Kim or Choi or Park, no doubt.

—Excuse me?

—That's what we call them in the palace.

Victor looked up at the towering pine that was spreading a wide shadow.

—You must not covet the court ladies of the palace.

The official seemed to have sensed the ripples in his heart.

—All the women in the palace belong to His Majesty. To covet the King's women is to commit an unpardonable crime that will bring your bloodline to an end.

Victor smiled a private, pained smile at the official's admonishment.

The stream flowed from the northwestern side of the reception hall's gate toward the south. Water flows when it is free, and pools when it is stopped. When the obstacle is removed, water flows once more. The official politely spoke again when they had followed the water up to another bridge.

—Auspicious waters. It flows with the hopes for the people of the palace to go about their care of the country with a clear and virtuous heart.

—I see that the desire to learn from water is the same in both the East and West.

Victor said this before he could be overtaken by old memories that were rapidly surfacing like the bubbles from a waterfall.

—Here we are.

They stopped before the Hall of Diligent Governance. A pillared wall surrounded it on four sides. The official pointed to the pavilion, rising amidst large flagstones, and told him that this was the seat of Korea's political decision-making. Its giant, solid wooden pillars held up a tiled roof adorned with colorful dragon heads. The palaces of the Qing Dynasty had floors made of baked mud bricks, but Korea's palaces stood on granite. A white, rocky peak above seemed to gaze down benevolently upon the Hall of Diligent Governance.

Victor sat on a chair in the waiting room until the King's attendant announced him.

The waiting room was small, but it looked out toward a path leading into a thick pine forest. Unlike China, where chairs were everywhere, Korea was said to resist their use. But here in the waiting room was what appeared to be a Western table and chairs, possibly Qing imports. The vase on the table held an early hydrangea bloom. As Victor admired it and took in the forest path outside the window, English biscuits were brought in for him, as well as, surprisingly, French wine and tobacco from Manila. An official informed him that the King was being delayed by his annual royal visit. Victor was perplexed. Seeing this, the official explained that the royal visit referred to the King partaking in ancestral ceremonies at the royal burial grounds. He had returned late the previous night, which was why he was delayed this morning.

Victor waited for a long time.

Presently, the official returned to announce Victor to the King. Passing through two doors, they came upon a wide hall. The King sat behind a table, his council standing behind and to either side of him and wearing their palace robes with their backs bent in deference to the King's presence. An interpreter was present to aid in the formal reception.

Victor looked up toward the center where the King sat. The dragons carved into his armrests looked real enough to be alive, and the eight-panel folding screen that stood behind the throne seemed to protect the monarch. And there the King of Korea's Joseon Dynasty sat, a man with a thin mustache and a generous smile.

—Welcome.

The official who brought Victor into the hall fell to his knees. Victor began to follow his example, but the King stopped him.

—That is unnecessary. You may follow your own customs.

Victor reverentially bowed his head.

—We have heard you arrived here on the third. Do not be disheartened that we summoned you almost ten days after.

—I have just heard of your royal visit, Your Majesty.

—Yes. We returned yesterday.

The King's movements were restrained, his voice low.

—Have you brought your letter of credence?

—I have.

The King's gentle eyes never lost their smile. The King seemed to like him, Victor thought. Trying not to ruin this first impression, Victor took care to bow whenever answering the King's questions.

Korea had long practiced a self-imposed seclusion from the outside world and was only beginning to open its doors. It was inevitable that the country would be thrown amidst powerful nations intent on their own gains. Outside cultures brought dramatic changes to daily life, the new dizzily mixing with the old.

—How did you find your voyage?

—There were some storms, but the waters were generally calm.

—And how is your president?

Victor handed over the letter from Marie François Sadi Carnot announcing his election as president of France. The King seemed satisfied as he listened to the interpreter's reading.

—We are glad to have a legation from France in Korea. You will inform France of our country's situation and usher in a new harmonious era between our two nations.

—I shall do my utmost, Your Majesty.

Korea was trying to balance the influence of outside powers. Russia was interested in obtaining a harbor of lower latitude than Vladivostok, Britain seized Geomun Island to block such Russian efforts and renamed it Port Hamilton, and China, which already had power over the Kingdom, used the Imoh Army Revolt as an excuse to establish an administrative center in Korea. Ostensibly it was to check Japan's expansion into the country, but it was more to interfere with Korea's internal affairs.

—You must find many difficulties living in a new country.

Victor bowed in appreciation of the King's concern.

—If there is anything you require, speak.

—There is one request I might make, Your Majesty.

—What is it?

—Allow me to take photographs inside the palace. I wish to capture the beauty of Korea's palaces.

—Is that all?

—It is.

He wanted to take a portrait of the King, but there was no need to try him in their first meeting.

—I confess I do have a camera concealed in my vest, but I wanted to inform Your Majesty as I felt I was doing wrong.

—You have a camera in your garment?

—I do.

—How small is it?

—It was made in America two years ago. One puts it in one's vest and takes photographs. The lens looks like a button from the outside. I do wonder if it was built to take photos secretly. Fifteen thousand of these models were sold as soon as it was invented. There must be many people who want to take secret photos. And I must be one of those people.

The King laughed out loud.

—Will you take a photo of me?

—It is impossible indoors. There isn't enough light.

—That is too bad.

The King's expression suggested he truly meant it.

—If it pleases Your Majesty, we could go outside. And I would bring the photo the next time I have an audience with you.

Victor had thought it unlikely, but the King acquiesced and rose from the throne. His council was thrown into confusion by his sudden movement. They urged him not to do it. One even said that photography stole the soul of the photographed.

—What is this nonsense? Did Ji Wuyoung not take a photograph of me once and show it to me? Do you persist, still, in believing such stories?

The King shook off their objections and stood beneath the entrance of the Hall of Diligent Governance.

To take a photo is to awaken the senses. Simply measuring one's distance to the subject is to store a new memory of that subject.

Victor, for the first time since entering the palace, properly aimed at what he was photographing and pulled the wire. The King's council, still up in arms, kept calling out to the King. "Your Majesty! Your Majesty!"

When the King returned to his throne, there was a satisfied smile on his lips as if he had done something terribly amusing. Victor was intrigued. The King seemed uncomplicated and introverted on the surface, but he clearly appreciated new cultural experiences. The King would have been happy to receive the gift of Sèvres porcelain that the French Ministry of Foreign Affairs had provided, Victor thought with regret. The porcelain should've arrived by now, but the Japanese shipping company had delayed its arrival.

—How diverting. In a short while, we shall hold a banquet in honor of your appointment here and see each other again.

—I am grateful, Your Majesty.

He was never to show his back to the King. Victor left His Majesty's audience by walking backward and sideways in observance of the rules. His forehead was beaded with sweat. He followed the same path he had entered, the dirt trails beneath his feet made into clay by the rain from the night before. He looked about, hoping he would see that court lady who seemed as light as a butterfly but had dark eyes full of sadness. But it came to naught.

When Victor returned to the legation office, he asked Secretary Guérin for the quickest photography studio in Korea. He wanted to see the picture of the court lady he had met near the Silk Stream bridge. He did not tell Guérin his real reason, saying only that he was curious how the photo of the King would come out.

—Are you saying you've managed to take the King's picture?

—I did, I'm telling you.

—Photography is forbidden in the palace. But how surprising that you've managed to take a photo of the King himself! Such a thing is permitted only through a complicated procedure.

Victor said it hadn't been difficult as the King had requested it himself. Guérin's eyes shone when Victor mentioned that the King had allowed him to freely take photos inside the palace.

—Congratulations!

Victor was taken aback.

—You see, this tells you how much the King welcomes you here. There are diplomats who have waited for months to have their first audience with the King, and many were promised an appointment only to be turned away at the palace gate. Being kept waiting for hours in the waiting room is a given. But you were granted an audience just days after your arrival, and the fact that the King went against the palace rules for you to take his picture is a rather unexpected favor.

Victor felt reassured. But the King's favor was surely not for him but for the French government. That night, as part of his official duties as

French legate to Korea, he wrote a letter to the French Foreign Minister reporting on his audience with the King.

Your Excellency, I have met with the King of Korea today. His Majesty seemed very intent on learning about foreign cultures.

Victor put down his pen and went out to the courtyard of the legation. The face of the dark-eyed court lady on the Silk Stream bridge kept filling the blank space of the letter, and he had felt as if he were writing on her face.

Hearing his footsteps in the courtyard, a Jindo puppy, still awake, came up to Victor. Palace official Cho Byeongsik had given the dog to him as a gift. It was born in a southern region called Jindo, the namesake of their breed. The reason he brought it over at barely a month old was that the puppies had to be young enough to imprint themselves for life on their owner. It was the kind of dog that would spend days or even years searching and waiting for a lost owner. The little dog had fluffy white fur, which Victor patted before walking up to the phoenix tree. The puppy followed a step behind. The aristocrats of Plancy had many white dogs at their home in Plancy village. Whenever Victor went there to see Marie, the dogs would come running out to greet him first.

In the dark, Victor took out a cigarette and brought it to his lips. He exhaled long plumes of smoke into the air. It had rained the night before, but now the sky was filled with stars. The leaves of the phoenix tree swayed. From somewhere came the cry of a nightingale.

Sometimes a dog does not guard a house but a person's solitude.

—I should've asked her for her name.

Victor addressed his remarks to the puppy underfoot.

—How can I see her again if I don't even know her name?

He bent lower and stroked the puppy's back. It had been only a moment, but the dark eyes of the court lady had already wrapped a vise around his heart. It was like looking down at a pocket watch he thought he had lost long ago.

She had clearly said, "*Bonjour.*" She said it so naturally. Her pronunciation and enunciation . . . She knew how to speak his language!

Victor stood up as if to shake off these meandering thoughts. He felt disgusted at himself for loitering around the courtyard. He dropped his cigarette and ground it out with his shoe. He wished to remain unmoved. He trod back to his quarters and sat down once more, taking out the governmental order he had received with the letter of credence.

> *Your duty is to carefully observe whether the agreement signed between France and Korea on June 4, 1886, is being carried out. Of specific interest, as important as our political issues with Korea, is the agreement concerning French missionaries in Korea. While Korea seems to unhesitatingly accept European culture, there remains a long history of prejudice against Christianity.*

Victor folded the order again and put it back in its drawer.

The reason the King welcomed the French was that France's influence was unthreatening. The King could not express his real intentions before the legates and consuls of Japan, England, America, Russia, or Qing Dynasty China. A single word from the King was enough to reconfigure the web of conflict between these powers.

France had signed its treaty with Korea only two years before.

In the meantime, France was more concerned with Vietnam, resulting in frequent clashes with China, which was also attempting to expand into Southeast Asia. France and Korea now had ties, but there was no real exchange between the two nations yet. France's chief interest in Korea was not economic gains but the religious issue of the spread of Catholicism. Its missions based in Paris had secretly sent three priests into Korea during the Kingdom's era of seclusion, and they had all been executed. This was followed by the martyrdom of eight thousand Korean Catholics and nine French priests.

That early summer night, listening to the sound of the young Jindo pup that softly whined as it tried to go to sleep, Victor lit the end of his cigarette, wedged it between two fingers, and began to write his letter.

2

The Dancer

Your Excellency,

Korea has requested that the American government send over American military officers to aid in the reorganization of their armed forces. They have also appointed emissaries to Paris, London, Berlin, Rome, and St. Petersburg.

Despite the treaty, there are situations in which our priests still face trouble doing their work.

I believe the Ministry of Foreign Affairs must take a special interest in this matter.

As Your Excellency has no doubt been informed, the garrison from the Aspic returned to Jaemulpo Harbor on June 23. The American garrison will remain until the end of this month, and the Russian military left a garrison of six when they left their legation. But I believe such measures are no longer necessary. All seems peaceful.

I believe that Yuan Shikai's intent upon realizing Qing's decline in influence upon Korea was to bring about internal turmoil through spreading rumors and to consequently justify China's military presence in Korea by making it seem that the latter's government was incapable of maintaining the peace.

June 23, 1888
Victor Collin de Plancy

Was it her dark pupils? Her red lips? Her skin that was as bright as her eyes? Jin's face was like a flower. Her eyebrows were as neat as lines, and the pupils nestled within her thick lashes were black and clear and deep. Her cheeks were pink, her fingers white and long, her breasts and hips full, her forehead flawless, her brow generous, and her wrists and ankles thin. What should be dark was dark, and what should be red was red. What should be slim was slim, and what should be bright was bright. Where she should have curves, she had curves.

Finally, Jin placed the dancer's lotus crown on her head. She was ready for the banquet. The waiting room was busy with the dancers preparing for their performance. Her yellow robes, the color of the oriole, seemed a touch more brilliant in the glow of Jin's white skin. The tight red belt accentuated her slender waist. She attached her seven-colored sleeve extensions and waved them about, checking their fit, before looking outside the pavilion.

The drizzling rain that had come down since the morning was not letting up.

The trees of the palace took on a refreshed sheen on rainy days, but the dirt paths unpaved with stepping stones became muddy underfoot. The strands of rain were thin but persistent, and the banquet attendees were sure to be annoyed by the mud on their shoes.

I'll get to see Yeon again.

Thinking of Yeon, Jin gazed out at the drizzle outside. It must have been raining in Banchon as well. *I wonder how Suh is doing.*

They said that the evening's banquet was to welcome the new French legate.

Jin had danced at many banquets for foreign legates, but this was the first time she was to perform for a French representative. France . . . She had never visited, but it was the closest foreign country to Jin's heart, having learned French from Father Blanc when she was a child. Blanc was now Bishop of the Apostolic Vicariate of Korea.

The Queen had summoned her the night before when Jin was at work in the royal Embroidery Chamber. The Queen was in the habit of personally tasking Jin with a solo dance performance when there was an important event at the palace.

—I have heard that the French legate invited for tomorrow's banquet is a sensitive and earnest man.

—Yes, Your Majesty.

—He lived for a long time in China and speaks their tongue well. He respects artisans and is no stranger to books. I think this gentleman is a good fit for Korea.

—I see.

—France's attitude toward Korea is different from China's or Japan's. They are far from us, so they will keep neutral. Their presence will help our country.

Jin bowed her head low as she listened intently to the Queen's words.

—Let your talent shine so that he may think well of Korea.

—I shall, Your Majesty.

As Jin was about to leave, the Queen stopped her by calling out, "Lady Attendant Suh!" Jin stopped in her tracks.

—I believe in you!

I believe in you. The Queen's words weighed heavily on Jin's shoulders as she left the Queen's Chambers. The once gentle Queen had become ruthless in the face of the many insurrections and political blows that threatened her life. The Queen, who once kept Jin so close that she had hardly even bothered to utter Jin's name, had one day begun to address her as Lady Attendant Suh. She could not trust new people and surrounded herself only with family. Whenever the Queen suspected someone was against her interests, she cut them out without hesitation, even when she had no evidence of wrongdoing.

—What are you thinking of so intently?

A peony swayed before Jin's eyes, bringing her out of her reverie, brought on by the patter of the rain.

There stood Soa, looking as crisp as a bloom that had stood in the light rain since morning.

What Soa had waved in front of Jin was the peony prop that ten court dancers used for the Dance of the Beauties Picking Peonies. Soa had also finished preparing. Her flower crown was in place, and she wore yellow and green ceremonial dancer's robes over a dark blue skirt. Her green dancing shoes peeped out from under the hem.

—It won't do for a dancer to look so glum before a banquet.

Soa smiled brightly as she said this and jiggled the peony flower again in front of Jin's face. Jin moved her head back to avoid it, causing the peony and glittering adornments on her own seven-colored lotus crown to sparkle from the sudden motion.

—I hope there are no mistakes.

—You're changing the subject!

—I'm fine . . . I'm just thinking about a special request the Queen made yesterday.

—What was it?

—She wants the French legate to have a good impression of our country.

—But Her Majesty always says that.

—Yesterday was different. Anyway, you had better dance your best today and receive a gift from the Queen.

—Not while you're dancing as well. And I'm only in the group dance.

Soa made a thoughtful face and looked at Jin sideways.

—Seeing how she asked you to do the Dance of the Spring Oriole, tonight's banquet must be quite important for her.

The Queen's animosity toward the King's father, the Regent who lived in Unhyeongung Palace, was enough to halt a running horse. At the same time, the Queen's concern for the sickly Crown Prince was delicate enough to surprise a blade of grass. Afraid for her life, the Queen often changed where she would sleep from day to day, and sometimes she even changed sleeping quarters in the middle of the night. She was ready with an icy reprimand for anyone who dared to show the slightest sympathy for the Regent. And any official voicing even light criticism against the Crown Prince would find himself dismissed from his position.

The Queen's anxiety had a way of infecting Jin and occupying her thoughts. Sometimes, the Queen burst forth with the accusation that none of the foreign powers in Korea cared about them. She accused these so-called modern civilizations of secretly caring only for their own interests. She lamented that they smiled to her face during the day and bowed their heads to the Regent at night. She could trust no one. Was that why she became so dependent on the words of the palace shaman woman?

A deep sigh issued forth from Jin's lips.

The usual protocol was for the shaman to be present at court only when there were ceremonies or rites to be held, but the anxious Queen had requested her to stay permanently. The Queen was especially dependent on the shaman regarding the Crown Prince. This was why there were always many rituals, both small and large, being held in the palace. Jin thought that at least the Queen, whose heart seemed as if it were turning into ice, had the shaman woman to lean on. But it is the way of the human heart to wish for the stream when given a puddle, the river when given a stream, and the ocean when given a river. It is most human to stand before an ocean and still think it is not enough water. While Jin was glad for the Queen, the shaman woman was jealous of how much the Queen favored Jin. One spring morning, as the Queen took a rare walk in the garden where the hydrangeas bloomed after the spring rain, the shaman pointed to Jin and said accusingly to the Queen, "That child is like a musk-scented deer."

She said this in Jin's presence.

When the Queen demanded an explanation, the shaman said, "Jin is so striking that she is fated to unknowingly steal the hearts of others." It sounded like a compliment at first.

—She is so exceptional that if she does not die young, she should be exiled to a faraway land.

The shaman went on.

—If you keep her close, she will steal the King's heart.

The shaman's words unsettled the Queen. Surely it was only a jealous scheme to throw Jin into disfavor with the Queen? Jin was about to ask Soa, *If the Queen had been herself, don't you think she would've seen through the shaman's intent?*

—Ten thousand blossoms bloom and turn the palace red . . .

Soa, who had been murmuring the lyrics to the music of the Dance of the Beauties Picking Peonies, suddenly turned toward Jin.

—What is it, Soa?

—I found a book to read at night. Will you read it aloud to me like you do for the Queen?

—If you like.

Soa smiled wide, flashing her white teeth. Jin smiled as well and swallowed her question. No one could resist Soa's smile, especially the smile in her eyes that reached all the way to her cheeks.

Not even a day had passed after the shaman woman had spoken when Jin was transferred from the Queen's Chambers to the Embroidery Chamber. The meaning was clear. The Queen's Chambers' ladies were closer to the attentions of the King, and Jin was to be kept out of his sight.

On the day Jin moved chambers, the Queen gave Jin a long look.

—Do you remember what happened in the Year of the Black Horse?

1882. Jin bit down on her lip. How could she ever forget the grievous events of that year?

—When it comes to you . . .

The Queen, who usually spoke so determinedly and with flashing eyes, trailed off into a brief silence before speaking again.

—When it comes to you, I do not wish to have a man come between us.

Jin felt her heart drop to the floor.

—Your Majesty!

—These are the ways of the court.

The Queen spoke these words sharply, then fell silent. Jin was also silent. *Yes. These are the ways of the court.* Jin wanted to look into the Queen's eyes, into the very words she was hiding. Had the Queen wanted to say that there was no telling what might happen between a man and a woman? Whether a court lady caught the eye of the King or not, all ladies of the court belonged to the King. Didn't the Queen's words mean that at court, only the heart of the King may prevail?

But even so . . . Jin could not help the tears that welled in her eyes. It wasn't because she was sorry to move chambers. Even in the Embroidery Chamber, Jin could be called by the Queen at any time to read for her or take down her dictation in neat court calligraphy. Jin would dance for her on days the Queen felt low. As a Queen's Chambers attendant as well as court dancer, Jin helped the Queen with her correspondence or passed on letters to courtiers on days when there were no performances. Such duties would not change much after her move. But still, her heart felt as empty as a small leaf fallen from a great tree.

—Oh, the banquet must be about to start.

Soa gave a last wriggle of the peony in her hand at Jin and walked to where the dancers in the group dance stood waiting. The pavilion, briefly peaceful as the dancers rested after having finished their preparations, was again awash in a murmuring hubbub.

Victor had learned that the banquet changed locations from the King's reception hall to the Pavilion of Festivities only after he had arrived at the palace. The change was because of the rain. The Queen had judged that the overcast drizzle would darken the interior of the Hall of Diligent Governance while the pavilion's open interior would afford an arresting view of the pond as raindrops fell on the water.

Victor had requested a private audience with the King before moving on to the banquet where diplomats from other nations would be present.

He wished to present his appointment gift of Sèvres porcelain from the French Ministry of Foreign Affairs, as the package had finally arrived in Korea. The palace guard had asked Victor what his silk-wrapped package contained, and when Victor said it was a gift for the King from the French government, the guard had Victor enter through the middle gate of the palace's main entrance. Victor's interpreter explained that the middle gate was used only by the King himself, and Victor was being afforded this privilege as he was carrying a gift for the King. Korean protocol made Victor nervous. In his previous post in China, a Qing official had assured him upon hearing of Victor's new posting that Korea's customs were similar to China's, and there would be few difficulties adjusting. But Victor was finding that Korea had its own way of doing things, and despite its larger similarities, there were important differences in the details.

Victor understood why the banquet had been moved when he saw the Pavilion of Festivities. The scene was one of unearthly beauty. The sight of the lotus pads and the light rain that fell on the water of the pond would have a soothing effect on any troubled soul. Upon the square pond stood an island, and the breathtaking pavilion standing upon that island made even Victor stand taller. Three bridges on the eastern side led to the island. The western side had steps descending into the water, presumably for boats. Tiny concentric circles from the raindrops rippled outward across the surface of the pond before dispersing.

The King gave a warm greeting as Victor arrived at the banquet.

—Welcome!

Next to the King sat the Queen, and next to the Queen sat the Crown Prince. The Queen, who had been caring for the Crown Prince, turned her gaze to Victor. Victor bowed deeply. He had repeatedly heard of how the Queen was wise in the ways of the world, that she was a voracious reader familiar with many disciplines, and that she exercised a decisive influence upon the King. But no one had told him that she was also beautiful. Her dark eyes shone with sharp intelligence, and her translucent skin sparkled like a pearl, so clear he thought he might see his reflection on it. From her emerald tunic, designed to demurely conceal the body, rose the delicate lines of her long and poised neck.

—You have been well?

—I have, Your Majesty.

Even as he answered thus, Victor was thinking of the hectic first days of his appointment caused by persistent rumors among the populace, that foreigners were kidnapping and selling Korean children. There were even rumors of cannibalism. Words can spread as if they had sprouted wings. The rumors put the servants of foreigners in a difficult position, as they were suspected of colluding with the supposed kidnappers. Then one day a servant was killed in the street, and before anything could be done about it, more than ten others were murdered in two days. The local servants at foreign residences, fearing for their lives, quit their employs in droves.

In that regal pavilion, Victor suddenly remembered a phrase he had read in China, that a king was a boat and his people the water, and the water may make the boat float, but it can also overturn it.

The people made the most nervous by these rumors were the Japanese merchants who lived in Korea. Because they spoke some Korean, they were suspected of being spies and ringleaders of the kidnapping operation. A rumor spread that an enraged mob was about to attack the Japanese legation. The Japanese, already having experienced two such attacks in the past, including the burning down of its legation building, braced itself for another bout. But the attack never came. Instead, the building where the American and British legations were located, as well as the customs and telephone offices, faced daily skirmishes with the locals. Each legation held emergency meetings and requested security from the Korean government. Korea's Ministry of Justice and the Police Chief posted decrees in the towns. But the decrees only encouraged the rumors that the children of Korea were being kidnapped by foreigners.

Victor had a feeling that the Chinese were responsible for the rumors.

Upon his arrival in Korea, Victor had hired Kim Holim as his interpreter, a man who spoke fluent Chinese and was recommended to him by the Chinese legate Yuan Shikai. Kim Holim would often visit the Chinese legation, even after becoming an interpreter for the French. It eventually came to Victor's attention that the man who had been spreading the rumors—that Bishop Blanc's orphanage, the first of its kind to be established in Korea, was incarcerating children for the purpose of harvesting their blood—was none other than Kim Holim. But Kim had already fled in fear that Victor would hand him over to the police. And the only place Kim would have heard of such rumors was at the Chinese legation, the fact that similar rumors were spreading in Tientsin and Peking being evidence of a sort.

Not to mention how the Chinese legate began to withdraw from participating in diplomatic meetings, citing sickness, since the day the rumors started spreading. The Chinese legation was the only foreign mission to not participate in the joint efforts against the rumors. But why would they do such a thing? It was likely they were forcing Korea to admit it was unable to control its own populace, giving the Qing the impetus to maintain their troops in the country. A ruse to keep in check Japan's growing influence on the peninsula. It chilled Victor to think how the conflict between Japan and China over Korea seemed irreconcilable. He would always have to contend with it as long as he was in Korea. And if his hunch was right, the Chinese had just succeeded in involving other countries in their conspiracy.

—And has your military regiment gone back?

The Queen's calm voice still conveyed a determination not to beat about the bush like the King. Victor glanced at the light rain falling on the pond. The Queen's cold voice seemed to contain the accusation, *And wasn't calling your military into Seoul's fortresses the first thing you did when you were appointed here?*

The foreign diplomats, fearing an uprising, had requested the American, British, and French military docked at Jaemulpo Harbor to send regiments of twenty each to the capital. They had judged the local police to be insufficient in their ability to defuse an uprising. This was an unprecedented and coordinated move on the diplomats' part. The joint regiment entered Seoul after just a day's march.

Only then were the officials taken aback and started giving assurances that they would post the notices that the diplomats had drafted themselves. The officials guaranteed the safety of the foreign legations and requested they send away their military. In the end, the King stepped in. He promised to capture and prosecute those who attacked foreigners or the buildings they resided in and to reward those who helped arrest the attackers. He issued a decree to track down the perpetrators of the rumors until they were found.

Only then did the mob calm down.

The more one speaks, the more one invites misunderstandings. Especially when one speaks out of turn.

—I'm afraid we had no choice but to bring in the regiment.

—Did I say otherwise? I was only asking if they had gone back, now that peace has returned.

The Queen surely knew the soldiers had gone back. In lieu of replying, Victor mopped the sweat from his brow and bowed from the hip. Tonight was a banquet night, and he was about to present a gift of Sèvres porcelain to the King. He told himself it was not the time or place for such sensitive matters.

—It was worrying. But we are glad it is done with.

The King's tone remained gentle.

—I apologize for the concern this may have caused you.

—The rumors are at fault.

Victor had requested the official Cho Byeongsik to find Kim Holim, the source of the terrible rumors plaguing Bishop Blanc. Victor was determined to verify where he was getting them from. Cho Byeongsik conveyed Victor's request to the King, who ordered a search. According to the decree, Kim Holim was to be beheaded the moment he was determined to be the source of the rumors. Thinking a beheading was too much, Victor asked Official Cho to consider exile as an alternative punishment. Not until much later did Victor learn that Kim Holim, apprehended at a Buddhist temple, was executed in a way unique to Korea. He was tied up and laid on the ground, and sheets of wet paper laid upon his face. The wet paper had blocked his nose and mouth, asphyxiating him to death. Official Cho had not informed Victor of his arrest or execution, and it was over by the time Victor learned of it. Victor was sure, then, that it was the Chinese legation that was responsible for the rumors. The truths that Kim Holim would have confessed to during his interrogation would have put the Qing in danger, and determining that the fates of countless Korean officials would also be compromised, they had, Victor deduced, shut him up for good.

As if to shed himself of a nightmare, Victor spoke to the King in a bright voice.

—Your majesty, the Sèvres porcelain that the French government sends upon my appointment arrived only yesterday.

—The Queen tells me that France is unparalleled in its production of artisanal works.

The King smiled at the Queen. It was part of his considerate nature to try to smooth the moment of tension between the Queen and Victor.

—I am grateful that you think so. But today, I am astounded by this pavilion. To have such a beautiful building . . . It is Korea that is truly a nation of artisans.

Victor bowed again and glanced at the Queen, who continued to look down at him. She had reached out to hold hands with the Crown Prince sitting next to her.

—The King appreciates good porcelain. I am curious as to what French porcelain looks like.

The Queen's words were now perfectly polite, belying her previous harshness. There was even a serene smile on her lips. Victor placed the silk-wrapped porcelain on the table before the King.

—Do unwrap it.

Victor obliged, untying the knot of red silk. He had heard that in Korea, only the King could use red, and so he had obtained red silk with some difficulty. The silk unraveled, revealing a jar drawn with a design of a French castle, plates of mythical figures, and a low teapot with ear-like handles on each side.

Beautiful objects are accompanied by moments of silence.

The King leaned toward the Sèvres porcelain. No one spoke a word. On the waters by the pavilion, the little rings created by the falling rain made ripples far and wide.

—We have known France puts much effort into creating its artworks, but these are even beyond our expectations.

As if eliciting her agreement, the King turned and smiled at the Queen.

—I have heard that even China imports porcelain now.

—Is that so? The Chinese?

—They use Sèvres porcelain in their imperial court.

—The imperial court?

—Yes. It made me wonder why the Chinese court would import French porcelain, but it must be because it is this lovely.

Victor was reassured by the Queen's words. He almost smiled as he realized that he inadvertently cared more about her reaction than the King's.

—Sèvres is the name of a place in France?

—It is, Your Majesty. Their factories were originally in Vincennes, but Madame Pompadour, who was the favorite of King Louis XV, loved their work so much she had them moved near her home in Sèvres. The city attracts not only potters but artists. Sèvres discards any porcelain that has even the slightest flaw. To prevent flawed works from being distributed, they forbid glaze from being applied on disapproved pieces. Therefore, to determine authenticity, one must look for the enamel finish and whether they have their characteristic ears.

—Fascinating. Truly admirable. We thank you for bringing such precious gifts. Please convey our gratitude to the French president.

—I shall, Your Majesty.

The porcelain was wrapped again in the red silk and taken away. The Queen, who had maintained a polite expression throughout the porcelain's presentation, returned to her grim stance.

—Having heard of Your Excellency's good taste, I am sure you will find Korean celadon of interest. I hope you take the opportunity to examine our white celadon in particular. You will find it quite satisfactory.

—I shall.

Victor gave another deferential bow to the Queen. A gesture according to protocol, to the Queen who even in admiring the Sèvres porcelain did not forget to introduce the excellence of Korea's celadon.

The legates began arriving, heralding the beginning of the banquet.

The American legate Hugh Dinsmore was the first to arrive, followed by Russia's Karl Weber. Britain's Colin Ford and Japan's legate Masuki Kondo arrived next. They broke the ice by talking about the rain that had been falling since the morning. China's Yuan Shikai was the last to come, and the first thing he did was to give out a boisterous laugh. His formidable bulk was matched by an attitude of sheer confidence.

The legates, as they stepped up to the pavilion, paid their respects to the King first and foremost. The King asked after the health of the heads of state in the other countries. Victor, standing at a remove, watched as the legates answered the King in cheerful voices, smiling perhaps because it was a banquet evening. As Ford, another recent appointee, tried to bow to the King in the Korean style of putting knees and hands to the ground, the King stopped him.

—We regret how we were not able to see the legate Watters before he left Korea. We have heard he came to court, only to be turned away.

Ford, who had never had an audience with the King until this moment, bowed deeply at the King's careful words.

—Try to forget the unfortunate events of the recent past and enjoy yourselves tonight.

As soon as the King's words were spoken, the banquet shifted into a more festive mood. Frogs sitting on the vegetation by the pond plopped back into the water as the banquet attendees began to move. The diplomats, all in their dress uniforms, sat in chairs toward the middle of the pavilion, their interpreters stationed between them. Some stood, leaning against the pavilion's balustrade. The sound of Korean and other languages intermingled like music. Junior court ladies from the Refreshment Chamber moved busily among the diplomats with trays of hors d'oeuvres and drink. A few diplomats were already imbibing wine.

Two dancers carrying a small octagonal table with a vase full of peonies appeared, followed by musicians. The appearance of the dancers, who placed the table with the peonies in the middle of the floor, hushed the conversing diplomats. The center of the pavilion became a stage. The first performance of the palace dancers was the Dance of the Beauties Picking Peonies. The musicians settled in a semicircle behind the table with the peonies.

Victor sat with Guérin near where the King was and drank British tea out of his teacup as he looked toward the pond where the rain fell. The lotus flowers and buds trembled, drenched in the rainwater. He turned his gaze to the stone beasts that supported the railings of the balustrade. The pavilion was grand from a distance but also beautifully detailed up close. Just when he thought of taking a photograph, he heard the decisive clack of the *bak*, a bamboo percussion instrument that heralded musical transitions. Eight dancers wearing green and yellow and indigo appeared at both right and left of the stage. The flower crowns on their heads jiggled whenever they advanced or retreated. At the sound of the *bak*, the dancers divided into two and made a final turn around the stage. With another *clack*, they gathered their hands together and stood toward the northern side.

The dancers recited the following poem.

Ten thousand blossoms bloom and turn the palace red.
The crowds of red and yellow flowers strain to be seen.
A new jade flute sings the music of peace.
Butterflies flutter above the fragrant petals.

The musicians then played the "Song of Everlasting Spring and Youth." It had a solemn and supplicating sound. Whenever the dancers circled the peonies, their crowns caught the light around them, and the green of their dancing slippers flashed underneath their skirts.

—Is it true that the crimson of their robes symbolizes the south and summer?

Guérin was unable to answer Victor's question, and said instead, "Doesn't the crimson color symbolize the north?"

—I thought the north was winter and the color black.

Guérin cocked his head and smiled, saying, "Perhaps it is best to appreciate the dance as is." He probably meant that it was a banquet, and they were there to enjoy.

Having learned that they would have the opportunity to see dances in Korea's palaces, Victor had tried to learn about them and their meanings. It was his nature to prepare beforehand. He asked Guérin, who knew less of palace dances than he did, and his interpreter. He also looked through books, but there was too much to know about the colors of the clothes, the headpieces, and the sashes around the dancers' waists. Victor turned toward the peonies in the middle and concentrated on the movement of the dancers. Even in the steps where they guilelessly caressed the flowers, a practiced sense of order was paramount. The dancers moved with a restraint that betrayed not a hint of private emotion. There were eight dancers picking flowers off the table, but to Victor, they moved as one. The dancers cast off their sleeve extensions and twirled until the last clack of the *bak* sounded, upon which they brought their hands and feet together. The music ceased.

While the Korean officials and lady attendants remained silent, the diplomats burst into applause.

—Is it the custom to clap after a dance?

The Queen asked this question with a smile, observing the surprise of the Joseon officials. The Queen often held teas and banquets with the diplomats' wives, and so it was impossible that she did not already know the answer.

—It is a sign of appreciation for the dancers' efforts.

This was said by the American legate Dinsmore.

—And how is it done in Russia?

Weber, caught off guard, put down his teacup with a clang. He quickly swallowed the biscuit in his mouth.

—If the performance is particularly moving, we even stand to clap.

The Queen, still holding on to the hand of the Crown Prince, smiled.

—I see. Then we shall clap as well. Especially since the next dance is to be performed by the finest dancer in all of Korea.

The Queen's words raised many eyebrows.

The peony table was removed from the stage, and a wide straw mat with a colorful pattern was spread in its place. At the sound of the *bak*, a dancer with her hands held in front of her took tiny steps onto the stage, as if she were carefully balancing herself on wooden sandals. The crown on her head sparkled, and her yellow silk robes glowed atop the straw mat. The dancer slowed to a halt and stood alone onstage. Once the *bak* ceased, a lovely voice flowed from her lips.

As I walk beneath the soft and pretty moon,
my silk sleeves flutter in the wind.
Enchanted by my beauty before the flowers,
my lover gives his heart for me to cherish.

The dancer finished her recitation of the lyrics, threw her hands behind her, and turned her head. Victor, who had been taking a sip of wine, bolted upright. The dancer's eyes . . . Victor froze, waiting to see those eyes again. He scrutinized the dancer as she turned and turned on the mat, her arms spread wide like that of a bird spreading its wings to the sky.

It's her!

Victor gave out a low gasp. The woman he had met on the Silk Stream bridge the day of his first audience with the King. The court lady he had spontaneously greeted with a *bonjour* and who had effortlessly answered *bonjour* back!

She was a court dancer.

Victor felt the breath leave his body. He was rising from his seat without knowing it.

His gaze was arrested by her as she moved as lightly as if floating in the wind. Guérin and the other diplomats shot glances at Victor, who was by now half out of his chair. The Queen also noticed him. Guérin tugged at his sleeve, but he couldn't make Victor sit down, too absorbed was he in the dance.

Guérin tugged at Victor's arm harder and whispered in his ear.

—The Queen is watching you.

Only then did Victor regain his senses and sit down.

Was it like a branch shaken by the wind?

Was it like the scattering of golden sand?

The dancer raised one hand high and the other hand low, lifting and dropping her feet in rhythm. She took three steps forward and raised her arms above her head. She did a movement symbolizing the raising of a tower. Was she catching flower petals blowing in the breeze? Her hands meandered freely in the air. There was a faint smile on her face as if she were privately admiring flowers in bloom. The smile was part of the dance, but it took Victor's breath away. Her right hand floated up and down like a blossom fallen on flowing water, and her left sprinkled imaginary petals in the air. The dancer's face was infused with melancholy as she withdrew her smile. Victor sensed in her an emotion that the previous eight dancers had not conveyed.

On the day of his first audience with the King, Victor had gone to Hwang Cheol Photography in Namchon's Jingogae neighborhood to develop the photographs he'd takem with his concealed vest camera. He had first met the Korean photographer Hwang Cheol at a photography store when he lived in China. Hwang spoke Chinese fluently and was so passionate about cameras and photography that his excitement carried over to those around him. Hwang had planned to learn photography in China and then visit Japan to observe the studios in Nagasaki, Kobe, Osaka, and Kyoto. When Victor heard Hwang had a studio in Jingogae, Victor felt as if he had chanced upon an old friend. Koreans did not like being photographed. Photography supplies were, consequently, hard to find. Thinking he might be in frequent need of Hwang's help during his Korea posting, Victor had taken it upon himself to visit the studio in person. He had also been eager to see the face of the court lady again, the one he had met on the Silk Stream bridge.

Hwang's eyes had grown wide when he learned that Victor had photographed the face of the King. Only Ji Wuyoung had managed to have done so in the past. Even then, the King's council had kicked up a great fuss, and Ji had barely managed to get away with it. Perhaps Hwang had been eager to see the King's face himself, but thanks to his expedience, Victor was able to see the court lady's face as well, if only through a photograph.

In the picture the court lady's eyes regarded him without teasing or surprise. They showed only friendliness, as if she knew who he was. There was also a shot of her without her smile, just turning to follow the senior court lady who was leading her. There was another one of her in her green jacket and long indigo skirt, descending the Silk Stream bridge. Would he ever meet her again? He had placed the photos in a drawer and looked at them often. But here she was now, dancing right before his eyes.

He was not the only one gazing intently at the dancer as she directed her line of gaze at one spot and flipped her wide, fluttering sleeves. Whether he was taken by the Dance of the Spring Oriole or seduced by the beauty of the palace dancer, the King also had a satisfied smile on his face and did not take his eyes off her for a moment. Yeon, who was accompanying the dance on his bamboo *daegeum* flute with "Sangyoung Mountain" from the *Music of the New Willow Leaves*, was also transfixed by Jin's dancing. The stares of the three men lingered upon her as her dance progressed. The Queen watched the King and Victor, both of whom seemed to have lost their hearts to the dancer. The King turned from the dancer to the Queen, and their eyes met. The King gave an embarrassed grin.

That child is like a musk-scented deer.

She is so exceptional that if she does not die young, she should be exiled to a faraway land.

If you keep her close, she will steal the King's heart.

Despite remembering the shaman woman's words, the Queen made herself smile when her eyes met the King's. She had tried to forget the prophecy. She sighed as she recalled the memory of Jin's devastated face when she had ordered her transferred from the Queen's Chambers to the Embroidery Chamber. The Queen had known her since Jin was five. Jin wanted to leave the palace when her companionship of the Dowager Consort Cheolin ended, but it was the Queen herself who had called Jin to the Queen's Chambers and made her a junior court lady.

The light rain falling on the pond surrounding the pavilion was drenching the spiderwebs on the reeds and lotus pads. The Queen frowned as she looked out at the water. Jin had been at the Queen's side as she grew into a young woman, as well as through the humiliations of the Year of the Red Tiger and the Gapsin Coup. During every crisis that threatened her life, there she was by the Queen with her head bowed. *The child is like a musk-scented deer.* Until the shaman had said so, the Queen had never considered Jin as a woman. She was a dear child, a lovely girl, a beautiful dancer, and a wise confidante. It was against the internal rules of the palace, but the Queen often made her sit close to her. She had Jin read to her and write letters and sometimes tasked her with styling her hair. Upon the shaman woman's words, the little child with the tearful eyes to whom she had fed spoonfuls of pear flesh was transformed into a woman of unparalleled beauty.

With the sound of the *bak*, the dancer walked in a large circle, her robe flapping like that of an immortal hermit of the mountains crossing a heavenly bridge. Her dance silenced the entire pavilion, save for the music of the *daegeum* flute that encircled the banquet like the sound of the wind. When the dancer gently brought her hands together, and her sleeves fell narrowly to her sides, the Queen was the first to clap. Jin gave a start at the sound. The diplomats also began clapping. Even the interpreters, who seemed uncertain as to whether they should or not, awkwardly put their hands together. To clap for everyone is the same as clapping for no one. Only Victor, among the diplomats, was not applauding the dancer.

—The French legate is not impressed by the dance.

Victor, too enraptured by Jin to even think of clapping, turned his head to the Queen. The music had ceased, and Jin had gathered her sleeves and was moving away from the stage like a bird flying back to its nest.

—Lady Attendant Suh.

The Queen called for her. Jin, whose feet were already making her exit from the stage, could not believe her ears. Did the Queen just call her name? For a moment, she thought she was hallucinating.

—This banquet is in honor of the French legate, but it seems he is the only one not applauding. Perhaps he does not like your dancing.

—Your Majesty.

Jin breathed in and bowed low. Hearing the Queen say the opposite of what he was feeling, Victor felt he needed to speak up, but the tense mood stifled his voice. The diplomats looked from the Queen to the dancer and back again.

—And what shall you do about it?

—Forgive me, Your Majesty.

Jin's forehead was beaded with sweat.

—How shall you satisfy the French legate?

Jin was as surprised by the Queen's reaction as anyone else. Nothing like this had ever happened before. When the dancers finished a dance, they brought their sleeves together and disappeared from the stage as if they had never existed in the first place. Clapping was forbidden in the palace. Jin was unable to exit the stage as she waited for the Queen to speak again. The droplets of sweat on her forehead fell upon the straw mat below.

The Queen was not unaware of how exceptionally Jin had performed the Dance of the Spring Oriole. It wasn't only because the Queen personally asked her to. From her first step onward, Jin approved of how the ground itself felt against her feet. Her waist had smoothly ridden the rhythm, and her sleeves lightly fluttered as if underwater. She couldn't see his face, but once she realized it was Yeon playing the *daegeum*, her heart swelled with her longing for the woman Suh and her gladness for Yeon's presence. This longing and gladness had eased her nervousness, freeing her heart for the dance.

—Did I not ask you a question? What will you do for the legate?

No one can be struck by beauty without even a trace of envy.

The Queen glared at Jin, whose whole body, despite the robe covering its length, radiated with the vividness of a living songbird. *How beautiful she is*, the Queen's heart sighed. She was as silent as the dancer herself who was like a tree in summer, a peach blossom, or a measure of silk.

The Queen's silence heightened the tension of the banquet.

Jin stood frozen on the mat, unable to exit the stage as the Queen looked down at her. The King was dismayed by the Queen's strange reaction. Only the prince, as if bored, turned toward the pond where the rain fell. Nobody was watching Yeon, but he had also set his flute on his knee and fixed his gaze on the dancer's back.

Thinking that punishing the dancer for his delayed applause was excessive, Victor began to stand up to placate the Queen, but Guérin pulled him back down whispering, "You will only make it worse."

Victor sat, his head turned to the dancer. She seemed lost in thought. Victor hadn't even been aware that the dance had finished. He hadn't noticed the applause of the other diplomats. Victor had forgotten he was at a banquet with other emissaries and officials and had even forgotten the King himself. He hadn't noticed the music had stopped; his mind had been full of the movement of the dancer.

—Did I not ask you what you plan to do for the legate?

The Queen's voice was harsh.

Jin, who wordlessly kept her back bent toward the Queen, now opened her mouth to speak.

—If it pleases Your Majesty, I will grant any wish the French legate desires.

A murmur arose from among the diplomats.

The Queen turned to the King.

—Your Majesty. Did you just hear what Lady Attendant Suh proposed?

The King smiled, uncertain.

—Would you permit Lady Attendant Suh to grant a wish of the French legate's?

—We trust the Queen in this matter.

Only the King had realized it. That the reason for the Queen's acting this way was because she saw him spellbound by Jin's dance.

—Do I have your word?

—Of course.

A strange smile appeared on the Queen's lips.

—Your Excellency!

At her call, the eyes of everyone at the banquet converged on Victor. It was so quiet that the sound of the rain falling on the pond could be heard.

—Lady Attendant Suh is the finest dancer in Korea. She says she is willing to grant you a single wish in repentance for her failure to satisfy Your Excellency with her dance. What say you?

Victor was mortified.

—What say you? The King himself permits it.

—It is so sudden. I am not sure of what to say.

—Is that a refusal?

Jin, whose head was bowed before the Queen, was glancing sideways in Victor's direction. Their stares collided in the air. These were not the friendly dark eyes that had answered his greeting with a *bonjour* on the Silk Stream bridge. They were filled with suspicion and resentment toward him. It was Victor's belief that in the event of an unexpected situation, honesty was the wisest form of diplomacy. He could see no other way out of this moment other than to show his true feelings.

—Your Majesty, I must say that it is an honor to make a request to the court dancer. I am only sorry that I am unprepared for such a joyous opportunity. If it can be arranged, could I have Lady Attendant Suh visit our legation office?

—The French legation office?

—Yes, Your Majesty.

—What for?

—I wish to show her our offices in return for her showing us her beautiful dance. If it can be permitted, I would like to photograph her as well. I am also unfamiliar with the capital, and it would be good if we could see the city together.

The Queen seemed to consider his words. Victor said what he said only because the situation forced him to, but a hope sprung within him that his wish would be granted. If the dancer came to the legation office, he could be with her at a closer distance. They could have a quiet moment together.

—Your words imply that you enjoyed Lady Attendant Suh's dance.

—Of course, Your Majesty.

—Then why did you not clap?

—I have never seen such a beautiful dance before. I was so taken by its beauty that I had quite forgot to applaud.

There was another murmur at his words, which subsided. The Queen turned to the King again.

—What are we to do, Your Majesty?

The King slowly turned his head to the dancer. *If it pleases Your Majesty*, she had prefaced her proposal with, but the granting of a wish to this foreign legate would inevitably compromise her standing as a court lady. It was impossible for a court lady of the palace not to know this. Only then did the King recognize her as the attendant who was always by the side of the Queen, ever since that night when the Queen's Chambers burned down.

He broke his gaze from the dancer and turned to the Queen. It was obvious to everyone that Victor had not applauded because he was too overwhelmed by the beauty of the dance. The King knew it hadn't escaped the Queen's notice as well. Had she not always been so observant, so clever in her reasoning? The Queen was only trying to read what he was thinking through this ruse.

—We leave it to the judgment of the Queen.

—It is not so simple, Your Majesty. You must consider it carefully.

—A promise is already made to the legate.

—But it is Your Majesty's decision. For who shall go against the decree of the King?

The Queen was pushing for the King to declare his permission in his own words. The King gave a hollow laugh.

—Fine, then. Lady Attendant Suh is to grant the French legate his wish.

Relieved laughter and applause arose from the gathered diplomats. A smile, so faint it was both there and not there, appeared on the Queen's lips. Jin sighed deeply as she stood still on the mat. The woman Suh had counseled her to always consider the Queen's position, how Her Majesty's life was under constant threat. Only then would Jin be able to understand the Queen's actions. Her eyes, unlike when she had looked at Victor sideways, were now completely emotionless. There was not a trace of resentment or censure. Only Yeon, sitting behind Jin with his *daegeum* perched on his knee, stared at the French legate with suspicion.

As Jin retreated from the stage with her hands gathered before her, and the mat was rolled away, the old festive mood returned to the pavilion.

3
Your Name

Your Excellency,

Since 1885, Korea and China have been connected through the telegraph between Seoul and Peking. The Chinese government, responsible for its installation, has held a monopoly for twenty years. They suspend or deny service at a whim. Meanwhile, the Japanese proposed laying a cable between Nagasaki and Busan and connecting it to Seoul at their own expense. We understand what Japan would gain from a direct line with Korea. As of this writing, Japan's telegrams can only be sent by permission of the Chinese government, and even then, the messages are rerouted through Tientsin and Shanghai at considerable expense.

Wishing to avoid further interference from foreign powers, Korea refused Japan's offer. Knowing that ridding their communications of Chinese supervision and extending their network to

Russia's on its northern border through a new line would be in its best national interests, the Korean government decided to establish their own telegraph company and lay the lines themselves.

The extremely difficult task of laying the lines in the mountainous regions was given to Mr. Halifax, the sole European in the venture, and a Korean team that managed to finish this endeavor in three months. Four telegraph offices were opened, and their fares set as follows.

Seoul to Gyeongju . . . 16 jeon.

Seoul to Jeonju . . . 18 jeon.

Seoul to Daegu . . . 20 jeon.

Seoul to Busan . . . 22 jeon.

The equipment is mostly handled by Koreans. The employees were trained in the necessary skills and in English for a year, now allowing them to undertake their duties. I believe that the Koreans will be able to run their own telegraph offices without the help of foreigners, just as the Chinese have.

July 27, 1888
Victor Collin de Plancy

While the grass grows, the steed starves.

The proverb he once read in Shakespeare came upon him with new meaning as Victor awaited his reunion with the court dancer. The promise made in late June came to fruition one summer morning in late July.

The cicadas on the phoenix tree filled the legation garden with noise. Victor woke earlier than he ever had since coming to Korea. Not that it was much of a waking up, as he had hardly slept the night before. As soon as he opened his eyes, he listened for the sound of rain outside his bedroom window.

Korea had a long monsoon season. The rains weren't rough, but the sun hid behind clouds. The fortress of the capital was muddy and damp, the air perpetually humid. The topsoil of the vegetable patch in front of the legation had washed away. The gardeners would have to concentrate their efforts on restoring the lost footpaths for the time being. The monsoon ended two days ago, but Victor couldn't help feeling anxious that it would rain again.

Instead of rain, all he heard was the loud singing of the cicadas. He stretched.

Cicadas heralded the end of the monsoon. Bishop Blanc had told him that the sun would shine all day if one heard cicada song at dawn. Victor did not want to greet his visitor in the rain.

Blanc had lived for so long in Korea that he knew the country's laws, traditions, weather, and the way its people lived almost as well as any Korean. Blanc took over as the Seventh Bishop of Korea when Ridel, the Sixth, passed away. Since Blanc became bishop, there was more tolerance toward the Catholic faith, and its persecuted believers, once driven underground, were more content than they had been in a long time.

Blanc, once he became the bishop, established the orphanage he had planned since he first arrived in Korea. He bought a house in the Gondangol neighborhood and modified it with the help of the woman Suh, a year before Korea and France signed their first trade treaty. At his orphanage, the first ever in Korea, he brought in children who had nowhere else to go. Korean Catholics helped, but most of the caretaking was done by Suh and Yeon. Suh, who had no children of her own, put all her care into the orphans, making them clothes, teaching them to write, and preparing their meals. Yeon helped her. Suh and Yeon were as hurt by Yuan Shikai's rumors as Blanc was. When it became clear they were in danger, Blanc had appealed to the newly appointed French legate for help. Thanks to Victor's quick and firm response, Blanc's honor was safeguarded, and Blanc befriended Victor, with whom he often discussed the goings-on in Korea.

Victor sat up, having listened to the cicada song as if it were joyful music. What should he show the court dancer first? He had thought about it ever since an official visited to inform him of the date of her visit, but he couldn't decide. Should he show her a painting? A photograph? He smiled at this welcome bit of pleasant worrying.

And should he follow Blanc's advice and take on a Korean name?

Victor had thought about doing so on his own and smiled when Blanc read his mind. One of the best ways of becoming friends with a Korean, Blanc had said, was to have a Korean name. Blanc's Korean name was Baek Gyusam. Blanc reasoned that Koreans called their friends by name, and foreign names were probably too difficult to pronounce. Victor decided to follow Blanc's advice.

His smile faded. He had confessed to Blanc that he was in love with a beautiful Korean woman and wished to learn at least a few Korean expressions for her. Blanc had laughed good-naturedly and agreed to teach him, but his smile had disappeared when he heard that the woman was a court lady of the palace.

One is often forced to decide whether to follow their society or their nature. A diplomat must follow society. Even if the laws of that society are wrong, they need to be upheld.

—Korea has Korean laws.

Blanc, usually of a humorous and genial, even carefree nature, looked worried.

—A woman of the palace may not have a life outside of court without the permission of the King.

Victor's silence deepened Blanc's concern.

—We do not live in a republic. There is no knowing what will happen to you if you let a woman of the palace into your heart. And does Your Excellency not represent France in this country? You must never forget that we are not in France.

France.

Blanc's admonishment that they were not in France cut him to the bone as he waited for the day he would meet the court dancer. Even France did not mean complete freedom. The trials his Irish immigrant father had to endure were also because of the laws that were written for the nobility. His father had to move to Paris, then Belgium, and again to Plancy as a printer to pursue his dreams of becoming a writer and an aristocrat. In the end, his family was prosecuted for illegally using an aristocratic name and banished from the village. But to ask for royal permission if he wanted to see the woman he loved, and to wait an entire month! Such things would never have been tolerated in France.

Victor shook off these thoughts as he rose and dressed. This country tended to dredge up the past at unexpected moments. But perhaps it wasn't this country but the court dancer, with whom he never so much as had a proper conversation. Victor had attended divinity school in Paris after leaving Plancy. But unlike the rest of his cohort, he then entered university for Eastern languages after graduation. Everyone thought this decision strange, his father especially so. Victor left for Peking after obtaining his degree in Law and Chinese. He wondered if he had chosen the East to get away from his father, the man who stopped at nothing to shed his immigrant status. The man who was obsessed with the idea that becoming a perfect Frenchman meant becoming an aristocrat.

Victor's life in the East began in Peking. He had no special reason to choose Eastern languages, but he was happy with his choice as it led him to East Asia. China, Japan, and Korea were lands of mystery. The French, and the nobility especially, adored the many objects he brought back from his posts. The books, celadon, and ornaments of the East were coveted items for bored French nobles who amused themselves by curating their collections.

Victor had a leisurely cup of coffee and came out to the courtyard. The Jindo dog circling the phoenix tree came up to greet him. The dog had grown quite dignified in the past two months. Wagging its tail, it sat at Victor's feet, prompting him to stroke its back. This was how they said hello to each other.

—Today is a very special day!

As if in understanding, the Jindo dog playfully licked the hand that stroked its back. Victor attached a leash to its collar. Knowing that this meant it was being taken out for a walk, the dog leaped up with its front paws in the air. This was the happiest part of the dog's day. From his experience of the past month, Victor knew just how hard it was to wait for someone. A walk would shave off some of that time.

—Let's go.

Victor, leash in hand, opened the legation gate.

A day is also a short life. Especially certain days.

It was a little before eleven in the morning when the palanquin carriers deposited Jin at the French legation gate. Her visit had been announced for eleven. It was the first clear day in ages. The world was bathed in sunlight. On the palanquin, Jin had looked out to see the houses putting out anything that needed to be dried.

The rains had washed away the path through the vegetable patch, making it difficult to determine what was the path and what was the patch. Jin watched the palanquin carriers awkwardly tiptoe through the mud before she turned toward the legation gate. Today, she was not the court dancer wearing the silk tunic in the Pavilion of Festivities but a lady attendant of the Embroidery Chamber wearing a dark green jacket and a long indigo skirt. She was as she had been when Victor saw her on the Silk Stream bridge. Her black hair was in a long braid twisted and fastened into a bun. It was the style worn by court ladies of her rank. In her right hand, she held a long outer jacket that was as green as her tunic. There was a hint of curiosity in her peach-colored face as she pushed open the legation gate and looked in.

The first thing that filled her vision was the green leaves of the phoenix tree on the far side. The leaves of the hydrangeas were a deep green where there had once been flowers, the trumpet vine was bursting with blossoms, and the juniper and yew stood in perfect formation at eye level. On one side were peaches and four-o'clocks that resembled a pattern on an engraving, their trunks rising to the same height with rose moss growing below. A brief glance was enough to know that the garden received someone's constant and devoted care.

Jin was about to take a red-slippered step into the courtyard when a glass window of the legation building slid open. Victor peered out.

When he spotted Jin, he quickly slipped on his leather shoes and came out of the building.

—I was about to come greet you at the gate.

Her arrival had been so abrupt that his words came out in French. What he said was true. He was about to go to the gate with his interpreter and Guérin. There was some time remaining, but he had been glancing out the window since early morning and had spotted her red shoe poking into the courtyard.

—I arrived a bit early.

Jin drew the jacket over her arm toward her body and bowed from the waist. Victor stared for a moment at Jin, who had just spoken to him in effortless French.

Welcome. I'm glad to meet you. Hello.

He hadn't had a chance to use these few Korean expressions he'd learned for her. Instead, he had burst out with "I was about to come greet you at the gate" in French and ended up hearing Jin speak French instead.

—It is an honor to have you here.

Victor bowed to Jin, just as she had done. Jin smiled faintly at Victor. Those eyes. Those dark eyes were again not hostile but friendly, and she was smiling. Her pupils were even darker up close. Without realizing what he was doing, Victor opened his arms and gave Jin a hug and a kiss on the cheek. It happened before Jin could do anything about it. She stood frozen and gave Victor a hard stare.

Oh.

He sighed as he saw Jin, the friendliness gone from her eyes, staring up at him like a stranger. Her posture was stiff with dismay.

—I've forgotten we're in Korea. How strange. You are not unfamiliar to me. I keep wanting to act in the French manner with you. This is how we say hello. Please understand, it is only a sign of friendliness.

Jin's expression turned cold, and she looked away.

Victor remembered a piece of advice he had heard in England, that one should ask for forgiveness if one had done wrong to a man, and even if one hadn't done wrong to a woman.

—I have offended you greatly.

—. . .

—Please forgive me.

The cicadas on the phoenix tree amplified their cries. Jin, who seemed unassuaged by Victor's repeated entreaties for forgiveness, suddenly turned her dark eyes toward him.

—Would you grant me one request, sir?

Her voice was clear and calm.

—If you forgive my offense first. Then I shall grant you any request that is in my power to grant.

A thin smile appeared on Jin's lips. Victor felt relieved.

—What is your request?

—Please let me visit Gondangol.

The Gondangol neighborhood? That was where Bishop Blanc had his orphanage.

—The lady who raised me lives in Gondangol, but as I am a court lady of the palace, it is difficult for me to see her when I wish. It is only because I wish, with all my heart, to see her before I return to the palace that I make this request. Please refuse if it is too difficult.

Jin demurely lowered her head, wondering if she had perhaps spoken too soon, seeing as she had just stepped into the courtyard. Guérin in his Western suit and the Korean interpreter in his Korean robes were walking toward them in quick steps from the door of the legation offices.

Victor's answer was immediate.

—We shall do so. Come in, for now.

—Do you mean it?

—Do I mean what?

—I can visit Gondangol?

—We shall leave as soon as we finish lunch.

—Together?

—Yes. Did I not tell you back then, that I wanted to see more of the capital? Gondangol is one of the places I wanted to visit.

Jin's face was now awash with happiness. She was going to see the woman Suh, whom she had not yet had the chance to visit since Suh's move from Banchon to Blanc's orphanage in Gondangol.

—This shall be an unforgettable day for me.

Guérin's eyes widened at how Jin and Victor were conversing with each other without the aid of the interpreter. The Jindo dog came up to Victor and sat next to where he stood. Two Korean men who worked at the legation paused on their way through the courtyard and peered at Jin.

—I'm Secretary Guérin. We met before, at the banquet.

Understanding his words, Jin bowed her head at him as the interpreter looked at her with a surprised expression.

—Do you understand the language of France?

—Only just enough to converse.

—Can you speak it?

—Only just enough to converse.

Having given the same answer to both of the interpreter's questions, Jin politely bowed her head at him.

—I am Choi Ga, the legation's interpreter. My Christian name is Paul. They call me Paul Choi here. I am pleased to make your acquaintance, my lady.

Two people born in different countries but speaking the same language is as refreshing as striking water in the middle of a desert.

The three men led Jin into the legation offices. Victor could not help thinking she was like an armful of flowers sparkling with droplets on a summer day after rain, but he dared not look back, and instead listened to the conversation Jin and the interpreter were having.

—How did you get here?

—The Queen loaned me a palanquin.

—A palanquin?

—Yes.

Jin's face had lit up at the prospect of seeing the woman Suh, but now she was lost in thought. She had hardly seen the Queen since the evening of the banquet. It was the longest time she had ever gone without talking to her since entering the palace. Even her roommate Soa was worried. Jin looked for Lady Suh whenever she wanted to ask after the Queen, but once she had Lady Suh's attention, she found herself unable to ask. The two were used to frank and lengthy discussions of the Queen's welfare, as they were senior and junior lady attendants affiliated with the Queen. But Jin felt a strange coldness from Lady Suh. While she had always been strict with her underlings, Jin was able to sense Lady Suh's affection underneath it all. But now Lady Suh all but refused to bring up the Queen. She did visit Jin the day before to inform her that she was to visit the French legation the next day. The events of the banquet a month ago had crossed Jin's mind when she caught Lady Suh's concerned gaze.

—There can be no mistakes. The Queen has many worries.

Jin was unable to discern what exactly Lady Suh was talking about. Was Her Majesty worried about the country, or was she worried about Jin?

—Since Her Majesty had no messages for you, she will be talking to you directly.

Jin wanted to ask what the Queen was worried about but Lady Suh had already walked off. Jin was tense all day, waiting to be summoned. Not until the middle of the night was she told to go to the Queen's Chambers. The Queen was in her bedclothes with her hair down as if she were just about to go to sleep. She silently looked at Jin standing at her bedchamber door. After about five minutes, the Queen spoke only a few words.

—You must visit the French legation in the morning.

—Yes, Your Majesty.

—I shall lend you a palanquin.

—Yes, Your Majesty.

—Tell me everything you remember once you return.

—Yes, Your Majesty.

—That is all. Leave.

Despite having heard the Queen say "Leave," Jin found herself unable to comply. It was too empty a meeting after an entire month of not seeing the Queen. She hoped that she would say something more, but the Queen was silent. Jin softly bit her lip as she left the Queen's Chambers. Why?

Why was the Queen so cold to her? Jin could not fall asleep that night as she tossed and turned next to Soa.

Her spirits lowered, Jin began taking in her surroundings.

She had never seen glass windows on a pagoda-tile house before. She had also never seen an oil streetlamp such as the one that stood in front of the French legation's courtyard. Guérin explained that the inner part of the compound was the legation office and the back part a dining room, library, and bedroom. Here and there on the porch, facing the courtyard, were chairs brought from France. To the right was a Western-style annex with a large parasol out front. Its windows were all glass and in the Western style, with curtains.

—These are part of the legation offices.

Jin looked in. She saw a wide wall made of brick. There were wooden desks and chairs with gently curved backs. Jin turned to Victor, who stood there without speaking.

They say that whoever keeps you awake at night is the woman you love. You are she. Victor had written this in a letter to Jin the night before. There were several such unsent letters inside his desk.

—I still do not know your name.

—Ah, that's true!

Victor almost burst out laughing. Neither of them had asked the other's name. He had written love letters deep into the night to a woman whose name he didn't know. All that had inspired him were her dark eyes.

—Victor Augustus Collin . . .

He stopped in the act of saying his full name. *Victor Augustus Collin de Plancy.* He did not want to give such a long name to her. The *de* in his name was given only to nobility. His father had endeavored his whole life for that article. And that was why Lord Plancy had accused his father of misappropriating his title and sent him to court. Victor's father defended himself by saying how his fame as a writer had honored the village of Plancy and how much he had contributed to the village over the years. He even brought up the fact of his blood relation with Georges-Jacques Danton several times. Losing the trial and being banished from Plancy did not dampen his efforts. His father managed to change their family registry not a year since relocating to Paris. And he was finally able to affix upon his son all the aristocratic names that he so longed to say. At one point, this desire to belong to higher circles turned Victor's name into Victor Emile Marie Joseph Collin de Plancy.

Victor stopped and spoke again.

—My name is Victor.

—. . .

—And what is your name?

It was a long time since anyone had asked her this question.

The woman Suh had called her Baby, Yeon called her Silverbell, and her roommate Soa called her Jinjin. The Queen called her Lady Attendant Suh. According to the woman Suh, Jin's mother had called her Ewha. *There were so many pear flowers in front of your house. When they bloomed, the blossoms made it impossible to see your house.* Jin couldn't remember the woman whom Suh referred to as her birth mother. Nor being called Ewha. Jin would have believed the woman Suh was her mother, but Suh was always adamant that Jin honor her birth mother. Suh was sorry that she did not know whether Jin's family name was Park or Yu or anything else and blamed herself for this. She said these unknown parents had hidden their name for some mysterious reason. That they never uttered it, even after years of hiding in Banchon. Sometimes, Suh would sigh deeply in the middle of Jin reading aloud to her. *I don't know where you are from, but it is surely a household with many books. You are such a quick learner.*

Later, Jin's name became a problem when the Queen ordered her to enter the palace as a court lady. They decided to enter her as the adopted daughter of Lady Suh's younger sister. Jin asked, then, why they never formally gave her a name. The woman Suh replied, "We thought someone would surely come to my house one day to claim you. And that someone would give you your rightful name."

—I am not important . . . What name would a lady of the court possibly have?

—. . .

—Lady Attendant Suh is fine.

Jin's face darkened as she examined the pictures on the legation office walls.

Because he couldn't think of a single witty thing that might lift her seemingly sad mood, Victor ended up blurting out a suggestion he had planned to keep only in his heart.

—I would like a Korean name. Would you give one to me?

Paul Choi and Guérin were more surprised than Jin herself, judging by the look they gave Victor. Jin, not quite understanding what Victor had just asked, turned to the interpreter for clarification.

—The legate wishes to have a Korean name and has asked her ladyship to make one for him.

—Me?

—Yes.

Not having expected such a thing, Jin turned her dark eyes to Victor. *There can be no mistakes. The Queen has many worries.* She didn't know why she thought of Lady Suh's words at that moment. Was refusing him a mistake? Was accepting him a mistake? Why was this man asking her to make up a name for him? Jin eyed Victor with a hint of suspicion, but her heart was with the Queen. She didn't answer him as they moved from the offices to the back part of the compound where the library and dining hall were. To be more precise, she *couldn't* answer him.

—There are books in that room.

Victor led Jin to the library, a large room stacked with books. Jin wandered through the space that was unusually wide for a Korean house, one possibly modified for its purpose, her face shining with delight as if she had discovered a new universe. So many books, tightly shelved in one place! The shelves reached up to the thick beams above, and each shelf was packed with books. There were Chinese and Japanese books on one side and Korean books on another. Jin moved with ease into the maze of shelves, at her fastest pace since coming to the legation office. Victor took note that it was the library that Jin showed the most interest in. He smiled at the thought that he had uncovered something that truly interested her. Jin passed the Chinese, Japanese, and Korean books and stood before a shelf filled with volumes of French history and philosophy. Montesquieu's *Persian Letters*, an encyclopedia with more than thirty volumes, Lamartine's *Poetical Meditations*, and the collected works of Mallarmé, Rimbaud, and Verlaine. Jin, browsing through Victor Hugo's *Les Misérables*, Stendhal's *The Red and the Black*, and Flaubert's *Sentimental Education*, took out an edition of Baudelaire shelved next to *Madame Bovary* and opened it. She flicked through the pages. Her eyes fell on the opening stanza of "Invitation to the Voyage."

My child, my sister,
Think how sweet
to go and live there together!
To love at leisure.
To love until death.

Jin couldn't take her eyes off the poems in the book. She read one after another, feeling as if she were about to fall into its pages before remembering where she was. She looked up at Victor.

—Is this what you wanted to show me?

—No.

—. . .

—There was something else I wanted to show you.

Jin stared at him.

—I wanted to show you Paris.

Victor saw her pupils tremble. What he really meant to show her was the village of Plancy that his family had been banished from. For some reason, he thought that he might bring himself to visit it again if he could go there with this lady by his side.

To have a place to go with someone means one has fallen in love.

—I would like to go to Paris with you someday.

With you. Jin's eyes that had trembled like the surface of water became calm once more. She gently closed the book she was holding and put it back in its place on the shelf.

—I cannot leave the palace. The only reason I could come here at all is because of a special dispensation from the Queen.

Her voice was emotionless and firm. Jin moved her gaze toward a group of books in one corner of the library. *Infernal Dictionary*, *Critical Dictionary of Relics and Miraculous Images* . . . Victor saw her looking at them.

—Those were written by my father.

Jin turned to Victor again.

—Was he a writer?

—He was.

Having failed at his ambition to write in Paris, Victor's father had gone to Belgium before moving back to his home in Plancy. He founded a publishing house through the help of some old friends and printed mostly religious texts. Victor liked the smells of the printing press. It was where he spent most of his childhood days. Would that printing press still be there? And the lake? Did the heron still fly to those waters in their season?

Reluctant to leave, Jin kept looking back at the books as she made her way out of the library. The fingertips of her left hand, the one that wasn't carrying the jacket, grazed over the spines as she passed.

—Would you like to borrow some of them?

Jin's eyes lit up for a moment, but she was silent.

—If there are any that you would like to read, please help yourself.

—But how would I return them?

—I shall find you.

—You?

—Yes.

It would be impossible. A court lady and a foreign legate could never have a private meeting in the palace. Guessing why Jin wasn't answering, Victor smiled.

—Perhaps I should give you a few volumes instead. What do you like to read?

Could she possibly accept? Jin hesitated, but her desire for the books overwhelmed her caution.

—I would like to read a book from France.

She answered with a resolve that belied her hesitation.

—Is there any book in particular?

—I have never seen French books until today. My roommate at the palace, Soa, enjoys being read to. If Your Excellency could choose a book that she might like?

When Victor looked as if he didn't quite understand her words, Paul Choi stepped in. Jin had said she wanted to read to Soa, but it was the Queen she was thinking of. She wanted to read these strange books to the Queen. It would take time for Jin to translate the French words into Korean, but she was already curious as to how the Queen, who had read many books from China and Japan as well as Korea, would respond to these unfamiliar texts. While Jin thought of the Queen, Victor thought of his mother. She married at twenty-seven. His father was fifty-nine. It was his father's second marriage and his mother's first. His old father's desire. The sound of his young mother reading aloud. The woman before him had the power to conjure up these memories from the other side of time.

—I shall have something selected while we eat.

The four people came out of the library and entered the dining hall where the table was set. Victor took Jin's green jacket from her hand, and after hanging it up, he went to the gramophone he had brought from Paris and put on Berlioz's *Symphonie fantastique*. Music is a blessing upon all people. As Guérin slid out Jin's chair for her, he told her that the symphony was one His Excellency had carefully chosen for her. Jin listened to the sounds that were so different from the *daegeum* Yeon played or the music of the *geomungo* or *ajaeng* zither. It was a sound so sweet it could make a leaf dance on a windless summer's day.

Upon the table were transparent cups and champagne. There were four neat settings of forks, knives, and spoons. A middle-aged Korean woman wearing an apron, who worked as the legation chef, served each of them a bowl of creamy soup, glancing at Jin as she did so.

—Today's entrée is coq au vin.

Guérin said this with a smile as Victor came back to the table from the gramophone.

—It is a chicken dish. I believe Koreans would like it. His Excellency arranged the menu himself. You must enjoy it. He was like a little boy as he chose the music and the menu.

As even the interpreter Paul Choi joined in on the teasing laugh, Victor concentrated on uncorcking the champagne.

—That bottle is also the best one we have in our legation offices. It comes directly from the Champagne region. The best champagne. He brought out for your ladyship what he never brought out even for Bishop Blanc.

As if trying to distract Jin from Guérin's words, Victor poured the champagne into the clear glass sitting before her. The dew-like bubbles of the wine sparkled in the light.

—Does Bishop Blanc visit often?

The other three looked at Jin in unison.

—Do you know Bishop Blanc?

—My lady! Are you a Catholic?

Guérin and the interpreter Paul Choi spoke at the same time. Victor was also surprised at her mention of Bishop Blanc.

—I've known him since I was little. He is the one who taught me French.

—Is that so!

Victor was overjoyed. The thought of Blanc being the bridge to this woman whom he had thought he was complete strangers with was like discovering a great mountain to lean on. He couldn't help the large smile that brightened his face. And no wonder, for he had been worried about what to do after Jin returned to the palace. But then he remembered Blanc's concerned expression when Victor revealed that the woman he was in love with was a court lady, and his smile faded.

While Victor filled Guérin's and Paul Choi's glasses with champagne, the cook placed a salad with olive oil and balsamic vinegar dressing next to each soup plate. There were also small bites of bread and cheese from Normandy, as well as butter.

—My lady, are you a Catholic?

The interpreter Paul Choi asked again.

—I cannot say I am.

There was a slight pall of disappointment in Paul Choi's face at Jin's vague answer. Blanc had been against Jin becoming an official Catholic. He had seen those who had suffered double the indignities for being both Catholic and being in the King's service. He advised her that until Korea gave Catholics complete freedom of religion, it was enough to follow the faith in her heart only. The woman Suh was of the same mind. She was against Jin converting to Catholicism, but Suh herself and Yeon were already faithful followers.

—We were destined to meet you. We should've invited the bishop as well.

Victor smiled again at Guérin's words.

—Perhaps next time.

The fragrance of the champagne wafted around the table. The three men held up their glasses and turned to Jin.

Was it Li Bai who wrote, *I sat to drink alone with the flowers, but the moon came with my shadow, and we were three?* Li Bai, whose poetry never failed to make an appearance in any evening of drinks with the Qing officials in China.

—Would you care for some?

To Jin, who hesitated, for she was uncertain whether she should drink champagne in the middle of the day, Victor recited another poem by Li Bai.

I go to bed for I am drunk
You should go now
And when you return tomorrow morning, bring your zither

—Champagne can hardly make you drunk.

—It is only to bring out the flavor of the dish.

Guérin and Paul Choi coaxed her. Jin relaxed and held up her glass. The sound of their clinking glasses rang clear and bright in the air. The Queen enjoyed conversing with the wives of the King's foreign political council or with Lillias Underwood, wife of the King's physician. When she was told stories of the lands across the ocean, her eyes were not those of the Mother of the Nation, which were fierce and concerned, sometimes heartbroken and anxious. They were eyes that shone with anticipation and discovery of the endless stories that filled the pages of books. There would be champagne with the refreshments at those conversations as well.

Jin took a sip of champagne and closed her eyes. It spread in her mouth a fragrance as sweet as the music floating in her ears.

Victor took up his spoon and had a taste of the cream soup before buttering his bread and eating that as well. When the cook brought out the coq au vin, he tasted it first using his fork and knife. He was discreetly showing Jin how to dine in the Western style. Jin watched Victor as she tried the soup herself and used her fork on the salad, betraying no awkwardness. From time to time the sound of the cicadas crying from the phoenix tree overwhelmed Berlioz's *Symphonie fantastique*.

Jin slowly tasted the unfamiliar flavor of the coq au vin, and a faint smile appeared on Victor's face as he wiped his brow. He was thinking of Jin when she first entered the legation grounds, how he had forgotten she was Korean and embraced her. The lovely scent of that moment had suddenly come back to him as they sat there around the table.

He also remembered the eyes of the woman who had glared at him as he apologized for greeting her in the French style.

—Bishop Blanc's Korean orphanage is also in Gondangol.

What was she saying? Guérin, who was refilling the champagne glasses, and Paul Choi, who had dropped a clove of roasted garlic on the sleeve of his tunic and was wiping it with a napkin, both looked up at Victor.

—The reason I requested we visit Gondangol is that I want to see the orphanage.

—Did you? We had the same thought.

Victor smiled again at Jin. Jin turned her gaze to the two paintings hung on the wall of the dining hall. Victor noticed her interest in them.

—This one is Monet's *The Gare Saint-Lazare*. Over there is Seurat's *A Sunday Afternoon on the Island of La Grande Jatte*. The Monet is a photograph of mine, and the Seurat is a copy.

Jin looked carefully at the paintings as if matching them to Victor's words. Paintings from the country of this polite, pleasant diplomat. The capital of which was Paris. What kind of a place was it, this place where the books in the library were published, where the music that lingered so in the ear was made, and pictures that filled one's vision were painted?

For the first time, Jin became intensely curious as to what Paris must be like.

One of the joys of life is to partake in a favorite dish with a person one cares deeply about. Victor was glad that Jin ate the French-style chicken without reluctance. How long was it since he had happily watched a woman partake in a meal? Guérin proposed that they have their coffee underneath the parasol in front of the legation annex. The four stood up to move. Before Jin could push her chair out, Victor was behind her to help pull it out of the way. As she waited for Victor to bring her jacket back from the other room where the music came from, Jin examined some framed photographs mounted side by side on the wall. Were they the legate's family? Foreign women and men smiled out at her from their little frames. There was a white-haired man and a lady wearing a pearl necklace. There was also Victor in his diplomatic dress uniform. Among the older photos, there was one of a young boy of about five or six that caught her eye. Whatever he was thinking in that moment, his mouth was firmly closed. He was frowning as if he'd been told to look in front of him when the snapshot was taken.

—That's me as a boy.

Victor had approached her and seen the photo Jin was looking at.

—It's the youngest photograph of me.

Jin nodded and drew her long jacket from the coat hanger he held out and draped it over her arm.

—I wondered what you looked like when you were young.

When you were young. The words evoked memories of Banchon and the woman Suh, of Yeon who wrote on any surface, and the sad dowager consort whom she served as a companion. Yeon, who did not speak but played his flute. Where could she see such an image now? Yeon was a Jangakwon musician now. She had left the banquet without getting a good look at his face. Would she get to meet Yeon at Gondangol?

—The people of my country do not like being photographed.

—I'm aware.

—They think their souls will be taken if they are photographed.

—Is that also what you think?

You. Victor had used an intimate form of the pronoun. She gave him a look.

—Are you also afraid of being photographed?

—I do not know. I have never been.

—Then may I take a photograph of you?

As if it just occurred to him, Victor went to his room and returned with his photograph of the King. Jin gazed at it intently. The King posed before the Hall of Diligent Governance.

—I took that photo. I took it about two months ago. But is he not the same now as he always was?

Victor held out another photo. Jin examined the image in her hands. It took a moment for her to recognize that the court lady in the photo was her. It was unimaginable to her that she was photographed, and the eyes that looked up at him were full of surprise.

—It is you.

Jin did not hide her perplexed expression as she looked him in the eye.

—I met you, on a bridge, the day I first visited the palace.

Jin knew. She hadn't forgotten how a foreigner had said *bonjour* to her as she crossed the Silk Stream bridge with Lady Suh. She had also learned that the foreigner was the French legate at the banquet. Lady Suh had greatly admonished her that day when she had returned his greeting in his language. Lady Suh, who was generally of a peaceful temperament, gave her a scolding. *How dare a court lady greet a stranger? Must you be taught every rule of the palace from the beginning?* This was why she remembered the incident.

But when had the legate taken her picture?

Fascinated, Jin gave the image of herself a close look. Time swallows all and passes, never to return. There were two photos taken on that bridge, and Lady Suh was in them as well. Jin was clear, but Lady Suh was a blur. Perhaps because of Lady Suh's spirited walk. It surprised Jin how passing moments could be retained so exactly. The moment she had inadvertently replied *bonjour* and turned to catch up to Lady Suh who was walking ahead of her, and the moment she turned to look at the legate again—these past moments had not disappeared but lived on in the photograph.

—May I have these?

—If you let me photograph you today!

The two smiled at each other for the first time. Leaving Victor to make the preparations, Jin came out to the legation courtyard. The cicada cries pierced the ear, and the midday heat hit her like a wall. Paul Choi was alone, lost in thought, waiting for dessert underneath the parasol of the annex. As Jin approached, he smiled and spoke.

—I've never seen the legate like this. He is very hardworking and thorough when it comes to his duties, but I've found him a bit cold and almost unapproachable. But today he's quite different.

—. . .

—He's pleasant and friendly. Can you tell?

—I'm not sure what you mean.

Having attended some business or other, Guérin appeared outside of the main legation building. He shielded his eyes from the bright sunlight, squinting one eye as he shrugged. It meant that he was hot, perhaps. Seeing Guérin made Paul Choi, who was about to say something, turn quiet again. The cook brought out cups of coffee and slices of cake to the white table underneath the parasol. Victor presently joined them from the legation's inner compound carrying a large leather case. The cook, who had gone back inside after laying the table underneath the parasol, now followed him carrying a bundle wrapped in silk. As she placed it on an empty chair underneath the parasol, she stole another look at Jin.

—Shall we take a commemorative photo?

Victor opened the leather case and took out the wooden box camera and affixed it atop the tripod that it came with. This was not the concealed vest camera he had used to take surreptitious photos in his first audience with the King. Victor slipped into the black cloth behind the camera.

—Everyone, please look in this direction.

Paul Choi and Guérin looked toward the camera. Jin felt a little awkward and decided to look at the phoenix tree on the other side of the courtyard and not at the tripod. There was a Jindo dog resting underneath it, exhausted by the heat. She heard a click coming from the camera.

Victor's head popped out of the black cloth, and he spoke to Jin.

—Please come forward a bit.

When Jin went to the tree he had indicated and stood next to it, Victor disappeared again underneath the black cloth. Did he not even feel the heat? He pressed the shutter toward Jin countless times. Jin drinking coffee, Jin propping her head with her arms, Jin occasionally smiling at Guérin's attempts at levity. Jin eventually looked in Victor's direction as he took these photos at a distance.

—Did you say you wanted a Korean name?

Jin said this as Victor came to join them underneath the parasol. He beamed.

—How about Gillin? *Gil* for auspicious, *lin* for clearness. It sounds close to Collin.

Jin traced the characters on the table. Gillin. As Victor uncertainly pronounced the Korean name Jin had given him, a breeze, as if thinking of the beads of sweat on Victor's forehead, caressed their heat away.

4
Live Here with Us

Your Excellency,

Since the signing of our treaty in 1886, Bishop Blanc diligently sought building lots for his priests' housing, churches, a printing press, schools, and for the abandoned children, orphanages. We obtained agreement from all owners, paid for their housing, and received the deeds for their property. We've knocked down their useless thatched cottages and started building the foundations for what we need. But Korea recently began to claim that the hill the bishop wishes to build on is owned by their government. They heard the bishop's contention but did not accept it. There is also the matter of a shrine being nearby. American missionaries have already settled in this land, but our situation remains uncertain. I explained to the official Cho Byeongsik that Article 4 of our treaty states, "They have the right to practice their religion" and that building a place to pray in the opened port and city were part of this deal. He insisted it did not apply within the capital's fortress. We must continue our dialogue regarding these matters. Bishop Blanc wishes to begin construction as early as next spring, but it will require great patience in negotiations.

August 5, 1888

Victor Collin de Plancy

Postscript: I have succeeded in creating a rough map of Seoul. I send Your Excellency the first copy. You can see where the land for the mission and the shrine are. They are approximately one hundred meters apart.

Was it morning sunlight? Bright light filled the room. Outside the window, in the orchard across the water, were pear trees weighed down with yellow fruit. Despite this hanging harvest of pears, there seemed to be unseasonal petals flying in the sunlight like snow.

Where was she?

—Is it good?

The child nodded as she accepted another spoonful of white pear flesh. The woman with the inner glow looked sadly upon the child. It was the Queen. The Queen cut deeper into the fruit, revealing the moist white insides of the pear. The person who sat before her was the Queen from the inner chambers of court, but they were sitting in the woman Suh's house in Banchon instead of the palace. It was the room where she had learned French from Blanc with the flute player Yeon by her side. The woman Suh's needlework was neatly folded in a corner of the room. The Queen was also not wearing her green tunic but the woman Suh's clothes. The Queen scraped the inside of the pear again, filling up its bowl, and gave the child another spoonful. The child almost closed her eyes as she kept accepting the Queen's white pear flesh in her mouth.

The sweetness that spread in her mouth lasted only a moment.

—Here I live! Here I stand, alive!

Now the Queen's hair was unornamented save for a long silver hairpin holding her bun in place, her dress that of an ordinary housewife. The words she shouted made Jin's blood run cold. It broke her heart to see the Queen wearing a simple skirt and jacket and her hair tied back into a bun. The Queen's eyes, which were once so luminous that they made others take a step back, were bloodshot, and her face had gone past pale and was now white as a sheet.

—To hold a funeral for me while I live . . . how can this be! When I stand here, alive!

The shrieking from the deathly white Queen jolted Jin from her sleep.

It was too real to have been a dream.

Jin tried to keep her eyes open, but they slid shut on their own accord. She lifted her hand and placed it on her forehead. She touched cold sweat. Her hand was already moist with sweat. In the Year of the Black Horse, the Queen had escaped from the palace, cast off her regalia, and disguised herself as a housewife. Jin had just dreamed of the Queen as she was back then, climbing up the mountain trail where the palanquin could not take her. That was not so very long ago when the Queen lived in hiding without contact with the King. One day, the Queen heard the news that the King's father, the Regent, ordered the Queen be considered dead and her funeral to be held, sending the Queen into a fury.

Jin tried to open her eyes again, and through her narrow vision, she could just about see Yeon in his linen trousers and jacket. Kang Yeon. Despite her confusion, her eyes trembled with gladness at the sight of him. Farther off sat the woman Suh, and next to her, Victor. "Ah," said Jin as her eyes flew open. Her swollen eyelids shuttered upward.

—Can you hear me?

—Ça va bien?

Suh and Victor spoke simultaneously to Jin. Yeon sat close by, his expression overflowing with sorrow. Suh placed a hand on Jin's forehead and looked at her with eyes full of concern. Yeon had grasped Jin's hand without realizing it, and he carefully placed it down and let go. As Jin tried to sit up, she felt a pain in her left breast.

—Keep still. The wound will worsen if you move.

Yeon seemed to be in pain as he watched Jin lie down once more. Jin's eyes grew wide seeing the bundle of linen wrapped around Yeon's left arm and the blood soaking through it.

—What happened?

The moment she asked that, a scene unfurled in her mind, rendering her silent.

Sometimes, an unexpected incident of a single moment can tow an entire life along in its wake.

It was past noon when Jin and Victor left the legation, with Guérin and Paul Choi seeing them to the gate. Victor had offered to hire a palanquin, but it was Jin who insisted they walk. She wanted to walk. Ever since she was kept away from the Queen's presence, Jin got up at dawn every morning—carefully, so Soa wouldn't wake—and walked to the Queen's Chambers and back. When she returned, there was dew adorning the hem of her skirt. This walk, which she did without telling anyone, assuaged her heavy heart a little. On the way from the palace to the legation, Jin had looked down from the palanquin at the streets that the monsoon had swept afresh and was struck by the desire to walk on even this muddy ground. How long was it since she had been outside the palace? She wanted to spread her shoulders and stride, something she would never be allowed to do within the palace walls.

Victor had taken off his suit jacket and rolled up his sleeves for the walk to Gondangol. He held a silk-wrapped bundle of French books under one of his white arms that were revealed to the strong sun. But Jin soon regretted choosing to walk instead of taking the palanquin. They were stared at for being a foreigner and a court lady, not to mention for her fine palace attire. The unusual sight of the two together had disrupted an otherwise tedious summer afternoon. An official in red robes and a young noble wearing a *cholip* straw hat glared at them as they passed, as did a clogs seller and a straw-sandal seller, their wares stacked high on their carrying racks like in a circus trick. Everyone stared at them, the woman in front of a cotton gin with her face peeking out of the long jacket thrown over her head, even the little children who had taken their tunics off and were playing in their trousers. Victor noted that the strong facial features of the Korean men with their prominent foreheads and high cheekbones resembled those who lived in France's Bretagne and thought no more of it, but Jin lowered her head, her face turning red, not because of the heat but rather from embarrassment.

It was easy to find the orphanage Blanc had built. It had started as a single Korean-style tiled-roof house, but they bought two more houses to accommodate more children. The boys lived in the lower house, which was thus called Namdang, and the girls lived in the upper house, which was therefore called Yeodang. It was immediately clear upon arriving in the neighborhood that the three tiled-roof houses were the place they were looking for.

Jin quickened her pace once the orphanage was in sight. Just then, two men with their hair tied in the topknot of adulthood walked out of an alley across from the Namdang. Their faces were red as if they'd spent the day drinking, and one had on his back an empty carrying rack. Their eyes passed over Jin. They were about to be on their way when they caught sight of Victor behind her. They turned rough and began shouting.

—A white bastard! He's here to steal the children!

Jin was glad Victor didn't understand Korean, and she was just about to turn away when the man with the carrying rack began swinging a stick at her. It all happened in the blink of an eye. Was it a hoe? A knife? Something flashed in the hand of the man standing behind him. The last thing Jin remembered before blacking out was the door to Namdang opening and Yeon running out of it as the man with the weapon rushed toward her.

The physician, who had left the room after administering emergency aid, came back inside where Jin lay. He regularly visited the orphanage to help with the care of the children.

—Your wounds are deeper than they seem, my lady.

The woman Suh's expression hardened, and Yeon's face fell at his words. Victor, not understanding Korean, looked Jin in the eye.

—He says I will be fine.

Victor glanced at the concerned faces of the woman Suh and Yeon. He guessed that she had not told him the truth.

Jin's eyes kept trying to close so she used all of her strength to keep them open for as long a moment as possible. The blot of blood kept widening on the linen bandage wrapped around Yeon's arm. Jin lifted her hand and caught it.

—Does it hurt a lot?

All I do is hurt you. Jin's eyes grew sad as she gazed at his wounded arm.

—It's my fault . . .

Yeon shook his head.

Victor, who couldn't have known Yeon was mute, looked nonplussed at how Yeon was answering Jin not with words but with his eyes and head-shaking. Victor thought Yeon's dark eyes underneath his thick eyebrows resembled Jin's in some way. Victor also didn't know that Yeon already knew of Victor. Or that Yeon was keeping Victor at a distance and trying to avoid eye contact. Yeon remembered Victor as the only man who had not applauded Jin's Dance of the Spring Oriole at the Pavilion of Festivities banquet, humiliating her before the Queen. Yeon wasn't surprised Jin had appeared with Victor. He hadn't forgotten that on the evening of the banquet, the Queen had halted Jin as she was exiting the stage and said, "Perhaps he does not like your dancing. And what shall you do about it?" Even if Victor had seen Yeon that evening among the musicians playing the *daegeum*, Victor would not recognize Yeon's face. The Yeon wearing the Jangakwon robes at the banquet and the Yeon in his ordinary clothes and his hair in a braid down his back looked like completely different people.

—Why did you attack when you should've avoided it?

The woman Suh worriedly examined Yeon's arm after telling Jin what the physician said, that his treatment would soon stop the bleeding. Suh had been so shocked by Jin's chest wound that she hadn't had the wherewithal to look after Yeon. Now that his arm was wounded, he wouldn't be able to play the *daegeum* for the time being. Jin kept looking at Yeon's hurt arm. In both the Year of the Black Horse and the Year of the Blue Horse, Yeon had kept getting injured for Jin.

—Water . . .

Her mouth was parched, and her voice came out cracked. Before Suh could get up, Yeon sprang to get her some water. Bishop Blanc appeared through the open door. Jin smiled at the sight of him. Blanc had come running after hearing Jin was hurt, but he stopped in his tracks when he saw Victor.

—Your Excellency!

Blanc's expression turned from confusion to dismay. He remembered Victor saying he was in love with a woman of the palace and asking him to teach him Korean so that he could greet her in Korean when they met. Was Jin the court lady the legate was in love with? Blanc's face grew dark.

Yeon came back into the room with a white celadon bowl full of water. Victor saw that he did not greet Blanc with words either, only giving him a look with his dark eyes. Jin managed to drink a few gulps of water with Suh's support. Blanc watched worriedly as Jin settled back down.

—How could this have happened?

—I believe there are still rumors that foreigners are kidnapping Korean children . . .

Suh was about to add that Jin appearing with a foreign man by her side seemed to have agitated the drunks as well, but she swallowed these words. It was strange enough for her that Jin, a court lady who should be in the palace, would show up at Gondangol, with the French legate no less.

—My heart is still racing.

Suh had managed to maintain a calm demeanor until that moment, but her eyes were now filling with tears. Jin reached out and enclosed

Suh's hand in hers. Suh had more white in her hair and wrinkles on her face than she had the last time they had seen each other.

Jin tried to smile, but the pain in her chest would not allow her to smile properly. *Was desire as heedless as this*, Victor thought, as he fought down the urge to kiss the wounded woman's lips. He had felt it when he saw Yeon easily take Jin's hand and when his eyes had watched Jin hold Yeon's hurt arm with a sorrowful expression on her face. The scent of her whenever he had been close enough to her as they walked from the legation to Gondangol. These rousing moments that had arisen despite the heat were now converted by his jealousy of Yeon into a compulsion to kiss her.

—What happened to the perpetrators?

—They were taken to the constabulary.

Victor watched them discuss amongst themselves as if they were four members of the same family.

—We must send word to the palace. You can't go back in this state.

—But I must return.

—Not like this!

Jin thought of the Queen, who was expecting a detailed recounting of her visit to the French legation.

—We won't send anyone. I shall go myself.

The woman Suh meant that she would go to the palace and talk to Lady Suh and request that Jin be allowed to stay outside until her wounds healed.

—But I must return.

Jin's stubbornness made Suh glance at Blanc. Blanc looked at Victor. Victor said he would summon a palanquin and move her to the French legation. He assumed that because the palace thought she was at the legation, this would be for the best. Jin, who would not bend in her wish to return to court, tried hard to keep her eyes from closing. When Blanc told Suh of Victor's suggestion, Suh said the shaking of the palanquin could worsen Jin's wounds. Victor reiterated that she should be moved to the legation before the diplomatic officials at the palace got wind of what had happened. He added that the legation had their own doctor who would aid in Jin's swift recovery.

Yeon, who had been still, began writing on the floor in front of Suh. Tell Lady Suh what happened. She will tell you what to do.

—Yes, I shall.

Victor watched Yeon as he traced the letters on the floor. He couldn't read Korean, but he finally realized that Yeon was mute. The possibility had not crossed his mind.

—Please send word now.

At Blanc's plea, Suh stood and opened the closet. She took out the clothes she wore to the palace for her rare visits to Lady Suh and left the room to change. As if she had come to the end of her endurance, Jin's fluttering eyes finally slid shut before the physician spoke.

—We must leave her to rest.

Blanc and Victor stood up. Only Yeon could not bear to. He kept staring down at Jin's closed eyes.

—They're like brother and sister after all . . .

At Blanc's mumbling Victor thought, *So they are not brother and sister.* He thought the two might be siblings seeing the familiar way they acted toward one another and how they somewhat resembled each other. As the three left the room, the few children gathered there, curious about what was going on, stared in unison at Blanc. A child reading a book in the shade of a tree also came running up, book in hand. Blanc approached the children and patted each one on the head.

—There was a disturbance, but all is well. Do not worry.

As Yeon emerged from the room, some of the children moved toward him as if carried by wind. Blanc couldn't help but smile at the sight of Yeon surrounded by children. He was fond of saying that those who do not have hearts like children shall never enter Heaven. The remaining children left him to crowd around Blanc as well. A child shouted at the sight of Yeon's blood-soaked bandage on his arm. Yeon was silent, but the children chattered in a near collective roar. Not even the stringent cries of the cicada could drown out their noise.

—Can you understand them?

Victor asked Blanc as he stared from a distance at Yeon, who was surrounded by children.

—Yes.

Blanc answered curtly as he wiped the sweat from his brow.

—Who is he?

—He is a musician at Jangakwon.

A Jangakwon musician?

—Meaning he plays court music?

—The *daegeum* flute. From what I know he plays every Korean instrument, not just the *daegeum*. He is excellent at the *ajaeng* zither.

—Can he hear?

—He can.

—How can a mute man be a court musician?

Blanc glanced sideways at Victor. He found Victor's interest in Yeon a bit odd. The Victor Blanc knew was a responsible and thoughtful diplomat who never betrayed what he was really thinking. He had a way of effectively getting things done while at the same time guarding his silence when asked for his opinion, prompting the other person to speak first. Victor was normally a reasonable and cool-headed man. His showing interest in a mute Korean musician seemed a little out of character.

Blanc had lived in Korea for so long that he was practically Korean, and Victor's way of thinking about Korea had made Blanc uncomfortable for some time. He was grateful for Victor's help in addressing the obscene rumors about his setting up the orphanage to suck the blood of Korean children, but Victor was also the cunning mind behind the plan that got French troops to patrol on their horses unhindered within the fortress of the Korean capital. It was to be expected that a diplomat should be looking out for their own country's interests using whatever means they had. But Blanc had hopes that as the first French diplomat to be formally appointed to Korea, Victor would have a better understanding of the Korean people. Blanc was already disappointed in how he showed more interest in Korea's celadon and books than its people. It was in keeping with his reputation as a collector. Blanc knew that the legation annex was already full of Korean paintings, books, celadon, and folding screens. Not to mention the fact that these goods were destined for France.

—Korea's treatment of the disabled has that in favor of the French. They do not particularly discriminate against or exclude them. Not even as royal court musicians.

Victor gave Blanc a look. How could he be so steadfast in his defense of the Korean people, even in the face of rumors so unreal they wouldn't be believed in a story, rumors that had been so persistent they led to an attack against him? Victor realized in that moment that Blanc was more a man of religion than a man of France.

—I am curious to hear the music of a mute man.

—You've already heard him.

—I have?

—He was there on the evening of the banquet held in your honor.

Was he?

Meanwhile.

The Queen, who was discussing the new Western-style hospital Gwanghyewon with the wife of the royal physician Dr. Horace Underwood, saw Lady Suh's face break into a surprised expression at a note passed to her by a junior lady attendant. As Lady Suh began stepping backward to leave, the Queen stopped her in her tracks.

—Is someone here?

Lady Suh hesitated.

—What is the reason behind your surprised expression?

—Forgive me, Your Majesty.

—Is it from Unhyeongung Palace?

Whenever Lady Suh made that face, it usually meant there was news from the Regent at Unhyeongung Palace. The hospital Gwanghyewon was established in the Jaedong neighborhood, following the recommendation of Dr. Horace Allen, who treated Min Yeongik when he was hit by a sword. The new hospital was said to be treating seventy to eighty patients daily. Allen was also conducting four to five surgical operations a day. Underwood himself, the King's physician who had studied medicine in America before coming to Korea, was also helping at Gwanghyewon and teaching Korean students physics and chemistry. Listening to Mrs. Underwood speak, the Queen had thought of her first son, who had died only five days after he was born. The child had been constipated and was given ginseng sent from Unhyeongung Palace and died two days later. It was because of a fever. If Gwanghyewon had existed back then, they might not have done such a foolish thing as to feed a baby ginseng. She would not have lost the prince so meaninglessly. The thought had been taking root deep in her mind like a tuber of arrowroot.

—No, Your Majesty. Lady Attendant Suh, she went to the legation . . .

—What of her?

—. . .

—What of Lady Attendant Suh?

—She is wounded.

—Wounded?

—Yes.

The Queen's pupils trembled. She asked through the interpreter present for Mrs. Underwood to excuse her before turning again to Lady Suh.

—How did this happen?

—She was attacked.

—Attacked? Why would she be attacked?

—There seems to have been a misunderstanding when she was seen walking with the French legate. They thought she was a spy.

The Queen gripped her hand with the cupronickel ring into a tight fist atop the low table. Korea's diplomatic policy was to maintain the balance of power between China and Japan, but since the Gapsin Coup, it was Chinese influence that was in the ascendance. China sent Yuan Shikai with the instruction to treat Korea like a vassal state. Yuan's power almost rivaled that of the King's. The Korean monarchy had returned to power using Chinese strength, but the Queen found herself frequently at odds with Yuan's measures. She thought that China and Japan were no longer enough. They now needed the power of Russia, America, England, and France.

—How serious are her wounds?

—The message is that she cannot return to the palace today. They request that she be granted a few days of treatment before she comes back.

—Who delivered the message?

The Queen asked this, wondering if it was the musician Kang Yeon, who had helped her in both the Year of the Black Horse and the Year of the Blue Horse.

—The woman Suh who does the housekeeping at the orphanage in Gondangol, Your Majesty.

Lady Suh bowed her head low.

—Where is she wounded, and how?

—Her left shoulder was pierced by a knife.

The Queen's eyelashes trembled. She closed her eyes. It is very human to endlessly make the contradictory request for a person with large feet to leave small footprints. Mrs. Underwood regarded the Queen with a concerned expression and thought, *Poor thing*. The Queen opened her eyes narrowly and spoke to Lady Suh in a cool and utterly unemotional voice.

—Tell Lady Attendant Suh to stay at the French legation until she is healed.

Lady Suh stood motionless, thinking she had misheard. Oh, why did she send that child outside of court? The Queen, having given a command that contradicted her will, could not bear to open her eyes again. Even as Lady Suh had beseeched the Queen to allow this very thing a moment ago, she knew the request was so extraordinary as to be unprecedented. Lady Suh could not believe that the Queen had so readily given her consent. *Tell Lady Attendant Suh to stay at the French legation* . . . Regret swept through the heart of the Queen. It was the Queen herself who had craftily sent Jin outside the palace. She remembered the King and the French legate at the banquet held in the Pavilion of Festivities. The King, his heart stolen by the dancer in her rendition of the Dance of the Spring Oriole, could not take his eyes off her for a moment, and the legate had completely forgotten his surroundings, acting as if only he and the dancer existed in that time and place.

—Tell her to remain there until further notice.

Lady Suh dared to raise her head to catch a glimpse of the Queen. Was she thinking of banishing Jin from court? Her heart dropped to the floor. It was almost unheard of for a court lady to spend a night outside of the palace. Even getting permission for a single night was difficult, but to remain outside until further notice? And not any lady attendant but Jin, who was frequently called to the Queen's Chambers? Lady Suh hesitated as question begot question until the Queen's voice reached her ears again.

—That is all. Leave us.

Here was the adamant voice the Queen used when her decision was final.

—Yes, Your Majesty.

The Queen turned toward Mrs. Underwood again.

As Lady Suh came out to the courtyard of the Queen's Chambers, the woman Suh, waiting restlessly by the hinges of the Gate of Dualities, walked toward her sister to faster close the distance between them.

—What does she say, my lady?

Lady Suh was younger, but the woman Suh never forgot to address the senior court lady according to her proper honorific.

—She orders Lady Attendant Suh to remain at the French legation until further notice.

—How can this be?

—These are her instructions, and so we must follow them.

The woman Suh seemed disappointed. She had hoped Jin could stay with her until her wounds had healed, at least. She had never been allowed to spend a night with Jin since Jin had entered the palace as a court lady. She could not even see her whenever she wanted. Suh could enter the palace only through special permission if she wanted to meet Jin, and such meetings were never enough for the two of them.

Lady Suh walked her sister to the Gate of Dualities.

—Has there ever been a case such as this?

—Never. Nor have we ever had to report on the actions of a mere junior lady attendant. The Queen ordered that she be told in detail everything that Lady Attendant Suh does.

—But why?

—I don't know. Is she terribly hurt?

—It will take her some time to heal.

The woman Suh stopped in her tracks and turned to Lady Suh.

—I understand that this is the order of the Queen, but I want to keep her with me tonight. She couldn't possibly send any other orders in the middle of the night, would she? I can take her to the legation tomorrow. May I do so?

Do not say I cannot, were the unspoken words that were nonetheless audible through the determination in her voice.

The night embraces everything. Including, firmly, the pain of day.

Jin, whose forehead was drenched in cold sweat from the pain, managed to crack open her eyes. She could see Yeon sitting next to her, dabbing away the sweat from her forehead. He could not speak, but his eyes were eloquent enough. The woman Suh sat on her other side, sleeping on the bare floor. She seemed to have dozed off while keeping vigil with Yeon.

—The Queen has ordered you to stay at the legation until given further notice.

Jin felt disheartened as she recalled the words Suh spoke since returning from the palace before Jin had fallen asleep. Was it a dream? The legate, upon hearing these words through Blanc, had made a happy face. Suh, her expression disgruntled, sat down by Jin. Jin had felt her strength leave her at the Queen's message, and she slid into sleep.

Yeon's face was tinged with pained concern as he dabbed the sweat that gathered again on Jin's forehead.

What time is it? Jin had merely thought the question when Yeon immediately picked up a fountain pen and small notebook beside him and wrote the time, *sagyeong*, or an hour after midnight, before showing it to Jin. Jin had never seen the writing implements before. Seeing her questioning expression, Yeon picked up his pen and notebook and wrote that the pen was given to him by the French legate, the notebook by Blanc.

—The French legate?

Yeon nodded at her question. Jin had seen feather pens on the desks of the legation office that day, but she had never seen a fountain pen before. There was a wild horse etched on the silver barrel. Jin looked at the pen that wrote with ink that flowed from its tip, and the notebook made from sheets of mulberry paper sewn together with cotton thread. Yeon followed her gaze and settled on the implements as well. The French legate, who had sat next to the sleeping Jin, remembered something as he got up to leave, and took out the fountain pen from his pocket before handing it to Yeon. Yeon could not understand the legate's French words. Blanc took out a small notebook he always carried with him, uncapped the fountain pen, and wrote, *You can take it from him. He says it is something you need very much.* Yeon watched the ink flow from the pen as Blanc wrote the words.

—He says he wishes for your success.

Why would he gift such a thing to me? His heart pushed him to refuse, but Yeon found the pen already in his hand. The letters that formed from the blue ink that flowed wherever his hand moved were like butterflies in flight.

—And the legate?

Yeon wrote that he had returned to the legation, saying he would come back in the morning. As Yeon wrote, he realized why Blanc had urged him to accept the pen. Now he didn't have to write his words on the floor. When Yeon seemed disconcerted from having been offered a gift from someone he had only just met, Blanc said he should play the *daegeum* for the legate once his arm healed. That the legate wished to hear his music.

Yeon stopped Jin from trying to sit up. Her wounds could worsen if she kept moving.

—I'm thirsty . . . I'm suffocating.

Since Jin refused to stay down, Yeon decided to support her instead. She could sit up but not on her own and leaned on Yeon instead. Yeon lifted a bowl of water to her lips. Once she drank the water, Jin discovered a silk-wrapped bundle next to her pillow. Victor had carried it with him from the legation that day. The bundle contained books from France. Jin stared at it. If all this hadn't happened, she would be in the palace right now, reading those books to Soa. What would she have said upon hearing French words for the first time? She would have fallen asleep immediately. And after Soa was asleep, Jin might've spent the night translating the French words into Korean to read to the Queen.

When there is no light in one's heart, even the brightest room seems dark.

—Take me outside.

Yeon's face fell.

—I need air.

The two looked at the sleeping Suh at the same time. She sat with her arm for a pillow, her forehead creased in wrinkles. Both Jin and Yeon were too injured to go out into the courtyard on their own. Jin could just about sit on the edge of the long porch that lined the courtyard and dangle her legs but only with Yeon's support. Once they sat down, she needed to lean on him once more. Jin gazed out into the dark at the date tree and persimmon tree planted in the orphanage courtyard.

—There's a moon.

The full moon rose in the black night. The two looked up at the sight of it surrounded by countless stars.

—It's like that time in the Year of the Black Horse.

—. . .

—I had no idea you could use a sword. When did you learn?

Jin laughed softly. She kept forgetting Yeon was mute. The Imo Mutiny had risen out of discrimination between traditional and modern weaponry. Not only was the traditional military pushed out into the periphery, but its soldiers had also gone for months without pay. When they finally received their rations, they were enraged by the fact that the rice was half-rotten and mixed with sand and chaff. The food storages were raided, and weapons were stolen. They were rearing for a fight, and once it sparked, the situation flared out of control. It began with the traditional military, but they were soon joined by poor civilians disgruntled with the forces of the Enlightenment movement. The houses of high officials were burned, and the Japanese legation was overrun. Soon, angry soldiers and peasants surged toward the palace.

Jin sighed deeply as she leaned against Yeon.

The mob was after the Queen. They considered her the reason for their impoverishment, having pushed reform by creating a separate modernized military and opening the nation to trade, allowing foreigners to seize power. Thinking that his father, the Regent, was the only one who could calm the angry mob, the King brought him back into the palace. The Queen had to flee. Accompanying her as she escaped from the palace with the help of Hong Gyehoon was the mere junior lady attendant Jin. Just as they escaped, a group of soldiers, who recognized Jin as part of the Queen's retinue, pursued them from behind. The Queen was made to hide in the long grass near the road, and Jin boarded the palanquin in her stead, not long before they were captured. When the soldiers realized the occupant of the palanquin was not the Queen, they brandished their swords at Jin. It was in that moment she heard someone call out, "Silverbell!" A man wearing a black head cloth over his nose and mouth appeared between the soldiers and Jin. He held a sword in one hand. The palanquin bearers had long run away. Jin also made a run for it, but she stopped suddenly.

Silverbell? Was it Yeon?

She had never seen Yeon handle a sword instead of an *ajaeng* or the *daegeum*. In the dark, she stared as the man with the black head cloth fought against the soldiers. His swordplay was too effortless for him to really be Yeon. Only the soldiers made a sound. The man with the black head cloth was silent. He managed to keep fighting them off until Hong Gyehoon arrived at the scene. A soldier who had wounded his arm stepped away. As the other soldiers began retreating, the man with the black head cloth also slipped into the dark. He seemed to have sustained a serious arm injury of his own. The Queen and her guardians hid during the day and traveled only at night as they put as much distance as possible between themselves and the capital, but Jin felt the presence of someone following them the whole way. When they ran out of provisions, someone left them a bundle of wrapped balls of rice by the roadside, and when they needed disguises, clothes seemed to appear from thin air. One night when the moon had risen, on a mountain trail where it was impossible to keep hidden, Jin finally came face-to-face with Yeon. The exhausted Queen had found it impossible to continue, and Jin had gone looking for water alone. Jin made Yeon lay down his injured arm on her lap as they gazed out at the moon over the valley.

Home is where they know you hurt. It is where they mourn your passing.

—I wish we could go back to when we lived in Banchon.

Jin whispered this as if to herself, leaning against Yeon. Where could that mountain trail be, where Yeon had followed her like a shadow despite his wounded arm?

—I want to live somewhere far away from here.

Yeon looked down at Jin, who had just contradicted herself after saying that she wanted to go back to Banchon. Jin always reminded him of the woman Suh's old house in Banchon. He could recall young Jin's voice saying, "Live here with us," as he had tried to follow Blanc. Back then, when he wandered from house to house, eating and sleeping where he could before he met Blanc, the only people who had asked him to live with them were Suh and Jin.

Where does she mean by . . . far away from here?

Yeon gazed up at the moon. If she had not become a court lady, what would she be like now? Yeon often wondered this when he was alone.

—Say something.

Jin hadn't said that to him in a long time.

—You can speak. You shouted Silverbell today.

It wasn't just that day. That dawn when the Queen's Chambers burned and she walked out of the palace alone, Yeon had shouted, "Silverbell!" as he came running toward her. And when Jin was surrounded by rioting soldiers as she escorted the Queen to safety during the Year of the Blue Monkey, Yeon had clearly shouted, "Silverbell!"

The door to one of the buildings slid open, and a child walked unsteadily out of it, rubbing his eyes as he made his way to the outhouse.

You know how to speak. Yeon hadn't taken her words seriously when she first said them, but he had at one time wondered whether she was right and opened his mouth to try to say something. But he couldn't hear the voice that Jin had said she'd heard.

If he could speak, what would he say to this woman? Whenever Yeon thought this, he played his *daegeum* instead or plucked at the *yangeum* or *ajaeng* or blew the *hyangpiri*. He used musical instruments instead of his voice. Sometimes all day, or all night. When he played music, he would think of Jin dancing, graceful as a butterfly in the wind, or a crane.

As the two sat on the edge of the porch and looked up at the moon, the woman Suh began to stir. Surprised that Jin wasn't lying where she was supposed to be, Suh quickly sat upright. She was beginning to get up when she saw the shadows of the two against the paper-screen door. She leaned back again.

—I want to dance.

Suh felt her heart break.

—Underneath this moonlight. To the music of your *daegeum* . . .

Yeon lowered his shoulder so Jin could more easily lean against him. His heart felt so full he could hardly breathe. He thought he would never get to play the *daegeum* for Jin in a place for just the two of them and not at some court banquet. If it weren't for her injury, he would have loved to see her dancing like flowing water in the moonlight.

—No one in the world plays the *daegeum* as well as you.

Yeon wanted to say the same thing to her. That there was no woman in the world who could dance as beautifully as she. When Jin danced, she didn't seem of this world. She was as light as air, smooth as silk, and fresh as newly sprouted grass. The silhouettes of the two trembled in the room. Suh gazed at Jin's shadow leaning against the shoulder of Yeon's shadow. Not for the first time, she regretted with all her heart that she had ever allowed the girl to enter court.

5
Confession

Your Excellency,

Before I came to Korea, you decided on our budget, promising an increase in my salary, which is as yet only temporarily set.

With this in mind, I hereby submit to the Ministry of Foreign Affairs our planned budget for this legation. The budget takes into account the fact that other foreign diplomats receive twice the amount in wages than French representatives, and I receive far less than my counterparts in Tientsin, Guangdong, and Yokohama. I wish to emphasize that expenses here are greater than anywhere else. Not only do Korean officials visit foreign diplomats frequently, but they also tend to stay longer than those of other countries. It is essential we provide them meals and wine. In addition, we need to invite them to dinners on occasion if we are to cultivate a closer relationship with them. In truth, the successes of the American and Russian legations in obtaining greater influence is due to their active courting of Korea's higher officials. This proves difficult on our part due to our limited funds. Please bear in mind that our treaty with Korea does not guarantee tolerance for Christians, and there are many occasions in which we are unable to meet with officials regarding our many religious disputes. I have done my best to meet with highly placed officials, not to mention continuously maintaining contact with those who say they disapprove of France because of Catholic missionary efforts. Should Your Excellency approve of such measures on my part, I respectfully request an increase in funds from twenty thousand francs to twenty-five thousand francs toward these endeavors.

August 10, 1888
Victor Collin de Plancy

Victor stood up from his chair in the waiting room for the King's audience. He was too nervous to remain seated comfortably. His mind was also on the letter in his pocket, the one Jin had given him before he set off this morning, to give to the Queen. What could she have written? His curiosity grew until it turned into nervousness.

It was fall. The summer days in which cicada song and the humid heat seemed to stop time itself had disappeared with the first cool breezes. It was Victor's first Korean autumn. The white clothes that the Koreans wore were in harmony with the deep blue of the sky. The autumn descended on the palace and made the trees look lusher than before. The pine trees, having shaken off the strong sunlight, looked greener than ever, and a few leaves on some of the other trees had already begun to turn. The colorfully painted rafters of the pagoda-tile roofs seemed more vibrant having overcome the heat of the summer.

Victor began to pace in the waiting room.

The King, without any consultation with China, sent out Ministry of Internal Affairs official Cho Shinhee to Russia, France, England, Germany, and Italy as adjunct legate. At the same time, Park Jungyang was sent to Washington as the Korean legate to the United States. According to the treaty signed with China, "Korea must request permission before sending Korean representatives to Western countries," and to follow these terms meant the King needed to have China's consent before sending out legations, a measure stipulated in executive guidelines. Korean representatives must be accompanied by Chinese representatives when visiting the foreign service headquarters of their posted countries. Chinese representatives were to speak for Korea in official meetings. In other words, the only thing Korean emissaries could do was stand in silence behind Chinese representatives as the latter conducted Korea's business.

—An article in the treaty states that orders shall change with the times.

Jin said this upon hearing Victor's explanation. But the article about changing orders was probably added as a measure for China to pressure Korea under whatever timely pretenses it saw fit, not to enable Korea's eventual self-determination.

—The Korean legate to Japan has already submitted his letters of credence to the Japanese emperor without consulting China.

Victor looked Jin in the eye. Jin looked back at him, her gaze clearly stating that the Korean legate to France should be able to do so as well. It was apparent to him that she was more than just a beautiful woman. Each day his love for her deepened, rendering him restless in his sleep. It surprised Victor that Jin would state her opinion so boldly on the matter of Korea's uncomfortable positioning between world powers. He remembered the time when Lucien Liouville, who taught at the divinity school built in the capital, took his Korean students on a walk along the fortress and unknowingly jumped over the palace walls. Even when Blanc told him they were in danger of being unduly punished, Victor thought the matter could be cleared up easily, until Jin had given him some calm words of warning.

—To unlawfully enter the palace where the King resides is grounds for beheading or banishment. You must meet with an official and negotiate a release before that happens.

She also suggested that there was a way to resolve the situation amicably, by meeting with the American O. N. Denny of the King's foreign council with whom Victor was well acquainted. And Jin was right. According to the law, crossing even the outer walls of the palace was grounds for execution or at least banishment.

Jin had been staying at the French legation since the past summer following the Queen's orders. The French physician affiliated with the legation treated her in the Western way, and her wounds were almost healed, but as autumn approached without word from the Queen, she retreated into silence. There were days when she did not speak a single word, where she shut herself in Victor's study instead. In contrast to Jin's wishes, Victor, whose infatuation for her grew with each passing day, found himself from time to time wondering if there was a way not to send her back to the palace.

Victor was lost in thought when a palace official came up to him and said the King was waiting for him.

The King sat alongside the Queen when Victor entered his presence at the Hall of Diligent Governance. With the interpreter official between them and himself, Victor stood on the flower-pattern mat before the King and bowed deeply.

—We have called you here to request your help. As you know, the Ministry of Internal Affairs official Cho Shinhee has left Korea under the title of adjunct legate. He was given the positions of Korean legate to not only Russia but England, Germany, and France. It is our wish to engage in more active exchanges with the West. Help Cho Shinhee to do his work as legate when he arrives in France.

The Queen stared at Victor. China's power had virtually subsumed the King's ever since the military rebellion. In the Year of the Black Horse, it was the Queen who made the King bring in the Chinese army to banish the Regent, who was unaware the Queen had been hiding in Janghowon. The Queen managed to return to the palace with the help of the Chinese, and the Regent was taken against his will to China. In the Year of the Blue Monkey, threatened by the rise of the

Enlightenment Party reformists Kim Okgyun, Park Youngho, and Hong Youngsik, the Queen was forced to bring in the Chinese army again. The Chinese drove out the Japanese military, upon whom the reformists had depended, and the Gapsin Coup was over in a mere three days, but the Chinese interfered with every aspect of Korea's domestic politics as a result.

—Korea is not a vassal state of China.

The King seemed to think that Victor could influence whether France would treat Korea as a vassal state or an independent one.

The Queen, who sat perfectly still despite the guilt she felt in her heart, began to speak.

—Does the French legate think that it is appropriate for the Korean legate to be accompanied by the Chinese legate when he visits France's Ministry of Foreign Affairs, and for our representative to stand behind him at all times?

Victor answered this question indirectly by using America as an example.

—I have heard that the Chinese legate attempted to accompany the Korean emissaries in America but was thwarted and that the official meeting with the president happened without Chinese presence.

The touch of fierceness in the Queen's eyes softened. The King also managed a slight smile.

—We hope that France may also treat Korea's legate as the representative of an independent nation.

This would be no easy thing. For France to do what the Korean King asked was to ignore China's wishes. France had already fought China for control of Vietnam. France did not consider their national interests to lie in Korea. This was why they were later than America, England, or Germany in engaging in Korean politics. Victor's main priority when he was sent to Korea from China as legate was not politics but to prevent the oppression of the Catholic missionaries. Having just won the war for Indochina, France would not want to disturb China again if there was nothing to be gained from Korea.

—Allow the Korean legate to reside in the French capital, just as you live here in ours.

In politics, each action underscores at least five motives. Victor refused to say he would try and could only bow his head politely.

—There are many things we will need to discuss with France.

—Yes, Your Majesty.

—Are there any requests for us?

Victor bowed politely again, glancing at the Queen's unreadable expression instead of the King's innocent demeanor.

—I do have one request, Your Majesty.

—What is it?

—Before we speak of it, I would like to present you with the photograph I took of you. And I also have something for the Queen.

The Queen stared deeply into Victor's nervous eyes.

—I have a letter for you from Lady Attendant Suh, who is staying at our legation.

Victor observed the Queen's expression as an official came down to the flower-pattern mat and took the photograph and letter from him. She remained utterly calm. It made Victor nervous that she did not ask him a single question about Jin despite how curious she must have been about her.

The King could not take his eyes off the photograph. He always did seem interested in matters of culture over politics.

—How does it compare to the one Ji Wuyoung took?

The King handed over the photograph to the Queen. The Queen's mind was preoccupied with the thought of Jin's letter, but she nevertheless closely examined the photograph the King gave her.

—Is it not more detailed than any painting?

—It is fascinating.

—Would the Queen also sit for a photograph?

The Queen set down the photograph with a firm smile. The King turned to Victor.

—Did you not say you had a request?

Victor braced himself.

—What is it?

—I beseech you to grant an impossible wish.

The King and Queen both looked at Victor. The Queen's lips were firmly shut.

—It concerns the court dancer staying with us at the legation.

The Queen, who had seemed imperturbable, showed a slight tremor in her eyes. The King glanced at her with a look that seemed to say, *A dancer staying at the legation?*

—Lady Attendant Suh, Your Majesty.

The one who performed the Dance of the Spring Oriole. The King sat up. He didn't know exactly when that girl had first caught his eye during his visits to the Queen's Chambers. Her face was of both an exquisite beauty and shining intelligence. Her eyes shone, and her skin was the color of apricots. The natural red of her cheeks had the vibrant glow of someone who had just returned from a quick errand. It was Lady Attendant Suh who had brought him the news, in the Year of the Black Horse, that the Queen was hiding in the village of Janghowon with Yu Taejun. And it was also Lady Attendant Suh who was unfailingly by the Queen's side when the Queen fled to Gyeongungung Palace. The Queen depended on Jin more than ever when a close senior lady attendant named Ko Daesu, at the Enlightenment radical Kim Okgyun's behest, carried out a bombing plot in the palace. Whenever the Queen found herself unable to remember something, all she needed was to glance at Jin, whereupon Jin coaxed the Queen's memory on internal affairs as if she were an extension of the Queen herself. But one day, the girl vanished. And the King dared not ask the Queen about her, thinking it improper. He had wondered what had become of her until the evening he saw her perform the Dance of the Spring Oriole at the banquet for the French legate. Her beauty was breathtaking.

Just as Victor was about to speak, the Queen spoke up first.

—I'm afraid I'm in need of some air.

Her distraction made Victor hesitate. The King looked at the Queen again, wondering what was wrong. Her face had turned white.

—Why are you so pale?

—I only need a moment.

—Are you feeling poorly? Should we call the physician?

—No, Your Majesty. I only need a moment.

Lady Suh was dismayed by the Queen's unscheduled movement. It was unheard of for the Queen to leave the King's presence mid-conversation. When the entourage of junior lady attendants waiting outside began to follow the Queen, she gave a sharp command for only Lady Suh to accompany her. Freed from the stifling atmosphere indoors, the Queen stretched her shoulders and took a deep breath. She gave the building a piercing look.

—Lady Suh!

—Your Majesty.

—What request do you think the French legate will make?

—It is quite beyond me, Your Majesty.

The Queen frowned. Her face remained pale above the green silk of her royal tunic.

Even if there were another mountain after this mountain, there would still be a path. Thinking so was the only way to survive.

Unlike Lady Suh, the Queen could guess what request the French legate was about to make. She had no official channels into the French legation, but she received reports on their affairs from the cook who worked there. She knew of Victor's astounding care toward the treatment of Jin's wounds. Indeed, the Queen had obtained the appropriate medicine from the King's physician himself, but she did not send them on.

Victor had apparently considered the legation physician inadequate and requested that Dr. Allen at Gwanghyewon bring new medicines and make house calls. When he learned at a diplomacy club event in Jeongdong that the Russians had an ointment that prevented scarring, he went to the Russian legation the next day to beg for some.

The Queen also learned that the French legate went running with a Jindo dog every morning. Afterward, he gathered flowers from around the legation and placed them on the floor near Jin's head. These flowers filled one edge of the floor and were now being laid down in layers. He would also boil a clear soup himself and bring it into Jin's room. It was almost saddening to see how much he was hoping she would enjoy the soup.

—Lady Suh.

—Yes, Your Majesty.

—Do you remember when Lady Attendant Suh lost her way in the palace and was crying?

—Do you mean that time when you scraped the pear and fed it to her?

—Yes. How old was she then?

—She was five, Your Majesty.

The Queen had thought back then, *If I hadn't lost a newborn princess to a mysterious illness, she would be as old as this crying girl is now.*

—Five . . . What would that make her now?

—She is nineteen.

The Queen mumbled something, and then stood up straight.

—I have done wrong!

—Your Majesty . . .

While unable to fathom the Queen's exact thoughts, Lady Suh was filled with sympathy. What on earth made her so restless? The Queen suddenly raised her head and restlessly walked toward the gardens before stopping in her tracks. Lady Suh called out, "Your Majesty!" The Queen's eyes filled with tears. In a low voice, she said to Lady Suh, who was so surprised she had forgotten to stand with her back bowed, that they must go back. Lady Suh had seen the Queen clench her fists so tightly she almost crushed her own hands, or so angry that the fine veins in her eyes became visible, but she had never seen her in tears. The Queen disliked showing any vulnerability. Oblivious to Lady Suh, the Queen, as if making up her mind, calmly walked back inside the Hall of Diligent Governance.

When she took her place again, the King gave her a worried look.

—Are you feeling better?

—Please forgive me for worrying you.

—Nonsense. Do not forget to care for yourself.

The Queen glanced at the gentle King and turned to Victor. Victor felt nervous once more as he met the Queen's gaze. He showed his deference by slowly bowing his head but felt as chilled as if he'd entered a cave. The Queen looked as if she'd read his mind.

She broke her gaze and spoke politely to the King.

—Do you remember the recent banquet at the Pavilion of Festivities?

The King gave an involuntary cough in lieu of an answer.

It is impossible to completely fathom the heart of one who is in love. Love always hides another motive.

—Do you also remember Lady Attendant Suh's promise to visit the French legation?

Of course, the King remembered that evening, the night he had first seen the dancer as a beautiful woman, but he tilted his head. A strange smile appeared on the Queen's face, then diminished. While the Queen had confused everyone else at the banquet, the King sensed the flames that flickered in the Queen's heart. The Queen, as firm and daring as she was when it came to dealing with rapidly changing political realities, also happened to be a woman. The King was troubled by her anger whenever she suspected the King had so much as glanced at another woman. His palms were damp from the tension that evening, but the dancer had cleverly turned the tables by offering to grant a single wish for the French legate.

—That day when Lady Attendant Suh visited the legation as promised, she was injured by a knife brandished by a drunkard.

—How terrible.

The King hid his surprise under a disguise of calmness, nodding. So that was why she had disappeared. He had discreetly sought out Lady Attendant Suh after the banquet but to no avail. And every direct order he issued was bound to end up in the ear of the Queen. As the Queen realized she could no longer hide the dancer from the King, she had sent her to the legation. The Queen's plan all along was to prevent Jin from ever returning to court, even if the dancer hadn't been assaulted.

—So she has dwelled at the legation all this time.

The King turned to Victor.

—We now see what has happened. But what is your request?

Victor bowed more reverently than he ever had before.

—Please allow the dancer to remain in the legation.

—The dancer?

—Yes, Your Majesty.

—What is the meaning of this?

Victor steeled himself, thinking that if he hesitated now, his desire would remain forever unconfessed. He felt as if he were being whipped by rough waves.

—I have fallen in love with the dancer.

The interpreter, who had been conveying Victor's words to the King and Queen, was so taken aback that his eyes opened wide. He thought he had misheard.

—What is so surprising?

Daunted, the interpreter asked Victor if that was truly what he wanted him to translate.

—*Faites ça.*

The interpreter broke into a sweat at Victor's answer.

—He says he has fallen in love with the dancer, Your Majesty.

Silence fell.

The Queen closed her eyes. She had expected this request. Victor was said to come out to the legation's courtyard every night and gaze in the direction of Jin's room. He would listlessly walk about the courtyard, until Jin, who whiled away the tedious hours by reading as many French books as possible, turned out the light in her room. The Queen had thought this day would come, but she did not think it would be so soon. She had thought she had the autumn, at least, as Victor was not an ordinary man before the King. He was a diplomat representing France. Such an affair, a diplomat coveting a king's woman, could easily cause a scandal.

No matter how deep his love for her was, to say it out loud was not an easy thing. It was like sparking a dry haystack in the heat of frustration when there was still a danger of shifting intentions and being unable to control the resulting fire.

It was the King who broke the terrible silence.

—How can this be?

Victor felt as bare as a branch empty of leaves.

—Because she is beautiful.

The Queen narrowed her eyes. She felt an anger she couldn't quite comprehend toward Victor. When one didn't have anything to say, it was better to say nothing at all; the Queen, who wished Victor could be silent for at least a moment, wondered how he could be so bold with his pronouncements. She had already discerned, at the banquet, the legate's feelings toward Jin, and even though she had brought about these events, she found herself disapproving deeply.

If this were not the Korean but the Chinese court?

He would not have said he had fallen in love with the Chinese emperor's woman so easily, she thought. The Queen straightened her back.

—Dancers are not celadon jars.

The Queen's voice was as cold as ice.

—Nor are they books or painted screens.

The Queen knew the legate was enthralled with Korea's celadon, books, and folding screens, hoarding whatever he could. She heard the annex at the legation was full of these objects, so numerous that it was impossible to know how many of which.

Victor bowed once more and beseeched them.

—If Your Majesty permits it, I would like to marry the dancer.

The hall was shocked into silence once more at Victor's words. Were the legate's feelings toward the dancer the same as what he felt for celadon or books? Suspecting as much, the Queen narrowed her eyes again at his blatant presumptions.

—Is this true?

The King seemed greatly disturbed.

—In the village where I was born, there lived a girl named Marie. She was my first love. My father opposed the match, and I was forbidden from seeing her again.

Marie. The daughter of Lord Plancy. She was the only girl in the village with black hair and dark eyes. Victor was only a boy and Marie a girl, but his father, Jacques, did not like his associating with her. And perhaps that was the reason his love for her only grew. One day, Jacques caught them lying asleep together like spoons, atop a pile of straw in a barn on the outer edges of Lord Plancy's estate. He was never to see Marie again. It would be more accurate to say that Marie could not see him. Victor would never be sure what his father had said to Marie's family. He searched for her night and day that spring. Then finally, that summer, Marie was found dead by the bank of the river that flowed through Plancy. This was just before the rains would bloat the river and flood the village. What was discovered next to Marie was not Victor, but one of Lord Plancy's dogs.

Victor did his best to tell Marie's story to the King and Queen. All night he had thought about how to properly convey his love for the court dancer, but even he hadn't foreseen himself to be talking of Marie before them.

The King had a question.

—Lady Attendant Suh resembles this Marie?

—Yes, Your Majesty.

The Queen asked her own question.

—And if she had not resembled her?

—Lady Attendant Suh is as beautiful as Korea itself. If she hadn't resembled Marie, I still would have fallen in love with her.

It was the Queen's turn to be taken aback. Not even she could have predicted the ardor of the legate's words.

Is there hope for this love after all?

Sweat dripped from Victor's forehead as he awaited the King's answer. It was Blanc who had told him that only by entering a hopeless love could one understand love's true meaning. What could Blanc have meant by this? Victor was already lost in his love for Jin.

—And how is Lady Attendant Suh?

The Queen's distraction made Victor turn toward her.

—She spends her days reading books.

It would have been more accurate to say she spent her days awaiting the Queen's orders.

—Books from France?

—Yes, Your Majesty.

The court dancer was likely reading in Victor's study this very moment. She almost never left Victor's study as she awaited word from the Queen. She would wander through the library and choose a book to read, and once chosen, spend the rest of the day with it. She read through the night on some days, and soon was reading all through the day in the study. Sometimes at dawn or late at night, one could see Jin in the legation courtyard, standing by the phoenix tree. Jin always looked in the same direction when she stood underneath that tree. He had thought it strange at first but came to know why. Paul Choi told him that Jin was looking toward the palace.

—Have her wounds healed?

—They have.

Her wounds had healed rapidly as if heeding her desire to return to court as soon as possible. It astounded her physician. But Jin seemed sicker once her wounds closed. She burst into tears on the day that the woman Suh visited from Gondangol. Afterward, her face betrayed no emotion. She was perfectly cordial and spent her days sitting and reading quietly, back straight. Sometimes, during the hours when she thought no one was watching, she would go outside to the phoenix tree and dance underneath its canopy. When Blanc visited, she conversed with him in a calm manner and watched in silence as Blanc taught Victor Korean. Blanc once asked her whether she might teach Victor while she was staying at the legation.

—I must be ready to return to court tonight if word comes.

She left the room after giving this short answer.

Victor, thinking Jin might be bored, suggested they go together to the diplomats' club in Jeongdong, or out to Saegumjeong on a donkey.

His suggestions were always met with the answer that the palace could send word at any moment, and she could not leave the legation until then.

He did see her smile once. The woman Suh had sent medicinal herbs from Gondangol by way of Yeon, and Victor had been the one to announce him to Jin. The news that the Jangakwon musician had come to see her brought a vibrant smile from Jin, who had been holed up in Victor's study with a book. That was the day Yeon played the *daegeum* for Victor in return for the gift of the fountain pen. Jin's joyous face as she listened to the strains of the bamboo flute was so distracting to Victor that he hardly took in the music. Jin saw Yeon off, walking as far as the vegetable patch in front of the legation. Victor watched the pair walk side by side down the path through the patch. He also watched Jin walk back alone, her head bowed in sadness.

—Legate.

The Queen's voice was low.

—You must return another time.

Victor was distraught. This meant she would not give him an answer today.

Those who love are inevitably made to wait.

A month had passed after the night of the banquet before the court dancer visited the legation as promised. The days of that month surely held the same number of hours as any other day, but each day of that month had been interminable. Victor had a feeling of what was in store for him if he left court without an answer.

—I shall discuss this with His Majesty and send word.

Victor's disappointment had not escaped the Queen's notice. She had closely observed his feelings toward Jin for a long time. That his feelings were true was a relief, but it was oddly unsettling as well.

The Queen bit her lip, feeling a wave of bitterness. Lady Attendant Suh at the legation couldn't possibly even dream of how Victor had just confessed his daring love before the King.

—This is no small matter. There are rituals to observe in the discharge of a court lady.

—It is why I beseech Your Majesties so fervently.

Victor knew it was now or never. He tried to seem as obsequious as possible, bowing low and using his most respectful voice. He would gain nothing but whispers behind his back if he retreated now. It was already going to be a major scandal among the diplomats. They were polite enough, working together in a foreign country for the sake of their home nations, but there was no telling how such politeness would turn. It was clear how they might twist the story of a diplomat who fell in love with one of the King's women. If such a distorted retelling ever got back to Paris, his career as a diplomat would be over.

He must not give in. He knew the Queen's excuse was only an attempt to hide her intentions. What would move her, to stop her from retreating behind the King? Victor made some quick calculations.

—Your Majesty, I shall discuss with my superiors the matter that has eluded you in Japan, of founding a residential Korean legation in France.

The King's frown was replaced with an expression of interest at these words. Victor was itching to read the Queen's reaction, but he kept his gaze fixed on the King.

—Is this a possibility?

The King's eyebrows were raised.

—Our conflict with China regarding Indochina is over, and France is ready to give its relationship with Korea more consideration.

—A resident legation would be of great help to Korea.

But the first thing to do before trying to shed China's influence was to procure enough funds. The adjunct legate Cho Shinhee had run out of money and was unable to move on to Europe from Hong Kong. China had conspired with Britain to keep him there, and Cho Shinhee had been ill for a time, but funds were the biggest reason he couldn't fulfill his duties. It was the King's ambition to maintain diplomatic ties with foreign countries on an equal footing, but the way things were, he couldn't even afford to pay local staff on time.

The King glanced at the Queen. She, more than anyone else, had borne the brunt of their uncertain finances. The Queen, who usually spared no expense when it came to the Crown Prince, had decided not to hold a hundred-day prayer event for his health due to the cost.

—We shall consider your proposal.

The Queen said this again to Victor, who showed no sign of moving off.

—Please leave us. We shall send word.

Defeated, Victor left their presence. As he walked down the stone steps of the Hall of Diligent Governance, he felt his knees begin to buckle. A helplessness he had never felt, even at the grand imperial court of China, pressed down on him.

The white Jindo dog greeted him when he returned to the legation.

Victor's eyes grew wide when he looked up from petting the dog that had run toward him through the vegetable patch. Jin was standing before the legation. To one in love, the object of one's affections is like a bird that might fly away at any moment. Jin walked over to him. It was a strange moment for Victor, as it was the first time that it was she who was approaching him. He felt as if he were hallucinating. It was also the first time he had seen her step outside the legation gate since she had seen Yeon off.

Jin stopped before him.

—Were you waiting for me?

—Yes.

Victor knew it wasn't him she had been waiting for but news from court. Nevertheless, his face, dark since his audience with the King, lit up with a smile.

—Shall we take a walk?

Before Jin could turn him down, Victor started walking around the vegetable patch. He took a few steps and looked back at her. Jin started to follow him. They walked over an irrigation ridge around the patch that had broken in the rain. Beans sprouted at the breach.

—I've given your letter to the Queen.

Jin suppressed the urge to ask him what she had said to him and bent down to push the sprouts into the boundary of the patch.

—She says she will send word soon.

—Did she read it?

—She only accepted it. She must've read it by now.

Victor's shoulders, ever straight, slumped as he asked the next question.

—Do you want to go back to court?

Jin didn't answer. Victor had seemed surprised when she handed him the letter and asked him to give it to the Queen should she be present during his audience with the King. He had acquiesced but looked displeased as he took the letter from her.

Victor turned around and faced her.

—Are you not comfortable here?

He looked her directly in the eye.

—I did not write asking to be reinstated to court.

Jin looked back at him, then turned away. She gazed at the roof of the Russian legation in the distance.

—I wrote asking if I could remain here.

Victor's eyes filled with surprise.

And what else had she written? Jin sighed as she remembered. She had stated that she had private records from the Year of the Black Horse, that Soa should be tasked with bringing them to the Queen for safekeeping. Jin seemed like she was doing nothing but reading all day, but she was also thinking hard about why the Queen was not calling her back to court. The reason came to her in a flash one dawn. She remembered what was said to her when she was sent from the Queen's Chambers to the Embroidery Chamber. *With you, I do not wish to have a man come between us.* She had always been near the Queen, but since that day, she could only approach her when summoned. And that evening of the banquet. The King had sent word three times afterward that he was looking for her. But each time when she got ready to see him, a lady attendant of the Queen's Chambers came and informed her that her presence was no longer necessary. Then, suddenly, the order had come for her to visit the French legation.

—Is that true?

—It is.

Jin walked past Victor, who stood there, stunned. The Jindo dog trotted out in front of Jin. It seemed to lead, this being a familiar path that the dog ran with Victor. Victor stretched his hand toward the wildflowers out of habit, the same flowers he offered every morning to Jin. The dried bouquets now made a low wall on one side of Jin's room.

—Did you read today?

—Yes.

—What book was it?

—The poetry of Rimbaud. I also read some Flaubert.

—What do you think of Rimbaud?

—I find him melancholy and anxious. A poet must be someone who sees what others cannot see. I don't know why, but I felt as if a large boulder were settling down on my heart. Even though I didn't understand all of it.

Victor gazed at Jin's black hair as he listened to her beautiful voice. He had been holding back his words, but his control slipped as he fought the urge to stroke her hair.

—I want you to be with me.

The words came out before he realized it. He had wanted to say these words for such a long time.

—If you knew what I said to the King and Queen today, you would despise me.

Jin stopped in her tracks and turned to look at him.

—I told them that I love you.

—. . .

—And I asked them to let you stay here with me.

Her dark, deep gaze seemed to penetrate his own blue eyes.

—My heart is filled with you. And I cannot imagine my days without you.

The evening wind blew, keeping them both company. Jin broke her hard gaze and turned away. Victor knew his words would offend her, as it was clear she wanted nothing more than to return to court. He followed her, determined to accept whatever abuse she would hurl at him.

—Will you take me to France?

Victor froze. He thought he had misheard.

—Someday . . . someday, I mean.

—Is that how you really feel?

Victor could not see the tears that gathered in her eyes.

—Will you accept my love?

That dawn when she realized that the Queen wanted to send her into the arms of the French legate, Jin had met the morning standing underneath the phoenix tree, looking toward the palace. It was pointless. Even with the realization that she may never return to court, there wasn't a single thing she could do. Soa's face had briefly flitted by in her memory. And one more thing: the diary she had kept for the Queen as part of her duties during the terrible Year of the Black Horse.

—I've already had word from the palace.

—When?

—Four days ago.

Four days ago? Blanc was the only person who had visited the legation on that day.

—Lady Suh brought a missive to Gondangol, and Bishop Blanc passed it on to me.

Was that so? Blanc had had a long conversation with Jin, but Victor hadn't known about letters being exchanged. Why hadn't Blanc told him about it? Victor began to feel anxious.

Was it word for her to return to court?

A man's mind is a tangled skein. The more one tries to untangle it, the worse the tangle becomes.

—It was an order to remain at the legation until Your Excellency leaves Korea.

Victor couldn't believe his ears. He felt he had been defeated by the Queen. She had not given him the slightest hint that she had sent word to Jin and instead made Victor beg. Not only that, she had refused to give him the answer he was desperate for, making him be the one to mention the possibility of a resident Korean legation. She had read his mind like a book.

—Why did you not tell me?

—I suffered.

Victor said nothing.

—Would you give me some time to decide?

—Time?

Jin was silent. There were many things she wanted to say, but she kept her lips closed. Victor spoke again in a sad voice.

—When will I hear your answer?

—The day I decide, I shall place my fragrance pouch in the pages of Hugo's *Les Misérables* in the library.

Jin showed him the small pouch she carried in her sleeve. It was thin and red, embroidered with yellow floss, the length of her palm. Soa had made it for her.

—Will it mean that you accept my love?

Jin did not answer but lowered her head. A sparrow on the grass fluttered up to the sky. Whether she accepted the French legate's love or not, she would never be able to return to court if the Queen did not change her mind. What happened to court ladies who could not return to court? She breathed deeply. Victor spoke as if it were up to her, but it wasn't. She hadn't been formally banished from court, but it was as good as if she were. And even a banished court lady could not wed whomever she pleased. Just as it was not up to her to become the French legate's wife. The Queen knew this, and her sending Jin to the legate meant she was sending her away forever.

Victor felt pity for Jin, who stood with her head bowed, unable to answer him. It was as if a little bird fallen from its nest was seeking shelter underneath his awning. Even if the woman did not love him, he wanted to be the steady roof that sheltered her.

—It was difficult for me when I was not allowed to speak my mind. Compared to that, waiting for your answer will be sweet. I only hope it is not too long a wait.

Victor saw Jin put out her hand toward the thick rushes, but not the tears that had gathered in her eyes. When she learned Victor was to have an audience with the King, Jin had rubbed ink from an ink stone for the first time since coming to the legation. She stayed up all night writing her letter to the Queen. She complained, she ranted, but in the end, she crumpled these missives and wrote down only two lines. The first declared that she would serve the French legate as ordered by Her Majesty, and the other stated that her roommate Soa knew where her records from the Year of the Black Horse were kept and that the Queen should take these into her safekeeping.

Meanwhile, the Queen spread out before her the notebooks that had been wrapped carefully in a length of linen. They were Jin's diaries, fetched from Soa by Lady Suh.

Diary of the Sixth Month of the Year of the Black Horse.

The Queen instantly recognized Jin's calligraphy on the cover of the notebook. Her finger trembled as it flicked over the first page.

> *Third day of the sixth month.*
>
> *Her Majesty is moved to Min Eungsik's house.*
>
> *We had to change the disguises we wore when we left the palace. Her Majesty has a sore throat and cannot speak. I gave her peppermint oil late last night, but she couldn't drink it. Perhaps because she went to bed on an empty stomach, she dreamed something unpleasant and called out. Her forehead was drenched with sweat. I dabbed it off. She woke up before dawn, came out to the porch, and leaned on a pillar until the sun rose, her eyes in the direction of the palace.*

The Queen frowned as she read on.

They detailed, over fifty days, how she had escaped the rebelling soldiers with her life, moving from Min Eungsik's house to Yeoju, then Janghowon, then Chunju. The act of recording is also an act of calming oneself. Even if one was only copying the broadsheets posted after the

Chinese military entered Korea or making a record of the two days spent in darkness when the Queen suffered from an eye infection. Or the time when a boil appeared on the Queen's back, and she had to either sit or lie down on her stomach with a medicinal patch stuck to her.

Still frowning, the Queen kept turning the pages.

Twenty-ninth day of the sixth month.

A squall. Her Majesty is devastated that a state funeral was held for her despite how she still lives. She sits up straight with the boil on her back, shedding tears all day. She does not say a word. Late at night, she lets down her hair and cries over and over again, "I am a dead person." I made her a medicinal brew of bellflower root and licorice, but she refused it. She did not sleep.

Second day of the seventh month.

I read to her, but she seemed not to listen. She is on tenterhooks thinking of the Crown Prince. In the middle of dictating a letter to the King, she shouted, "What letters would a dead person be writing?" She snatched the letter and crumpled it.

When the Queen got to the part where Jin had made her way to the palace with a letter saying she was still alive, she exclaimed aloud, "That poor thing!" She slammed the notebook shut. Lady Suh looked up, startled. She was nervous as she saw the Queen's eyes narrowing. This meant she was about to make a decision. Such decisions sometimes meant death.

After she sent the French legate home disappointed, the Queen had removed herself from the reception hall and torn open Jin's letter as she stood in the gardens. There were only two lines in the letter. Was that it? The Queen was bereft. Not a single word more than to say that she would follow her orders and to get the diaries from Soa.

And yet . . . the Queen's eyes narrowed again.

She had felt herself hesitating as she read the diaries from the Year of the Black Horse. She could feel the writer's desperation as she detailed each movement of the queen she served. And the Queen finally understood Jin's intentions regarding the Year of the Black Horse diaries. She wished the Queen to read them and to reconsider her decision, to recall Jin back to court. She thought of how the girl must have cried when she received her letter four days ago. *But how would you possibly know my true feelings?* The Queen, her hand still touching the cover of the notebook, called for Lady Suh.

—Where is the King?

—He is in the reception hall, Your Majesty.

—Who is with him?

—The Crown Prince and his Foreign Minister.

—Prepare my writing implements.

—Yes, Your Majesty.

As Lady Suh rubbed the ink stone, the Queen began speaking again to Lady Suh.

—I shall wed Lady Attendant Suh to the French legate.

Lady Suh became pale, and she looked up at the Queen.

—She'll be better off at the French legation than this prison. Do you not agree?

—Your Majesty, as an initiated court lady of the palace . . .

—I am aware that it is out of my purview. That is why I shall obtain a dispensation from the King himself.

The Queen, her frown deeper than ever, cut off all discussion on the matter.

6

Take Me to the Louvre

Your Excellency,

The Korean king shows much interest in the cultural goods of France. He told me that he has heard of the beauty of France's architecture and wishes to hire a French architect for Korea's palaces. I began negotiations through the Bank of Paris in Tientsin, which ended quickly thanks to M. Salabelle's agreement, his pay agreed at three thousand won a year.

The King requested the loan of some illustrated books to give him a better idea of our architecture. Despite my considerable library, I do not have any books in this field. Therefore, I presented to him the seven volumes of Guizot's History of France, *and he was much moved by the illustrations therein. He wished to keep the books for himself. He also seemed interested in the uniforms our military men wore . . .*

I request books be sent of our national architectural treasures—the Louvre, the Tuileries, the Palace of Versailles, and the greatest monuments and cathedrals of Paris. The King has also expressed interest in our military these past few months. If General d'Amade were to visit, he should have a very welcome reception and have an audience with the King many times over. The King has already requested a full description of the rules of our infantry, cavalry, and artillery units. I had to inform him that I did not possess such information and that I would have to send a request to Paris. The King desires expedience in this matter, and so I write to Your Excellency herein.

December 10, 1888
Victor Collin de Plancy

The leaves of the phoenix tree fell softly that dawn.

Before she set out for Gondangol, Jin went to the library and took down *Les Misérables* from the shelf. It was the story of Jean Valjean, who spent nineteen years in prison for stealing a loaf of bread. She had read it three times, which made her think of him as a friend more than a character. The book was one that Victor had recommended during that time when she virtually lived in the library. He told her that the author was the most beloved in France. Despite skipping a few parts that she couldn't understand, Jin had immersed herself in the book, reading and rereading the stories of "the miserable ones."

Jin opened the book to a random page and cast her eyes over the waves of French words. It was the scene where Valjean was caught stealing the silver candlesticks owned by Bishop Myriel, who had given him shelter for the night. If it weren't for Myriel's kindness, what would've become of Valjean? Jin smiled. The joy of reading came from imagining the answer to that very question, *What would've happened?* When Myriel had testified that he had gifted the candlesticks and Valjean was not a thief, Jin had felt her heart would burst. What would've become of Valjean otherwise? He would not have lived a new life under a new name. Jin carefully placed her fragrance pouch on the part where the rough heart of Valjean, having known only poverty and loneliness, realized the power of love. She saw a flash of Yeon's face on the pouch. She stood still for a long time.

—The leaves of the phoenix tree have fallen.

Jin was startled out of her reverie by Victor's voice. She thought he was still asleep, but there he was, looking out into the courtyard.

—It would make a good *geomungo* zither.

Victor gestured to the phoenix tree. Jin came over and stood next to him. She murmured, "geomungo . . ."

—I shall be visiting Gondangol this morning.

—Is something going on at the orphanage?

There wasn't. She simply did not want to see Victor's face today, having placed the fragrance pouch into *Les Misérables*.

—What do you plan to do there?

—I shall tell you when I return.

Jin made haste to leave, and Victor walked her to the gate.

The cabbages were harvested, and the vegetable patch lay bare. The cold winds hushed the birds. Winter approached, and the ground would freeze. Victor, still unaware that Jin had planted her acquiescence of his love in the pages of *Les Misérables*, watched her go. She never looked back. It was now months since he had gone to the library every morning to see if the pouch was there in the copy of Hugo's novel.

When Jin first suggested she help out the woman Suh at the orphanage, Victor refused to allow it. He could never forget how she was assaulted on that fateful day of their first visit. While the incident had given him an excuse to extend her stay at the legation, he still thought it was dangerous for her to go there. Disappointed, Jin had once again shut herself in the library. Victor proposed a compromise. She was to ride out on a palanquin and return before nightfall. Jin stated that she would ride the palanquin only when she was returning; she wanted to take in the sights of the people going about their business in the morning. Victor had no choice but to accept. He could not refuse anything she said, for to him she was like a bird that could fly away at any moment.

Victor made her soup every morning. He loved sitting across from her as they ate their soup together. Victor would then go running with the Jindo dog, and Jin would head on out to Gondangol. She enjoyed the morning breeze as she walked there. A freedom was in that breeze, something she never felt when she was in the palace. She walked among the people who carried their kindling or vegetables on their cows to sell by the roadside, the women with the water pails balanced on their heads, the butcher's and other stores and the silk market that had not yet opened, feeling her restlessness calming as she made her way. She had to make this walk every morning if she were to feel motivated for the rest of the day. The woman Suh sighed, thinking that Jin was diverting herself to the care of the children so she could forget what was happening at court.

What Jin did at the orphanage mostly was teach. In the morning, she taught Korean to the two French nuns who did administrative work at the orphanage, and in the evening, she brought the boys and girls together to teach Korean history. When there was time between teaching, she showed them a simple dance movement or told them about life in the palace. The children listened wide-eyed as if to a fairy tale. In the late afternoons, the woman Suh heated up some water and washed each child. She had a designated bathing vat in the backyard of the orphanage, with an earthen stove and an iron pot to boil the water nearby. Bathing two or three at a time meant everybody got a bath about once every two days. The children ran away from her as she chased after them for their bath, but once she gave up, they jumped into the vat themselves.

As on any other day, Jin was helping Suh with the bathing. When Suh washed their hair, Jin cleaned their little feet, and when Suh scrubbed their backs, Jin lifted their arms and washed their armpits. Suh watched Jin as she stood the children in a line and dried their hair before putting them in their linen clothes. She found herself asking her a question.

—Are you worried about something?

Jin looked up from helping a girl put on her jacket.

—Do I seem so?

—You haven't said a word all day.

—Oh, Mother.

Suh gave a start. Jin would refer to Suh as her mother to others, but it was the first time she had called her that to her face. The little girl, now fully clothed, put on her shoes and ran out toward the orphanage courtyard.

—I put the fragrance pouch in the book this morning.

Suh stopped in the middle of gathering the old clothes the children had left behind. Jin had told her that she would be with the legate when she left the fragrance pouch in a French book. They were silent for a while.

—He waited a long time for me.

Suh nodded. She saw how much the French legate loved her. She had watched him wait for Jin to open her heart. If he hadn't wanted her love, he would not have waited so long for this king's woman to accept him. She felt it was a good thing but was saddened by the thought of how Yeon would feel. She had known for a long time that while Yeon never mentioned it, Jin was the only woman in his heart.

—I want to dance.

To Yeon's flute, she wanted to say but didn't. Suh stood up and left the backyard. When she returned, she had a wrapped bundle in her hands. She placed it wordlessly before Jin. Jin didn't ask her what it was. She already knew they were her marital bedclothes. She had asked Suh one day as she sewed, "What are you working on?" And Suh, after a silence, answered, "These are for you." Jin was looking down at the bundle when a boy came up to her, his cheeks flush with excitement, and said, "Someone is here for you." Jin asked, "Who?" The boy couldn't answer.

Jin wiped her wet hands and came out to the courtyard. Victor stood by the gate.

Had he seen the fragrance pouch she had left between the pages of *Les Misérables*?

Victor, in his suit vest, watched Jin walk toward him. His direct gaze made Jin feel self-conscious. How strange the human heart was. She felt unable to treat him in the same, natural way that she did before placing the fragrance pouch. Sister Jacqueline, one of the French nuns, saw Victor and greeted him. She stepped into the courtyard and smiled at Jin. The mischievous children also looked to and fro from Jin's face to Victor's.

—What brings you here?

Perhaps it was the children who made her self-conscious. She glanced at their little heads popping out from the orphanage doors.

—I came here to take you to the photography studio before seeing you to the legation.

Hwang Cheol's studio. Victor now developed his photos there and relied on Hwang for camera parts imported from China and Japan.

—Why the studio?

Victor only grinned.

—Are you going somewhere with Hwang Cheol?

—No. I want us to have a commemorative photo taken.

He had seen the fragrance pouch. The downy tips of Jin's ears blushed.

—I want to commemorate this day with you.

She had slipped a letter in the pouch instead of dried flowers. It said that she would prepare tea for him late one night, but she hadn't thought it would be that very same night. She had meant, whenever the night it would be that he discovered the fragrance pouch in *Les Misérables*. Jin was unaware that Victor had flicked through the book day and night in hopes of getting her answer. The woman Suh came out and invited Victor in. But Victor said it would be better to leave now and looked at Jin.

—Then leave first. I shall meet you outside the gate.

Victor left through the gate, a few children trailing after him. Suh fetched the silk bundle from the backyard. Some other children, who were picking from the cloud of red dates on the date tree, ran to Jin to stroke the silk bundle. Jin stroked their heads.

—He's waiting for you.

As Jin made it to the gate and turned to look at Suh, Suh made a waving-away gesture meaning Jin should be on her way. Suh's eyes were moist. She stood watching Jin disappear. *I must sew her some quilts before it gets too cold.* Suh brushed off her skirt and took the children by the hand and led them back inside.

Jin and Victor, as they left the orphanage and entered the main road, were as silent as a married couple who had just argued.

Since coming to the legation, Jin's steadiest conversation partners had been the Jindo dog and Victor. She would whisper her hidden thoughts to the dog, but it was Victor who told her endless stories of what life was like across the ocean. He talked of the steam engine, sticking stamps on letters, the music of violins and organs, and stories from Greek mythology or the saints of the Middle Ages. Of a philosopher named Nietzsche, who shocked the learned people of Europe by declaring that God was dead. He also mentioned how paintings from China and Japan were all the rage in France. When he declared that the world might be ruled by one strong country in the future, Jin led him into a discussion that lasted for three hours. And the nights when they compared French books to Korean ones were too short for them to reach any conclusion.

But here they were now, guarding their silence as they loosely kept pace with each other.

There was a portrait hanging at the entrance of the studio of the minister plenipotentiary Min Young-ik and his group. Min was close to the Queen, and so Jin was familiar with him. Dr. Allen had saved him when he was attacked by an assassin sent by Kim Okgyun, winning the Queen's favor and enabling Allen to set up Gwanghyewon. Mixed in with the people wearing traditional clothes, Western suits, and student uniforms was Seo Gwangbeom of the Enlightenment movement, holding up a photograph from his travels. Victor approached Jin as she gazed at Min Young-ik in the photo.

—I thought it was a shame that we couldn't hold a wedding here in Korea. Which is why I thought we might take a picture instead.

The first words he'd spoken since they left the orphanage. Hwang Cheol had been talking to another guest but greeted Victor warmly in Chinese as they entered. His guest happened to be Hong Jong-u.

—What a coincidence! We were just talking about Your Excellency.

—Good things, I hope?

—You must've done many bad things to be wondering about that.

Hwang Cheol gave a hearty laugh.

—Hong Jong-u is preparing to leave for his studies in Paris and wished to meet you. He's going to be the first Korean to study in France. He needs your help.

—I am happy to assist.

—He wishes to study law in Paris. He wants to see what he can learn for Korea. It is unprecedented, so he is not sure what to do.

—It would help to carry an introductory letter from someone of good standing.

The tall Hong Jong-u, with his black, wide-brimmed *gat* hat and simple white robe, bowed to Victor and glanced at Jin. He said he already had a passport issued by the Minister of Diplomacy, but he would absolutely need Victor's help.

Hwang Cheol did not only take portraits. He also lugged his cameras around to capture scenery such as of the fortress walls, Gyeongbokgung Palace, and Inwangsan Mountain. Sometimes Jin and Victor would accompany him, with Jin disguised as a man. They were soon joined by Hong Jong-u. Victor always took photos of Jin at these locations. Hwang Cheol teased Jin and Victor about their hours-long conversations about Eastern and Western books, poetry, and paintings, wondering aloud how two people who lived together still found so many things to talk about. Hong Jong-u was displeased. He said he found it odd that a court lady, who should be at court, was living in the French legation.

Jin had caught the Queen's interest in all things foreign. Listening to Victor talk of the world outside was like seeing it with her own eyes. Once Hwang Cheol and Hong Jong-u joined their conversation, their horizons expanded to Hong Kong, Shanghai, and Japan. Victor set the tone of their conversation when they discussed how France had wrested French Indochina from the Chinese. Jin was surprised at his knowledge of the East, and it had been an occasion to see Victor in a different light.

—But what brings you to the studio today?

—We're here to take a commemorative photo.

Hwang Cheol and Hong Jong-u looked at him, questioningly.

—We trust you to take a good portrait of us together.

Hong Jong-u frowned. Hwang Cheol called upon his assistant to prepare the shoot, saying they had to make haste before they lost the light. There was still some illumination from the glass window. Victor stepped onto the straw mat and waited for Jin to join him. Jin, conscious of Hong's frown, took her position beside Victor.

—Perhaps we should have dinner together since we're all here.

—We must see Bishop Blanc. But we shall invite you both to the legation soon.

Happiness makes the days feel busy.

Jin shot Victor a questioning look, but Victor only smiled. Taking the photo took a long time. It took twice as long to set up the studio's camera than Victor's state-of-the-art equipment. Victor asked Hwang Cheol to take special care in developing this shot. He wanted the print to last forever.

Hong Jong-u respectfully said to Victor that he would visit the legation soon. He didn't so much as nod at Jin.

Blanc was surprised by Victor's sudden visit. He greeted them at the annex of the traditional Korean house he used as a church. It was still his dream to construct a proper cathedral in Korea. Victor took out a small wooden box and opened it before him. There was an old ring with three leaves engraved on it.

—It belonged to my mother.

The French legate's mother?

Jin felt nervous. Every person in the world had a mother, but she did not until this moment imagine what Victor's mother would be like. Nor what any of his family were like.

—Are you proposing marriage?

—I am.

Happy people are prone to making promises.

The lack of hesitation in Victor's reply made Blanc give Jin a look of concern. He seemed to ask whether this was what she wanted as well.

—Please make it so.

Victor's face brightened at Jin's reply. But Blanc looked despondent.

—But why so suddenly?

—It isn't sudden. I've been waiting for this moment for a long time. By Korean law, initiated court ladies are not allowed to hold weddings. It is not my place as a foreign diplomat to break local laws. But thankfully I have this ring, so I would like to make a promise before the bishop instead of a wedding.

—Your Excellency!

—I know what you're worried about. I have thought about it for a long time. I want her to be my wife.

A pall came over Blanc's face. How long would Victor feel this way? Promises made in the heat of passion were forgotten once passion cooled. How could he take Victor's oath seriously? Blanc sometimes had doubts about his profession, despite his having entered Korea as a man of God. What was wrong with leaving the Koreans to live in the manner they wanted? France occupied Indochina and took the people's timber, rice, coal, and pearls. That was imperialism. Was missionary work ethical under such pretenses? To assuage his doubt, he would often ask for increases in his orphanage funding from Paris. He understood Victor's wish to marry Jin, but he also couldn't with good conscience allow Victor to do whatever he wanted. He was worried that Victor was thinking of Jin as if she were a pearl or a tusk of ivory pilfered from Indochina.

Blanc's silence made Victor nervous.

—We will always be together.

Then there was Yeon, Blanc thought. Blanc himself had brought Jin and Yeon together. Anyone with the least amount of sense was clear on what Yeon felt for Jin. Blanc had wanted to lead the mute boy into priesthood but the boy had chosen to become a court musician instead. Because Jin was at court. He had accepted that there was nothing to be done, as Jin was a court lady. But for her to become the wife of the French legate! Unimaginable. How devastated Yeon would be when he found out. This clever, bright girl whom he had known since her youth. Who knew his teaching her French would lead her to such a fate?

But everything that exists has a beginning somewhere.

Jin listened to the sound of the fallen leaves being swept on the legation courtyard. The winter chill had crept upon them. She could hear the whining of the Jindo dog from time to time, the dog that had been a gift from the Minister of Diplomacy to Victor when he first arrived in Korea. It had grown big, but this was its first winter. The first time it saw the wilting of the orchids, the retreat of the fiery maple, and the fall of the phoenix tree leaves that were as large as a person's face.

Jin looked down at the ring that Blanc had put on her finger for Victor. When she turned from the study, she found that the legation cook had placed on the table a French dish of lightly sautéed beef, mushrooms, vegetables, and garlic. A red chrysanthemum cutting stood in a vase between the two settings, and a bottle of wine lay in a long basket. Neither person spoke as they ate. Jin felt suffocated by the atmosphere. It was so tense that the clang of the fork on her plate filled the room. She left the table as soon as she was finished.

Suh had packed not one but two sets of marital bedclothes. One of the sets was meant for Victor, seeing how it had long sleeves and legs. Within the folds of the linen was some sandalwood scent that Jin had used when she was at court. Her throat constricted with tears, and it was only much later when she heated up some bathing water and dropped the sandalwood scent into the water for her bath.

When she was ready, she blew out the lamp.

She heard Victor, who had been standing in the courtyard, take off his shoes and come in through the glass door. His footsteps stopped in front of her room. She waited for his knock, but it never came. Nor did the sound of his steps retreating.

Jin got up and slowly opened her room door. Victor stood there in the dark. She stepped aside, and he entered. He was so tall he had to bend to come through the doorway.

Jin lit the candle on a French candlestick Victor had once gifted her. Their shadows soon danced on the walls. She had blown out the lamp because she wanted to use this very candlestick. Victor saw the piles of wildflowers drying on one side of the room. The pinks and violets had faded without moisture to sustain them. Foxtails and reeds were mixed in with them. A tea set was neatly laid out on a low table beside the flowers.

Victor looked at Jin's hand peeking out from her wide sleeve. The ring that Blanc had placed there was still present, which was a relief. And yet he said something silly.

—Thank you for following my wishes today.

It was the ring worn by his mother when she wed his much older father. He had lied when he said to Blanc that his mother had given it to him. He had stolen the ring from his mother when he wanted to propose to Marie in Plancy. But he never got the chance to even show it to her. His family home had been turned upside down when the ring went missing, and he had simply kept it with him ever since. The ring had surfaced from deep inside a drawer when he was packing for China in France. He had looked at it and slipped it into his bags.

—Would you like some tea?

As Jin stood to fetch the tea set, Victor gently hugged her from behind. Her clothes rustled, and he could smell the sandalwood.

A wind blew, strong enough to finish off the last leaves on the phoenix tree. Its fruit, shaped like sailboats, would also scatter far and wide in the wind.

Victor gazed down at Jin's half-moon forehead, her dark eyes, and small, plush lips.

—Do you know why I went to Gondangol today?

Was it not because of the photograph and Blanc?

—I did want to take a photograph with you and have Blanc put the ring on your finger. But more than anything else, I was worried you would not return.

Victor closed his eyes at the scent of her hair.

—I was helpless the moment I found the fragrance pouch.

—. . .

—How strange it is. I'd been waiting to see that pouch for so long, but once I saw it, I was taken by the fear that you would never return. I could not sit here waiting for you to come back.

Why had he thought she would never return?

Grateful that he had allowed her to work at the orphanage, Jin always returned to the legation as promised in a palanquin before sundown. She made a Korean-style dinner and sometimes had tea and conversation with Guérin or Paul Choi. Victor once asked her, with the air of making a difficult request, whether she would accompany him on a moonlit walk. They had gone as far as the Gate of Greeting Autumn and visited the Diplomats' Club in Jeongdong. The Russian legate, whom Victor had befriended, also visited the French legation. The diplomats treated Jin as Victor's legitimate companion. Whatever they thought in private, they accorded her respect in public. There were evenings when the Board of Trade and Diplomacy officials and the French people at the legation dined together. The cook's face would be flush with the pleasure of picking out new pottery and having to go all the way to Mapo Harbor to procure fresh ingredients. Even Guérin, who once regarded Jin's presence at the legation as an inconvenience, remarked that the legation seemed more like a home since Jin's arrival. Other than the times she felt sad thinking of the Queen, Jin found her days filled with contentment.

—I think I can rest easy now.

How different their minds were. Victor was anxious that she would not return to him, but Jin feared that he might give her up. Now that she knew she could not return to court, there was nowhere else she could turn to. That fear had made her place the fragrance pouch in *Les Misérables*. And that wasn't all she feared; she was afraid of what would happen to Yeon's heart.

—I love you.

Victor tenderly cradled Jin in his arms and kissed her forehead. His hands trembled as they undid the ribbon at the top of her bedclothes. Her round shoulders emerged from the linen. When he loosened the string of her skirt, the white band that wrapped her chest was revealed. Her breasts swelled as Victor fumbled through the knots and released them. Jin covered her wound with her hand. It was healed, but the scar remained. Victor gently lifted her hand and kissed the scar. Jin winced. Victor buried his face in her freed breasts. There couldn't possibly be anything else in the world that was rounder or softer. They were like white clouds, the white moon, like pure water.

Who is this man, to me?

It seemed like only a moment had passed between Victor's hands laying the flowers in her room to their releasing her skirts layer by layer. Jin's hands stayed his. She cupped his face with her hands. Their gazes met, as did the rhythm of their breathing. Jin's dark eyes looked into Victor's blue ones in the candlelight. Jin's hand traced Victor's forehead, eyes, nose, and lips. They were like the mindful touch of a blind man who had to find his way without his cane. When Jin reached his lips, she felt tears well up in her eyes. Victor's lips moved slowly toward Jin's face and licked the salty moisture that had gathered underneath her eyes. He remembered the name Jin had made for him the first day she had come to the legation.

—I am your Gillin, and yours only.

Jin closed her wet eyes and whispered to him.

—Take me to the Louvre.

—I shall.

—Take me to Notre Dame.

—I shall.

—To the Bois de Boulogne.

—Yes.

—The Latin Quarter.

—I shall.

—To the opera.

Jin's eyes remained closed as her lips recited the place names of Paris, its buildings, and its parks. Victor was astonished. When had she learned these names, names like beads strung on a necklace? She spoke as if she had lived in Paris and was remembering all the streets that she had walked and the places she had been. The Luxembourg Garden, the Champs-Élysées, Les Invalides, the Île de la Cité . . . Victor stopped the musical recital of the place names with a kiss.

—I shall go anywhere in the world with you.

Jin took her hands off his face and released her hair from its tight bun. Her braid fell to below her shoulder. Victor took his clothes off and embraced Jin as if he would never let her go. Her luscious hair touched his chest.

Victor's lips slid from her earlobes, her neck, the cleft of her breasts, her belly, her hips, and back to her breasts. Victor buried his face in them again and lay still as if to hear her breathing. How could he have known he would fall so hard for her, for this Korean woman with dark eyes? Just as he had slid into the charm of her beauty, Victor slid into her warm body. The fallen leaves from the phoenix tree blew into the middle of the courtyard and were tossed to and fro.

Jin was the first to open her eyes at dawn. The early light lit the paper sheets of the screen doors aglow, and the room was as calm as if it were underwater. She had become used to waking up to the fragrance of drying flowers by her bedside, but now that fragrance was mixed with the scent of the ocean. She had never slept undressed before. The bedclothes Suh had sewn for her remained crumpled next to the futon. Suh had made them for their first night together, but she hadn't had the chance to wear them or to place them underneath her to catch the spots of blood as was their purpose. Victor, who must have been uncomfortable sleeping on a futon instead of a bed, had a faint smile on his lips in his sleep. His neat mustache made her recall the events of the night before, and she blushed. The touch of it, both as rough as a calligraphy brush and also as soft, had grazed her face, her lips, her breasts, and even her toes. Victor breathed deeply. Jin made to get up before he woke. But Victor, whom she thought was asleep, whispered, "My bluebird!" and pulled her back underneath the covers.

It was a year before the Eiffel Tower, in commemoration of the centennial of the French Revolution, stood tall by the Seine River in Paris.

PART THREE

1
The Reading

Your Majesty,

The city's market is arranged like a go board. There are goods, strange and luxurious, stacked like clouds. The great number of customers that crowd about them attest to how rich the city is. Scattered like stars throughout Paris are ponds, exotic flowers, odd trees, and lush forests. They say it wasn't always like this. A hundred years ago, the houses were low and small, the paths so crooked you couldn't see far beyond where your feet were planted. Napoleon changed things when he returned to France after conquering several European countries. He razed the old city and altered everything within ten li*'s from the Tuileries Palace. Twelve roads radiate from the Arc de Triomphe, with palaces, houses, and grand structures like the Palais-Royal rising along* *them. Museums stand next to botanical gardens and prisons. Trees provide shade along the avenues where carriages run day and night. The West looks to Paris as a model city, and there are new inventions every day. From its cuisine to its clothing, children's toys to adult games, the entire world seems to love Parisian creations. Electricity is part of daily life, and trains and steamships take you everywhere. And so, Paris is called not a city of France but a city of the world.*

There's a happiness to the smells of the morning.

Jeanne, the servant, baked bread downstairs. The smell of fresh bread crept in through the slender gap of the doorway. Victor would greet the scent of bread in the morning with a smile of contentment. The scent brought home the fact that he was back in France. That, as well as the taste of wine and cheese.

In the high-ceilinged room, Jin put on her light blue dress, sat down before her escritoire, dipped her feather pen into an inkwell, and started a letter. Next to her atop its linen wrapping was the French-Korean dictionary, the first thing she had packed upon leaving Korea. It had been handled so many times that its yellowed pages were barely clinging to the spine. Roses were embroidered along the tasteful décolletage of Jin's dress, and the lines of her corseted waist flexed gracefully each time she moved. Her skirt skimmed her hips and widened as it fell toward her ankles before covering her feet. The white nape of her neck was revealed underneath the upsweep of her hair, which was pinned into a chignon.

Jin wrote, *Your Majesty*, and stared down at the letter.

Morning light shone through the rose-pattern lace curtains and made her writing paper glow. She couldn't understand why the words *Your Majesty* felt suddenly unfamiliar. Was it because several months had passed since she had spoken the honorific out loud? A suspended drop of blue ink fell from the tip of her pen onto the paper. Jin removed the spoiled top sheet and began again on the one below.

Your Majesty,

It has already been five months since my arrival. I was blinded by the sunlight when I first stepped foot on the harbor at Marseilles, but now the season has come when water turns to ice. The French are excited about the upcoming Christmas holiday. They say it is the birthday of Jesus, whom we call "Yaso" in Korea. It is a month away, but they are already preparing for the Christmas Eve feast. They call this feast the Réveillon, and they drink their best wine. Victor is carefully choosing which wine to drink on Christmas Eve. He is filled with plans, as he hasn't celebrated it in his home country in a long time.

I wonder whether you've forgotten me. Or whether you think of me from time to time.

Although it took me this long to write, I have thought of Your Majesty every time I see something I have never seen before.

It took sixty days to reach Marseilles from Jaemulpo. We transferred to a steam ship in Shanghai and made our way to Saigon. Except for our six days in that city, we lived on the water as we sailed through Singapore, Colombo, the Suez Canal, and the port of Alexandria. It was a long and difficult journey. Seasickness left me clinging to the edge of the deck. Nausea and dizziness took away my initial excitement in setting sail for a new world, replacing it with despair for the voyage ahead. I imagined how it would be if Your Majesty had come on board. Not even the storms would've made you waver. Thinking of your steadfastness gave me strength. While I suffered in our cabin, Victor read to me from Jules Verne's Twenty Thousand Leagues Under the Sea. *They say the author is from Nantes and wrote the book after sailing the wide oceans of the world on a yacht christened* Saint Michel, *which was only thirty* ja *long. There were days when I endured only by focusing on these tales of mysterious creatures that lived in the ocean deep. Several passengers had come aboard healthy only to be carried out on the backs of others; my seasickness was on the less serious side. For even on the nights I felt my very organs turn, there came the mornings where I could still watch the red sunrise.*

Jin dipped her pen again but hesitated as she hovered over the paper. She felt lost. What would the Queen think of her penmanship, when she had seen only Korean writing done with a brush? She was also bothered by how she referred to herself as *I* instead of *your servant*. But after a pause, Jin corrected only her grip on the pen and did not correct the *I*'s to *your servant*'s.

Only a boat that endures the storm may reach the harbor.

After their long voyage to the other end of the world, they had finally reached the harbor at Marseilles. Illustrating Victor's point that one could sail from Marseilles to anywhere in the world, its blue waters were busy with tugboats towing ships from Morocco, England, Penang, America, Singapore, Shanghai, and Japan. One of the books Jin had read at the French legation as she waited for the Queen's summons was *The Count of Monte Cristo*. She struggled over almost every line but was so taken by the story that time flew by. The novel opened with Edmond Dantès arriving at Marseilles, revenge burning in his heart. When Jin took her first step on the shore, she consoled herself by thinking that unlike Dantès, she was not there for revenge but love. She became determined to not cage herself in but to explore as much of her new world as she could.

The bustling port of Marseilles, awash in the smells of fresh fish, baking bread, produce, and seaweed, was much larger than any of the other harbors Jin had visited on her voyage. The first thing she noticed was the different shades of skins and hair of the people who were waiting for the ships at the docks. There were all kinds of races: Europeans, Africans, Asians, Arabs . . . but Jin, in her Parisian dress, still stood out. Everyone looked at her, from the white women spreading their parasols against the sun to the Northern African laborers on the docks. Their Algerian carriage driver kept glancing at Jin as he drove them to the train station. Jin did not avert her eyes. Instead, she looked directly back at them. She looked directly at everything, not wanting to miss her first impressions of her new country: carriages she had never seen before, the island of If upon the blue water where Dantès was imprisoned for fourteen years for a crime he didn't commit, the thick steam of the steamships from around the world, the bright sun, the people of many races. And the statue of Mary atop a cathedral spire, shining in the sun.

Your Majesty,

The reason it took me so long to write is that Victor fell ill as soon as we arrived in Paris. He would often suffer from laryngitis in Korea, but this time the condition was accompanied by fever. A fever that assaulted him five or six times a day. We were worried he would die. We knew his illness was a culmination of the fatigue of his years of living overseas, unleashed by the relief of having come home, but then his inflammation worsened, and he could not speak, eat, and at one point, almost couldn't breathe. He had to be hospitalized. Even then his fever wouldn't abate, which worried us all. Thankfully, the hospitals here are very good. They are similar to the Gwanghyewon but much larger. There are tens, no, countless nurses and doctors. Hospitals here are not mere places of healing. They seem to be realizations of the Catholic ideals of charity. Dr. Allen of the Gwanghyewon is, as Your Majesty is well aware, himself both a doctor and a missionary.

Jin paused and glanced at the silver pocket watch on her escritoire. Victor had forgotten his watch again. Nine-twenty. Her history tutor, Simone, was always punctual. She would ring the doorbell in exactly forty minutes.

Jin stood up, drew back the curtains, and looked down at the square.

A carriage stood waiting in front of the house across the beech grove. It seemed that a lady of the house was about to set out.

Jin never felt more like she was in a foreign country as when she viewed the houses of her neighborhood in Paris. Each four-story building was a single house, with floors connected by stairways. Sixty houses stuck side by side surrounded a square-shaped plaza. Each house had windows overlooking the square with its beech grove, fountain, and wooden benches. On hot summer nights and sunny autumn days, the people of the houses came out to enjoy the spray of the fountain's cool jets of water or to read and doze on the benches.

The first floors of the buildings formed a gallery of shops that was fringed with a continuous canopy. A shopper could make a full circle around the square underneath it, sheltered from rain. The shops sold all sorts of daily necessities such as bread, fruit, meat, wine, fabrics, and vegetables.

Jin sometimes accompanied the apple-cheeked servant girl Jeanne when she went about the shops. This astonished Jeanne, but Jin enjoyed looking at the variously shaped cheeses, the red cuts hanging in the butcher's, the sweet fruits and colorful vegetables, and the shoes and fabric store with its unimaginable variety of textiles. As the servant women haggled in their rapid French, Jin was reminded of the time she went out to Mapo Harbor to buy fish with the legation cook.

Something caught Jin's eye as she looked down at the shimmering square.

Their young charge, Vincent, walked quickly through the beech trees. He held a bouquet in his hand. He must have gone to the morning flower market. Jin tilted her head. Buying flowers was Jeanne's task. Were they meant for Jeanne? Jeanne would blush and deny this, but Jin knew how fond the young man was of Jeanne, who in turn didn't seem too reluctant to accept his attentions. Vincent disappeared underneath the canopy of the shops. Jin poked her head out the window, straining to see what flowers Vincent was holding. All she got was an eyeful of the canopy glowing in the sun.

She sat back down and looked over what she had written so far. How could she convey the speed of the locomotive that had brought them from Marseilles to Paris? The inadequacy of her own words gripped her like a physical thirst. Jin took up her feather pen and dipped it into the ink once more.

Your Majesty,

Here I am, learning of France.

My French has improved, and I now learn about philosophy, history, literature, and music. It still saddens me to remember the late Bishop Blanc, who first taught me French. He was worried for me right up to his passing. He told Victor several times that he must always believe in me, and that he must love me as he loves Korea. I'm told Bishop Mutel is to take his place. He should have arrived from France by now. Victor seems to have known him from before and says he will be very good for Korea. That he will realize Bishop Blanc's plans for building the Jonghyeon Cathedral and establish a new school, just as he has in France. I am aware Your Majesty is not enamored of the Catholic faith so please forgive me for mentioning these things. The people here may not attend church often, but most call themselves Catholic and defer to the faith's tenets. Cathedrals take pride of place in every town. Paris has a cathedral that happens to be hundreds of years old and is a proud symbol of their history.

Jin was so absorbed in her writing that only a firm knocking sound made her look up.

Vincent stood outside the door, holding a bouquet of red roses. Roses were said to be a flower that bloomed in the morning with a thousand hopes. The people here loved roses, especially red ones. They planted them everywhere, their vines growing not only in small gardens but often in the most unlikely of places. The morning flower market was largely a rose exhibition. There were always buckets of them no matter the season. Vincent's cheeks were flushed; the air outside must have been cold. His brown curls tumbled over his forehead as he offered the bouquet of red roses to Jin.

—What's this for?

Jin, uncertain, took the bouquet from him. Vincent was much taller than Jin and looked down at her from far above. He took off his cap. His hair underneath was soaked in sweat. He must have run a great distance. He smiled shyly. He was really just a boy despite the considerable stubble that grew back every night, and the shyness of his smile matched his youth. One of his suspenders had fallen off his shoulder.

—I have a request, Madame.

—What is it?

—I hear you are going to the reading room at Bon Marché.

He must have heard it from Jeanne. Victor had already said he could come straight from the Ministry of Foreign Affairs. It was an event organized by Monsieur Planchard, one of Bon Marché's proprietors. The invitation said that there would be a reading followed by a viewing of the sculptures in the gallery next to the reading room.

—Madame!

Vincent dropped to his knees before Jin. Taken aback, Jin tried to get him on his feet.

—What's the meaning of this! Stand up at once!

Jin gave an involuntary glance around the room.

—It is my wish to head a department at Bon Marché someday.

Jin already knew this from Jeanne, who had also told her that because of Vincent's low birth, he would never be an attendant at Bon Marché, much less a manager.

It's a foolish dream. The attendants there are full of pride for their positions. Even the young bourgeois men living along the Seine wish for nothing more than to work there. But a cheesemonger's son being a manager at Bon Marché? Unheard of, Madame!

Despite her adamant refusal to take his dream seriously, she didn't seem too put off by his ambition.

—Do you want me to do something for you, Vincent? At least get up, first.

—Only if you promise to grant my request.

—How can I grant a request I haven't heard yet? Please get up.

Vincent slowly rose from the floor.

—Now, what is it?

—Monsieur Planchard was here for your salon recently, Madame. He is one of the proprietors of Bon Marché. Could you please put in a good word for me?

—You bought me flowers just to ask me this?

Jin's amused smile made Vincent grin in relief.

—You would put in a good word for me, Madame?

—But I do not know Monsieur Planchard very well. I've only met him that once!

Vincent blinked his long-lashed eyes innocently. When one is young, all you need for happiness is the prospect of a future. Jin had never known Vincent to be so passionate about anything. He began speaking to her in a voice as excited as if he had come aboard a ship about to sail.

—But, Madame! The people who came to the salon that evening were completely taken with you. Your every word, the Korean food you prepared . . .

Vincent closed his eyes, reminiscing, then opened them again.

—They were mesmerized by your dancing. I almost dropped my tray. I've never seen dancing like that. It was as if you had shouted to everyone in the room, "Freeze!"

His earnest expression made Jin laugh. French dancing was swift and fluid, but Korean dancing was stately and had pauses. That must have been what he was referring to as *Freeze!*

—You silenced everyone. Even the Minister of Foreign Affairs could not take his eyes off you. He promised to hold a ball and begged for you to attend. I've never seen such rapt faces. They looked as if they had made a new discovery. Monsieur Planchard was the most taken of all. I think you were the only one unaware of it. He never left your side! If you ask him, I am sure he would not refuse.

The words spilled out as if rehearsed. Jin had never heard him say so much.

—If I get the chance, I shall ask. However!

Vincent's face had brightened like a boy's at the prospect of his wish coming true and now darkened with apprehension.

—You must give these flowers to Jeanne, Vincent.

—But these are the most beautiful flowers in the market!

—Which is why you should give them to Jeanne.

He blinked his big eyes.

—Because you are fond of her.

Jin smiled. Vincent, shy again, scratched his head with the hand he held his cap with. The two looked more like young friends than mistress and servant. Jin held out the bouquet and gestured, *Go on!* Blushing, Vincent took the bouquet from her. He was about to leave when Jin stopped him.

—But why do you want to work there? Is the work here too hard? Or the pay too little?

Jin had no idea how much he was paid. Victor took care of such things.

—Not at all, Madame. It is good here, but at Bon Marché, they will move you up if you prove yourself. A department head is as good as a proprietor. It is great work. I wouldn't envy a king if I worked there! They even give incentives at Christmas.

—Incentives?

—Extra money to sales attendants who sold more over the past year. Isn't that wonderful? There, even a sales attendant can become a proprietor, Madame.

A proprietor at Bon Marché? Jin couldn't help being impressed. Was Vincent's dream, then, not department head but proprietor? She did not think this dream hopeless. Instead, it made her see both Vincent and Bon Marché in a new light.

—To be honest, Madame . . .

In contrast to his confidence a moment ago, Vincent had retreated into shyness again.

—If I become an attendant at Bon Marché, Jeanne would accept my love. That is my biggest reason.

Vincent grinned and hurried back down the stairs. Jin watched him disappear down the hall before sitting down again in front of her letter to the Queen. Her gaze lingered on her feather pen.

People make cities, and cities make people.

Vincent had come up from Plancy, the same village where Victor was from. He was the son of the cheesemonger and had been introduced to Victor by Victor's mother. His tasks at the house had come to include taking the mail to the post office, calling for carriages, cataloging and maintaining Victor's collection, submitting forms, and doing handiwork about the house. Victor would have had to give up much of his leisure time if not for Vincent. She had heard Victor, who was not easy to please, praise Vincent on many occasions. Victor trusted him, but here was the boy hoping to become a sales attendant at Bon Marché. Victor would hate to see him go.

The Queen could not have meant that she was curious about Jin when she had asked her to write her letters. What the Queen really wanted to know was the laws these faraway people lived under, their thoughts, and their daily lives. How was Jin to explain Vincent's ambition to the Queen, about his regard for Bon Marché as the greatest place in Paris to work, a place he was ready to devote his life to? Jin felt overwhelmed at the task and put her pen down over the letter once more.

In the winter, darkness descended by five o'clock.

All she had done that afternoon was an hour's history lesson with Simone, and yet the day had flown by quickly. Aided by Jeanne, she donned a purple gown, put on a hat adorned with feathers, and sprinkled herself with sandalwood fragrance. The streetlamps were lighting up one by one by the time she had finished preparing. The nights lengthened with the shortening days. Jin watched the scenery go by outside the window of the carriage that Vincent had called. The buildings and the shop fronts glowed in the gaslight of the streetlamps. Jeanne had told her that the "novelty shops" used to close at sunset, but now, thanks to the gaslights, they remained open into the evening. And what were these novelty shops? Jeanne told her that they sold the latest in dresses, fabrics in every color, parasols, shoes, and perfume. Jeanne professed she enjoyed walking by them with their wares displayed in the gaslight, but she was hardly the only woman in Paris who wanted to immerse herself in the spectacle of the latest fashions, the paved streets making it all the more accessible for carriages. She enthused that walking down the storefronts among the new wares made her feel as if she were in another world. Jin had once accompanied her on her evening off, and at one of the fabric stores bursting with goods of every color and texture, she had purchased thick white backing cloth, embroidery floss, a set of needles, fabric scissors, and a measuring tape. Jin then cut the cloth into squares, backstitched the edges, and embroidered a peony in the center of each, and gave away the finished work to the guests at a salon Victor held at their house.

The streets were lit up in a festive mood. The glass doors of the shops shone with brilliant light, and each door had a sign saying, "Controlled Prices." The waves of lights reached their peak at Bon Marché, catching the eye from afar. In contrast to the plain whitewashed walls of its old building, the new Bon Marché, designed by Eiffel, stood grandly in the midst of the lights. It was seductive enough to lure in any pedestrian for a quick look if they happened to be passing by, the friendly greetings of the attendants aiding this urge.

Jin's carriage stopped at the busy curb in front of the new department store building. Victor had been waiting to accompany her to the event in the second-floor reading room, and he helped her out of the carriage. He kissed her lightly on the cheek. He didn't forget to whisper, "My little bluebird," or to give the carriage driver a tip on top of his fare.

—What is this scent?

Jin raised her eyebrows at Victor's question.

There is a tree that leaves its scent even on the blade of the ax that strikes it; that tree is white sandalwood.

—What scent?

—This one, coming from you.

—It's sandalwood . . . do you dislike it?

—Not at all. I could get drunk on it.

Victor remembered the scent of sandalwood from the first night he spent with Jin. How could he ever forget it? To him, it was the scent of the East. It was the subtle scent of not only Jin but also of the ancient

Buddha statues he collected from China and Korea. Was it because of the sandalwood? Victor felt an urge to embrace Jin but wrapped his arm around her waist instead.

Jin smiled back at the polite greetings of the shopping attendants and thought, for a moment, about Vincent. Each attendant was so well-mannered and helpful, smiling as if they were born to smile, light-footed in their eagerness to help. But even they couldn't help stealing glances at the dark-haired, dark-eyed Jin, dressed up like a Parisian woman. The glances followed her as she made her way up the spiral staircase past the displays filled with tempting objects and all the way to the reading room. Planchard greeted them at the door.

—Welcome.

As Jin and Victor said hello, Planchard introduced them to his wife, who was standing next to him. Madame Planchard smiled at Jin, her smile bringing out the fine wrinkles by her mouth. Talk of Victor having returned from the East with a dark-eyed woman was making the rounds amongst her crowd. Madame Planchard tried to treat Jin like any other acquaintance, but it was difficult to do so. Her gaze kept getting drawn toward her. It was fascinating to see an Asian woman speak French so fluently. Her accent was slightly odd, but she gave off an air of being completely at ease. What had made Victor fall in love with her? Curiosity got the better of Madame Planchard as she gave up any pretense of discretion and stared at Jin in earnest.

As the audience went through their greetings, Jin took in her surroundings. There was a green carpet in the middle of the room, a group of people crowding over it. When Boucicaut, the department store's owner, had proposed building a reading room, even his architect Eiffel had thought it strange. A space not for more displays but for reading, which was not an activity that would help sell things, and in the central hall of the store at that, the busiest point of the entire building? It was only later that people realized the beauty of Boucicaut's idea when the Bon Marché reading room became the toast of Paris. It was a rendezvous point, a place where children could read as their affluent mothers shopped, and also functioned as a salon for Parisian society. The library had past as well as current newspapers for their patrons' perusal. Paper with the Bon Marché letterhead, envelopes, pen, and ink were also provided for letter-writing.

—Madame!

Jin turned to see Madame Planchard standing behind her. Victor was farther off, standing in the gallery behind the pillars, talking with Planchard. Was there a perfumery nearby? She could smell scents all around her.

—How is it in Japan? Do they also have department stores like this?

Madame Planchard must have mistaken her for Japanese.

—I have never been to Japan, Madame.

A slight look of consternation came over Madame Planchard.

—I see . . . Are you Chinese?

—No, I am Korean.

—Korea?

This happened often here. Jin smiled reassuringly at the disconcerted Madame Planchard.

Sometimes, misunderstandings forge relations.

Naturally, Madame Planchard, when hearing Jin was from the East, would have assumed she was Japanese, and if not that, Chinese. The order may have been different, but no one guessed Korean without prompting. Jin explained to the embarrassed Madame Planchard that Korea was a country situated between China and Japan.

—I've never heard of it.

Madame Planchard tilted her head, inquisitive. Jin was at a loss as to how to explain Korea to someone who had never even heard of its name. Even if it did happen to her quite often.

—It is somewhat similar to Italy.

—Italy? Then it must be a grand country indeed.

Jin smiled again. She had said Italy, but in truth, she knew nothing about the country. She had simply heard Victor give this answer once when asked what other country Korea was like. Jin thought that at least

Madame Planchard would now have an impression of Korea as a grand country.

—Then was Madame's dance a Korean one?

She was referring to the Dance of the Spring Oriole that Jin had performed at Planchard's request during the banquet celebrating Victor's promotion to the head of East Asian affairs. Because of the boisterous atmosphere of that evening, perhaps due to all the wine, the guests had made it impossible for Jin to refuse them the honor of seeing her Korean dance. Jin hadn't been ready to present any other dance except the waltz and had no costume with her. And so her first Korean dance on French soil had been performed in her blue dress.

They heard Planchard calling for his wife. Jin turned around toward the sound and gave a start. She had spotted Korean clothes through the pillars. Jin blinked. Was she seeing things? Madame Planchard led the way toward the gallery. Jin wasn't hallucinating; her eyes fixed upon a man in white Korean robes and a wide-brimmed, black-horsehair *gat* hat, standing tall and firm. A person in Korean clothes, this far away from home!

—Hello.

The man in Korean clothes greeted her in Korean. How long had it been since she'd heard Korean spoken?

—Have you forgotten me already?

—. . .

—It is I, Hong Jong-u!

Jin came over to him. Victor gave her a worried look.

—You said you would go to Paris, and here you are.

—Indeed, my lady. I arrived before you did. I thought we would run into each other one of these days. Let me introduce my companions. This is the painter Félix Régamey. And Monsieur Boex, editor and translator at Dentu.

Before Jin could say hello, Hong began to introduce Jin to the men in stilted French.

—This is the wife of Monsieur Collin de Plancy, who leads East Asian affairs at the Foreign Ministry. She is also Korea's finest court dancer.

So Hong had known of Victor's recent appointment. Had he always been this tall? Jin examined him closely. Despite his odd French, he spoke with no hesitation. To see a man wearing a Korean *gat* hat in Paris, at the ultra-modern Bon Marché no less! Jin carefully hid her surprise and went to stand by Victor.

Hong looked Jin up and down.

He seemed to regard her as someone who had carelessly and unthinkingly thrown away her old clothes for new.

—You look more Parisian than the Parisian women, Madame!

Hong gave a strange laugh. He had that same disapproving expression he wore in Korea whenever he had seen Jin with Victor. He was mocking her! Jin stared back at him. The clothes of the only two Koreans in Paris stood in stark contrast. Planchard, who had been watching from the side, interrupted their conversation.

—How fortunate we are to have not one but two Koreans in the same place. Well, the reading is about to begin. We shall save the rest of our greetings for later. But I do have the feeling that the evening will be full of more happy surprises.

—Are you feeling unwell?

Victor whispered this as he held her waist again. Jin only smiled. The audience gathered around a desk in the middle of the room. The author had not arrived yet, so the chair behind the desk stood empty. Jin saw Planchard and his wife standing underneath an arch across the room. She wanted to see where Hong Jong-u's party was but then she would have to look about the room. Jin kept her arm entwined in Victor's and did not turn her face. She wondered if Hong was also looking around for her.

—Are such events common?

—The readings have been going on for a long time in Paris. Sometimes they read the Bible . . . Once, there was a reading of Rousseau's *Confessions* before it was banned. They say it's the first time Planchard is trying something like this here. They may hold readings regularly if the response is good.

There was a stirring in the crowd near the entrance. The author, wearing a black suit over a white shirt with his curly hair swept back, made his way to the desk in the middle of the room. He was a thin man, about forty, pale, with a mustache. Planchard approached the author and introduced him to the audience as Guy de Maupassant, the most popular writer in all of Paris. The audience applauded. Planchard said a few words about how difficult it had been to bring Maupassant out to such a gathering and that he hoped they would find this precious time with the elusive author fruitful.

—He looks unwell, Victor.

Victor smiled at Jin's whispered words. Jin pretended to look toward the large clock on the wall as she surreptitiously scanned for Hong Jong-u. Her gaze went over the ornate furnace in the back and spotted him standing nearby next to Régamey. Her eyes darted away. It was easy to find Hong. Many of the people there were looking at him and not Maupassant. Ordinarily, Jin would have been the target of such looks, but tonight all eyes were on him. Hong was impervious to their stares and continued to regard the author with a focused gaze.

The grim-looking Maupassant opened his book and put on round reading glasses. He stated the title of the novel, *A Woman's Life*, but said nothing more about it before launching into the reading. It was the part where the aristocratic daughter Jeanne returned home from the convent and was packing up for another trip, mindful of the rain that fell outside.

—Jeanne had left the convent the day before.

She had become a free woman. The happiness she had longed for all her life seemed within her grasp. But then, the weather chose that particular time to take a turn for the worse. If the rains continued, her father might postpone her journey. The anxiety was unbearable.

Maupassant's reading drew a cloak of silence over the audience. The richness and clarity of his voice were unexpected considering how thin he was. Jin leaned against Victor and let the author's words wash over her.

Maupassant's voice continued to demand silence from the others gathered there. Jin closed her eyes and took in his clear, cold, and firm reading. Was it because it was his own work? Jeanne's entire life seemed to spring from Maupassant's voice alone. Jin could imagine the sound sliding from the author's forehead, cheeks, and arms. He interrupted his reading to skip and explain certain parts. Then, after about five parts, he stopped reading. He lifted his head toward the audience.

—I'm afraid my throat is sore.

The audience came out of their reverie to regard the author who sat behind the desk, rubbing his throat. Victor, whose arm was around Jin, and Jin herself, stretched a bit in sympathy. Of course his throat was sore. By then they were fifty minutes into the reading.

—Could one of you take over for me?

At Maupassant's unexpected request, the audience glanced around at each other. Over their murmuring, Madame Planchard stepped forward from beneath the arch. Her hands were gathered neatly before her, and her voice was full of anticipation.

—We have a lady among us from the land of Korea.

Korea? The murmuring persisted. The people started looking in Jin's direction.

—Her French is excellent. Shall we ask her to read for us?

Jin, surprised beyond all measure, stared at Madame Planchard. Madame Planchard smiled at her. Jin turned her gaze to Maupassant. Their eyes met. Maupassant pushed his glasses back up on his face.

—I, too, would like to hear Madame read.

Jin glanced at Victor. He seemed as surprised as she was. But he had read the room and whispered to Jin, "I don't think you can refuse. You will be marvelous!" He encouraged her to accept.

Jin, feeling as if she were walking on water, approached the center of the room. Maupassant gave her the chair and stood next to her as she took her seat. Planchard, just as he had with Maupassant when the reading started, introduced Jin to the audience.

—Madame comes from the faraway land of Korea. A mysterious country situated at the very end of the East. Madame was its greatest court dancer.

The mention of Jin having been a court dancer made the audience murmur again. Maupassant had prepared where he had wanted to read with bookmarks inserted between different pages. He indicated with his finger the scene where Jeanne was giving birth. Jin spread the book in her hands and sat up straight.

—A feeling of joy passed through Jeanne. She had taken her first step in a new direction.

Her voice was shaky at first, but she soon found her normal tone. The murmuring crowd settled down into an underwater silence. They seemed taken aback at how a dark-eyed woman from the unknown land of Korea was reading aloud, fluently, from a novel written in French.

—Jeanne was liberated. She found stability and felt happy. It was the kind of happiness she had never experienced before. She felt a new stirring in both her mind and body. She realized she had become a mother.

Jin slid into total concentration upon the text.

—She wanted to see how the baby was doing. The baby was early, so early there was no hair or fingernails. Whenever the baby squirmed like a larva, opened his mouth to cry, wrinkled his face into a frown, and when she touched his tiny, premature body, Jeanne was swept up in an irresistible joy. She was coming back to life after having been destroyed by Julien's betrayal. She had fought through despair, and now accepted this love that was more precious than anything else in the world.

Jin's calm voice began to waver. As it did, Maupassant slowly opened his eyes and turned to look at Jin.

The slight tremor in Jin's voice made the audience listen all the more attentively to her.

The voice, clear as dew, seemed to reprimand the men in the story, the men who had treated the woman like a possession, repeatedly betraying her trust as if it meant nothing to them. The voice also seemed to console Jeanne as she grasped at her love for the baby and tried to overcome the wounds given to her by her husband and other children.

Jin finished, and someone began to clap. The applause spread within the room like concentric circles upon a watery surface. Maupassant applauded the longest. He came up to Jin, who had stood up by the desk, to embrace her.

—It was as if you had written it yourself, Madame!

Jin gave her seat to him and was making as if to return to Victor when she decided to slip out of the reading room instead. She could hear Maupassant resume the reading. She walked over to the store with the display of lace across from the reading room, trying to hold back the tears that threatened to spill. She could just about make out a case of colorful perfume bottles next to the lace display. Jin looked back at the gallery next to the reading room. There were fewer people there, as almost everyone was attending the reading. Jin walked to it quickly. Its golden dome ceiling was supported by pillars with oil paintings hung on the walls between them. There was a large bronze statue of Aristide Boucicaut, the founder of Bon Marché. As if it were a statue of the savior Himself, Jin quickly walked toward it and sought sanctuary behind it. When she was sure no one was watching her, she sank to the floor. The tears she had been suppressing sprang forth. "Calm down." Jin put a hand to her heart. "Calm down, please." She whispered to herself in Korean, but it was no use.

What had happened to her? Her heart had begun to swell when she read the part where Jeanne gazed upon the newborn. Jin could feel Jeanne's hope and excitement, and even the wriggling fingers of the baby that had been born despite all the despair and sadness. The letters had wavered through her tears, and her voice could hardly keep still. When she had looked up from her reading, her wet eyes had met with Maupassant's. A tear had fallen from her eye then. And so, Maupassant had seen the tear that Victor hadn't.

—Why do you sit here, crying?

Jin was so surprised she forgot she was crying and looked up. Hong Jong-u's wide eyes were looking into her tearful ones.

—Did you come all this distance just to hide away and cry?

Jin's lips trembled.

—I see you are human after all. I was beginning to think that Lady Attendant Suh was devoid of emotion.

Jin narrowed her eyes at him.

—What is it? Does the title offend you, my lady? Should I call you Madame instead?

Call me whatever you please, Jin seemed to say as she turned away from him. At least, she thought, his mocking had helped her calm her tears.

—Wipe your tears with this. Surely Madame must never be seen losing her composure.

Hong took out a handkerchief and held it out to her. It was a French handkerchief, incongruous with his Korean robes.

—That won't be necessary. I shall not use it.

—You wish to show your weakened, teary self?

He was reprimanding her. Jin took the handkerchief from his hand. Doing as he said seemed the fastest way to get rid of him. She gently patted away the tears on her face as Hong watched.

—What made you so emotional?

—I know how the novel ends.

She couldn't say to him that Jeanne's fiery love for her baby had made her think of her own mother whom she could not remember. She could not, moreover, tell him of the baby she had lost a year before they had left Korea. She could hardly tell him that her tears were not for anyone but herself.

—You have read it?

—Yes.

—How does it end?

—Find out for yourself.

Jin handed him his handkerchief and said no more. The novel ended with Rosalie, who had had a baby with Jeanne's husband Julien, gazing at the face of the newborn Jeanne's wayward son Paul had abandoned, and saying, "Life is not better or worse than one expects." Jin briefly wondered if Hong Jong-u, who spoke and acted as if the world were as clear as black and white, would understand such an ending. The thought made her smile bitterly, for she realized she had been harsh in judging him.

—I have a favor to ask.

Hong's tone had turned from mocking to polite. There is a sense of release after burst tears. Jin's eyes, clearer for having cried, took in Hong's sincere expression.

—I am translating a Korean book into French.

—Which book?

—*The Story of Chunhyang.*

—You plan to publish it in French?

—That is so.

Jin saw Hong in a favorable light for the first time. When she was with her books, she sometimes thought of the Queen, who thought nothing of staying up all night reading. In Korea, she had once translated a part of *Les Misérables* with the thought of giving the Queen a taste of French literature. Despite this, she had never thought of translating a Korean book into French.

—The quickest way to make Korea known is to translate Korean stories into foreign languages. These people know of the Chinese and Japanese, but they do not know of us. They don't even know that we have our own language. Is that not frustrating? I'm being helped by Boex and Régamey, to whom you've been introduced, but there is only so much they can do.

Jin thought of Victor. What would he say if she told him that she wanted to help Hong Jong-u? She had the impression that Victor did not have a good opinion of him.

—What can I do to help?

—Many things. Writing is so different from speaking, but I can hardly even speak it. Every one of my sentences needs polishing . . . Will you help?

—. . .

—For Korea.

Was the reading over? Jin stepped away from the Boucicaut statue and looked toward the reading room. People were crowding out of it.

She felt tense, as if burdened with a secret.

—They must be looking for us. We shall speak later.

Hong began to stride away, his distinct Korean robes fluttering about him. Victor spotted Jin following Hong as the two approached him together.

—What happened?

—I had a request for Madame.

Hong said this with a polite bow of his head. Victor gave Jin a quizzical look. Before she could speak, Madame Planchard and Maupassant walked up toward them.

—Madame, today's reading was a great success. Do take in the sculptures and paintings in the gallery. A reception is being held on the first floor outside.

Jin saw Boex and Régamey coming up to Hong. They must have looked for him when he had disappeared. Publishing a Korean book in France? She hadn't had time to appreciate Hong's plan at first, but now she thought of how wonderful it would be if it came to fruition. Jin, standing next to Victor, examined Hong's companions. The three acted as if they were old acquaintances. How had they even befriended each other? Jin was impressed by the daring of Hong to wear his Korean clothes in Paris, and his natural ability to make friends. He was now engaged in conversation with Planchard. Jin slipped her arm around Victor's. He was still looking at her questioningly as if wondering why she had been with Hong a moment ago. Jin whispered in his ear.

—I'll tell you when we get home.

Planchard was explaining how it had been Boucicaut's idea to have an art gallery inside Bon Marché. His wife caught Jin's eye and smiled. The look she had given Jin when they'd first met, regarding her as if she were some spectacle, was replaced with a friendly glint. Jin smiled back at Madame Planchard. People milled about the paintings and sculptures. The artwork was apparently for sale, as an old woman and a gallery attendant were conversing over the price of a sculpture in front of them. Victor slipped away from Jin and approached Madame Planchard. Jin turned to look at the statue of Boucicaut behind which she'd been hiding moments ago. Hong stood before it, gesticulating as he argued about something with Régamey and Boex.

—Madame!

Jin turned to see Maupassant standing before her. Jin smiled, happy to see him. Then she remembered that he had seen her shed a tear after her reading. She blushed.

—Your reading was extraordinary. They say you are from Korea. It makes me wonder what this country is like. I never would've expected someone so beautiful from such a foreign land to be reading aloud from my work.

—It shall be an unforgettable experience for me as well. You write so knowingly of a woman's soul that I was surprised to discover you were a man.

—Ah, tonight was not the first time you read my work?

—The women of Paris cannot get enough of your books. And I happen to be a woman of Paris myself.

Maupassant was listening to the flow of French issuing forth like music from the Eastern woman's lips. The mention of her having read his work delighted him.

—Must you stay here with the hypocrites? Or would you step out with me?

Maupassant's spectacled eyes lingered on Jin's dark ones. His eyes were shadowed from lack of sleep. *Hypocrites.* Victor, who had finished speaking with Madame Planchard, entered into the awkward silence that ensued. Maupassant, who was reclusive by nature, spoke to Victor in a low voice.

—I wish to hear the stories of the East from your wife. Will you allow me to see her again?

—That would be an honor, but it is entirely up to her.

Victor seemed to be urging her to answer, whatever that answer may be. He looked at her expectantly.

—I hear you live on the Rue de Babylone, Madame. That is close to where I live. I take a walk around five every afternoon. Perhaps we can walk together . . .

From a distance, Hong Jong-u's laughter burst through the sound of Maupassant's voice. Jin involuntarily glanced in his direction. He seemed to have been introduced to Madame Planchard and was animatedly telling her about Korea as Régamey supplied additional explanations.

—Is there a place you wish to explore?

—Perhaps the morgue.

Victor, more surprised than Maupassant, gently gripped Jin's arm. Jin had been astounded by the Notre Dame on the Île de la Cité when Victor had taken her there. She could not believe that human hands had wrought such beautifully detailed and sublime construction. To Jin, whose very arms trembled from awe, Victor had calmly explained that the construction of the western towers had taken a century after the foundation stones were laid and that the very tower before them had watched over the history of France. *A century.* It made her feel so awed as to be bereft. *That tower will stand there long after I am gone.* She could not take her eyes off of the spires that pierced the sky, or the countless faces of kings looking down at the people below. Then she saw the statue of the Holy Mother standing at the main entrance of the cathedral, surrounded by the twelve apostles. A sudden memory of Bishop Blanc brought tears to her eyes. She wondered if she should seek confirmation into the faith. Inside the cathedral, she stood for a long time underneath the stained-glass rose window, awash in its lights of blue and red and indigo. She felt her soul being absorbed by its beauty.

—There are several morgues in Paris. Which one would you like to visit?

—The one behind the Notre Dame . . .

They had left the cathedral, Jin still overwhelmed by what she had just experienced, when she saw a long line of people on the street. They were visitors to the morgue who were waiting to gawk at the bodies on display. Morgues had become popular entertainment in Paris. So many people would gather there on Sundays that newspapers occasionally wrote about it. Victor kept turning down Jin's suggestions about visiting the morgue. He couldn't understand why anyone would want to see the dead bodies of strangers.

—But what about them?

Jin pointed to the line of people, but Victor avoided her question. It only made the morgue as intriguing to her as the interior of the Notre Dame. She wanted to know why Parisians enjoyed looking at dead bodies so much.

—The morgue it is.

Victor frowned at the prospect. Jin didn't know whether she should accept such an invitation from another man. She glanced at Victor, who didn't seem happy with the idea, but could find no reason to refuse.

—All right.

Jin assented while looking at Victor's face, not Maupassant's.

—Then I shall take your leave. Madame should also free herself from these disgusting people. I shall contact you through Monsieur Planchard.

This wasn't the kindly Maupassant who had watched over Jin's reading. He seemed angry, as if he'd been insulted. He bowed politely, but only to Jin, and stalked out of the gallery.

2
Feather Pen and Blue Ink

Your Majesty,

What surprised me the most upon arriving in this country were the modes of transport. Of these, the train is the most astonishing. All of France is connected by rail. Parisians eat fresh vegetables and meat from all over the country and can go anywhere as swiftly as they please. Rail is what enables the wondrous lives of the people of this city.

They say that steamships with screw propellers leaving Le Havre can arrive in New York City in ninety days. I could not help but marvel at the variety of modes of transport featured in a novel by Jules Verne titled Around the World in Eighty Days. *There are twenty-three tramlines in Paris and each run on steam. In addition to the electric tram that runs in front of the Louvre, there are fifty-three coaches on these lines. The rich have more conveniences thanks to these new methods, but the poor suffer because of them. A few days ago, I saw a woman in rags scraping cheese by a wall on the street. They say that many poor laborers survive by scraping the cheese off packaging from places like Switzerland. One sees fewer chimney sweeps since the establishment of a new company that installs furnaces, but I saw one yesterday. He wore a black fur hat pressed down on his head and had covered his eyes with something like glass. I still remember their strange, otherworldly look.*

March 12, 1892
Yi Jin

There are nights when one wants to be awake alone.

Jin gently moved Victor's arm from her chest to the bed sheet. His thin snore had made her think he was asleep, but he slowly opened his eyes. Her movement also made Quasimodo, their white cat asleep on their nightstand, open his eyes. The cat had been a gift from the Minister of Foreign Affairs when his own Turkish Angora had kittens. When Vincent had gone to the minister's residence to collect it, the kitten had been small enough to fit in Vincent's palm like a ball of yarn. Vincent named it after the character in Victor Hugo's *The Hunchback of Notre Dame*. Saying Hugo wouldn't mind, as the author had died three years ago, Vincent would call for the cat in his boyish voice, "Quasimodo!"

Victor drowsily moved his arm underneath her head and kissed her cheek.

—What is it? Do you want to sleep on the floor again?

Jin still had trouble falling asleep in a bed despite becoming acquainted with them since her days at the French legation. In Korea, she would silently leave Victor behind in their bedroom and sleep on a futon in the study. But in this house, all that awaited her across the hall was another unheated floor, some chairs, and a sofa. She ended up lying down on the floor next to the bed once Victor fell asleep. Usually, she would return to the bed at dawn before Victor woke, but sometimes he would wake before her.

It dismayed Victor to see her like this.

—French floors are not heated like in Korea. You will become ill.

—I shall try to adjust.

Jin placed Victor's other hand on her chest. She hadn't been trying to sleep on the floor tonight. She had wanted to go to their salon downstairs and take one more look at Hong Jong-u's manuscript. She was beginning to enjoy translating Korean into French. Victor's hand stroked her cheek, neck, and breasts, then moved down to the small of her back and pulled her toward him. Jin stretched out a hand and gave Quasimodo's silky back a stroke.

—Jin!

Victor's pronunciation of her name had improved greatly since their days of traveling out of Korea.

—We shall have much time to ourselves over the next four days.

—It's been a while since you've had some rest.

Victor had just returned after two days in Marseilles on a work trip. He was supposed to stay there for four days, but he had finished early.

Victor loosened his hold on her waist.

—Do you remember?

—. . .

—What you said to me on our first night in Korea.

Our first night in Korea. Jin could feel heat gathering underneath her ears. Their first night had turned into four nights. Victor had not shown up at the legation offices during that time. To Guérin and Paul Choi's consternation, Victor had simply said he was ill and had spent that time in Jin's room.

—You asked me to take you to the Louvre.

—Ah!

Jin buried her face in his embrace and smiled.

—I thought you'd chosen me so I could take you to Paris. I am telling you this now, but I was taken aback at how you had memorized the names of so many Parisian streets.

—I knew of no other way to tell you how I felt.

—I love you.

Victor, once again, was unable to say the words that hovered over his lips. *Do you love me?* Whenever he felt tempted to ask her that, ever since their days in Korea, he told her he loved her instead.

"Gillin!" Jin whispered his Korean name and placed her face on his chest again. Victor's mustache tickled the curve of her ear. The harder earned the love, the more passionately it burns. Victor slipped off the shoulder straps of her Korean nightdress. In bed, Jin always wore the nightdress the woman Suh had made for her as if Jin was determined never to forget her. Victor was swept up in a fit of desire whenever Jin whispered his Korean name. He knelt above her and lovingly cupped her face in his hands. Then, he slowly slipped into Jin's body. The more his body fell into a rhythm like rough waves, the more Jin found herself being conscious of the cat Quasimodo. Soon, Victor buried his face in her breasts. Jin lifted an arm and stroked his back. She could feel his drops of sweat. As she caressed his face, she asked him a question.

—What made you love me?

Victor lay down again and put his arm under the nape of her neck.

—Your eyes drew me in.

—My eyes?

—Yes. Your dark eyes. When my gaze first met yours on that bridge in the palace, I thought my world had gone white. I was astounded when you said *bonjour* to me. Then, when I saw you dance, I thought my soul had left my body. You were like a butterfly, like a bird. You are the only one who does not know how seductive you are. Did not Planchard and Maupassant fall in love with you at first sight? Even Guimet. That's not all. Even Vincent is at your every beck and call.

Jin giggled. She had met Emile Guimet through Hong Jong-u, who had secured work at Guimet's museum. Victor probably referred to the deference Guimet had shown her during that meeting.

—Monsieur Guimet is not really interested in me but in the fact that I am from the East. Like any spectator would be.

—Hong Jong-u is infatuated with you as well.

—Him?

—You're the only one who does not notice. He is deeply enchanted with you.

—Are you serious?

—Ever since Korea.

—Ridiculous . . . he treats me like a foolish woman. He would've had nothing to do with me if I didn't speak French. He takes every opportunity to mock me for putting on Parisian airs when I'm a Korean woman.

—That's how he expresses his interest. Does he not espouse the need for a royalist reformation, even as he lives here in a republic? Think of how you would seem to such a man. You and he are the only two Koreans in Paris, but it upsets him to think that you are forgetting Korea.

Hong Jong-u is infatuated with me? The idea struck Jin speechless. How long had Victor thought this? Why had he let them continue to meet to discuss the translation and twice a week at that?

Victor spoke in a low voice.

—About those four days. Why don't we visit those places in Paris in the order that you spoke of during our first night?

—You remember the order?

—I do.

—Say it for me.

—The Louvre . . . Notre Dame . . . Bois de Boulogne . . . the Latin Quarter . . . the opera . . . Luxembourg Garden . . . the Champs-Élysées . . . Les Invalides . . . the Île de la Cité.

Victor thought of when Jin had said, "Take me to the Louvre," with sadness, resignation, and perhaps a touch of hope in her clear voice. He stroked the full length of her black hair.

—I can't believe you remember that in order.

He hadn't tried to. He had memorized it naturally. Perhaps love was like that. Victor pulled her to him as if to grasp a bird that was trying to fly away and kissed her neck and breasts.

The face of one asleep after lovemaking is one of happiness.

But Jin was still awake after Victor had fallen into a deep slumber. She regretted each passing minute of the night. She slowly sat up. Quietly, she gripped her nightdress to herself and slipped out of the bedroom. Her foot was on the first step of the staircase leading down when Quasimodo walked into her path.

—Shh!

Jin lifted Quasimodo into her arms. The softness and warmth of the cat's fur seeped through her nightdress. She stroked the underside of his neck and rubbed her cheek against it. Quasimodo, having had enough, wriggled in Jin's embrace. She shushed him again, and slowly walked down the stairs and opened the door to the salon. She could smell the scent of the wooden Buddha that Victor had brought from China. Aside from the Buddha statue, the salon had a Korean celadon, fans from Japan, and books from China. The exotic atmosphere of the room made visitors look about with awe, like tourists.

—Stay quiet.

Only when they were in the salon did Jin gently put Quasimodo down on the floor. The cat extended his front paws and arched his back in a feline stretch.

Jin walked straight to the table with several drawers that stood in the middle of the salon. In the middle of the table was a feather pen, an inkwell, a fountain pen, and letter-writing paper, ready for whenever they were needed. The table, also from China, was long enough for ten people to sit together, and was used to serve tea during their salon sessions.

People would often visit Victor when they prepared for a posting or a visit to the Far East. They wanted to hear Victor's stories before embarking on a voyage across the great water. More and more people were supposedly interested in the Far East, but to most of them, that meant China or Japan, not Korea. They would try to pronounce the name of the country once, but for the most part that was all the effort they would muster. Missionaries headed for the East would also seek Victor's advice. They seemed to be more cautious when leaving for Korea than China or Japan. When Jin asked Victor why that would be, Victor said it was because they still talked of the suppressions in the Year of the Red Tiger and the Year of the White Sheep, which made Korea seem like a dangerous place.

Aristocrats who owned every Western luxury under the sun often turned their interest to Eastern objects, and this group also sought Victor for advice. Chinese books, paintings, calligraphy, and pottery were their favorites. Quite a few came for appraisals. In the spirit of maintaining good relations with the gentry, Victor did the best he could in appraising the Buddhas, lacquered furniture, or celadon that they carefully collected and presented to him. There were those who were disappointed to hear that their wares were Korean and not Chinese. Victor would then ask Jin for help. Some of these well-heeled collectors would be assuaged when Jin carefully explained the symbolism of the flowers and birds on the screens, paintings, or celadon, the different uses of the brushes and inks, or the meanings behind the *hanja* characters in the books.

Jin opened a drawer and took out the translation manuscript along with Blanc's French-Korean dictionary, the same one she had thumbed through since she was a child. The manuscript was her final edit of Hong Jong-u's first draft before it went over to Boex for further revisions. At first, she had taken on the work just to provide a few comments, but soon she became interested in the task of translation itself. Having intended to just skim over it, Jin had found herself reading each line, correcting the obvious mistakes and circling questionable choices, going through the language to make sure it flowed properly. Before she knew it, hours had gone by. Her attention was also arrested by how Hong's *Story of Chunhyang* was not the classic in its original form. The translation was replete not with Hong Jong-u's desire to tell a Korean story but to tell the story of Korea itself.

Jin was so absorbed in the revision work that she did not notice that the sun was rising or that Quasimodo had jumped up onto the table. The cat licked the back of Jin's hand and stretched out beside the manuscript.

Dawn is a soulful time.

Jin stroked Quasimodo's back as she continued to read. Quasimodo flipped over on his back and fell asleep, one of his hind legs pointing in the air, a foreleg curled so tight it looked as if it had been rolled. What was in this animal's bones that made it so flexible? Jin glanced at Quasimodo whenever the cat curled into a ball or stretched or contorted itself, even in its sleep. It did so freely and effortlessly. Korean dance also required great flexibility. She had to learn how to relax on command instead of using brute force, to conserve enough strength to maintain her positions for the right amount of time. Only when she controlled her breath could she softly flutter like a butterfly, soar like a bird, or hover like the air itself and land as lightly as if to stand on still waters.

Jin broke off her gaze from the sleeping Quasimodo, collated the manuscript spread out before her, and returned it to the drawer. She then took up the feather pen, ink, and letter-writing paper on the desk.

Your Majesty,

Jin stared at the inky blue Korean script that spelled out *Your Majesty.* This kept happening. She would be bursting with things to write, but once she sat down to write them, a blackness would descend to block out the words. As if someone had called for her, Jin put down the pen and slid her chair back.

She had intended to take a vigorous turn about the room but found herself throwing her arms in the air and turning her ankle in a dance step. Her Korean nightdress wound around her body. Soon she immersed herself in movement and danced as if she wore her extended sleeves of many colors and the beautiful flower crown. Quasimodo sat up from his languid sleeping position, gathering his soft paws and solemnly watching Jin dance. The Queen had enjoyed her dancing. She would often break the palace rules for her. The young Jin should have entered Jangakwon to properly apprentice with the other court dancers, but the Queen had Jin learn separately in a small wing of the Queen's Chambers. The Queen also used to have Jin dance in the courtyard of the Queen's Chambers, to personally track her progress.

To be an apprentice in the arts is to invite the possibility of having one's talents flourish beyond those of the master.

Whether it was in learning palace calligraphy or embroidery, Jin did not learn in a class but under private instruction, like the daughters of nobility. The Queen also had Jin read aloud to her whenever possible. "So, what have you read today?" She would call Jin to her room late at night and have her read aloud from the book Jin had read that day, falling asleep to the sound of Jin's voice. When Lady Suh would try to dissuade the Queen, saying the other court ladies were jealous of Jin receiving preferential treatment, the Queen would turn melancholy and say, "If the Princess had lived, she would have been just like her." Once she asked Jin if she was lonely and had Soa transferred from Jangakwon to room with her. From then on, Soa became Jin's dancing friend and roommate. Soa . . . *I wonder how Soa is doing?* Jin, her eyes closed, moved as if in answer to the clack of the *bak* that announced the start of a banquet, as if the thoughtful, slender face of the Queen were watching her at a distance, as if she could hear the strains of Yeon's *daegeum*. In this great city, the memories of Korea, the Queen, Yeon, Soa, Blanc, and Suh were as shapeless as snow when her eyes were open. Only when she closed her eyes did they become clear.

As one who dreams of the new enlightened world but could not step one foot outside of this palace, I envy you.

It seemed like a long time ago when she had, for the last time, performed the Dance of the Spring Oriole for the Queen. Jin's movements became as light as if she were stepping on white clouds. Her forehead beaded with sweat. She heard the voice of the Queen saying that Jin should break from the chains that bound her and learn new things and live a new life. Jin's eyes were studded with tears.

The salon was connected to the kitchen. Jin was unaware that the servant girl Jeanne had entered the kitchen to prepare breakfast and was now silently watching her, awestruck. Jin spun round and round in the salon like a gyre of golden sand in the wind.

3
Who Am I

Your Majesty,

I read the newspaper every morning. It tells us of everything that is happening in the country. Political affairs mostly, but also things like how many people gathered at the Grevin Waxworks Museum on the Montmartre, or what the weather will be like the next day. I also read about what performances are being held at the opera and learn what books are coming out without having to visit the bookstore.

You can also hear about other countries. Reading the newspaper is important, as it makes one aware of many different opinions. I think of writing down your letters for you whenever I read the newspaper. I also remember my younger court lady days, rushing to and fro as I delivered the letters in the palace.

They say that not every Parisian read the newspaper at first. Subscriptions were so expensive that only the nobility or the rich could afford them. There was also much censorship and oppression of the press before the Revolution. But since the Revolution, it was declared, "Freely shared communication of thought and opinions is a valuable right of man, and all citizens may freely speak, write, and print." This made me wonder. What would happen if a newspaper were printed in Korea, one that would show what went on at court? Would that not be good for the country? If everyone in the world knew what they were doing, the Chinese and Japanese would be more careful with how they conducted themselves. Then how would events like the Imo Military Incident be recorded? But I suppose Your Majesty wouldn't want such a publication in the first place.

July 4, 1892
Jin in Paris

Cities are made of spectators.

Jin was such a spectator, and spectacles abounded once she opened the front door. She took everything as an opportunity for observation: the architecture, the exhibits, publications, and people. Of course, Jin knew that she herself was also a spectacle for the Parisians. That wherever she went, all eyes fixed on her. Jin was used to being the center of attention since she began the art of Korean dance. But while the gazes of her audiences were tinged with awe, the gazes of the Parisians were only curious. And it was through their curious gazes that Jin understood she would never become truly Parisian. She could wear the latest fashions, but she was immediately categorized as an Eastern woman in Western clothes. Even Jeanne and Vincent had stared at her at first. If it hadn't been for Jin's friendliness, they would be staring at her still. But whenever she thought about this, she recalled Victor's life in Korea. What a spectacle the blue-eyed Victor must have felt like in her country.

Even when they were by the Eiffel Tower or at the Luxembourg Garden, Jin was always stared at. When she stepped off a carriage in front of the Louvre, the lined-up museumgoers treated her like she was their first exhibit of the day. Jin endured their stares in silence as she waited for Victor to get the tickets. When he returned, she wrapped her arm around his.

—Why do Parisians stare at dead bodies when there are so many other things to see in Paris?

—I told you not to talk about that again!

Victor was normally patient with Jin's endless questions, but he shut down any discussion of the morgues.

—That was the only place where people did not stare at me.

—There's another place. We're going to the opera tomorrow. No one will stare at you once the performance begins.

—I'm finally seeing an opera!

—The minister and his wife will be there. Monsieur Planchard and his wife, as well. And Monsieur Guimet, he was the one who invited us.

—Why did you wait to tell me this now?

—I just got the message myself, before we set off from home. I wanted to tell you tomorrow morning . . .

That must have been in the letter Vincent had handed to Victor that morning. Jin smiled. Victor was in the habit of sharing good news in the morning, embracing her as she woke.

—Oh yes, Monsieur Maupassant will be joining us.

This last bit of news widened her smile. Maupassant had kept his promise and taken her to the morgues just four days after the reading at Bon Marché. Before setting off to work, Victor had begged her not to go, but Jin said she had promised. The crowd lined up behind the Notre Dame astonished Jin more than the dead bodies themselves. Jin had been stared at ever since she had arrived in the harbor at Marseilles—no, since she had left Korea—but at the morgue, she was free from the attention of others. They were too keen on the bodies to pay her any mind. Jin had seen countless new things since leaving Korea, and a dead body was again a first for her. A display of two drowned sisters, a recent addition, drew the largest crowd. They looked exactly like their picture in the newspaper. Spectators were forbidden from standing before one display for more than five minutes, but viewers tended to linger at that one. Jin unconsciously took Maupassant's hand. She wanted to be as calm as the other Parisians at the morgue, but it wasn't long before she slipped out and looked for a ladies' room. She was afraid of vomiting and soiling Maupassant's shoes.

A violist played his instrument in the Louvre courtyard where flocks of pigeons took flight.

Jin gazed at the violist's hands as they played the viola. How might Yeon be doing? The grand boulevards of Paris were bustling with pedestrians, carriages, and street vendors. The buskers brought an extra liveliness to the scene. There were many of them along the boulevard connecting the Champs-Élysées to the Louvre. Even in the clamor of the carriages and the vendors calling out their wares, the buskers calmly played their music. Passersby would sit at one of the outdoor tables of the cafés as they drank coffee and listened, and others walking the boulevard would stop to watch. The boulevard enchanted cashiers, suited aristocrats, and aproned maids alike.

—Keep your arm in mine, don't get yourself lost like last time . . .

Victor held on to Jin as they waited to enter the Louvre. The former palace filled the eye even on the Champs-Élysées, where there were countless things to see. Victor told her how impossible it was to see all two hundred and fifty rooms of the Louvre in one day, especially after seeing the Place de l'Étoile and the Arc de Triomphe.

—You're making fun of me again.

Jin slipped her arm out of his grip and looked at him sideways.

—But you're always losing your way when you're out with Monsieur Maupassant. At the morgue, the Pantheon, and the cemetery at Montparnasse.

—I never get lost with you by my side.

The smile on Victor's face faded as he gave her a questioning look.

—But why is it that you go to cemeteries so often with Maupassant?

Jin realized he was right. All the places she had been to with Maupassant were related to cemeteries.

—How true. I didn't realize.

Jin had felt sick at the sight of the girls' corpses on display at the first morgue she had visited with the author. In the midst of trying to find a place to compose herself, she had gotten lost. Oddly enough, the thought that she was lost made her forget her nausea completely. Jin stood in the middle of the morgue's maze at first, uncertain of what to do. She looked through the crowd—a woman in white, a young vagabond, an old man from the provinces, tourists, children—but she could not find Maupassant anywhere. Tired of searching through the anonymous corpses, she left the crowd to rest in a ratty underground corridor.

Remembering the fear, she pulled Victor's arm closer.

Too tired to mount the stairs or even call for help, she had sat in that underground corridor until the morgue was about to close. Maupassant, searching for her, insisted the doorman help him scour the morgue. When the author found her crouched in the dark, his relieved voice shouting "Madame!" was so loud that it rang in her ears.

—What are you doing here?

—I lost my way.

Maupassant crouched down and looked at her for a moment. He gently helped her up and hugged her. He was out of breath. Jin returned his embrace. Supporting Jin, whose legs kept threatening to give way, Maupassant led her to a bench by the Seine and had her sit until she gathered her strength.

—Were you frightened?

—I was nauseous. Why do people look at dead bodies?

—Perhaps they're arrogant. They want to look at death in the face and think there isn't much to it after all.

Maupassant had admired the fragrance of the Chinese tea Victor served him the afternoon that he brought her home from the morgue. Since then, Jin served him tea on his visits. His gaunt face broke into a smile as he said he would like to visit her country, Korea, one day. The author seemed to relax his normal cynicism in Jin's presence.

Once it was their turn to enter, Victor wrapped his arm around Jin's waist.

The Louvre, standing grandly on the Rue de Rivoli and the right bank of the Seine, was more than just a beautiful façade. Its interior divided into narrow and complex corridors, especially past the Daru gallery and up the stairs where countless rooms extended in all directions. Victor told her that artists and ordinary citizens had lived in the Louvre for a time, after Louis XIV left it for the Palace of Versailles.

Victor led the wide-eyed Jin from room to room, his footsteps echoing in the space.

—No one can see all the artwork in one day.

The sculptures, the paintings, the great chandeliers descending from the ceilings, the accoutrements of the aristocrats in glass display cases . . . Jin passed all of them as she was led through the rooms.

—This is incredible. Are these all French?

—There is far more stored than is displayed.

Victor stopped in front of a hall showing artifacts from Ancient Egypt. He led her to a large granite statue.

—A sphinx. It means monster in Greek.

—The face of a man and the body of a lion!

—The face of the pharaoh. The Greeks thought the sphinx was a monster, but the Egyptians must have regarded them as guardians of their temples.

Jin examined a list of pharaohs' names posted next to the sphinx.

—Is it not preserved almost completely?

Its large size cowed every other exhibit in the hall. Jin began noticing that there were many other Egyptian sculptures on display beside the sphinx. She walked silently among them, noting that they all had their heads turned to one side. Their feet pointed to the side as well, so much so that Jin found herself looking only at the feet of the statues to confirm this. There were jars with handles, muscular warriors poised for battle, and a small carving of a woman said to have come from a tomb. Jin turned to Victor.

—But why are all these Egyptian things here, Victor?

—Don't you think they'll be better preserved here than in Egypt?

—Do you think those pharaohs think the same?

Victor smiled and led her to the chamber where the sphinx was again. He led her out of the hall and through another maze of corridors, looking for something. Jin stopped in her tracks. Victor looked back to see what had arrested her. She was gazing at a statue of a woman with no arms, the torso slightly turned, an almost undetectable smile upon its lips. Jin, as if called by the statue, walked reverently up to it.

—Venus de Milo.

Jin couldn't take her eyes off of the armless statue of Venus carved from white marble. The fabric wrapped around her legs seemed ready to slip off at any moment. How could she smile so? Jin's eyes shone with admiration. The neck supporting the face with the mysterious smile seemed to be soft and hard at the same time. The proud breasts swelling between the broken arms, the lovely curve of the belly and hips. Jin wanted to reach out and touch the goddess. The absence of the arms only accentuated the beauty emanating from the balance of her body.

—A man named Milo carved this?

—Milos is an island and not a man. They call her the Aphrodite of Milos Island as well. No one knows who sculpted her. She was discovered by a farmer who was tilling his land near a temple.

—Is Milos a French island?

—No, it's in the Aegean.

—Then why is this here?

Victor looked into her wide, inquiring eyes. He felt as lost as if he were trying to stop someone who had taken their shoes and socks off to walk the Seine's riverbed barefoot. How could he answer this question? He had come to the Louvre many times but had never heard anyone ask, "Why were these artworks here?" They belonged to the Louvre, so of course they were here. He cleared his throat.

—At the time, the French navy was docked at Milos. They brought the statue to Paris and gave it to the Marquis de Rivière, who later gifted it to Louis XVIII. That's why it's here.

—Does the navy collect sculptures like you collect Korean books?

—I'm not sure.

—And that goddess?

Jin pointed to another statue in the entrance to another hall, a carving of a goddess with an arched back and wings open wide.

—The Goddess of Victory. It was excavated on the island of Samothrace, so it's called the Nike of Samothrace. The island is also in the Aegean Sea.

Samothrace. Jin did not ask what a goddess of Samothrace was doing here. She had noted the troubled expression that crossed Victor's face. She knew of the Aegean Sea but not this island of Samothrace. She felt sad for the goddess. *Dragged here across the sea to be imprisoned in this palace*, she thought.

Victor suggested they move on, but Jin wished to stay beside the Venus de Milo a bit longer.

—There's a break down her left side. She couldn't have been like this in the beginning . . .

—I'm sure she was damaged before being buried or was broken when she was dug up.

Jin closely examined the angles of the statue's broken arms. It looked as though the original statue had only the arms down to the elbows, and it was just the left arm that had broken off. Perfection can be off-putting. The effect from the wounded arms and leg of the beautiful goddess made the viewer more sympathetic to her. Her lack completed her beauty.

—Let's move on.

Victor gently persuaded her, as he was afraid she wouldn't move away from the Venus de Milo otherwise. Jin reluctantly followed him while stealing a final look at the Goddess of Victory, who seemed ready to take flight at any moment. Only then did she realize the museumgoers were looking at her. Drawing herself in from the brief feeling of freedom that her immersion in the sphinx, Venus, and Nike had given her, Jin straightened her back.

Having walked past the Rubens, Corots, Rousseaus, and Turners, Victor stopped inside the room where the Eugène Delacroix pieces were.

—These are my favorite pieces in the Louvre. I never fail to drop by here, even if I see nothing else. How do you find them?

Jin examined the paintings that Victor marveled at. The caption read, "Eugène Delacroix, *Liberty Leading the People*." Over the bodies of the dead charged a mob led by a woman holding up a tricolor flag. The charging woman's bared breasts were ample and healthy. A nobleman holding a rifle followed her, as did a young boy wielding two handguns and shouting with what seemed to be delight. Other parts of the canvas were dark, but the goddess was framed by a thin fog and bright light like a halo.

—They're revolutionaries. Men struggling to establish a republic, stepping over the bodies of their fellows, charging. Exciting, isn't it?

—I think the focus is on the goddess and not the revolutionaries. She looks as if she'll jump out of the painting. Full of passion. Nothing can contain her.

Jin followed the goddess's palpable movement with her eyes. To her, she was almost dancing. She found herself unconsciously lifting her arm in a similar fashion but discreetly reached for Victor's arm instead.

—And so, the strong possess the Venus and the sphinx.

Victor didn't hear what she had mumbled to herself. Jin felt conscious of the emptiness of her hands and held on tighter to Victor's arm. Why this sudden urge to resist the grandness of the Louvre?

—Is Delacroix a French artist, Victor?

—He is. From Saint Maurice. His father was a diplomat.

—A diplomat like you?

Victor grinned.

—He attended a public art school and visited the Louvre often. They say you could see him copying Rubens or Géricault all day long. This museum was like his playground.

—So his paintings are where they're supposed to be.

Victor gave Jin a look that seemed to ask, *What do you mean?*

—You said the sphinx came from Egypt. The Venus came from the island of Milos, and the Goddess of Victory from the island of Samothrace in the Aegean Sea. I meant that Delacroix is at least in his proper country, as he was French.

Victor looked disconcerted, as if he found it difficult to answer her. Jin, feeling awkward, changed the subject.

—You were right. One can't see the Louvre in a day. I think I shall come here often, so let's stop here for now.

—Would you like that?

Jin nodded, giving *Liberty Leading the People* one last look, imagining she could hear the shouting of the crowd.

—Let's leave by the Seine entrance and not the boulevard. The sun will set soon. Let's go to one of the many beautiful bridges over the river.

They had to go through another maze of rooms to exit the museum. Jin held on to Victor, fearing she might lose her way as she had with Maupassant. *Why do I keep getting lost in Paris?* she wondered. She remembered how she had lost her way in the palace as a child and met the Queen for the first time. She laughed bitterly.

—What made you laugh just now?

—It's a secret.

—A secret?

Victor reached out and playfully tugged at Jin's nose.

—You said this place used to be a palace. I just remembered losing my way in the palace as a child at court. That's why I'm holding on to you so tightly.

Many people walked along the river at sunset. Parisians seemed to prefer being outside than staying in. Jin saw aproned women selling flowers from their baskets. A young man buying a rose to push into his buttonhole gave Jin a look. Dogs and children were also out by the river. The bridge that connected the Louvre to the other side of the Seine was the Pont des Arts; she could hear the accordion music of the buskers on the other side of the bridge. They walked down the bridge's walkway, which was made of wood, refreshing to the eye. There were potted plants and wooden benches. The bridge was known for buskers and painters. There were few such people on the Pont Neuf, where each pillar was elaborately carved, but the modest Pont des Arts had an artist every few steps. The artists at their easels were hard at work painting the Seine. Some painted Les Invalides, Notre Dame, or the Eiffel Tower. Jin and Victor walked among the other flaneurs. The people on the bridge were different in what they wore but the same in their leisurely pace. They were also the same in how, if they happened to glance at Jin, they turned around to stare at her, whether musician, painter, or flaneur.

A beautiful scene can invoke hidden thoughts. Jin stopped in the middle of the Pont des Arts and leaned against the railing as she looked out onto the Seine. Paris at sunset was a city poured with gold. Birds flew up toward the stunning rose window of the Notre Dame and the top of the Eiffel Tower, the latter visible from everywhere in Paris. Jin was wrapped up in her thoughts as she gazed upon the scene before her until she presently called out Victor's name. A shadow darkened her eyes.

—I was wondering about something.

Victor looked into her eyes, which now seemed filled with despair.

—What is it?

—I heard that in the Year of the Red Tiger, Korean books from the Oegyujanggak archive at Ganghwa Island were brought here by Admiral Roze. Are those in the Louvre as well?

—No, they're in the National Library.

Victor waved toward the north.

—You just follow this river. It's forty minutes on foot, fifteen by carriage. They're safe there.

—Like the Venus and the sphinx?

—Jin, if the Venus and the sphinx had stayed unexcavated where they were, we would not have been able to see them today. They might have even been rubble by now. Who would've acknowledged their beauty? It's because they're in the Louvre that they're so perfectly preserved.

Jin felt frustrated.

—Why? Why do you think the Venus and the sphinx would've perished if not for France?

—I've seen with my own eyes treasures being mistreated or neglected. It made me feel very sad. They're not mistreated anymore once they reach the Louvre. France has the power and the means to bring them here.

—Then you're the same as the British, the Germans, and the Americans, Victor! Like Japan or China or Russia thinking they're protecting Korea.

Jin stood up straight. The willow branches along the Seine bowed over the surface of the water, almost touching it.

—People here look at me like they look at the things you've collected, Victor.

—What on earth are you talking about!

—I'm no different than the exhibits in the Louvre. Look.

Jin turned her back on the river. An old and rich-looking woman, a servant in tow, slowly walked by as she stared at Jin. The servant girl who carried the old woman's shawl also stole a glance. Four masked clowns putting on a raucous show looked back at Jin as they passed. A boy in a vest ran toward them and slowed down in front of her, smiling at her in curiosity at first and then openly gaping. This, in a country that preached freedom, equality, and charity in its cathedrals and hospitals. It took several months to assimilate the countless words that she had never imagined existed. Tutors had corrected her French and taught her history, philosophy, and literature. She learned French music and even the cancan in her attempt to embody France in body as well as soul, but on the streets of Paris, all she received for her trouble were stares. It was the same whether she was walking with Maupassant or Jeanne. Jin could not be free of the attention of strangers, whether they were from kindness or curiosity. And without that freedom, there could be no equality.

Jin turned from the onlookers and looked out at the sunset-drenched Seine again.

Someone once said Paris was not a city but a world.

It was easy to feel this way from where she stood, in view of the awe-inspiring Romanesque, Gothic, and Renaissance architecture that surrounded her. Jin felt as if she were standing alone in the middle of Paris. Victor approached her and hugged her shoulders. He thought he might understand the welling despair in Jin's heart. But he was still worried about her. The river flowed wordlessly underneath. Jin and Victor, after gazing out at the Île de la Cité in silence, finally moved on.

They did not exchange a word as they stepped onto the other side of the bridge.

It was just as crowded as the right bank. Pedestrians passed on either side, stealing glances at Jin. Victor looked down at the fat pigeons that were so used to pedestrians that they didn't even bother to look up.

—Do you think you are the only one who is stared at?

—. . .

—Have you forgotten what it was like for me in Korea? You were knifed because you were with me. Koreans made a spectacle of me, too. But I didn't feel hurt by it. I was only uncomfortable.

—But you have power. You can withstand the stares of others.

What was this woman talking about? Victor lowered his arm from her shoulders to her waist.

—If I have power, then so do you.

—Victor, no matter how kind you are, you are a Frenchman, and I am a Korean woman. Your thinking that Korean books and celadon are better off here than in Korea is because of your power, not mine.

—Jin!

—The Queen greatly regretted the loss of the Oegyujanggak books that Admiral Roze stole. Those books were not printed into many copies as books are here. They are each unique. What use are Korean documents and books to France? They're plunder to you but living knowledge to us. They include records of court rituals.

Victor said nothing.

He was thinking of the time when he laid out, in the legation courtyard, the Korean books he was going to send to the School of Oriental

Languages. Jin had wistfully stroked them. He recalled how her expression turned disapproving whenever they touched upon the subject of his collecting Korean celadon and books. One day she asked, "What are you going to do with all that?" She would follow him to the bookseller who sold woodblock-printed books, or to Gwangtong Bridge where they spread out old books for sale, but there was reluctance in her step. Victor had sent his collected books to the School of Oriental Languages when he lived in China as well. He regarded it as one of his diplomatic duties.

Victor knew of the gorgeously illuminated manuscripts that were once housed in a temple in Ganghwa Island, which Rear Admiral Pierre-Gustave Roze had brought back as plunder. There were three hundred volumes of various sizes. There was also an astronomical map, scrolls, maps of Korea, and armor that still had their helmets attached. Admiral Roze and his soldiers had discovered large oak boxes during their ransacking and had hauled them aboard thinking they would be filled with treasure. What they were filled with were books. Some of the soldiers had been so enraged that they'd tossed some of the books into the ocean.

"Why do Koreans put their books in treasure chests?" The question was asked again and again among them.

Silent rivers run deep.

Jin slipped her arm into Victor's again and sat down with him by the waters of the Seine.

—Admiral Roze took his ships to Ganghwa Island because Christian missionaries were executed in Korea.

—I know, Victor. What happened to the Catholics in Korea was tragic. It breaks my heart to think of these people who went to a strange country to spread God's word and were killed. But bringing a fleet into Ganghwa Island is an act of invasion.

—Jin!

—That's what I think, Victor.

The statues carved into every pillar of the Pont Neuf, the oldest bridge on the Seine, were drenched in gold. The river seemed close enough to dip her hand in. Jin could almost see the face of the Queen on the surface of the water. That face, so filled with worry whenever China and Japan and the Western Powers played their power games over Korea.

Victor thought back to the nights he read the *Anthology of Great Buddhist Priests' Zen Teachings* at the legation, savoring each page. He had lucked into obtaining a copy and found it filled with profound sayings that aided in the realization of the Buddhist way. What would Jin think if she heard that he had taken that beautiful book to the antique collector Henri Werber? He cleared his throat. On one of his photography walks in Seoul, Victor had come across a book reader reading aloud *The Story of the Good Wife Sa*. Most of these paid book readers at the market were young men, but the one he met then was an old woman wearing tattered straw sandals. Her reading voice was so evocative that many had gathered around her. He was taking photos of her when he noticed the books she was selling at her feet. He looked through each one of them and was struck by the last one in the stack. It was bound by red thread sewn through five holes punched along the spine and had an abbreviated title on the cover. The second volume of two, printed on mulberry paper . . . but there was something unusual about its form. He examined the intricate colophon stamped on it and saw characters indicating that it was printed using movable metal type. Surprised, he checked the printing date: 1377, Heungdeoksa Temple. 1377? That meant this tiny country had managed to predate Gutenberg's movable metal type by decades, even if the size and shape of the type were inconsistent and wooden type was mixed into some of the characters. Victor bought the book with all the money he had in his pocket and quickly returned to the legation. He walked the quickest he had ever walked in his life, afraid someone would come shouting after him for the book.

The two now walked toward the plaza where the Sunday market was, where they could buy flowers and birds for low prices.

Sensing that Jin disapproved of his sending books overseas, Victor had not told Jin about his discovery that evening. He had only the second volume, and when he discovered the first page had been torn out, he sighed sadly. How could that old book reader be so careless? He let it be known that he was willing to pay a high price for old books, and booksellers showed up at the legation with huge bundles. With Paul Choi, he searched the neighborhood around Heungdeoksa Temple where the book had been printed, trying to find the first volume of the *Anthology*, but it came to naught. Did the old saying go that truly knowing someone's heart was to know the heart of the Buddha? Victor found someone who could appreciate the value of this book of collections of questions and answers harvested from a vast number of Buddhist texts. That was Henri Werber. Victor still yearned to find the first volume of the *Anthology*. Did this woman know how deep his obsession was for Korean books? Victor felt disheartened by her reaction, and even a little angry.

Perhaps to sell birds by the Seine, a bird seller passed by carrying a long pole with a birdcage attached.

—Gillin!

As she stared at the birdcage, Jin called out Victor's Korean name in a sad but loving voice. The grand buildings and the towers of the cathedrals seemed to stare down at the two.

—Who am I?

Victor, walking by her side, stopped and hugged her shoulders. Jin gently lifted his arm away. *Who am I?* She never had to think of it in Korea. *Who were my parents, who brought me into this world?* She felt she would stumble as if she were walking on nothing. Her eyes, still staring at the bird seller as he walked farther and farther away from them, were filled with melancholy.

4
The Ball

Your Majesty,

In Germany, a pair of brothers named Lilienthal observed the flight of birds and wished to fly themselves, so they fashioned an aircraft with wings that allowed them to soar. I am not sure how it works, but they say they flew using the pressure from the difference in the speed of the air above and below the wing.

Victor, who is difficult to impress, was very excited at this news. According to him, the day may soon come when we won't need sixty days on the ocean to go to Korea, but only two or three by air.

May 3, 1893
Jin in Paris

The guests began to arrive at the garden of the Minister of Foreign Affairs' residence.

The minister's daughter was married at Notre Dame that day, and the minister was holding a ball for the occasion. The garden in spring was abloom with white lilies, new rosemary, red tulips, and pale daffodils. There was a neat path meandering through the trees and flowers, with honeysuckle running alongside it.

Beyond the flowers basking in the golden sunlight of the evening, round tables were set for meals, with plates and cutlery laid with precision. The servants bustled among the tables, setting down wine, cheese, and other food. A space before a grove of cherry trees was prepared for a chamber orchestra, and the musicians looked trim in their crisp white shirts and black vests.

Jin wore her light blue dress and a felt hat with lace and a narrow brim, and thin gloves that came up to her wrists. The dress was Victor's favorite. Victor wore a bow tie with his white shirt and a morning coat over his striped vest, the formal attire that he wore at all diplomatic dinners. Jin checked whether Victor's bow tie was crooked. It hadn't been to his liking, and he had tied and retied it several times as Quasimodo watched. Jin had asked whether the frock coat wouldn't be a better choice because it was cooler at night, but Victor insisted on the morning coat, saying that the striped vest and bow tie went better with it.

As the two were greeted by the minister and his wife, they saw the Planchards, who had arrived before them, waving hello. They hadn't seen each other since seeing Bizet's *Carmen* together at the opera. *Ah, the opera.* Reminded of it by the sight of the Planchards, Jin trembled at the memory. Planchard's golden watch chain glittered against the vest underneath his frock coat. Clad in a pink dress, Madame Planchard lifted the veil on her hat before speaking to Jin.

—Madame, how opportune. I've wanted to speak to you about something.

—To me?

Madame Planchard smiled at her.

—It is a bit complicated. I hope we shall talk later.

Just after this friendly exchange, Régamey came up to them and greeted Victor. Jin instinctively looked around him.

Régamey grinned as he followed her line of vision.

—Are you looking for Hong Jong-u? There he is.

He pointed to the entrance. As ever, Hong Jong-u wore his Korean robes. He had just bumped into Henri Philippe from the Travelers' Club; they gesticulated wildly as they greeted each other. Henri Philippe wore striped trousers, a white shirt with a winged collar, a simple gray vest, a silvery tie to match, and a morning coat like Victor's, which contrasted with Hong Jong-u's white robes and black *gat* hat.

—The traveler Henri Philippe. How surprising he should come here.

Victor didn't need to tell Jin who Henri Philippe was. She had met him the day she had gone to a café in the Latin Quarter to meet Hong Jong-u and return his manuscript. Without bothering to ask whether she was up for it, he had taken her to the Travelers' Club, where Henri Philippe was introduced to her as an aristocrat and explorer. There were many such nobility and politicians at the club. Hong had been invited to talk about the Far East, where none of them had ever been. Henri Philippe was intrigued by Jin when Hong introduced her as a former Korean court dancer. *This is that woman?* He had heard of her but had never seen her before. Hong Jong-u was a passionate speaker. There were many Korean stories he wanted to tell but his French was lacking, so Jin ended up interpreting for him. Which had been his plan all along.

Music, however, is a language understood by all.

The party took on a lighter atmosphere when the orchestra began playing "The Swan" from Saint-Saëns's *The Carnival of Animals*.

—And there is Monsieur Guimet.

Régamey's words made Jin look toward Hong; she saw Henri Philippe and Guimet greet each other. Something Hong said made Henri Philippe and Guimet burst into laughter.

—Monsieur Hong's French must be very good by now.

Régamey laughed at Victor's observation.

—Monsieur Hong is sure to get along with anyone in any country, whether he speaks their language or not. He has a certain charm. I introduced him to Monsieur Guimet and got him a job at the Guimet Museum, but now he is closer to Guimet than I am.

—Does he still reside at the Serpente?

—No, he lives with me now.

—At your home, Monsieur Régamey?

—My studio. I am painting his portrait. His love for his country is considerable. He always keeps with him a photograph of the King and the King's father, the former regent. The photographs have enabled me to draw their portraits as well.

Régamey, who was an archival painter and managed the Guimet Museum, was also famous for painting the portraits of Victor Hugo and the chemist Pasteur. His interest in the East was what sparked his friendship with Hong.

The tuxedoed minister walked to the middle of the garden. His wife, wearing a hat with a wide brim and veil, followed. The guests settled down at the tables or came out to the clearing from the trees.

—Thank you all for coming. The newlyweds, married under the many blessings of our guests, have reached Marseilles by now. Tomorrow, they set off for Italy. As the couple is not here, do think of it more as a party than a reception. Please partake in the wine and enjoy the music. Do remember this moment as a pleasant one.

The guests clapped. Jin raised her head to observe the Parisian women. Madame Planchard, sitting across from her, was saying hello to such a continuous stream of people that her smile never disappeared from her face. Jin had gotten into the habit of watching the women of Paris since her trip to the Louvre. They tended to be slender with skin flushed pink, their features clearly defined. Sometimes she found herself comparing herself to them, which dismayed her. She was so intent on her observations that she didn't notice Hong Jong-u had walked up to her.

—Hello, Madame!

Had he already forgotten? Hong plopped down beside Régamey, his manner brusque as usual. Confessions sometimes break relationships. They had shared a carriage ride back from the Travelers' Club event where Hong had suddenly said in a low voice, "You and I are the only Koreans here in Paris." Jin had said nothing, waiting for him to explain what he meant. Then suddenly, Hong leaned forward and reached out his hand, pressing down on Jin's shoulder. Jin's body fell back against her seat, and she saw his face approach hers. His eyes were wide open and brimming with frenzy. He said he had loved her since their days in Korea and attempted to kiss her. Jin pushed him away. When he persisted, she slapped his face, hard. They hadn't seen each other since.

The music changed to Johann Strauss's "The Blue Danube."

Hong's pretending nothing had happened made Jin uncomfortable. To avoid looking at him, she fixed her gaze at the servant girls as they brought frottage made from mushrooms, chicken cooked with white sauce, glass bottles of cider, and roasted veal. The skillfully executed dishes were delicious to the eye, an impression aided by the scent of herbs. Some of the guests who had been conversing over wine began moving to the clearing to dance.

—Dance with me.

Victor held out a hand to Jin. Grateful to get away from Hong, Jin took Victor's hand and allowed him to escort her to the clearing. The other dancers, keeping time with the rhythm of the waltz, stole glances at her, overcome with curiosity over their first sight of an Eastern woman.

—The people are looking at me again.

Victor leaned into the sandalwood scent under her ear.

—They aren't looking at you so much as admiring you.

Jin lifted their joined hands and executed a smooth turn. There was a time when she learned the waltz twice a week from Laura, a dance teacher introduced to her by Madame Planchard. In the beginning, Jin had to familiarize herself with the basic steps of Western dance before she could attempt the waltz itself. Her body, trained in the art of Korean dance since a young age, was reluctant to learn the new movement. It was difficult adjusting to three-four time as the Korean dance in her bones resisted this foreign rhythm. Victor would never know how much she practiced, repeating Chopin's waltzes on the record player. Quasimodo was her audience. One day, she saw the cat jumping higher and higher against the wall at a feather toy, so to tease him she would place it even higher. Quasimodo, tired of dealing with the wall, ran up the drapes. Jin chased after him, and amidst her playing with the cat, she realized she was stepping in three-four time. Laura marveled at how quickly Jin managed to learn her steps after that, as well as the newest variations of the waltz. In three months, Laura declared she had nothing more to teach Jin and asked her to teach her Korean dance instead. But Laura gave up soon enough. Her own body, used to the rhythms of the waltz, had trouble accepting the calm and contemplative movement of Korean dance.

—I wish to dance with Madame.

Jin gripped Victor's hand, but Victor politely handed it to Hong. It was strange, still, to be dancing with any man other than Victor. And Hong, at that, with his robes. Jin resented Victor, who headed back to their table. Hong, reading her thoughts, whispered to her to stop grimacing, that everyone was watching.

—Wouldn't you rather give them a good show?

Jin had never heard Hong speak so quietly in Paris. And when had he learned to waltz? He led her with unexpected ease. Jin's efforts to keep a distance between their bodies made her seem like the novice of the two.

—I apologize for the other day. Those people at the club, including Henri Philippe over there, are highly regarded in Paris. They're explorers, but they know nothing of Korea. I became sentimental as I talked to them of our country. You must forgive me.

He had never seemed so chastened.

She had often wondered why he was so rude to her. But Hong was also the only person she could speak in Korean to. Whether he sank into one of his silences or talked heatedly about the country they left behind, it gave Jin a chance to think of Korea.

His sudden change of manner was odd, but his words assuaged her a little.

—When did you learn the waltz?

—I didn't learn it. I only observed it with my eyes. My robes are good cover. My steps are terrible.

As soon as he said this, he stepped on her foot. Jin laughed. The thirty-eight-year-old man suddenly seemed like a child.

—I'm glad you're feeling better. Thanks to you, our book was published yesterday. It's the first time a Korean translation has been published in France. Careful, I'll probably step on your foot again.

—Is that so? I can't wait to see it.

Jin's smile crumpled into a grimace. Hong's powerful knee underneath his robes had forcefully knocked against hers.

—Monsieur Boex will bring it. They've chosen the title. *Fragrant Spring*. It wasn't easy. I had to sing the "Love Song" that appears in the work to Monsieur Boex in my hotel room.

Jin had already heard from Boex that Hong had invited him to his hotel room and passionately sung "Love Song" to him during his presentation of the work.

—I'll buy you a shot of absinthe at Les Deux Magots in celebration of its publication.

Whenever Hong visited her house or Jin didn't meet him at the Guimet Museum, the two would go to a café in the Latin Quarter or the Boulevard Saint-Germain and talk about the manuscript over shots of absinthe. Boex would sometimes accompany them. Absinthe, a cheap drink made from wormwood, made her throat catch fire. But the burn was part of the pleasure of sipping absinthe at an outdoor café, watching the crowds go by.

—Your French is excellent, and there are many things you can do for Korea here, but why are you not interested?

Jin gave a bitter smile that was neither negation nor assent. *And what could I do to serve Korea?* Hong made it impossible for her to keep rhythm. His initial grace was gone. Holding on to each other, the two ended up taking the same three steps back and forth.

—Monsieur Boex asked me what I planned to work on after *Fragrant Spring*. What do you think? What about *The Story of Shim Cheong*? They like fortunetelling in these parts, what about a book of divination? It's important to draw them in at first, I suppose. What about translations under your own name?

—I'm not good enough for that.

—Such modesty . . . You're more than adequate. I came here to learn about French civilization and bring back knowledge that will help Korea. I have never forgotten Korea during my time here. But learning is not enough. It's just as important to let people here know of our country. And our time of ignoring Western nations has run too long. We've let the divide between us grow too wide.

—Korea is all you think of.

—I have other thoughts.

—Such as?

—Of you . . . of Lady Attendant Suh.

Jin let go of Hong's hand.

The music switched from "The Blue Danube" to Chopin's *Grande valse brillante*.

Jin gave Hong a polite curtsey and turned her back to him. She began walking toward the tables. But then she turned and addressed Hong once more.

—I am Victor's wife!

She needed to make that clear. Her cold voice only made Hong take a step closer.

—In this country, the married people seem more licentious than the unmarried. But he has not even held a wedding in your honor!

Jin left Hong behind with the dancers and returned to her table. Victor wasn't there. He was dancing. Jin tried to catch a glimpse of his partner's face, but the other dancers kept getting in the way.

—Madame!

A beaming Madame Planchard approached her and sat down in Victor's seat.

—Did you know we hold a white sale every February and August?

Jin knew, thanks to Jeanne. They were held after the bargain sales at the beginning and middle of the year, during the period that seemed a little too early for the next season's new arrivals. Bon Marché and other major department stores sold mostly linen then. Jeanne pleaded with Jin to go to the sale together, saying all of fashionable Paris would be there. Jin had been deeply impressed by the presentation of the wares. The department store looked as if snow had fallen inside, with white muslin descending from the ceiling and wrapped around the banisters of the stairs. The pillars between the displays and the cases themselves were all decorated in white. The women of Paris drifted among them like snowflakes, choosing white underclothes and sheets. Jin purchased white shirts for Victor, along with towels and a tablecloth. All at half-price.

—Do you remember the white fan you gifted me at the opera? The one with the red peonies embroidered on the white satin backing?

Jin's hands were idle one afternoon, and she had thought longingly of her days at the Embroidery Chamber of the palace and of her roommate Soa. She had removed the lace from an old fan and placed a piece of white satin against the ribs to measure. With the colored thread bought during her sojourns to the arcade with Jeanne, she had embroidered red peonies on the satin and given the finished fan to Madame Planchard as a gift.

—Many who have seen me carry it wish for fans of their own.

—Shall I make another one for you?

It would be easy enough, as long as she had more fan ribs.

—What I mean is, Madame, if you could make more of these satin fans whenever you can, I could sell them for you to these other ladies for a handsome price.

—But that is unnecessary. I am happy to make another fan for any lady who wishes it.

—Everyone asks me where I bought my fan. More than just one or two ladies. And there are many fans already, our department stores have several kinds. But the ones you make are distinguished. They are exotic and stately. I think it is due to your skill with the needle. You have a beautiful touch. Such attention to detail is an art in itself. In fact, I've stopped using my fan and had it framed on a wall!

—But how could I possibly accept payment?

—It is only natural to be paid for crafting something beautiful with your hands. I wouldn't say this if it were only a few ladies who've asked. And the ladies in question happen to have impeccable taste. I thought we might sell a few to them and then display the rest at the white sale . . .

— . . .

—I don't know how you will take this, but I am very intrigued by you, Madame. I wish for you to be enriched through your talents. Don't think too much about it, just make more fans like the one you gave to me. I shall take care of the rest.

Jin straightened her back and looked at Madame Planchard's face. Madame Planchard poured champagne into the empty flute placed before Jin. Golden bubbles, clear and bright, rose to the top. Régamey, his interest piqued by what Madame Planchard was saying, leaned toward their conversation as he sliced some roast suckling pig to put on his plate.

—Would you be interested?

Jin looked into Madame Planchard's eyes, which were full of good intent. She took a sip of champagne. There were, sometimes, such kind gazes, even among the Parisians who gawked at her. Maupassant's was one of them. Maupassant was also prone to say that lack of interest in one's own life was the death of hope, and lack of interest in the lives of others was the beginning of sin. But he himself seemed uninterested in his own life as well as anyone else's. He hated places where people congregated. If someone praised him, he would riposte that such words were better addressed to rotting cheese. Jin wondered how such a man could bring himself to come to a reading held at the Bon Marché reading room.

—Why do you think I should be enriched, Madame? Do I seem poor?

—Have I offended you?

—No. I am only curious.

—Madame, you seem mysterious, not poor. But you never know what the future holds. No one can know that. Money is safety. Even if a need to spend it never arises, you can always give it away, or buy whatever you desire, and more than anything else, you will have freedom.

Freedom. Could Madame Planchard, said to have come up alone from the provinces to become a shop girl at a boutique at Magasin de Nouveautés on the Left Bank, have obtained her freedom in such a way? Jin glanced at Victor, who was waltzing with a woman she didn't know and thought over that word, *liberté*, which Madame Blanchard had just spoken. Fish tend to gather in deep waters. Madame Planchard's considerate nature attracted many people around her. Whether it was from the champagne, Hong's words questioning the validity of her marriage, or Madame Planchard's generosity, Jin's face was a touch flushed.

—May I ask a favor?

Madame Planchard leaned forward, ready to listen.

—We have a servant boy named Vincent. He's clever and hard-working and optimistic, he makes everyone happy around him. His dream is to be a sales attendant at Bon Marché. I've been watching him, and I am convinced he could be an asset to your department store.

Madame Planchard, who had been tense as she listened, let out a laugh.

—How odd you are, Madame! Who would try to find her own servant another position?

—Vincent is not our servant, strictly speaking. He helps Victor. He's the son of the cheesemonger at Plancy, Victor's childhood home. He stays with us because he has no other relations in Paris.

—But it will inconvenience you to lose him.

—I shall persuade Victor. I want Vincent to live the life he wishes. Will you help us?

—Ah, then! We shall put him in charge of the vendor for your fans!

—Are you serious about putting my handiwork up for sale?

Régamey spoke up for Madame Planchard.

—Let her do so, Madame. Talent should not be hidden. I don't know about Korea, but here, the judgment of the market plays an important part in the shaping of talent.

—Here you all are.

Boex seemed to have just arrived at the ball, which prompted a flurry of greetings. Planchard came up to them and escorted his wife to the clearing for dancing. Boex sat down in the seat she had vacated. He put down a large envelope next to the roasted veal and looked around, mentioning that he was searching for Hong Jong-u.

Jin was also taking a look around at the ball. She didn't see Hong, but Victor came into view. Who was he dancing with? Jin had never seen the woman's face before.

—There he is.

Jin looked where Boex pointed and saw Hong walking toward the minister, who was visiting each table, talking to his guests. Jin, Boex, and Régamey looked at Hong at the same time. They were in for a surprise. Hong had just knelt before the minister. His white robes covered the flagstones in the garden. The minister in his tuxedo and Hong in his Korean robes on his knees before him resembled a scene out of a play. Hong kissed the minister's hand. But the subtlest method of insult is to ignore. Despite Hong's earnest show of respect, the minister simply stared down at him for a moment and moved on to another table. The insult was obvious to everyone. Hong remained on his knees upon the flagstones, even when the minister and his wife ignored him. Jin half stood out of her seat but sat back down. Her heart was filled with a pity she had never felt toward Hong before.

Régamey stood up and walked over to Hong.

—What just happened?

Jin had to ask as she poured Bordeaux, said to be indispensable among gatherings of diplomats, into Boex's empty glass.

—Monsieur Hong thought the minister would know him. Hong had wished to see him for a long time but had never been given leave to, so he came to this party despite being uninvited, and now he's being treated like a pest. I do hope I'm not found out, I don't have an invitation, either.

—Why would Hong wish to see the minister?

—Well, he's the Minister of Foreign Affairs, so Hong would want to make his acquaintance. Hong told me he was introduced to the minister when France signed their treaty with Korea. They say he worked under the King. Did you know?

Had he? Jin had no idea what work Hong had done in Korea. She had only known him because of Victor, who frequented Hwang Cheol's photography studio. He had occasionally accompanied them on their jaunts with Hwang Cheol, but Hong never deigned to look her in the eye, and his manner was like thorns. Jin had avoided speaking to him as much as she could. If Hong had never held an office in Korea, how could he have been at the treaty signing? Jin stared at Hong, who remained kneeling. The minister, who gave him no notice, lingered for a long time at Henri Philippe's table. The laughter of the two could be heard all the way to where Jin was sitting.

—Is this not Monsieur Boex?

Victor, returning from his waltz, greeted Boex, his dancing partner nowhere to be found.

—Monsieur Hong wanted to see me. His book has been published.

Boex took out a bound volume from the envelope he had set next to his veal and handed it to Jin. Jin gazed at the cover, emblazoned with the title *Fragrant Spring*, as Régamey came back to the table with Hong.

—Here it is!

Hong, as if he'd already forgotten the minister's insult, shouted triumphantly as he practically snatched *Fragrant Spring* from Jin's hands. He stared at the book for a while before laughing his characteristically boisterous laugh.

—Look at Chunhyang!

Hong held out the book to Jin with the pages open to an illustration of Chunhyang. The woman Suh had once told her, "Books are friends that can never betray, always keep them close." Jin looked down at the illustration. Régamey, a painter himself, also bent over it in curiosity before speaking.

—What seems to be the problem? Marold is an excellent illustrator.

The drawings were said to be a collaboration between Marold and Mittis.

—The drawings are fine. Except the illustrators have never seen a Korean woman. The pictures are of a Korean woman of their imagination.

Hong laughed, much amused. Boex, the publisher of the book, smiled at him as if in agreement. The Chunhyang of the book wore Korean clothes, but her features, skin, and hair were closer to that of a Western woman.

—If they had only one glimpse of you, Madame, it would've helped tremendously.

Hong had just addressed Jin as "Madame," perhaps because Victor was present. Victor smiled as he looked at the illustration.

—I believe it is thanks to Monsieur Hong that Lee Mongryong looks like a proper Korean gentleman.

Hong nodded at Victor's critique.

—Everyone at this table are good friends, but others cannot even imagine what Koreans look like. There is much work ahead to strengthen the friendship between our countries.

As they made these exchanges, Jin looked closer at the conical hat one of the characters wore. She caught a glimpse of Yeon in these illustrations of Koreans; why had she not had photographs taken of Yeon and the woman Suh? She felt a wave of regret. If only she had done so, to look upon them whenever she missed the two.

As the others thumbed through the book in merriment, gaslights started lighting up one by one in the garden of the house. The servants brought out vanilla ice cream with strawberry jelly to place on each table, as well as mille-feuille with their countless layers. Henri Philippe in his trendy striped trousers jauntily approached them. Hong greeted him, and Régamey introduced him to Boex and Victor.

Henri Philippe nodded politely to Jin.

—We meet again. Madame is more beautiful than ever. And is that a Korean book in your hands?

Henri Philippe had asked Jin, but Hong replied in her stead, saying it was the first Korean book to be translated into French. Jin passed it to Henri Philippe. Interested, he flipped through *Fragrant Spring* on the spot and looked up at both Jin and Hong.

—Would you like to come to the Explorers Club to introduce the work to the people? I think our members would be fascinated by the fact that it is the first Korean book published in France. Many were impressed by Hong's passionate lecture that afternoon.

Hong smiled brightly at Henri Philippe's words and bowed to him again. Henri Philippe turned to Jin.

Victor, who hadn't known about Jin's sojourn to the Explorers Club, gave Jin a look that said, *What is he talking about?* Just then, the minister approached their table. Régamey, afraid Hong would fall on his knees again, discreetly restrained him. The minister passed Hong and spoke to Henri Philippe and Boex.

—It is impolitic for French persons to deal with Koreans as if they were equals.

Victor glanced at Jin. The minister gave a pretense of talking in a whisper, but of course Hong and Jin, standing behind him, heard every word he said.

—It is perhaps best to ignore Korea and Koreans. Ah, but I do not mean you, Madame. *You* are a true Parisian through and through.

The minister, his manner one of bestowing a great honor, smiled at Jin, sitting right beside Victor.

Loneliness swept through Jin's heart; she felt she couldn't recognize a soul around her.

She was overwhelmed by the feeling that she was going uphill when everyone else was going down. Jin quickly brought a hand to her belly. Her ears filled with music, whispers, the sound of a knife falling on the flagstones of the garden, the sound of wine being poured, and the occasional sound of laughter. She tried to contain the pain unleashing itself in her stomach, her face turning white from the effort.

—I saw you dance the waltz a few moments ago. You dance it better than any woman who was born in Paris. I am glad you learned our ways.

The sounds of the dancing, chatter, and laughter were receding from her like a lie.

—Well. Enjoy.

Jin's eyelids trembled from her worsening abdominal pain. The minister gave her a courteous parting look and moved on to his other guests. His wife, following a step behind, looked back at Jin. Jin could feel sweat beading on her scalp underneath her felt hat. She caught the eye of the minister's wife, who gave a friendly smile before trotting after her husband.

Dusk fell over the garden.

Despite the strange mood between Régamey and Hong Jong-u, perhaps brought on by the minister's words, the dancers, bathed in soft gaslight, looked more romantic than ever.

—Victor.

Jin quickly dabbed away her sweat and called for Victor in a low voice, but Victor was too preoccupied with talking to Henri Philippe about China.

—Madame?

Boex was trying to get her attention.

—I have already talked about it with Monsieur Hong, but we are looking for the next Korean book to publish after *Fragrant Spring*. Is there a work you would recommend?

Boex slid a plate of mille-feuille toward her. Hong was filling his own wineglass, and Régamey was listening in to what Boex was saying as he dipped a spoon into his ice cream and strawberry jelly. Boex, in his considerate way, was trying to change the mood at the table.

—Would you be interested in trying your hand at translation, Madame? I can help you. I'm sure we won't have any problems.

Jin was silent with pain as Boex poured more champagne into her flute. Régamey, who had been silent since the minister's pause at their table, spoke up in a somewhat exaggeratedly cheerful voice in his own bid to lift the mood.

—Let's go to Montmartre to celebrate our new book. Yes, why don't we go to the Moulin Rouge? We shall stay out all night. Shall we?

Hong seemed enthused by the idea.

—Have you been to the Moulin Rouge, Madame?

Jin shook her head at Boex's question. She had read in the papers about how cafés and dancehalls—of a markedly different style than the ones on the Saint-Germain or in the Latin Quarter—were popping up in Montmartre. Among the bustle of the party, Jin looked down at her belly, which once again seemed to contort itself in agony. The twisting would seem to subside for a bit, but when the sweat on her forehead cooled, the sudden stabs of pain would begin again.

Régamey was rapturously describing the virtues of the Montmartre district to Hong.

—There's a new, joyful Paris being born at Montmartre, and something fascinating to see in every alley. As for the Moulin Rouge, all sorts of people seem to go there. We might meet Toulouse-Lautrec. He always sits in a corner like the Buddha, drawing the dancing girls.

The others had arrived at a consensus as to going to the Moulin Rouge while Jin sat in silent struggle.

She knew she wouldn't be able to withstand the worsening pain for long, but she nevertheless tried to keep upright in her chair.

Régamey, Boex, and Hong continued to talk of the Moulin Rouge cabaret at the foot of the Montmartre hill. Jin had heard of the Moulin Rouge from Maupassant. He had also told her about Toulouse-Lautrec. He was a very short painter whose legs had failed to grow since suffering an accident as a child. He showed up every evening at the Moulin Rouge and sketched the dancers. Maupassant had also told her that the artist would likely want to sketch Jin's form if he ever saw her dance.

—Madame, would you like to come to the Moulin Rouge with us to see the cancan?

Régamey was inviting Jin to join them. Victor would probably not like the idea of Jin going to the Moulin Rouge. She knew this since the day Maupassant told her about the place. That evening, she had relayed to Victor what the writer had said, and Victor—normally so guarded with his emotions—replied sharply that he didn't understand why Maupassant kept wanting to introduce her to such places out of all the things to see in Paris, ending further discussion. She could see Victor had one ear to their conversation in the midst of his talk with Henri Philippe.

Regardless of Victor's opinion of it, the cancan, which originated in the Moulin Rouge, was all the rage in Paris. It was common to see young people on the streets imitating the Moulin Rouge dancers, who would lift their skirts to their knees and kick up their legs, switching the leg they were standing on in the blink of an eye. But even if Victor consented, she could not possibly go in this state. She began rubbing her belly, discreetly wiping away her cool sweat.

Henri Philippe stood and politely held out a hand.

—Would you give me the honor of a dance, Madame?

Hong was staring at her from across the table.

—I have already received the unanimous approval of our committee!

Jin could barely focus on the outstretched hand as her face collapsed into a grimace. Taking this as a refusal, Henri Philippe, embarrassed, withdrew his hand. Victor looked at Jin. Jin wanted to say something but a wave of pain hit her once more and she could not form the words. Jin grasped her stomach, determined to see through the pain.

—Victor!

Jin managed to call out for him as she bent over the table in agony. Only then did Victor utter the single syllable of her name as he jumped from his seat and hovered over her. Jin forced open her eyes, trying not to lose consciousness. Through her faltering vision, the silhouettes of the waltzing dancers and the musicians underneath the cherry tree were rippling as if underwater. The wineglasses and leftover food on the tables were also wavering before her. She tried to unbend herself, but her face found the hardness of the table again. She could smell the cheese and strawberry jelly. She fought against her eyelids, which threatened to close. She thought she saw Hong's white robes flutter in the breeze and a bunch of yellow daffodils glowing in the gaslight.

—Jin!

Victor embraced Jin and tried to get her to sit up. Madame Planchard came over from her dancing and shook Jin's arm, calling out, "Madame! Madame!"

—What are you all doing! You must take her to the hospital!

Jin could faintly hear the sound of Henri Philippe calling for a servant to ready his carriage. Victor lifted Jin into his arms and quickly made his way out of the garden. The ladies and gentlemen of the ball looked puzzled as they followed Victor out with their gazes.

—Jin! Please, wake up!

Victor, who had brought Jin into Henri Philippe's carriage that awaited them before the minister's house, called out her name over and over again, but Jin's eyes slid shut.

5

The Oriental Room

Your Majesty,

There are many schools west of Paris. I have visited a few of them. The schools were created by the monasteries for the monks to teach novices how to read and understand prayers. Religion has great influence in these parts. Eventually, the schools began teaching more than just prayers to monks. They taught the catechism and the lives of the saints, which eventually led to the great success of the French language.

How can I describe the joy of reading in this country? Books from around the world are translated into French so that anyone can read them. New thoughts mix with the old. I envy how writers so freely express themselves in the language of their country. They say a writer named Balzac suffered from much debt throughout his life. He had to move several times because of this.

He also wrote an unfathomable number of works. He would write from midnight to eight in the morning, eat breakfast for fifteen minutes, and write again until five in the afternoon. He then would take a thirty-minute dinner, sleep at six, and rise again at midnight to write. If I ever return to Korea, I want to work to ensure that all children know how to read and write Korean. This is only a dream, and I do not know if I can ever return, but if I do, I want to spend the morning, when the mind is clearest, teaching children to read. Balzac gave me this hope.

October 9, 1893
Yi Jin in Paris

Jeanne knocked on the door of the room behind the salon.

It was the room where Victor displayed his collection of objects from the East. When no reply came, Jeanne cautiously pushed open the door. Jin sat on a cushion thickly padded with cotton, embroidering a bit of white satin. Yesterday, the pattern had been a red rose. Today, it was a lizard.

—Madame!

Jin was oblivious to Jeanne's knocking or her calling her name. She had learned on the day she fainted at the minister's ball, after being rushed to the hospital, that she had miscarried. Jin had not uttered a word for three months after. That was six months ago. She had planted the flower seeds Soa had given her, but they did not sprout. Jin took the pot outside to the square and smashed it to pieces. The orchid they had grown together was long dead. How could she have miscarried if she hadn't known she was pregnant? The miscarriage made her lose interest in Paris, and she rarely ventured out. The most she did was go to the nearby Paris Foreign Missions Society building to gaze at their large map of Asia, or to Les Invalides, where soldiers marched in threes and fours. She was unresponsive to Victor's proposals that they take a walk along the Seine. Victor even visited Maupassant, for whom he had no great fondness, begging him to take her out somewhere, even if it were to a cemetery.

Jin found her voice again because of the Oriental Room. Throughout the three-month period when Jin didn't speak, Victor changed the pieces exhibited in this room to Korean objects. The books and paintings from the other countries were donated to the Guimet Museum. Then, with Jeanne's help, he decorated the room like a Korean noblewoman's chamber. Excited to show her this new, secret world, Victor covered Jin's eyes with one hand as he led her to the room. When he opened the door and flung away his hand, Jin only looked upon the room in silence. Her gaze lingered longest upon the hanging peony scroll the Queen had bequeathed her when she left Korea. Victor's heart sank at Jin's lack of reaction. He had been full of hope earlier as he placed the vase with the white chrysanthemum pattern upon a lacquered chest of drawers stamped with butterflies and birds. Jin didn't even seem to notice the jewelry box with the pine tree engraving or the oak makeup box with the angled mirror placed on the floor next to the cushion. He had thought she'd rejoice at the sight of this padded Korean cushion, but she only gave it an expressionless look. Jin continued to be listless when he gestured toward the painted screens that stood before the long windows.

—It saddens me that this is all I can do for you.

Victor said this in a low, disappointed tone, his initial hopes dashed against her reaction. But then, Jin whispered, "Thank you, Victor," and kissed him on the cheek. Victor broke into a smile. Those were the first words Jin had spoken since her miscarriage.

Jeanne called out again, "Madame, you have a visitor!" Jin raised her head. This wasn't the Jin who had been rapt at *Carmen* at the opera, or the vibrant dancer at the minister's ball. The healthy flush of her cheeks was replaced with melancholy paleness, and her delicate clavicles were more pronounced than before.

—Who?

—A nun I've never met. I think she said she's from the Paris Foreign Missions Society.

The Paris Foreign Missions Society? A small bit of light seemed to break in Jin's eyes.

—Show her to the salon and offer her tea. I'll be out soon.

There was a new firmness to Jin's voice in contrast to her languid appearance. Jin put down the fan she was embroidering and drew the makeup box toward her, examining her features in the tilted mirror. The fingers that tucked in the more wayward strands of her chignon were more delicate than ever before. She stared into the mirror, at the deep shadows under her dark eyes. She rubbed the glass with a handkerchief. Her dark eyes trembled and were still again, large and whole. She lifted her shawl from her lap and wrapped it around her shoulders before entering the salon. The nun, who had been drinking the tea Jeanne had brought, gave a start at Jin's appearance.

—I hardly recognized you!

It was Jin's turn to be startled by the nun's Korean words, which drew forth from her lips like a sigh. This was Sister Jacqueline, who taught French to the Korean orphans at the Gondangol orphanage. Jin beamed. It seemed like a lifetime ago when Jacqueline had taught the children French, and Jin had taught Jacqueline Korean. Among the three nuns Jin had taught, Jacqueline had been the fastest to take in Jin's teachings.

—Have you returned to Paris?

—No, I'm only visiting. I have to go back soon.

—To Korea?

—Again, no. Penang this time. But are you unwell?

Jin smiled at Jacqueline. Jin's face was so gaunt that the tiny wrinkles of her smile were pushed almost to her ears.

—Have you not been eating?

All Jin could stomach lately was a cup of coffee and a piece of bread. She couldn't bear to eat cheese, which she had once loved. Jacqueline's presence reminded Jin of the fluffy steamed rice the woman Suh used to make for them. She felt that if she could get a bowlful of that, she could mix it with some water and eat it whole. In the past few months, her desire for a steaming bowl of gleaming Korean rice had grown as great as her desire to sleep on a futon spread on the floor.

Jacqueline, her eyes filled with concern, took another sip of the tea before opening her bag and taking out a package wrapped in white linen. She held it out to Jin; it was small enough to carry in one's sleeve.

Jin looked up at the nun.

—The musician Yeon gave this to me when I said I was coming here. He begged me to pass it on to you.

Jin sat up from her leaning position. Her shawl kept slipping from her shoulders. Her eyes were transfixed upon the white linen package.

—Open it.

Jacqueline leaned forward with the package, urging. But Jin only placed the package on her lap.

—How are things in Korea?

A shadow fell across Jacqueline's face.

—Turmoil. There's been a peasants' uprising down in Gobu. It was a small movement to begin with, but now it's becoming difficult to control. The palace felt threatened enough to request reinforcements from China. Which prompted Japan, sensitive to such things, to also send troops.

Jacqueline looked up again.

—But none of this is helpful to you now.

—What happened after?

—There is a Buddha carved into the face of a cliff somewhere down south. They say there's a book hidden in its belly button, and the day this book is taken from its hiding place, the country will come to ruin. The peasants, desiring a new world, are said to have broken the Buddha with an ax and removed the book.

Jin's face darkened. She spoke when Jacqueline paused again.

—What happened then?

—The royal family was taken into custody by the Japanese troops. There was a movement attempting to reinstate the Regent. In the end, Japan and China declared war, and a battle raged . . . and Japan won.

Jin lowered her head.

—I, too, hoped Korea would welcome new ways. But was this really the only way . . . ? I worry for the country.

Jacqueline started to say something else but stopped. She regarded Jin's lowered head. A silence flowed between them. Jacqueline gently asked her a question.

—And how has it been for you here?

—. . .

—Are you happy?

Jin smiled at Jacqueline.

—I have always hoped you would be happy, Jin.

—My life here is not so bad.

—Which means it is not so good, either.

—There are days when I am happy. And days when I think it is too much.

—You are aware that Bishop Mutel took over from the late Bishop Blanc? The cathedral he was building stopped construction during the war between China and Japan, but it's restarted now. The orphanage thrives, even without Bishop Blanc. All thanks to Madame Suh and young Yeon, of course. They devote most of their energies to educating the children. The children's favorite thing to learn is the *daegeum* from Yeon. I so wish to talk more with you, but I could barely make the time. I arrived in Paris yesterday. I couldn't wait to see you, and it happened to be close enough to walk. Would you like to come to the Paris Foreign Missions Society sometime?

—When do you leave?

—I believe I shall stay here for a month or two.

Jacqueline embraced Jin lightly and whispered, "May the blessings of the Virgin Mary be with you." Jin did not release her from the embrace. The two stood in each other's arms for a moment. After Jacqueline left, Jin brought the linen-wrapped package to the windowsill, swung open the windows, and leaned out. She followed Jacqueline's brisk progress until the nun was completely hidden underneath the beech canopy. Jin stared at the package, afraid of what it might contain. Then her hands quickly unwrapped the contents. Inside was a letter written with the fountain pen Victor had given Yeon.

The letter began with no preamble.

Silverbell,

Two months ago, I bought the house in Banchon where we spent our childhood together. Mother had mentioned that it was being sold. She doesn't know that I bought it. I'm thinking of having her live there when she becomes too old to take care of the orphans. I never dreamed I wouldn't get to see you for so long. Mother asks after you through Lady Suh in the palace, but even she has no news. Sometimes I think maybe I'm the reason you don't send us word. If that's true, then please know that I have accepted things as they are, that what's past is past. I know you are no longer the girl I met when I was led by the hand of Father Blanc to Banchon. And forgive the pettiness I showed you at the end. I thought if I said good-bye, I would never see you again, and I couldn't bear that.

Your life, Silverbell, has always been a mystery to me. It's full of things I can't begin to understand. I watched your ship leave Jaemulpo Harbor. I thought, I should've followed you onto that boat. I should've followed you, to keep that promise I made long ago. I would've followed you if I'd known I would never hear from you again. But what use are these leftover feelings?

We are doing fine. Korea is the same as ever, and I sometimes meet Lady Soa at the banquets. Sometimes, she performs the Dance of the Spring Oriole that the Queen enjoys so much. We always ask each other about you.

Please send us word, somehow, to reassure us of your well-being.

Jin read the letter twice before putting it down on the white linen wrapping on the table. *Please send us word . . .* the words hovered before her. He must've written it after some hesitation, hearing that Jacqueline was to return to Paris. He still called her Silverbell but also used the formal form for "you," wavering between the familiar and unfamiliar.

One must close one's eyes to see the things one misses.

Jin brought the letter to her nose as if to detect the scent of Yeon's hands. She stroked the letter and closed her eyes. She could sense through his concern for the woman Suh that she was not well. When Blanc had purchased two houses for the orphanage, the woman Suh had sold her Banchon house and given the money to Blanc. A dismayed Blanc had refused to accept her money at first, knowing that it was all she owned in the world, but Suh had even turned down his subsequent suggestion to give just half. Then, she had volunteered to cook for the orphanage.

Jeanne came in to collect Jacqueline's cup and saucer. She was bending over the table when she glimpsed the letter sitting on the linen wrapping. Her eyes shone.

—Is this Korean writing, Madame?

Jin smiled and nodded. Jeanne looked closer at Yeon's handwriting.

—They're like pictures!

Jeanne examined the mysterious Korean letters as if she were looking at a painting. When Jin rewrapped the letter and stood up to return to the Oriental Room, Jeanne called out to her.

—Are you all right? You don't look well. Would you like another cup of tea?

—Is Vincent coming today?

Jin tried to put on a cheerful voice to alleviate Jeanne's concern. Jeanne grinned and even blushed at the mention of Vincent's name.

A man's walk becomes purposeful when he has realized his dream.

Vincent had become an attendant at Bon Marché thanks to Madame Planchard, and his duties included coming to the house to fetch Jin's embroidery. Gloves and fans had become essential accessories at Parisian balls and gatherings, and the women would secretly observe and compare each other's fans. Victor wasn't too keen on Jin's preoccupation, which made Jin hesitate at first, but she was now settled into making them as she spent her days in the Oriental Room. She used mostly satin or silk muslin, but sometimes tried microfibers for a warmer look. Vincent was in charge of providing the fan ribs and ferrying the material to and fro. Once Jin handed over the embroidered cloths, Vincent would take them to a fan store by the Seine and have them completed. Jin used to do everything from the cutting to the finish, but once her fans became popular, she did only the embroidery. The demand was too high for her to complete the fans herself; Jin's fans always sold out first, without fail. Madame Planchard priced them several times higher than the other fans and made a separate display for them.

—I've put the finished fans in the other room, so please help Vincent find them when he comes.

What Victor dubbed the Oriental Room was called "the other room" by Jeanne and Vincent. Vincent brought the proceeds from the fan sales when he came, and Jeanne would carefully put the gold and silver coins in the jewel box with the pine tree engraving.

—There's also a party tonight, so Victor will be late. You don't have to make me dinner. Why don't you go somewhere with Vincent? Stay out as late as you want.

—But are you not going out yourself, Madame?

Jin smiled sadly. Victor must've told her that Jin was going to a party that evening and she needed help to prepare. Victor had said he'd go directly to Henri Philippe's house after work, but Jin was thinking of not going. This had happened several times before, so Victor would likely just accept that she was not coming.

Jin went back to the Oriental Room and shut herself in. She leaned against the door and stood there for a long time. She heard a scratching at her back. Jin rubbed her cheek and opened the door. Quasimodo the cat meowed as he entered the room and jumped to the top of the carved dresser.

—Come here!

Jin held Yeon's letter in one hand and gestured to the cat with the other. Quasimodo didn't come. Jin lowered her arm and looked upon the half-embroidered lizard on the fan lying on the cushion. She'd been working on it right up to the moment Jacqueline had arrived. She had finished the last batch of satin Vincent brought her, so to pass the time she put new satin on an old fan she occasionally carried and was embroidering a lizard on it. Jin had learned that Victor had once written a paper on lizards. She found the article in a zoological journal shelved among some old books. The paper described the mating and spawning habits of lizards of France and included illustrations. Reading it, Jin felt as sympathetic to Victor as she had to Yeon when she discovered he was mute. The thought that Victor, who so rigidly followed the rules, was once interested in the free lives of animals living in the wild, was strangely moving.

Quasimodo jumped lightly down to Jin's feet. Jin remained leaning against the door panel. Quasimodo as a kitten had been as little as a snowball, but now when the cat stretched, he was almost as long as Jin's arm.

When Jin sat down on the cushion again, Quasimodo leaped into her lap and settled down.

Jin stroked his neck while she read Yeon's letter again. Indeed, they had not said good-bye when she left. Yeon didn't want to believe she was leaving for Paris with Victor. He had refused to recognize them as a couple, even when Jin was living in the French legation as if they were married. When Jin said she was Victor's wife, Yeon had paused for a moment before writing, *But you are not married*. Jin grimly realized that this observation had been presented to her on two separate occasions: once by Yeon in Korea, and the other by Hong Jong-u in France.

Just before she left Korea, Jin had kept visiting the orphanage by night and Jangakwon by day in the hopes of meeting Yeon. He was nowhere to be found. She soon realized that Yeon was avoiding her on purpose, as he couldn't possibly be that unavailable. The woman Suh told her to not think too much of it, but Jin determinedly visited both the orphanage and Jangakwon on the day before she was to leave. She couldn't find him. She had even spent a whole day waiting by the gate of the French legation, sure that he would come and see her.

Someone knocked. Jin didn't answer, but the door cracked open anyway, and Jeanne's kerchiefed head peeped in.

—A strange visitor is here.

—What do you mean?

—He says his name is Hong.

Hong? Jin stared back at her.

—He is wearing strange clothes, and he seems very angry, so I did not invite him in. Shall I turn him away?

—Did he say his name was Hong Jong-u, Jeanne?

—I'm not sure . . . he's rather rude. Should I tell him you're busy?

—It's all right. Show him into the salon. I'll be right there.

Jeanne cocked her head but closed the door carefully behind her. What on earth was Hong Jong-u doing there at that hour? Jin wrapped Yeon's letter in the linen and slipped it into the carved dresser. She pulled the mirror toward her again and looked at her face. Her eyes were slightly swollen. She blinked twice and opened her eyes wide. She came out to the salon holding Quasimodo in her arms. Hong was standing at the window of the salon, looking out at the beech trees. He was so broad and tall that he covered half the window. Jin took a moment to take in his silhouette. She had seen him many times in Paris, but never, so closely, his back. Oddly enough, he seemed lonelier from the back.

—It's been a long time.

Hong didn't immediately turn at Jin's greeting. When he did, he grimaced and glared at the cat in her arms. Jeanne came in with tea and placed the cups and saucers on the table in the middle of the room. The servant girl openly stared at Hong.

—Why don't you take a seat?

Hong reluctantly did as Jin suggested and sat down at the tea table. His robes covered the chair and grazed the floor. Jin sat down across from him and placed Quasimodo on the chair next to her.

—They say you never go out?

—. . .

—You will never accomplish anything by being so weak.

Jin was irritated by his rudeness, even when she conceded that his words contained real concern for her.

—Why have you come here?

Hong cleared his throat at her cold reply. Jin was steadfast in her look and wondered what was taking him so long to get to the point.

—I am returning to Korea.

Hong practically spat this out as he lowered his teacup. Jin blinked. She leaned back in her chair and glanced at Jeanne. Jeanne, who had been standing and staring at Hong, took the hint and left, but couldn't resist looking back as she exited the salon.

—I wasn't sure if I should, but in the end, I have come to say farewell.

Since when had this man been unsure of anything? Jin sighed deeply.

—There is nothing more to learn from France? Did you not wish to use their ways for the benefit of our people back home?

Hong seemed thoughtful.

—I have learned many things here. I want to go back as soon as possible to use the things I've learned. I dream of a new Korea. Not through the ways that Kim Okgyun suggests. My thinking is different from his ilk. If Korea is to stand firm among the great powers of the world that threaten us, we need a strong monarchy first and foremost. I hope for the monarchy to lead the way in modernizing our country and leading us to prosperity. And there's no end to learning. I cannot keep learning indefinitely. I need to contribute to my country.

Hong cleared his throat again at the sight of Jin picking up the cat and holding it in her arms.

—And you shouldn't waste your time playing with cats!

Jin gave him a hard stare.

—You are always so sure of yourself. Since you've been friends with Régamey and the like, you must've gained an appreciation for their freedoms as well. Is it not the first rule of the French to respect what others think and not be so quick to pass judgment? Do not judge me by your standards, sir. I am well aware of your passion for our country. But that passion often blinds you.

Hong looked Jin directly in the eye. She had never called him "sir" before and had never expressed herself as clearly to him in so many words. She had always given him the impression that she had nothing to say to him.

—I apologize if I have offended you.

—Just as you have your own rules, I am living my life by my own. I live by my thoughts, not by the thoughts of others. To say that I am wasting my time is simply untrue. In France, I do not fall to my knees before those with power.

Even the sweetest honey will sting when applied to a wound. Hong's face turned red. He looked more disconcerted than when Jin slapped him for trying to kiss her. He hadn't forgotten the humiliation he had suffered at the minister's ball. Red-faced and silent, Hong sat still for a moment before taking out from his robes the photographs of the King and the Regent and pushing them toward her.

—I wanted to give you these before I left.

Jin pushed them back.

—I've no need of them.

—Do you wish to forget Korea?

—And whether I keep these tokens or not decides that?

Hong leaned back, discomfited by her stare. Hong had been the only other Korean in Paris, the only man with whom Jin could converse in Korean. And now he was going back.

In the face of her adamant refusal, Hong picked up his photographs and stood up from his chair.

He had made to leave immediately but then paused. He took out a large envelope and pushed it toward her across the table.

—These are my translations for the *Celestial Almanac* and *The Story of Shim Cheong*. No doubt they require much editing. I chose the first book because the people here are interested in fortunetelling, and so an interest in Korean fortunetelling may lead to an interest in Korea. Put in whatever facts you deem helpful. *The Story of Shim Cheong* is not just the story itself. I've added a long foreword on our country and changed the setting to fit our recent history. My only regret is that I will not be able to see the books published before I leave. They are part of a series planned by the Guimet

Museum. Take a look at them as before. And care for them as if they were your own until they are published.

—. . .

—I ask you this as a favor.

Jin didn't say anything as she regarded the envelope. It had been a long time since she took the French-Korean dictionary out from its drawer in the salon.

—Korea's geographical location makes it a battlefield between Japan, China, and now, Russia. You've served the Queen, so you know what I say is true. The only way for Korea to survive is if we make their ideas ours.

—. . .

—We have to make Koreans understand what is going on in the world. And let the people here know about Korea as well. Do this for us.

—Wait here.

Jin went to the Oriental Room and brought out some books wrapped in linen.

—I also ask a favor of you. I wish to give these to Her Majesty. They are only two books, so it will not be a burden. Give these to Lady Suh at court, and she will pass them on. Or give them to a musician named Kang Yeon at Jangakwon.

—What books are these?

—A translation of some of Maupassant's stories. And a Korean book.

But it wasn't the Maupassant translations or the Korean book she wanted to send to the Queen. She had gone into the Oriental Room thinking about the little stack of unsent letters. But after much hesitation, she picked up the translation and the book instead. The more she wrote those letters, the further she felt from the Queen, leaving her with an ache in her heart.

—A Korean book?

—I happened to come across it here. Are you going directly to Korea?

—I have some business in Japan. I was there for two years before coming here. I need to see some people and get some of my old things. I shall return to Korea after a few days.

Jin walked him to the door. She had never made such a friendly gesture to him before. Jeanne watched worriedly as Jin, who had not gone outside for many days now, followed Hong beyond the threshold.

Perhaps they were reluctant to part. Although neither had suggested it, they found themselves walking along the storefronts that lined the square.

—When do you leave for Marseilles?

—It will take a fortnight to take care of affairs at the Guimet Museum. I shall go soon after.

—Where will you stay until then?

—The Serpente.

Hong stopped. He turned to Jin and stood silently for a moment, taking her in. The heads of the cheesemongers popped out of their doors, ogling them.

Once they had made a full circle around the stores, the two said their farewells. Hong said he would not take a carriage. He said he'd begun to walk everywhere once he decided to return to Korea. He walked from the hotel to the Guimet every day. Jin nodded. One did notice more things on foot than in a carriage. Hong plodded away and didn't look back. Jin watched him disappear into the crowd.

6

At the Bois de Boulogne

Your Majesty,

I heard of an astounding event today. A colleague of Victor's returned from America and spoke of a massacre of hundreds of indigenous people who were resisting the American government. They say there were once 850,000 natives living in North America. Not even 40,000 remain, and they face extinction. The cavalry is said to have charged when the natives objected to the oppression of their peoples and the assassination of a leader named Sitting Bull. The natives, armed with arrows, could not have been well-matched against the cavalry with their guns and cannons. Countless fell. They say the snow-covered plains were red with their blood. I prayed for them, a people I've never met who lived in a land I've never seen. I prayed for the native women and children buried in that frozen ground.

This morning, I read in the newspaper that women in a British colony called New Zealand were given the right to vote. They say its legislature bowed down to constant pressure from their women . . . but I shall stop writing. What would be the point of writing to you about these things? The pile of letters I could never send to you continue to mount.

I do not even know what the date is today.

From Paris,
Yi Jin

Victor was stirred awake when Jin sat up in bed.

She seemed unaware that Victor was also sitting up and looking at her. She put on a coat over her bedclothes, opened the bedroom door, and walked out. Victor slid out of bed, threw on some clothes, and followed suit. Jeanne had told him that Madame was acting strangely. That Jin would leave the house in her bedclothes each dawn, barefoot. Victor didn't believe her at first. The servant told him that she didn't know where Jin would go except she always returned exhausted, swaddled in cold air, to go lie down in the Oriental Room.

—She's like that ever since that day at the Bois de Boulogne. Did something happen in the forest?

Only then did Victor stare at Jeanne.

—It's been a month now.

Jeanne looked uncomfortable talking about Jin behind her back. "Surely she's going for a walk," Victor had said, to which Jeanne replied, "Who goes for a walk before sunrise?" Her eyes pleaded for Victor to intervene on her mistress's behalf.

Victor could see from Jeanne's expression that the girl was sincere. Jin had treated her more like a friend than a servant, which Jeanne found fascinating and endearing at the same time. Victor understood that Jeanne was berating him. How could his wife be slipping away from their bed and wandering outside the house for almost a whole month without him knowing?

Jin reached the bottom of the stairs and unhesitatingly walked through the salon. She opened the door and paused for a moment, seemingly looking back. A wind came through, making her clothes flutter. It was the beginning of summer. If she had gone out in those clothes in the winter, she would have fallen ill. Despite Victor standing in the salon, her eyes passed over him as she gave the room a final look before pushing the door wide open and leaving. Victor was dismayed. The same as yesterday and the day before. At least she had thrown on a coat this time. She seemed to have forgotten that one must put on shoes before leaving or to lock the door. She simply left. And walked, as if leaving it to the wind to determine her direction. Victor followed her, holding Jin's leather shoes with the laces that came up to her ankles. This was the fourth time he'd done this.

Jin walked around the storefronts, closed at this early hour of 4 A.M., and walked into the beech grove. Two days ago, she'd walked to the Paris Foreign Missions Society. She had stared up at its shadowy façade for a long time. She walked around the courtyard of the five-story stone building before standing absolutely still in the middle of it. There, she raised an arm. Her body arched. She made a turn. From these awkward movements, she gradually fell into the steps of a Korean dance. Victor watched her, holding her shoes, until the dance petered out to a halt. Victor had approached her to put the shoes on her feet, but Jin passed right by him and walked back, retracing her steps to the house. Yesterday, Jin had awoken at the same hour and this time went past the Paris Foreign Missions Society to the plaza at Les Invalides. Having walked a long way through the empty streets at dawn, Jin leaned against a wall to rest. Victor came to her. He put the shoes on her feet and stood leaning next to her, but Jin seemed oblivious to him and her surroundings. Then, just as she had at the Paris Foreign Missions Society, she started dancing in the plaza at Les Invalides. Fear rose in Victor as he watched Jin dance with the birds and the trees and the litter of the plaza. He no longer recognized her as the woman he had fallen in love with. Had she really wandered the streets at dawn like this, for a whole month? Jin would retrace her steps back to the house and collapse into a fitful sleep in the Oriental Room. She seemed unaware of Victor sweeping the strands of hair from her forehead as she slept.

Often the sight of someone being alone is eloquent with the words they're unable to say. Victor watched Jin standing beside the carousel in the square. Carousels were a new fad taking over the streets of Paris. The Champs-Élysées and the Tuileries were noisy with them being ridden by children and hatted ladies. Did Jin want to ride the carousel? She stroked one of the wooden horses. Victor approached her and put her shoes on.

—I'm sorry, Victor!

Victor looked up from his crouched position as Jin whispered to him. It was the first time in the four days he had been following her that he heard her speak. But Jin's face became expressionless again. She turned to the beech tree grove. Gathering her coat around her as if chilled, she slowly began to walk. Victor sprang up and embraced Jin from the back.

—Jin!

Jin continued to head forward.

—Where are you going?

When Victor loosened his grip, Jin tried to walk away again. Victor tightened his hold.

—Where are you going to? I'll take you there instead.

Jin turned and looked up at Victor. Her face was full of clarity.

—To Korea.

Korea? Jin turned away from Victor's surprise and continued to walk away from him.

Where was she going now?

Jin did not remember that she left the house every morning at four, nor that she wandered, barefoot, among the dark streets populated only by stark buildings and the smell of the sewer. She also didn't remember dancing at the Paris Foreign Missions Society or Les Invalides. When Victor told her, she stared at him as if he were describing someone else and answered, "Why would anyone dance there?" Aside from the sleep-walking itself and her inability to remember it, Jin was fine. Rising from her exhausted sleep, she would partake in the breakfast Jeanne prepared them, choose what Victor would wear that day, make the bed, and open the windows to the square to let out the tepid air. She seemed so lucid that Victor almost suspected it was he who was dreaming. When he asked Jeanne after work what Madame had done, she replied that she did ordinary things such as embroider fans, have tea with visitors, or edit Hong Jong-u's manuscript with the help of her French-Korean dictionary. But each dawn, Jin would slip out of bed as if summoned and walk out the front door.

Did she mean to walk to Korea? Did she think, in her sleep, that the courtyard of the Paris Foreign Missions Society or the plaza at Les Invalides were places in the palace of the Joseon court? His thoughts darkened at this juncture. Victor had thought that Jin was content with her life in Paris. He could feel it in her letters to the Queen. He had come across them long ago and was reading them in secret. He found himself unable to stop. Jin apparently wrote letters to the Queen but never sent them. The neatly folded letters, wrapped in linen inside a drawer, detailed weekly Sunday mass at Notre Dame, the July fourteenth festivities on the anniversary of the French Revolution, and included vivid accounts of trains and engines that ran on steam. The letters also revealed a gradual sense of Jin becoming her own person. There seemed to have been an awkwardness of calling herself *I* instead of *your servant*, but now she wrote *I* freely upon the page.

Victor followed Jin with a heavy heart. Guilt makes one look back on one's life. He suddenly remembered Veronica, the woman he had run into again at the minister's ball. Did Jin sense her presence in his life? Watching Jin wander the empty streets at dawn, Victor was lost in self-reproach.

Jin had settled into her life in Paris by learning French history, philosophy, literature, and music from the tutors Victor had hired, soaking it all up like cotton to water. And except for the waltz, Jin's learning had been effortless. She enjoyed going to the balls at City Hall and led the discussions at salons, her cheeks flush with enthusiasm for debate.

She looked peaceful attending mass and listened in with interest on Parisian conversations along the Seine or at cafés. She played chess with Maupassant at a café near the Palais-Royal. Jin's stories of the East told in her inimitable, charming accent breathed fresh new life into Henri Philippe's Explorers Club. Naturally, Victor had thought of Jin as a true Parisian woman.

As for her holing up in the Oriental Room after the miscarriage, he had assumed she would feel like herself again eventually. But Korea? Korea was the country that had oppressed her and forced her obedience. He couldn't believe she wanted to return there and wanted it so much that she wandered the streets of Paris in the night. He tried to remember what had happened in the Bois de Boulogne a month ago.

Spring had brought daily festivities back to the woodland park.

Victor thought Jin would feel better after a picnic there. Upon his return from a five-day trip to Marseilles, Jeanne told him that Jin had not left the Oriental Room during his absence. Victor couldn't help feeling a burst of frustration. What did Jin want him to do? His shame at such feelings made him insist on the picnic. They left the carriage at the entrance of the forest and began to walk. The Bois de Boulogne was as crowded with people as it was with cedar and mulberry. Sunlight streamed through the canopy of Brazilian acacia and banana trees. The spring blooms were vivid with life. Vendors carrying their wares on long sticks sold tricolored flags, and old men played a game of rolling metal balls to knock against colorful wooden ones. Some languidly rode boats on the water, while others gave children horse rides for a few coins. Still others carried large wicker baskets and spread out a picnic on the shores of the lake.

Jin lingered longest at the menagerie. She smiled at an Indian water buffalo that walked backward, and along with the other people threw morsels at the hippos, orangutans, bears, camels, and kangaroos. She tasted ice cream from a vendor who carted a round container and watched horses as they raced along the tracks.

They left the menagerie and followed the forest path up north. Victor had forgotten that this was where members of an African tribe had been brought in. Jin and Victor walked toward a low fence where people were gathered and found that it was an enclosure containing an entire village. There were as many spectators there as the menagerie. Barely clad men jumped about with their spears as if they were hunting. Women with their breasts exposed carried buckets of water balanced on their heads. Their naked children stared back at the staring people, not blinking an eye. Victor had heard they had moved some Africans into the Bois de Boulogne for the amusement of Parisians, but he never dreamed they'd move an entire village. Jin's expression, which had relaxed into amusement at the menagerie, became contorted in pain. A naked child went to the toilet on the grass and wiped himself with a leaf, accompanied by laughter from the onlookers. When a woman in the enclosure comforted a crying child, her bare breasts shaking, the spectators jeered obscenely at her.

—Let's go, Victor.

When Victor looked back, he saw that Jin was already running toward the forest.

He realized his mistake.

Too late, he recalled his own laughter as he watched the people in the enclosure. What Jin hated most were people leering at her as if she were a spectacle. He had told her not to take it to heart, but Jin suffered regardless. She ignored it as much as she could but sometimes murmured, "Did you not say the most highly regarded virtues of this republic were liberty and equality? How highly regarded can they be, when they discriminate and stare so at those who are different?"

Victor could not catch up to her.

She wasn't at the entrance to the park. He waited for her in the carriage, but she did not come. The picnic was ruined by his having to search for her through the crowds. He finally found her at sunset, sitting on a bench that overlooked the lake. He was so exhausted from his search that he had no thoughts left in his head, not even the sliver of irritation he had felt at having their rare outing ruined. Not even his worry that Jin had suffered an accident by one of those reckless young carriage drivers who seemed to think they were at a race. When Victor sat down beside her, Jin leaned against him. She seemed as exhausted as he was. Victor held her shoulders with one arm.

—Gillin.

She hadn't called him by his Korean name in a long time.

—Why did you not keep your promise to me?

Victor did not ask her what she meant. So many broken promises. He hadn't even kept the promise he made in Korea, of holding a wedding for her when they reached Paris.

—You told me we would go to Plancy. Together.

He had said this. He thought he could finally face the town where Marie had drowned, as long as Jin was by his side.

—Why did you not take me there? Don't you want to go with me anymore?

—Things just happened that way.

—Would it have been different if the baby had lived?

—We can have another baby.

—No, we shall never have a baby together. You don't know this, but in Korea . . . this has happened before.

That evening, as they rode the carriage home, they did not say a word to each other. It was the first time that had happened.

The sleepwalking Jin stopped at a cemetery. It looked almost like a park. The people on the Rue de Babylone walked their dogs there around dawn and dusk. Jin pushed through a low gate and entered. Birds sleeping in the trees fluttered away in surprise. When Jin first discovered the cemetery, she had indeed thought it was a park. A boy wearing a pilgrim's cape was rolling a hoop. The boy's mother sat on a bench underneath a parasol, reading a book. Jin was surprised to hear from Victor that it was a cemetery. He showed her the weathered headstones hidden in the long grass, standing among the shorter trees: graveyards of the unknown who died more than two centuries ago. The letters on the headstones were so weathered that it was hard to read the names. Some headstones stood with no discernable letters at all.

Was she looking for a place to dance?

Whenever she came to a clearing, Jin would circle within as if to test the feel of it. Then, she would reject it and move on. She took a full turn and came across the bench where the reading woman once sat, her child playing with the hoop nearby. Jin sat down.

The roses blooming between the headstones gave off a sweet scent like that of children's skin.

Jin slowly got up from the bench.

She stood where the boy with the hoop had been, raised her arms, and turned. Victor thought she would dance again, but all she did was turn and turn. Then, too dizzy to continue, she collapsed to the ground.

—Jin!

Victor broke from his observation and ran to her. His hand clutched her shoulder.

—Are you all right?

He helped her to her feet and guided her to the bench.

—Victor.

Victor listened intently, ready for her to say something, but nothing came. Jin seemed to have fallen asleep. Fearing the coldness of the dew, Victor hoisted her onto his back. He remembered how the women of Korea would carry their children on their backs. Jin drowsily draped her arms around his neck.

—Who . . . who is she?

She sounded as if she were talking in her sleep.

—Who?

But Victor's question was met with silence.

Was she talking about Veronica? Victor adjusted his hold on Jin as he carried her home. He knew Veronica from before he was posted to China. He hadn't tried to hide the fact that he'd seen her again, nor was he avoiding the topic. It was just never a good time to bring her up. Veronica was the only child of noble parents who died in a carriage accident. She had survived the crash herself and grown up headstrong. Victor loved that about her, but her strength was also the reason their relationship could not last. Veronica had been afraid of marriage. When he received his orders to go to China, she told him that she wouldn't follow him. He had noted she hadn't changed much when he ran into her at the minister's ball. She was married to a baron for a time but was alone again now and as personable as ever. He continued to run into her at dinners. He later learned she was purposefully seeking him out when he wasn't with Jin. Supposedly it was because his feelings toward Veronica were largely indifferent, unlike his memories of Marie in Plancy, a state of affairs that stimulated her interest.

A white fog rolled over the dawn streets.

Victor walked through the fog with Jin on his back, his heart heavier than his load.

How could a person weigh so little? And yet her body was warming his back. He frowned as he thought of the promises he had made to her in Korea. He had been unable to convince his mother, who told him he could marry Jin only if he were ready to throw away the Collin de Plancy name, which they had clung to even when they were thrown out of Plancy. She had said he would be better off marrying Veronica. His mother regarded any attempt to wed Jin as a de facto resignation from the Ministry of Foreign Affairs. She could not have helped feeling guilty about his made-up aristocratic family name being a stumbling block whenever he was up for a promotion at the Ministry. Jin was curious about Victor's mother and wished to meet her, but his mother left her apartment in Paris as soon as she heard Jin was coming to Paris. She had not visited them once in the past three years.

Victor carried Jin home and laid her down on their bed. He thought she was sleeping, but she opened her eyes, slid off of the bed, and lay down on the floor. Unlike Korean floors, the floor in their Parisian apartment was not heated. Victor laid her down on the bed again, but she came back down to the floor and curled up into a fetal position.

Victor covered her with the sheets from the bed and sat on the edge of the mattress, looking down at her.

Quasimodo appeared, breaking through Victor's sad mood.

The cat stretched out next to the sleeping Jin's head and looked up at him. Victor, who was about to lie down on the bed, lay down on the floor next to Jin instead. Quasimodo stared at both of them. Victor gently turned Jin onto her back and lay her head on his arm. Jin moved closer toward him. Victor turned to his side and embraced her. She felt delicate in his arms. He ran a hand down her back and stopped. He could feel each vertebra against the palm of his hand. The once beautiful curve of her back was turning into hard edges. The chill from the floor made him pull her closer toward him.

Victor wished Maupassant were still alive. The author would tell her stories about shooting guns in the Franco-Prussian War, being taught by the notoriously strict Flaubert, the boat rides with friends, and the histrionic interferences of his mother. Jin had felt sorry for him whenever he worried about his worsening eyesight. What else could the two of them have talked about? Victor wondered. Maupassant might have understood why Jin wandered the streets of Paris at dawn. But Maupassant was no more. The author had attempted suicide by cutting his wrists on a beach in Nice. Jin was devastated at the news. *He was even worried about going bald. Please help him.* He was eventually institutionalized at a hospital in the outskirts of Paris, and Jin would take the carriage there to see him. She always took the French-Korean dictionary with her. Victor wanted her to go with Jeanne, but Jin went alone. He would ask, "What do you do when you meet him?" She would answer, "I read him the translations Hong Jong-u left me."

—He then edits the parts that sound awkward. I also teach him words in Korean.

—Is he lucid enough for that?

Jin seemed surprised at Victor's question. She said she didn't know why he was held there when he seemed perfectly clear-headed. *No one seems to visit him anymore, not even his family.* Then one day, she came home without having seen him. The author had refused to see anyone. He never did leave that hospital on his own feet. Jin read his obituary in the papers in silence. She seemed surprisingly relieved at his death. She only asked, in a sad voice, a single question: "How old was he?" Victor replied, "Forty-three." Jin murmured the number to herself. Victor thought she took it well, and soon forgot about the author. Jin did not go to his funeral, nor did she visit his grave. When Victor suggested it, she firmly declined, shaking her head. But now that he thought about it, Jin's state had begun to worsen after Maupassant's death. She distanced herself from the translation she had been so eager to show Maupassant. It finally occurred to Victor that this was when Jin began to spend her days in the Oriental Room or an armchair in the salon. He recalled her murmuring, "Victor, I think I can understand Maupassant now," a wisp of a voice coming from the depths of the armchair.

Victor stroked her forehead.

Her weakness wasn't the only thing he discovered as he followed her for four days. Victor found himself living his life before meeting Jin. She was the center of every thought he had since the moment he met her, so much so that he surprised himself. But now . . . how she still insisted on sleeping on the floor, even after the trouble of creating a Korean room for her in the house . . . he wondered if he had returned to who he was before . . .

Whenever Jin rose from their bed, Victor had assumed she was going to the Oriental Room. He could not have imagined she was wandering the streets of Paris if Jeanne hadn't told him. Victor sighed and brought his lips to her cold mouth, kissing her in her sleep.

Not long after, Hong Jong-u assassinated Kim Okgyun in Shanghai, and Paris became swept up in the Dreyfus Affair.

PART FOUR

1
Reunion

It took fifty days for the voyage beginning in Marseille to pass the Suez Canal, Colombo, Saigon, and Shanghai before docking at Jaemulpo.

Spring had come to Jaemulpo, and in contrast to when they left, it was bustling with the Japanese. Japanese signs dotted the storefronts, and there seemed to be more Japanese people on the streets than Koreans. Jin imagined she heard more Japanese being spoken than Korean during their two-day stay in the harbor town. China, which had once treated Korea as a vassal state and declared itself the greatest power in the East, had lost a war with Japan, an underdog keen on using Korea as a platform for its ambitions. China had been no match for Japan's steam-engine armada and ceded the Liaodong Peninsula to Japan. This allowed the Japanese to invade China's shores and penetrate deep into the mainland. England supported Japan while China asked for Russia's help. Korea remained caught in the middle with no escape.

There were new oil streetlamps in front of the French legation building.

The view of the Russian legation building caught Victor's eye. It hadn't changed in four years. He couldn't help but notice it whenever he was by the gate of the French legation. The Russian legation building was built in the Russian style and stood in stark contrast to the black-tiled roofs of the Korean houses that surrounded it. There was a limit to remodeling Korean houses to suit the legations' purposes. But that was also their aesthetic advantage; one could change the doors and put in glass windows, but the roof and structure still made them immediately recognizable as Korean. The French legation building had been changed as well. The interpreter Paul Choi led them to their temporary lodgings, a new Western-style annex to the left of the main building.

Guérin, who had been acting legate before Victor's successor Frandin arrived, was now in China. Frandin had returned to France at the news of his mother's death, and Lefèvre was acting legate in his place. The King requested that the French government appoint a new legate, but the seat was currently unfilled. It was a sign of how little progress had been made in France's relations with Korea as opposed to China or Japan.

Victor had taken leave to come to Korea for the sake of treating Jin's sleepwalking. Aside from her wandering the streets at dawn, Jin had seemed to feel more like herself again. She carefully edited Hong Jong-u's manuscript and saw to its successful publication by the Guimet Museum and held a party in the salon when the book came out. Victor had Jin accompany him on his business trips, thinking a change of scenery would help cure her sleepwalking. But wherever they went, Jin rose at 4 A.M. and left their room as if called by someone. She would have no memory of anything that had happened, so it was pointless to discuss it with her. The doctor said visiting Korea might do a world of good.

The cook and the Jindo dog were the first to welcome them back. Even with the other changes in the staff, the dog still lived in the courtyard and the same cook worked for the legation. As soon as Jin and Victor entered the courtyard, the dog, on the lookout for moles, bounded toward them. It seemed to remember how it used to go running with Victor every morning, and jumped up at Victor's face with joy, and circled Jin in a friendly, familiar manner. As the two settled down in the annex, the Jindo dog also moved to that side of the legation. Lefèvre's young son burst into tears when the dog refused to come back at his command. Jin comforted him, saying they were not going to stay forever. But the dog insisted on living near the annex, so its hutch and food bowl had to be moved there.

It took days for Jin to recover from the long voyage.

Jin had been fine when they had journeyed to France, while it was Victor who had fallen sick. But she wasn't fine this time. The cook made her congee for every meal. She said she hoped Jin would recover soon so they could go to the docks at Mapo to buy fish like they used to.

It was a full moon.

Victor did not fall asleep on the fourth night at the legation. He watched Jin. He had tried to watch her since the first night, but he couldn't fight the journey's fatigue. Blue light shone through the window. He wanted to know if coming to Korea, indeed, had done a world of good for her as the doctor predicted.

His old memories of her had flooded back as soon as they touched land. The passion he felt for her since the moment he saw her on the Silk Stream bridge. The joy of seeing her again at the banquet, his forgetting to clap for her dancing as he sat transfixed. The day Jin walked into the legation alone, his running toward her to embrace and kiss her. Her dismay at this strange greeting, and her composure despite her dismay. His anguish as he watched the light in her room from the phoenix tree during the days she awaited word from court. He had forgotten these moments when he was in France, but now they felt like yesterday. He sighed, thinking that despite the dreaded voyage back to France, it was a good thing they had come again to Korea.

Moonlight fell on Jin's face. All was calm, aside from the occasional movement of the dog. Jin in Paris had always slunk back to the floor to sleep, but here in Korea, she had no trouble sleeping on a bed. Her face was peaceful in the blue glow. Did the return cure her sleepwalking? As the gray light of dawn broke over the fading moonlight, he felt a measure of relief. Sleep started to overtake him. He lay on his back and was about to close his eyes.

—Gillin.

Jin quietly called out Victor's Korean name.

—Are you awake?

He turned to look at her, slipped his arm under her head, and held her close to him. Jin curled into his embrace.

—What were you thinking about so hard just now?

—You weren't asleep?

—Thank you, Gillin.

—For what?

—For coming here with me.

—Of course, I'm here with you.

—No. You could have sent me on alone.

—Why would I send you away alone?

But he could have. He never said it out loud, but the thought had crossed his mind. Jin was always able to read his mind. It hadn't been easy, taking such a long leave of absence. It would not have been possible if the minister, who was indifferent to Korea, hadn't cared about Jin. Victor kept stroking her hair. There was a hint of sandalwood in her thick black hair. A scent that he had thought was lost in Paris, but now returned.

—Concentrate on feeling better. Then we can go to the orphanage in Gondangol and visit all the people you wish to see. And you must want to know how Korea has changed since you left.

Jin lifted her head and kissed him softly on the lips. Her dry lips had turned moist again.

Broken promises create more promises.

—When we return to Paris, let's get married at City Hall. We'll invite our friends and hold a ball. We'll have enough food and drink for even the people we don't know.

Jin laughed softly.

—Are you laughing?

—Victor, I don't care about wedding ceremonies. It's enough that you came here with me to Korea.

It was true. She had been disappointed in Victor, who ceased all mention of marriage once they arrived in France. But she changed her mind after hearing about his family's banishment from Plancy and the scandal that had come with his name. She could almost understand his mother's position.

—How long has it been since I've heard you laugh?

—Did I laugh just now?

Victor pulled her closer. Her body was warm. He slid his hand onto her breast. Jin looked closely at each feature of Victor's face in the dawn light. She lightly touched with her fingertips his eyelids, nose, and mouth. To her, this man whose face she was touching seemed familiar and unfamiliar at the same time. Victor had always been like that to her. A man who never raised his voice and was always hardworking, thoughtful, and generous. He was a conscientious archivist when he recorded his observations, and a loving collector when he examined his books, celadon, and antiques. But she also knew him as a shrewd and level-headed strategist who would do anything to further French interests.

—Do you remember the scent pouch that I slipped into *Les Misérables* as a sign of my acceptance of your love?

The pouch with the red peony embroidery. How could he ever forget it?

—I've embroidered a lizard next to the peony. The lizard in your paper. I put it in the dresser in the Oriental Room.

That wasn't all she had put in there. She had also slipped in the ring that Victor had put on her finger the first night they spent together.

—Your watch is in the drawer of the nightstand.

—. . .

—Don't wear your morning coat to dinners in the winter. You looked cold.

Victor turned on his side toward her.

—Why do you speak as if you're not going to return to Paris?

Jin stroked Victor's chest.

—Because you never know what might happen, Victor.

Victor gripped Jin's hand. He sat up and looked down at her.

—What on earth are you thinking of doing?

Bathed in the weak early light, Jin lay her head down on his lap instead of answering. Victor couldn't have known. The reason she hadn't left the legation in four days was not that she was unwell. It was her dress. She didn't know whether she should dress as she did in Paris or change into a Korean dress or what to do with her hair . . . everything had to be thought anew.

It pained her to think that she was not the same person she had been when she left Korea.

This pain had begun as soon as they arrived at Jaemulpo.

The harbor was busier than when they had left. Everyone stared at her, Japanese, Korean, Chinese alike. It was the same when they stayed in Jaemulpo for two days and in the inns on the way to the city. She thought at first that it was because she was with Victor, but they stared at her even when she was alone. Jin was used to it, but when a little child suckling at her mother's breast on the porch of one of the inns looked at her as if she were a foreigner, she felt more pained than ever before. She realized she was a spectacle in Korea as well as France.

Did the dog think the coming of the dawn meant going on a run? The sound of its whining carried into their bedroom.

—Would you like to take a walk?

Victor lowered his face and rubbed his cheek against Jin's.

—And do visit Gondangol today. You've missed it so much. I'm going to see Müllendorf in the morning and hear what's gone on since we left.

Jin hesitated, but Victor managed to persuade her. The two changed and came out into the courtyard. The Jindo dog came up to them and waited for Victor to put on his shoes. When Victor came down from the porch, the Jindo dog eagerly encircled him. It was early, and the main legation building was silent. The two left by a side gate next to the annex.

The scent of fresh mugwort and pine assaulted their senses. There was a hint of the overturned earth from the vegetable patch. Jin lowered the shawl around her shoulders and breathed in deeply. A breeze brushed past her earlobes. The first Korean spring breeze she had felt in four years.

—Monsieur Collin de Plancy!

They turned and saw Paul Choi standing at the main gate. Jin's vision filled with the green leaves on the phoenix tree, the tree itself much taller since she last saw it. Paul Choi strode toward them.

—Do you always come to work this early?

—I spent last night at the legation. The change in scene made me get up early. I thought I'd come out for a walk.

The Jindo dog had bounded away from them and was looking back. Paul Choi smiled.

—They say Jindo dogs follow only one master all their lives. It must be true. It's clearly much happier now that you're here.

Victor grinned as he ran toward the dog. The dog must have remembered their runs after all, for it began running as well as leading Victor away from the other two.

—You surprised me at first. I thought you were someone else. Have you managed to rest a bit, my lady?

—Have I changed so much?

—Well . . . How should I say this? You seem like a different person. Perhaps it's the clothing. Would you like your old clothes? I believe the cook stored them for you.

Would I be able to wear them again? Jin couldn't answer that.

—Much has changed in Korea. I don't know if it's for good or bad. Japan's influence has grown in leaps and bounds since you left. There are Japanese swordsmen sauntering around the fortress as if they own the city.

Jin drew her shawl over her shoulders again.

Her heart was a confused mix of familiarity and sadness as she stood there in the spring breeze. It was the same feeling she had in Jaemulpo when she watched a mother nursing her child as she sold fresh fish at the market. Before she realized it, Jin had stretched out a hand to stroke the baby's sun-drenched head. The emptiness in her heart made her turn her gaze to the barges on the harbor and the dark seagulls that flew over them. It seemed that the King and Queen, who had tried to play the ambitions of the powerful foreign countries against each other for the sake of bringing stability to Korea, were still in a precarious position.

—A powerless country we are, being tossed to and fro at the whim of foreign powers . . . not to mention the power struggle between the Queen and the Regent, which could only end with one of them dying. Neither cares about the people, only power. There was a peasant uprising down south. It spread like wildfire.

Jin sighed deeply. Was Sister Jacqueline, who had already told her about the uprising, in Penang by now?

—The people suffer under corrupt officials and taxes. They can barely grow enough to eat themselves. The peasants of the uprising were pushing an idea of equality. That all people were the same under the sky. The people were on their side. Their leader was caught and executed, which ended the uprising, but resentment remains. Jeon Bongjun was caught by the Japanese when his subordinate gave him away, but he remained steadfast under torture. Even the Japanese were taken aback. He told them to display his head on a pike at a crossroads in the city. To sprinkle his blood on the clothes of passersby. He wanted the resistance to continue past his death . . . What a mess the country is in.

—. . .

—A man named Hong Jong-u killed Kim Okgyun in Shanghai. He preserved the corpse and brought it back on a boat. He's a hero now. And Kim Okgyun's body was posthumously beheaded at Noryangjin.

Jin had already heard this from Régamey in Paris. The news surprised everyone that Hong had known there. Was this why he left so suddenly? Jin felt she would suffocate. She widened her shoulders and straightened her back. She could see Victor and the dog running back toward them.

—Monsieur Collin de Plancy asked me not to tell you about Hong Jong-u . . .

Paul Choi muttered this, looking worried.

—What happened to him?

—After his return, there was an examination for selecting officials. They say it was held as a formality, just to give Hong Jong-u a position. The Queen herself conferred officialdom on him. Not to mention a house and slaves.

He hesitated before continuing.

—Things are not looking well. No one knows what the country is coming to. During the uprising, the Queen feared a repeat of the events of the Year of the Black Horse and called in Chinese troops, while the Regent, who used to hate the Japanese, befriended them . . . and they say court is nothing but frivolity and parties now.

He glanced at Jin's face when he said this.

—The Queen favors the daughter of a Japanese woman named So Chonsil. Some say this daughter is a spy. So Chonsil's daughter is said to have ordered several portraits of the Queen to be drawn, but to what end no one knows.

Portraits of the Queen? Jin looked back at Paul Choi in wonder. The Queen was not one to allow her portrait to be drawn. She had even objected to sitting for a photograph.

—One could hardly walk the streets when Kim Okgyun's body was being decapitated. They say someone called him a traitor and pulled out his liver and ate it. And there wasn't a Japanese person who did not pass by his head on display and not shed a tear. Then came a cholera epidemic, and the dead were so numerous that no one knows how many died. Quarantines were issued, and an edict went out against eating anything raw, but all for naught. Be careful out there. We live in a time where the King is being told seven different things by seven different courtiers.

Jin was silent. Before Victor and the dog could reach them again, she turned and walked back into the legation.

In the afternoon, Jin saw Victor off as he left to meet Müllendorf, before leaving the legation herself.

The woman Suh stared at Jin for a long time when the former court dancer entered the orphanage grounds. Suh couldn't believe her eyes.

The orphanage was the same, but it was clear there were more children than before. As the children crowded around Jin in her Western dress, Suh managed to wake from her trance and introduce the children one by one, each child calling out, "Here!" upon hearing his or her name. Jin thought she recognized some of them as her former students, but they had grown so much that she couldn't be sure.

Suh shooed the children away and brought Jin to the building in the back.

—The outbreak last year brought in many children. Most of them lost both of their parents at the same time. When they first came here, they'd do nothing but sit on the branches of the date tree or the porch . . . but children will be children. Look how playful they are now.

Jin remembered what Paul Choi had told her that morning as she looked back at the children. They had already scattered and left. *A disease that started with a fever and coughs, ending in two days with death.*

—I heard there was cholera. Was the orphanage affected?

—Thankfully, we didn't lose any children to that. By the mercy of God.

—Bomi is the only child I really recognize from my time.

—The ones who reached thirteen were sent to a French school by Bishop Mutel. Bishop Blanc had left a special request for the children before he passed. The plan is to educate them for a while and allow the ones who want to be priests to continue. Some of the children followed priests who were going to Japan. They promised to educate them there.

Suh's room was as austere as Jin remembered it.

A length of white linen hung on the side of the room as a cover for her clothing; she did not even own a common wardrobe or dresser. Inside a large basket was a jacket that was being sewn. Underneath the jacket was an assortment of needlework tools. Jin looked up to see a single shelf with rolled, uncut fabric, standing in a row.

—Do you still sew all the children's garments yourself?

—The nights are long . . . and I've nothing else to do.

Suh's room made Jin feel she had truly returned to Korea. The floor, once a light yellow, was darker with age and sporting a few burnt spots. Against Suh's protestations, Jin sat Suh down and bestowed upon her a deep homecoming bow. The floor felt warm as Jin's forehead touched it. Had she interrupted Suh in her laundry when she arrived? When Suh approached Jin on her knees and clasped Jin's hands, the old woman's hands felt cold to the touch. Jin gripped Suh's hands in return and caressed them. Suh's palms were as rough as tree bark. Suh extracted her hands and wrapped Jin's in hers. Bomi, who had been peering at them through the crack in the door, wiped away a tear and softly closed the door behind her.

—What has happened? Are you here for good?

When Jin didn't answer, Suh reached out and stroked Jin's face.

—Seeing you is like a dream. I thought we would never meet again. Have you come alone?

Suh's moist eyes were full of concern.

—No, I'm here with him. We have to go back.

Suh nodded.

—Have dinner with us. Yeon always comes around sunset. The children love him so much. Lady Suh might come as well. She's a sponsor of this orphanage. She comes once every ten days, and I'm sure she'll come today.

The woman Suh still faithfully observed the proper honorifics when referring to her younger sister. Jin took a closer look at Suh's face. It had always been a small one but now seemed smaller still. The wrinkles near her eyes seemed to almost close them altogether, and her hair was now half white.

She must have fallen asleep.

Jin lowered her arm from her forehead. She opened her eyes, and the room was dark. Had she slept until the sun set? She had sat knee-to-knee with Suh, deep in talk, when Jin coughed. Suh said she had just made some *shikhye* rice drink and went to get it, during which Jin must have dozed off. The floor was so warm with the Korean-style *ondol* heating, and she had laid down on it, just for a moment. The heat had immediately seeped through her entire body. It felt like a moment ago, but a good deal of time must have passed. Suh had come and gone; there was an old wooden tray with a white bowl of *shikhye* on it. Suh also must have taken off Jin's silk hat, carefully placed it next to the tray, and covered her with a blanket. Jin sat up and brought the bowl to her lips. She smelled its sweet scent. Jin drank it without leaving a single drop. She licked up the grains of rice that remained stuck to the bowl. She sat and stared at the bowl for a long time before standing up.

She was carrying the tray and bowl to the kitchen when she stopped.

Eight children were gathered underneath the date tree that was just beginning to sprout green leaves. A man, his back to Jin, stood facing the children. Each child held a bamboo flute in their hands. Jin wondered what was going on until she heard the sound of the man's flute. She immediately straightened her back. The children repeated what the man played, their notes all over the place. There was always one child who held on for a beat too long. But the music continued. The children's fingers seemed to dance on the flutes in the dim light. Jin thought of the musicians at Bon Marché and smiled. Sometimes the attendants would form musical groups and hold concerts after the store was closed, making an impromptu stage of the floor. They were very good. Jin once went with Jeanne to watch Vincent, who played the cymbals.

The music the children played was familiar. Jin's eyes trembled. It was a composition that Yeon used to play for her when they were growing up in Banchon. The children were so cacophonous that she hadn't been aware of it at first, but the man's melody was clear and true. The song ended as Jin approached the children. The man held up his index finger, meaning they should play it one more time. The second time around, their sound was more unified. By their fifth try, they were more than serviceable. Then the man did a solo. Could the bamboo flute make such a sound? Then Jin realized he wasn't playing the smaller flutes like the children were. This was the *daegeum*. Because the man had his back to them, she hadn't seen him switch instruments. *What an amazing sound.*

The children, who had been so serious as a united orchestra, began dancing joyfully to his tune.

—What fun you're having!

Bomi had come out of the kitchen at the sound of the *daegeum*, but when she saw Jin, she quickly took the tray from her hands. Jin smiled at Bomi. It must take great effort to play the *daegeum* like that. The children jumped and spun, stood on their heads and flipped backward. Bomi shouted, "Be careful!" The children laughed and stuck out their tongues. Jin walked toward them. She wanted to see the face of the man who could make children dance so. The man didn't notice she was approaching, as his eyes were closed in concentration. The children seemed to know the music well. Aside from the dancing children, there were others who had closed their eyes and were enjoying it silently, and those who clung to his clothes as they looked up at him.

Yeon's *daegeum* was said to make rain fall in the middle of a drought.

In May, Yeon would be off to the marshes to find good reeds. Every year he searched for the best examples, peeled back the protective membrane, and attached them to the *daegeum* to produce the perfect vibration for its sound. But the music that made the children dance was a different kind. It wasn't court music or folk music. The man playing the *daegeum* opened his eyes and met Jin's gaze. When his music stopped, so did the children's dancing. The man's eyes and forehead seemed to form a grimace before his focus wholly concentrated on Jin.

—Silverbell!

Yeon lowered his flute and called out to Jin. Bomi was so surprised that she dropped the tray, the bowl rolling on the ground.

—Sobaek is talking!

Jin slowly moved through the crowd of children as she walked up to Yeon. Yeon stared at her, not moving until Jin gathered him in her arms. *How could I not have recognized you?* Jin buried her face in his chest. She could hear Yeon's hard breathing. It made her remember the moment when she had embraced Maupassant at the morgue. She held Yeon for a long time as Bomi quickly picked up the tray and bowl and rushed back to the kitchen, and the children crowded around them in a group hug.

They lit an oil lamp in Suh's room, where the three of them sat around the low meal table that was brought in.

Jin stared at the table. White bowls filled with steaming white rice mixed with potatoes. There was fermented soybean soup, with the fragrant bean paste mixed in with rice water and boiled with shepherd's purse. There was also lettuce, wild rocambole mixed with sliced turnip and soy sauce, sautéed fatsia sprouts, well-aged kimchi, and a mugwort *jeon* omelet. Most of these were offerings from the warm spring earth.

—Let's eat.

Jin and Yeon hesitated despite Suh's suggestion. Suh picked up a piece of mugwort *jeon* with her chopsticks and placed it on Jin's rice.

—It will get cold. Do eat . . . Remember how you used to love spring food?

Jin picked up the piece of *jeon* with her chopsticks and slipped it into her mouth. The lovely taste of young spring mugwort filled her mouth. While Jin ate it, Yeon placed another piece on Jin's rice. The three of them laughed. It was just as they had done when they lived together. Once the slight but wily shoots of green mugwort broke through the plains of Banchon that were frozen all winter, Suh would go out with her basket to harvest them and make *jeon*. Little Jin would insist on helping her with the flouring of the dried mugwort and end up with flour all over her forehead and hair. When the lightly fried *jeon* made it to the table, a scene like the one they had just enacted would occur. Suh would place a piece of *jeon* on Jin's rice, then Yeon would place one.

Jin spread her rice with her spoon and poured in some of the bean paste soup. Yeon was taken aback by how quickly Jin mixed the rice with the soup after having hesitated before the food for so long. Even Suh, as she lifted her spoon to eat, was surprised at the speed with which Jin was eating.

—Don't eat so quickly. You'll get sick.

Suh stood up.

—I'll get you another bowl.

Her mouth full of soup and rice, Jin could not object as Suh opened the door and left. Yeon slid his bowl of soup toward her. Only then did Jin swallow the food in her mouth and put her spoon down.

The things that move the heart never change.

The first thing Jin did as she stepped onto the grounds of their old Banchon house was touch the bark of the apricot tree. Tiny white flowers like snowflakes dotted its branches. Befitting of flowers that had endured the winds of winter, the blooms seemed modest and shy. Jin had been listening during nights when the cold wind blew. It was said that when the winds were loud, there could be no apricot blossoms; hence, the scent of apricot flowers was to be listened for, not smelled.

She remembered how Blanc and Yeon had stood underneath that very apricot tree that spring evening when little Jin returned home from court on the back of Lady Attendant Lee. Lady Attendant Lee was so surprised that she fell over backward, causing Jin to bite her lip. That was the first time she had seen Yeon, who wore his old gray rags. She remembered the blood she tasted as she stared at him.

Jin stood underneath the apricot tree and watched the lights go on, one by one, in the woman Suh's sewing room, Blanc's old room where he taught her French, and the room Yeon had lived in. Suh had asked Yeon to accompany Jin back to the French legation after dinner. They had walked toward the legation when Jin changed direction to Banchon. Yeon wordlessly followed her lead. Jin walked slowly through Banchon. The children came out to their gates and stared at her. The people lined up at the butcher's also turned to look at her. The women washing clothes at the stream seemed to think, *Who could that be?* No one recognized Jin. They greeted Yeon with a nod and continued to stare until they were out of sight.

—"Does anyone live in the house now?"

They were the first words Jin spoke to Yeon since she'd come back.

Yeon nodded. Only then did Jin step away from the tree and enter the house. A house falls quickly into disrepair without a constant human presence. Jin looked into every room where Yeon had lit a lamp. They were all empty save for the room Yeon used, where a futon was neatly folded in the corner. She peered into the yard in back where Suh had once heated water and washed the boy Yeon in a large earthenware jar. Bamboo leaves still whispered in the spring breeze. The lamps made the house seem cozy despite its emptiness.

After Jin examined the house, she came to where Yeon sat on the edge of the porch and sat beside him. Jin recalled the letter she had received through Sister Jacqueline. *I bought the house in Banchon where we spent our childhood together . . . Please send us word, somehow, to reassure us of your well-being.* She had kept the letter in the Oriental Room and read it again and again. He called Suh "Mother." And mentioned that Suh didn't know he bought the house.

Jin opened her bag and took out a long leather pouch. She put it on Yeon's lap.

—It's an oboe. A French wind instrument. It's a much older instrument than a flute or clarinet.

Jin wanted to say more but paused. It was useless to talk in terms of flutes or clarinets, as Yeon would never have seen either. She had asked Vincent at Bon Marché to procure an oboe for her. She was happy to have bought something with the money she made from making embroidered fans. She wouldn't need that money in Korea, so she put the rest in a jar and placed it in Jeanne's room before leaving Paris. She'd thought of Yeon when she had first seen an oboe being played, by a street musician at the entrance to Luxembourg Garden. Yeon loosened the strings and took out the boxwood oboe.

—There's music inside.

Yeon had learned hymns from Blanc, so Western musical notation was not foreign to him. He turned the oboe this way and that and tried blowing on it. A squawk emerged from the reed and Yeon quickly put it down, with a smile.

Jin leaned her head against Yeon's shoulder.

Yeon again tried the instrument, which resembled the Chinese *guan*, bringing the mouthpiece to his lips. It was sensitive and high-toned. The reed made a different sound each time. A sound like tearing paper, which changed to something like a note. Yeon thought that, with an instrument like this, his sound wouldn't be buried in an ensemble, when he paused and set the oboe down gently on his lap. Jin had fallen asleep against his shoulder. Surely it was an uncomfortable position, but he could hear the change in her breathing.

Frozen still, Yeon looked out at the apricot tree.

There was once a wandering swordsman who called that tree by a different name: *homunmok*. The swordsman was one of Suh's lodgers. He called the tree *homunmok*, but Suh and Yeon called the man Homunmok, as he never told them his name. They didn't know how he came to be a vagabond, but he stayed in their house for a year. It took them some time to learn that he was a swordsman. Suh was wary at first because he was dressed like a Chinese person. When she learned Homunmok had been a swordsman in the old army before the new one with its modern weapons took over, she made Yeon kneel before him and begged him to teach Yeon how to use a sword. Suh was always clothing those who owned nothing and inviting all sorts of strangers into the house to give them a warm meal; Yeon was so used to Suh giving to others that it was strange to see her beg for something. Homunmok was silent at first but, four days later, he asked why she wanted a mute to learn sword fighting. Suh replied without hesitation that his being mute was precisely the reason. From that day on, Homunmok had Yeon run with him every morning through the bamboo and pine forest of Banchon. They endured cold water training together at the stream and would sit still and meditate for hours. Sometimes Homunmok would disappear without a trace and Yeon would wander the mountain paths at night alone. It was said that to handle the sword, one first and foremost needed to have his wits about him, second to which one required great strength. And he always needed to have the right heart. One could handle the sword only when one had these three things. But regardless of Suh's intention with Yeon learning the sword, and regardless of what Homunmok taught him about mindfulness, the only thing Yeon thought of when he trained was Jin. If the sword was to benefit a mute like him, then he was convinced it would benefit Jin too. A year later, Homunmok wanted to leave Banchon with Yeon, to become swordsmen together who used their skill for good. But Yeon did not follow him.

He sighed deeply and looked down at Jin.

To not have hope is harder than to have it.

The woman he thought he'd never see again. The woman he always tried not to love. He thought he was hallucinating when he saw Jin that afternoon standing among the children. He couldn't believe she was here, not even when she walked through the children and embraced him. It wasn't because of the satin hat or the leather shoes or her Western dress. He was simply too astonished to see her in Korea to return her greeting. Only when he saw her mix the fermented soybean soup into her rice did he think this was really Jin. His heart was arguing between the hour growing later and his regret at having to wake her. Yeon listened closely to the sound of her breathing.

The dawn light was breaking when Jin opened her eyes.

It took her a moment to realize she had spent the night leaning on Yeon's shoulder while sitting on the porch of the house she grew up in. As she avoided Yeon's gaze, Yeon took out a fountain pen from his pocket. It was the one Victor had given him. He fished out the small notebook hanging on a string around his neck from inside his tunic and began writing in it.

You were so deep asleep I couldn't bear to wake you.

—Where do you get the ink for that?

Yeon wrote again.

The nuns give it to me.

Jin regarded his writing before she stood up. She thought of Victor, who had gone to see Müllendorf. How he must have waited for her in the night. When she reached the French legation with the hem of her dress damp with dew, Victor was standing at the side gate to their annex, waiting for her. The Jindo dog, which stood waiting with Victor, bounded up to her as she approached.

2

A Changed Face

The Queen was playing a throwing game with some lady attendants in the palace garden.

There were two teams. Ten steps away was a bronze urn with handles on each side. The game involved throwing arrows into the urn or the loop of the handles. The first to throw 120 arrows into the targets won the game. Cheers resounded in the garden as someone managed to hit a target. Jin listened closely for the sound of the Queen's voice. The Queen playing a throwing game? It was unthinkable, but Victor, who had never seen the game before, was already regarding the activity with interest.

—What are they doing?

—A throwing game. There are winners and losers. Those who win are rewarded, and those who lose must suffer a penalty.

Lady Suh's reply was so firm that Victor dared not ask her any more questions. Lady Suh had a grim expression. Jin used to play the throwing game with the Dowager Consort Cheolin when she was a little girl. Whenever the young Jin managed to throw her arrow into a target, the normally reserved dowager consort would clap her hands and cheer. Jin so loved watching her laugh that she would practice with Yeon using sticks and a bottle. The Queen did not enjoy this game. She used to keep her distance. While the young dowager consorts outranked the Queen, the Queen was still more powerful in practice, so the mood of the throwing games tended to be careful. The Queen used to say, "I would sooner read another book than play that silly game." Seeing as the urn was filled with arrows, the game must have been going on for a long time.

—I see you may win again today.

Jin raised her head to see who it was the Queen so generously praised. The one who had just thrown an arrow into the urn was not a court lady but a Japanese woman in a kimono. Jin gave Lady Suh a questioning look, and Lady Suh replied that this was So Chonsil's daughter, the one who had the favor of the Queen. So Chonsil's daughter? Jin recalled Paul Choi telling her that she had commissioned scores of the Queen's portraits. She couldn't make out her face at this distance, but the kimono made her stand out from the crowd. Everyone was absorbed in the game, unaware that Lady Suh and Jin were approaching. Jin spotted her old roommate Soa. Jin's eyes trembled and her mouth almost broke into a smile. Across from Soa was Lady Lee, who used to fetch Jin in the morning and carry her back home at night when Jin was with Dowager Consort Cheolin.

—Lady Attendant Suh, Your Majesty.

Lady Suh had made the address. *Lady Attendant Suh.* Jin would always be that to Lady Suh. The ornaments in the Queen's hair sparkled in the sunlight. The court ladies stopped the game and turned to face Jin. Jin's clothing drew instant whispers and murmurs from the gathered ladies. The court lady at a distance, poised to throw the next arrow, also stopped to see what the fuss was. This was Soa. The arrow dropped from her hand onto the ground.

The Queen slowly turned toward Jin. The woman in the kimono to the left of her also stared at Jin. Victor took off his hat and bowed politely to the Queen. The Queen's narrowed eyes glanced at Victor and lingered on Jin's face. They moved on to the purple dress Jin wore. The murmur among the court ladies subsided into a tense silence.

—At ease, Your Excellency. How long has it been!

—It is an honor to see you again, Your Majesty.

To Victor, the Queen looked as formidable as ever.

Müllendorf had told him that the King and Queen were close these days to the Russian legate; they seemed to be trying to use Russia to check Japan's growing power at court. It was a reasonable policy from the Queen's point of view. Japan, having won their war with China, would want to use reformation as an excuse to install a pro-Japanese government, a threatening prospect for Korea. Japan wanted to use Korea as a platform for invading Manchuria. The King and Queen could only be glad that Germany, France, and Russia—countries that did not welcome the rise of a new power—were joining forces to put down Japan's ambitions.

—Let me see your face, Jin.

Jin.

Jin slowly raised her head toward the Queen. This was only the second time she was meeting her since being given her name by the King. Jin had wondered what the Queen would call her.

—Raise your head higher.

She did. The woman in the kimono standing next to the Queen also looked closely at Jin's face. The Queen spoke again.

—Would you like to try?

The woman in the kimono gave a slight start.

—Take an arrow. Let us see how good you are.

Jin moved among the court ladies to where the arrows were. Soa handed her the arrow she was holding. In the handoff, Jin briefly squeezed Soa's hand. Soa also quickly grasped Jin's hand before letting go. Jin, her form accentuated by the line of her purple dress, threw the arrow precisely into the bronze urn. The Queen alone clapped as everyone else stared.

—Jin, I believe this child has finally met her match!

So Chonsil's daughter, an almost imperceptible frown in her small eyes and mouth, gave the queen a brief bow.

—The legate is here so I must give him my audience. We shall continue this some other day.

Victor and Jin followed the Queen. So Chonsil's daughter, holding an arrow in her hand, stood until she couldn't see Jin anymore.

Geoncheonggung, the compound they were in, was the farthest court building from the main gate of Gyeongbokgung Palace. The King had built it in secret from the Regent and even his royal council. When the council found out, the courtiers loyal to the Regent were vociferous in their condemnation of the construction. But the King completed it anyway. The palace within the palace represented the King's desire to stand on his own feet.

But instead of taking them to the new compound, the Queen led them to the Pagoda of Far-reaching Fragrance.

The pagoda was striking in its beauty, even from afar as it stood on an island in a pond. The Queen stopped the retinue on the arch of a bridge overlooking it.

—Geoncheonggung was where the first electric lights in Korea were installed. Only nine years after a man named Edison invented them.

Victor gave Jin a look, perplexed that the Queen was suddenly talking about electric lights. Geoncheonggung, compared to Gyeongbokgung proper, was modest. The King had fled from the Japanese into Changdeokgung, but soon after returned to Gyeongbokgung. Jin understood why the Queen chose the obscure Geoncheonggung as her refuge in the palace. Its secretive nature was probably safer than the main parts of the palace. The Queen was probably reluctant to show its interior to Victor.

—We use the water from this pond to create the steam that generates Geoncheonggung's light. That's why we all call it "water-fire."

Before the installation of the electric lights, the palace was lit with porcelain or earthenware oil lamps. Candles made from beeswax and tallow gave off smoke and an unpleasant smell. Jin remembered the awe she felt when the interior of the palace was lit up as bright as day in the middle of the night. Courtiers often visited Geoncheonggung to admire the electric lights.

Jin glanced at the Queen's face as she stood looking out at the pagoda, but what she saw pained her so much that she lowered her head again.

The Queen's face had changed.

Her thin eyes and flawless, pale skin were still the same. But the grace that once shielded her intentions had vanished, as well as her regal poise. Instead, her face showed irritation, an indication of deeply seated tension and anxiety.

—Your acting legate, Lefèvre, is a very frustrating man.

She was talking about the matter of commissioning a residential French legation. The report the acting legate had sent, about the King's formal request for this appointment, sat neglected on the desk of the Minister of Foreign Affairs. Lefèvre was also not interested in this issue, being more concerned with negotiating the price of the Japanese-owned houses adjacent to the cathedral being built by Bishop Mutel. Victor bowed his head, unable to look the Queen in the eye. The Queen had surely not forgotten that this was something they'd discussed when Victor had requested Jin's hand in marriage before the King. According to Müllendorf, the Japanese legate Miura had informed the Queen that Japan was considering a permanent legation in Korea. The Queen had been pitting Russia against Japan in an attempt to stave off the latter's influence, but soon she would no longer be able to keep Japan out of Korea's affairs.

—I am sure that France would not like Japan's influence in this country to grow indefinitely?

But France did not want to make an enemy of Japan, either. France was more interested in Japan than Korea, and more interested in China than Japan. Which was why they were unhappy with Japan winning their war against China. If Japan invaded Liandong, France's position in China would weaken. France's policy was no different from Korea's in its leaning toward China when Japan became stronger and leaning toward Japan when China became stronger, in an attempt to keep the balance of power.

—I need your help.

—Your Majesty, the matter of a permanent legation is not something Lefèvre can decide on his own. France has to step in. And I am not here as a diplomat for my country, so it is not my place to advise in any capacity.

The Queen turned to him.

—You haven't changed. Do you plan on taking that girl back to France?

—Of course.

Victor looked up at the Queen, inquiringly.

—Of course, you say . . . But if it is such a matter of course, why did you not keep your promise when you took her away? In Korea, there are Korean laws. If you took her, you should have held a formal wedding ceremony and made it clear that she was your wife. I feel that we gave you ample opportunity to do so.

How did she know that they had never held a wedding ceremony? Victor glanced at Jin.

—You don't have to look at her.

Jin was utterly taken aback. No one had asked her about Victor since her arrival in Korea, and Jin had talked to no one about him. The Queen had known Jin was in Korea; they had sent word through Lady Suh twice, but no summons had come from the palace. Then, suddenly, they had been called to the palace that very morning.

—If you bring her here without having wed her, the girl retains her old status.

—Her old status, Your Majesty?

—She remains a court lady.

Silence flowed between the three. So this was why Lady Suh had such a grim expression.

—If you're thinking of taking that girl back to France, move fast. That is why I summoned you here. You have very little time . . . But leave her here with me at the palace tonight. I shall send her back to you in the morning.

The Queen left Victor and Jin on the bridge and walked away to the other side.

Nothing can replace an old friend. After Victor left on his own, Lady Suh brought Soa to Jin. With one young woman in her lady attendant dress and the other in Parisian fashion, the two slowly walked side by side in the palace where they had spent their younger years together. At one point, Soa reached out and held Jin's hand. Despite her Embroidery Chamber affiliation, Soa was sometimes called to watch over the Queen in her sleep. The Queen changed her ladies-in-waiting whenever she felt their faces became known to outsiders. She was also said to frequently change her place of sleep, and the court ladies wouldn't know until very late where the Queen's bed would be that night. Kings were known to do this, but it was unheard of for a queen. Wherever she slept, the Queen made sure Hong Gyehoon stood guard. This was the man who helped her escape the treasonous soldiers during the Year of the Black Horse.

—She only feels safe with General Hong by her side.

Jin hadn't sensed the Queen's desperation when Paul Choi explained the situation to her, but the news felt different coming from Soa. When the Queen led them to the pagoda, she kept looking back as if she were afraid someone was following her. Jin had also looked back; she could see a line of bodyguards approaching at a distance. Only when the Queen saw them did she seem to feel less anxious. Did she feel so threatened that not even the palace felt safe to her? Jin was afraid her knees would give out.

Late that night, Lady Suh led Jin from Soa's quarters not to Geoncheonggung but to the Queen's Chambers. Despite Jin's asking, Lady Suh would not tell her where they were going. When they reached the Queen's Chambers, Lady Suh finally murmured, "She hasn't slept here in a long time." This was where Jin had performed the Dance of the Spring Oriole for the Queen before leaving for Paris. Soa followed them to the Queen's Chambers but had to wait outside. The guards had blocked her from entering. Only then did she let go of Jin's hand.

Lady Suh guided Jin into the Queen's Chambers, where Jin suddenly stood rooted on the spot.

The Queen sat on her bedding in her white sleep clothes. Her hair ornaments had been removed, allowing her long black braid to fall to her shoulder. The Queen raised her head.

—Sit.

Jin sat before the bedding.

—Closer.

Jin sat closer.

—Sleep here with me tonight.

—Your Majesty . . .

—Yes. I know it's not done. I've heard countless times about how things are not done. I shall not hear of it from you. Do you not have many things to say to me? We could talk all night and not say all the things we wish to say. When will we ever have this chance again? Do not speak to me about what can't be done. Did we not share the same bed for countless nights during the Year of the Black Horse?

The Year of the Black Horse. The Queen's mentioning of that year silenced Jin's heart. Not only had they shared the same bed but sometimes the same quilt. There were days when the only way of knowing they weren't alone was through the body heat of the other. They had lain side by side and gazed at the moonlight glowing behind the paper screen of the sliding doors.

—An attendant is fetching some water so that you can wash.

The attendant arrived, and Jin washed her hands in the metal basin with the Chinese character for luck stamped on the bottom. She washed her face, too. She could scarcely breathe and took a moment to simply stare down at the water. Then, she took off her dress and put on sleeping robes. The Queen, her head lying on a pillow embroidered with a turtle shell pattern, flicked back the edge of the blanket with her own hand for Jin to climb in.

Jin lay next to the Queen.

There the Queen lay, just a stretch of the hand away.

She could smell her faint scent. Underneath the blanket, Jin placed her hand on her own heart. She was this close to the Queen, but she felt as lonely as that time she became lost at the morgue by the Seine and Maupassant found her at the bottom of a staircase.

—I had a dream last night. I entered a pagoda at dawn, but it was empty. There was a silk bundle there, which I unwrapped. Written on it was the name of someone I knew well. I was reading the name when someone told me she had died. I was so saddened that I began to cry, I felt my own life would end.

—. . .

—Such a strange thing. To be saddened enough to die, and yet unable to remember the name when I woke.

—. . .

—It would not come to me, despite all the pain the name caused. I can't remember the last time I slept through the night. I keep hearing footsteps. I see Japanese or Chinese people with swords, and once I saw you.

The Queen pressed her own forehead. A habit of hers, for when she was feeling distressed. *If only she'd go to sleep with good thoughts, then she wouldn't have bad dreams.*

After some restlessness, the Queen finally sat up.

—I believe I need a cigarette.

Lady Suh had said the Queen might request a cigarette if she were having trouble falling asleep. The Queen in the past would ask Jin to read to her on sleepless nights. Jin had read countless books to the Queen over the years. It seemed that she could no longer be lulled to sleep through the sound of reading. Jin got up and lit one of the rolled cigarettes prepared beforehand and offered it to the Queen. The flower patterning on the filter end was exquisite. As the room filled with the scent of tobacco, the Queen's voice, calmer now, came to Jin once more.

—Yes, so what do they say about me outside the palace? What do they call me? A fox-demon? A fox-demon who made the King stand against his own father, who brought the Chinese into court just for the sake of my position? A fox-demon who killed innocent peasants using the swords of the Japanese?

—Your Majesty . . .

Heartbroken, Jin gripped the cupronickel ring on her hand. It was the one the Queen had given her before she left for France. Victor had wordlessly watched her put it on as they prepared for their journey back to Korea. She had never worn it in Paris.

—Does it seem that way, too, to someone who has come back from breathing new air?

The Queen was never one to show what she was truly thinking. When she wasn't sure of her position, she would fall silent. She would make others talk more than she would talk herself. The Queen had once been astute like this, weighing the different sides of each position, ever logical in her thinking.

—Hong Jong-u told me how you were getting on in France. He says you have a talent for translating Korean stories into French. How did you come across the Korean book you sent through him?

—Through a painter named Régamey in France, Your Majesty. I found it in his studio. He didn't know it was a Korean book. There are many booksellers along the river Seine. He said he had only bought it out of curiosity and allowed me to have it in exchange for posing for him. The books the French stole from Ganghwa Island are stored in their library.

—Have you seen them?

—I have.

—That such a precious thing should end up at a used-book seller!

The Queen held out her cigarette stub, which still had some tobacco left. Jin snubbed it out and placed it on a table. The Queen lay down on the bedding again and closed her eyes.

To some, even a whole night can feel like a short moment.

—I have read the Maupassant stories that you translated. Is that all of it?

—No, Your Majesty. They are a selection. I'm afraid I'm not good enough to have done all of them.

—I see. I had a feeling there were more. I did not like them. How could a woman's life be turned into such a meaningless thing by one man? It seems that it is just as tragic to be born a woman there, over an ocean, as it is here.

—It was not a place of equality between men and women, indeed. Just ten years ago, women were not allowed to enter cafés. Even now, men may sit inside, but women may sit only at the tables outside. Perhaps because so many different people live there, they also have racial discrimination. But they have a tolerance that we do not have in Korea.

—Tolerance?

—There was a freedom to think differently and live one's own life. A way of thinking that respected the way others thought and lived. Parisians seemed to feel pride in being different from other people. That kind of thinking created the Eiffel Tower and built hospitals, department stores, and markets, and raised doctors, philosophers, painters, and writers.

—What do you think is the foremost thing that Korea should emulate?

—Establishing schools and teaching children how to read.

The Queen let out a deep, weary sigh. Jin continued.

—I believe teaching illiterate children how to read is the most urgent task. I felt that the most fundamental thing of all was to help the people express their thoughts freely. And giving the people opportunities to venture out into the world and learn of new ways would help Korea strengthen itself as a country.

—How ideal such a thing would be.

The Queen sighed again, tossing underneath the blanket.

—And how did Hong Jong-u conduct himself in Paris?

—He never took off his Korean robes and carried photographs of the King at all times. He never lost his devotion to Korea. Korea is mysterious to the French. He tried to tell them about it as much as possible.

—He carried a photograph of the King?

—Yes. He said he looked at it in times of difficulty.

Jin did not mention that he also carried a photo of the Regent as well. She recalled how Hong's face had reddened when she turned down his offer of the photos when he visited her before he left Paris.

—How was he with you?

—I helped his work.

—Is that all?

—Yes, Your Majesty.

—He has petitioned the King. Presented him with a detailed list of the wrongs the French legate has done to a Korean court dancer. It is legally indisputable.

Hong Jong-u? Did he know she was in Korea now? Jin suddenly realized that she felt a weight pressing down on her heart whenever she thought of him.

—When were you loneliest in France?

—When I wanted to know who I was.

—All right. Then who are you?

—I do not know. I am like the dust, like the grass, like the clouds . . .

—In the end, we are all nothing.

Her pronouncement was like another sigh. Jin turned to look at her. The Queen was asleep. Jin propped herself up on her elbow and looked down at her. When the Queen's breathing evened out, Jin gently lifted the Queen's hand from her forehead and laid it down.

Insomnia is like waiting for someone who would never arrive.

Jin felt the Queen sit up three times throughout the night. She sat there in the dark, lost in thought. When she first got up, her deep sighs grazed Jin's face. The second time, she lit a cigarette on her own. When had she begun to smoke so? Jin breathed in the smoke and watched the Queen through narrowed eyes. The Queen's hair in its thick braid, falling on her shoulder, was blacker than night. The third time she sat up, the Queen raised one of her knees and leaned an elbow against it, her hand to her forehead. Deep in thought, she occasionally pressed the flesh around her eye sockets. Presently, she turned to Jin.

—Do you sleep?

Jin's heart was so full she couldn't answer.

It wasn't just the Queen who had changed. Jin, herself, had changed. She couldn't rescue the Queen from the precipice she stood on, not with only the things she had seen and learned in Paris. Jin finally realized that she had been unable to send those countless letters to the Queen because she had known, all along, that she couldn't help her.

—You must be asleep.

The Queen's gaze lingered on Jin's features as if examining what she really looked like.

—How alone I am.

She lamented in a low voice.

—I was fifteen when I entered court. The Regent accepted me as his daughter-in-law because, perhaps, I had no one. If I had powerful parents, he would have feared to have me near. He must have approved that I was alone. The King's heart was elsewhere, so when I arrived at court, he did not even deign to look at me. My only pastime when I entered the palace was reading at night. I read until my eyes were tired to tears. Years passed. I was sorrowful and lonely at the time, but compared to how things are now, I was peaceful. I gave birth to a prince but lost him in five days. I made a promise to myself. To guard myself against it all. I felt I would shatter if I didn't. When I didn't stand up for myself, everyone praised me. But praise alone wasn't enough for survival. The only way to survive was to give birth to another son, a crown prince. That was my beginning. No matter what, I could trust only myself. So it all began with my determination to survive. Eventually, those who once praised me as virtuous began calling me a conspirator, and those who called me wise began calling me cunning. They said that I did not inherit the Regent's power but stole it from him. That our country is a mess because a queen dared to govern over a king. Was the Regent ever one to easily give up his power? Of course not. But no one cared about that. My only wish was for my survival to be the people's survival. Was that so ignoble? But it turns out, my survival brought suffering to the people. Such was the Year of the Black Tiger and the uprising during the Year of the Blue Monkey. I wanted to open Korea's doors because I thought the Regent's isolationist policy had done real harm to the country. I wanted to strengthen Korea. But that has become a story in which I use foreign armies to kill my own people. How could the story have turned out this way? Where did I go so wrong that the path I chose was a path of thorns, the animal I chose to ride was a tiger . . . I cannot dismount it.

The Queen paused in her pained lament.

—Do you sleep?

She stretched out a hand and stroked Jin's face.

The Queen lay down on the bedding again. She tossed and turned for hours, unable to fall asleep. Was she this sleepless every night? It was a long time before her breathing became even again. Jin lay silent and still, not wanting to disturb the Queen. Memories of the past and worries of the present came and went like waves with the Queen's breathing.

It was dawn when Jin left the Queen's Chambers. The events of the night before felt like a dream. She stopped at the Gate of Dualities and looked behind her. Soon, the day would break, and the Queen would return behind her cold mask, hiding the vulnerability she had shown in the night. And all would tread lightly before her.

Lady Suh's quarters were lit despite the early hour. When an attendant announced Jin had come, Lady Suh did not invite her in but came out herself. She was already immaculately dressed, walking toward Jin in her green silk tunic and blue satin shoes.

—Hong Jong-u has an audience with the King today. You must meet with him before you leave.

—Is the situation so serious?

Lady Suh gave Jin a look.

—How could you have thought to come to court in such attire?

Lady Suh was objecting to the dress that not even the Queen had found fault with. Jin curled her toes inside her shoes and gripped the cupronickel ring on her hand.

—Do not forget that this is court.

—Did you want to say that I was once a court lady?

—You are still a court lady. Have you forgotten our laws? Even if a court lady leaves the palace, she must live under its rules. That is her fate. You still do not understand why the legate brought you back here. He hasn't married you. What use is having lived in another world? Why, oh why, did you return? Don't you know that the moment you did, you would revert to your old status?

—. . .

—I've already met with Official Hong twice. He refuses to listen to me. I don't understand why he persists in this issue when everyone else is willing to forget you. Did something happen between the two of you? He will be asking the King to judge your situation. And Hong has the King's ear for having killed Kim Okgyun. Hong is the kind of man who fears not even the Japanese and says that any courtier who insults the King must be executed. If he persists in questioning your status, the King will have no choice but to listen to him.

Despite the harshness of Lady Suh's words, her hands clasped Jin's in sympathy.

—You must meet with Official Hong. You helped him in France, so don't you think he would cease his petition if he saw your face? If he gets his way, harm will come to the legate as well. You will have the safety of oblivion as long as no one mentions you, but if your name keeps coming up, the King will eventually have to make a decision. What will become of the legate? The only way out of this is to silence Official Hong and leave Korea immediately. The only way for you to survive is to be forgotten. I cannot stop thinking of Official Hong. He went to Shanghai and killed Kim Okgyun. Think of what he is capable of. He's had his audience by now, and it must be ending. Let us go together.

Lady Suh led the way. Jin realized that Lady Suh had not invited her into her quarters because she wished to waste no time in taking Jin to see Hong Jong-u. She could scarcely remember Lady Suh's smile at this point. Jin called out to her.

—I shall go alone.

Lady Suh turned and gave Jin a long look.

3

First Letter—Tangier, Morocco

When the summer started, the French legation interpreter Paul Choi brought Victor's letter to the orphanage.

Jin,

I'm in Tangier, Morocco. I have been busy settling in since I arrived. I tried to write earlier, but I'm afraid I'm only now putting pen to paper. Not unlike Korea, the country is beset by conflicting foreign powers; you would've marveled at how there could be another country in such a similar situation. It rained all day. Aside from hospital visits for my laryngitis, which persists whenever I am fatigued, things are settling down. But the thought of you makes me feel as if I stand before a dark ocean at night.

You said you would never return to court, but I don't know what has become of you since I left. I, too, think it is not right for you to return to the palace. But having come here instead of being by your side, there is nothing I can say in my defense. This was the real reason I found it difficult to write to you. How pathetic I am. I wonder what happened to you if you haven't returned to the palace. Are you at the orphanage? I don't know how I could've left you behind at the annex of the legation. I send this letter there, in hopes that someone will pass it on to you.

I spent four days in Paris before setting sail from Marseilles. They were under German influence for a long period, and it is felt everywhere. My task is to strengthen France's standing in this country. As it was in Korea, there isn't a day that goes by without incident. England's influence grows by the day, making matters even more tense.

I've spent much time thinking about how we came to this. I brought you to Korea to cure you of your sleepwalking. I don't understand how that led to my being alone in this place. I sometimes think you would be here in Morocco with me if I hadn't taken you to Korea, and sometimes that you knew this would happen all along. Did you? How could you be so accepting of it otherwise, if you hadn't?

I am sorry.

I was the one who left, but I am berating you as if you had sent me away. How strange it is. I left you there, but I feel as if you banished me. This breaks my heart. I've begun to talk of something I could never conclude. Know this one thing. We are not finished. Wherever I may be, you are my wife, and I am only here on duty. This is the thought that comforts me. When the situation allows, I shall return to you.

Jin,

Morocco is a land of white houses, of the endless Sahara Desert, the rugged Atlas Mountains, and the blue Mediterranean Sea. Europeans mix with Arabs and Africans. Christians mix with Muslims. If you were here, your clever eyes would have so much to take in. We would've met new people and seen new things, and who knows, we might've been born anew. I sometimes think of the time we went to the Bois de Boulogne together. I recall how devastated you were to see the Africans on display. The people here sit in tiny, dim rooms, weaving carpets. Their hands are quick. The carpets are strange and beautiful. You would love them, too. Entire villages are leather-dyeing factories, and their craftsmanship is extraordinary. I bought a carpet said to have been made a hundred years ago and sent it off to Paris. You shall see it someday. My only regret is that we cannot have these moments together. Jin! Please forget how cruel I was to you before I left Korea. I could not accept our situation as easily as you did back then.

I shall work hard to succeed in my mission here. I look forward to the day we shall meet again. Be well in the meantime.

May 2, 1895

Your Gillin, from Tangier, Morocco

4

Second Letter—Please Forget Me

After she received Victor's letter, Jin lit a lamp and wrote a reply, and gave it to Paul Choi the next day to send to Tangier.

Gillin,

I received the letter you sent from Tangier.

I had worried about your voyage, the one you took so hurriedly out of Korea, but your letter laid to rest my concerns. We parted as if we'd never see each other again, so I was grateful that you took care to write what was surely a difficult letter. Now I can truly feel at ease.

The Queen made it so that I did not have to return to court. Korea's situation is not improving. I left the French legation soon after you did. It was not a place for me without you. I moved into the house where I grew up in Banchon. It is a typical Korean earthen house. There is a bamboo grove behind it and a kitchen with a furnace, and several rooms. I never did visit your birthplace, Plancy, but then again, I never brought you to this house. Just as I did when I first lived at the legation, I go to the orphanage during the day and teach the children to read. I also teach Korean to a few nuns from your country who wish to speak the language. If only Hong Jong-u would forget me, then I believe I could find a way to do the work I want to do.

Do not worry about me. And please read carefully what I'm about to write.

You were kind to me. You were faithful and tried not to let me go. That is enough for me. Do not blame yourself for not keeping your promises, and do not castigate yourself for the cooling of your passions. I have never said this to you before, but I know how long you waited for me to make up my mind, even after the King had allowed our union. If it were only a matter of lust, you would not have waited so. I never forgot that you waited for me. Sometimes, when I couldn't bear to be with you, I thought of how you waited. The reason I was so accepting of your departure was that I accepted your feelings. If I did not let you go, we would be like flowing water trapped to stagnate.

I was happy to live as an "I" and not as "your servant" in your country. Even if I forget the Eiffel Tower or the Louvre, I will never forget the boisterous and free Parisians who walked the city's streets. To see Vincent realize his dreams, to be there when our lively Jeanne realized her love, made me so very happy. I was able to see many sides of your country through Madame Planchard's kindness and Maupassant's wit and devastation. I learned of charity, which uses our strength to protect those who have none, and freedom, the feeling of living my life the way I want to live it. I had lived in the palace ever since I was a young girl. I was afraid to smash the things that surrounded me, to feel the me inside of it all. As exciting as it was, the suffering was also like fire to the heart.

Gillin,

You can now let go of me. I understand what you meant when you said you didn't know if you loved me anymore. I do not misunderstand you. I do not resent you. I know your conflict and your determination not to give me up. Because that was my conflict from the beginning. I didn't know whether I loved you or not, but I could not leave you. But that was because I was "your servant," in a way. After you left, I greatly regretted how I refused your last wish to brush my hair. I was afraid it would make you regret your leaving. But if you didn't even have that little of regret, what would the years we spent together have meant? I was foolish not to have thought that then. In truth, you have given me so much, but I did not give you even that. I thought you were the strong one, and I the weaker. I must've always had that thought in the back of my mind, that you were French, and I was Korean. When in fact, you and I, we were only a man and a woman after all.

Gillin,

Let go of Yi Jin and be free. Only then can I become free, too. I shall always worry over your laryngitis even if I never see you again. And you will always want to brush my hair, even if you never see me again.

And that is enough.

June 3, 1895
Yi Jin, in Korea

5

In the Name of Love

Someone stood underneath the apricot tree of the Banchon house. Jin stared at the figure, who seemed to regard the dark house with interest. Jin's face lit up. It was Soa. Despite the darkness, Jin almost immediately recognized her. She joyfully called out Soa's name as she pushed open the low gate of the house.

—Why are you standing out here, instead of going in?

Soa, an indigo throw jacket neatly folded over her sleeve, did not move from underneath the apricot tree. She made no reply. Jin lit a lamp on the porch and turned to her friend.

—How did you leave the palace?

Soa walked over to the porch and sat down next to Jin.

When the woman Suh learned that Yeon had bought the old house in Banchon, she helped Jin move into it from her lodgings at the French legation annex. Bothered by Jin being alone in the house, she had Yeon move in with her. Suh came to the house on occasion to make the three of them meals, which made them feel like they'd gone back in time to when they lived together after Blanc had left Yeon to Suh's care.

—You're still in Western dress?

Jin grinned.

—Why do you keep wearing them when the legate is gone?

—I've no other reason, other than they're comfortable.

Soa gave Jin a deeply worried look.

—Why, what's the matter?

—That's what I wanted to ask. Did something happen between you and Official Hong?

—Hong Jong-u?

—He's made another petition.

—A petition?

—This time, it's not against the legate but the musician Kang.

Kang Yeon. Jin was silent as she waited for Soa to continue.

—You know our laws. Even if a court lady entered the palace as a child and left before she turned ten, she is not allowed to marry. Not even court ladies who have been banished from the palace. You've heard these rules a thousand times before, so I won't repeat the penalties. Official Hong is claiming that your living with the musician Kang is in violation of these rules. He's pushing for Yeon to be punished. Lady Suh told me to let you know. What on Earth happened in Paris that he's so determined to ruin you?

Hong Jong-u, again.

Jin bit her lip.

She remembered the time she had gone to see him. His audience hadn't ended, so she had ended up waiting for him for most of the morning. As Hong emerged with the other officials, he spotted her and stood stock still. The other officials stared at Jin's clothes. Hong, as if to hide something, escorted her to a more private setting. He looked her up and down before speaking.

—Why are you wearing such clothes in Korea?

Hong himself was dressed in the red robes of the court officials. Even before Jin could mention the petition, Hong made an unexpected request. That since she'd come back, she should stay in Korea permanently. Confused by his beseeching tone, Jin could only stare back at him. Hong was so tall that he blocked the rising sun as he looked down at her. He seemed different from when she had seen him in Paris. He hesitated before adding that he had held her in his heart for a long time.

—I know nothing of what you speak.

Jin avoided his gaze and kept repeating this line. Hong had replied that he would not be so helpless about her as he had been in Paris. That as long as Jin promised she would remain in Korea, he would find a way for her to be with him. Jin sighed, wondering what the two of them had been in a past life to deserve this fate.

To some, love is war.

Jin was worried that Hong, who would stop at nothing to get what he wanted, had begun another petition. His previous petition had been effective enough to send Victor away and leave her in Korea. There was no guarantee that Yeon would not suffer a similar fate.

—Does the musician Kang not say anything about it?

Yeon had told her nothing. He hadn't come to the orphanage, even after sundown. He usually came once his work was done at Jangakwon. The children who had played all day, sweating in the sun, would eagerly learn the bamboo flute from him when he gathered them around the date tree. He had said nothing to her when he left the house that morning. She thought she heard him play the oboe last night, right before she drifted off to sleep. Its sound was as clear as droplets of water falling on a stream.

—The Jangakwon people must've been informed of the petition by now . . . Why don't we ask the Queen for help?

—Lady Suh would already have told her.

—Try again. I mean, it's true that you and the musician Kang aren't really sister and brother.

Jin didn't reply. The Queen already knew that while she and Yeon weren't related by blood, they were raised as if they were by the woman

Suh, older sister to Lady Suh. The Queen was also aware that Yeon was the invisible man who had protected her during the Year of the Black Horse.

—Could the penalty forbid Yeon from playing the *daegeum* ever again?

—He'll be lucky if his hands are the only thing he loses.

—What happens then?

Soa wouldn't say.

She stood up, saying she had to go back to the palace. She could not stay out for too long without a special dispensation. She had waited a long time under the apricot tree for Jin to come home. Jin walked with her. Soa said nothing as they walked the Banchon paths and crossed the bridge. They could see the lamplight of the other houses winking through the pear trees.

—Even a nobleman who takes a court lady would be punished severely. Remember that official who was beheaded for making a concubine of a woman who left the palace at eleven years old? Sometimes they'll look the other way, but if there's someone determined enough to enforce the rules . . .

Hong had said himself that he had many things to do for Korea, that it was time to use what he had learned in France for the good of his own country. That only reformation could strengthen the country, and reformation could be implemented only through a strong monarchy. He'd told her that now that he had the King's backing, all he needed was Jin's support to be invincible.

—Remember that official who was banished for having a drink with a court lady?

Jin gripped Soa's hand in the dark. She meant for her to stop talking about it. The two paused and faced each other at the entrance to Banchon. Soa returned Jin's firm grip. Jin could feel the heat of the summer night on Soa's palms.

—It's good that you're not back at court. Nothing scares me more than being in the palace. We scarcely sleep at night. All we do is wait for the day to break. I think we've caught the Queen's insomnia.

Jin gripped Soa's sweaty palm. Soa spread out her indigo throw jacket and covered her head, with only her face showing. When she looked back after walking a distance, Jin waved. Soa was only returning to the palace, but for some reason, Jin felt Soa was going somewhere far away. She stood there long after Soa had completely disappeared into the dark.

Jin stood on the bridge and waited for Yeon to return.

It was the same wooden bridge on which Yeon had waited for a young Jin to return, carried on the back of Lady Attendant Lee. Since then, Lady Attendant Lee had risen to the rank of senior court lady. But Jin could still remember being carried by her and watching Yeon as he ran like the wind toward them from the bridge.

Living in the same house with Yeon was against the law?

Jin's face was flush with anger at Hong Jong-u. She could hardly think of him as the same man she once knew in Paris. Hong had been rough at times, but he was clearly of good learning and devoted to his country. This was what led to his assassinating Kim Okgyun, whom he perceived to be an enemy of the King. He would brook any humiliation if it were for the sake of his country. This was why she had spent so much time with Boex, going over the translation he had left behind. "To those who love, distance does not exist." Editing his French translation of this line had almost moved her to tears. But what was it that made Hong act so irrationally now?

Jin realized it with a jolt.

Was this the heart of a man who had been rejected? The very sound of the stream below her seemed to go silent. She had known Hong's petition was not the only reason Victor had left without her. Jin was aware that the biggest reason for that was Victor's change of heart. In Paris, she had felt that she was getting in the way of his ambitions as a diplomat. And her life in Paris had taught her that nothing, not even love, managed to escape the realities of change.

The urgent thought that she needed to send Yeon back to the orphanage made her look harder down the other side of the bridge.

If there was one thing that never changed in this world, it was Yeon's love for Jin. Jin ached at this realization. She was appalled at the prospect of his never playing the *daegeum* again because of her. Yeon without his music was unimaginable. Soa did not have to explain to Jin what awaited a man who was said to have an attachment to a lady of the court.

A little while later, she saw Yeon's shadow approach.

Jin hurried toward him. Yeon stopped at the sight of Jin almost running toward him in the dark. She came to a halt.

—Go back!

Yeon could hardly make her out in the darkness.

—You have to go back to the orphanage!

Jin tried to block his path to the house. The two stood there, listening to the sound of the stream below. Yeon stepped around her and continued to walk home. The crescent moon shone on the stream.

—I told you to go back!

Jin was now shouting at Yeon.

—Please!

The strength left her body as she collapsed on the bridge. *The only way for you to survive is to be forgotten.* Lady Suh's words pierced her heart. She finally realized what she really meant. She cursed Lady Suh in her heart for sending her into court as a child. A thought that had never crossed her mind before, even when she sent Victor away. Yeon saw her fall and came back for her. He picked her up from the ground.

—Listen to me. If you don't go back, they will destroy you.

Yeon slowly embraced Jin. Jin listened intently to the sound of his breathing.

Yeon's firm arms showed no signs of letting go. She could feel the length of his *daegeum* underneath his robes. She knew the sound of his playing, the way one knows the footfalls of one's beloved. To Jin, the *daegeum* was Yeon's voice itself. She realized another thing. That that was why the sound of his *daegeum* brought her dancing to such ecstasy that her feet hardly touched the ground.

Waves of sadness made it impossible for Yeon to let her go.

He had become a court musician because this woman had become a court dancer. It was the only way to be near her. He had refused to follow Blanc's advice to go to Japan and learn to be a priest, refused Homunmok when he offered a new life as a swordsman for the common good. He only wished to end his days by the side of this woman. But that would never be. The moment she left court to live in the French legation, Yeon had to fight the persistent urge to fall on his knees. When she left for France, he played the *daegeum* to any audience he could find—people, animals, the very air. He took care of the things that were left behind. This was not only because of the woman Suh's teaching, that it was his duty as a human being to love and care for others. It was more of a prayer of sorts that his good deeds here would somehow bring goodness to the woman who had gone so far away.

Yeon released her from his embrace and gently cupped her face with his hands.

Then, as if accepting something he could not change, he let her go and began walking away. Jin stared after him for a bit before running to close the distance between them.

Yeon was sitting on the porch when Jin came through the low gate. He took his notebook and pen from his bag. Yeon stared at an empty page that seemed as wide as an expanse of desert. Then, he wrote something and handed it to Jin. Jin lit a lamp and brought the words close to her face.

Once I go to the Jangakwon tomorrow, I'm being taken to China.

China? Jin looked at him inquiringly.

I'm going with an elder musician.

—What for?

Jangakwon business. We're buying Chinese instruments.

Jangakwon business? Chinese instruments? Jin stared at Yeon. She recalled Soa's worried face.

—It's because of me, right?

Was this exile? She dared not ask him.

Think of me as going to perform my music.

Jin's face broke.

I'll come back someday. Like you did.

Jin became angry. Yeon gripped her wrist.

It's no use. It's done. At least I was told beforehand, so I had time to say good-bye.

The ink drops from his pen were like drops of his blood. Yeon seemed to know that Jin had wanted to petition the Queen on his behalf. Jin tried to pull her arm away, but Yeon only gripped tighter. Jin buried her face on his knees.

She remained there, still.

Only a moment ago, she had wanted to run to the palace to see the Queen or even Hong Jong-u. But now she could think of nothing. Her heart was fit to burst, but no tears came to her eyes. She was swept up in a feeling of metal dust blowing in a dry wind.

How long did they remain so?

Yeon gently helped Jin up and onto the porch.

Please dance for me.

Dance? Jin looked at him with eyes that seemed to have lost all their light.

If only you could see yourself dancing.

—If only I could? Then what?

You're like a butterfly. Like a cloud. A flower.

Yeon smiled. She found it extraordinary that he could smile at such a moment. She stood up from the porch. She went to her room, and from the bamboo shelves took down a package wrapped in blue satin. Inside was the yellow dancing costume from her court dancer days. It also had the lotus crown inside. Soa had given them to her when Jin had left for Paris. But Jin had not taken them with her. The legation cook had kept them for her, and Jin had brought them with her when she moved into the Banchon house. Jin took off her dress and rearranged her hair so the crown would sit better. She slipped on the yellow silk, tied the red belt tight, and inserted the extended seven-color sleeves. She stood for a moment, wondering when she had last worn the costume.

Yeon rose when Jin entered the courtyard.

She stood with her back to the apricot tree. Yeon took out his *daegeum*. Without the sound of the *bak*, Jin listened only to Yeon's music as she took her first steps.

There was a time when she tried to become steel with this dance. To become the wind, and clouds. Tears began to flow, tears she hadn't shed for Victor when he left Korea, or onto Yeon's knees when he told her he was leaving for China. Yeon's eyes were also wet as he played his *daegeum*. Both were sweating as one danced and the other played music. Why was Jin remembering the Queen's words, her urging for Jin to release herself from her bonds, to learn as many new things as possible, and to live a new life? Jin danced as if she were building a high tower, as if she were plucking flower petals from the air. Yeon's music to her had the rhythm of breathing. Her tears ceased. She concentrated entirely on the form of her hands, her feet.

Daylight seeped faintly through the paper-screen door.

Jin bolted upright from a dream of being run over by a carriage while walking the streets of Paris during the Paris Carnival. Her forehead was drenched with sweat. She rubbed her ankles, which ached as if they had been run over by a carriage wheel. Jin looked down at the other side of the bedding.

Yeon wasn't there. In his place were only his notebook and fountain pen.

The tears Jin shed the night before when she danced to Yeon's *daegeum* were for pity. What was she to do about Yeon now? As she danced for him alone, and not for the court as she had done in his presence countless times, she had been caught up with the urge to run away and disappear with Yeon forever. And yet, while they'd been raised like two lost fawns in the arms of the woman Suh, Jin's heart had answered Yeon's love only with pity. The years of her pretending not to know how Yeon felt had disintegrated like a waking dream.

When Jin had returned to her room to take off her lotus crown and dancing costume, she took out her Korean clothes for the first time and put them on. Then she went to Yeon's room. It was the one where

Blanc had once taught her French. The room where Yeon had once played the bamboo flute for them. Yeon lay there with the lamp still on, and Jin climbed into the bedding next to him. Yeon stretched out an arm for her to rest her head. They lay there like two cucumbers hanging from the same vine. Then Jin sat up and asked Yeon to brush her hair. Yeon brushed her long, black hair for a long time. Before they knew it, they were touching each other's faces. Then, they lay facing each other, running their hands down each other's backs. They hugged each other tightly as if they would never part from that moment on. They fell into a deep sleep.

Jin, in her sleep clothes, slid open the door to the room.

Yeon was not in the courtyard. Neither was he in the kitchen or the bamboo grove. Already? Jin walked out to the low gate and looked out as far as she could. She couldn't see him anywhere. She paced underneath the apricot tree and came back to the room and picked up his notebook. The pen slid from the pages and fell on the bedding.

Silverbell,

To see your sleeping face this close . . . it's like a dream.

I remember the first day I came to this house. You were on the back of a court lady, and your eyes widened at the sight of Bishop Blanc. Do you remember? Mother heated water and bathed me in an earthen jar. That was my first day here. I couldn't follow Bishop Blanc because you were here. You made me stay. Live here with us . . . you said. From that moment on, I kept your words in my heart. I had always followed my father, who was forever running from something, until he drowned in the pond of a village that has since faded from my memory. Now I've only a bamboo flute to remember him by. What I feared the most in those days was the night. I didn't know where to spend the nights, those nights that would return relentlessly. A good night was when I could find a pile of hay to sleep on or shelter by a furnace that still had some embers glowing in it. That was my life until I met you. Live here with us . . .

Silverbell,

Last night I . . . became. I became everything I could become. I hope you realize your dream of creating a school where you can teach children. Hong Jong-u will help you. I met him yesterday and begged him to help you. Just as Mother did before us, maybe you can start in this house by teaching the children of Banchon. I wanted to be by your side to help you. I'm only sorry that I can't. I wanted to be by your side no matter what, but I couldn't follow you across the ocean. I couldn't even protect you when you came back to Korea. And that is the regret that will haunt me to the end of my days. That all I could do for you was to play my flute.

Silverbell,

I want you to find strength by thinking back to when life was even harder than it is now. And one more thing. No matter what you hear, do not look for me. I will be in China. For my sake, do not ask after me. I know this will be hard, but please do this. Do this for me. Know that any other thing you do for me will only harm me in the end.

Tears gathered in her eyes as Jin turned the rest of the pages of the notebook. Nothing was written on them. Jin reached out and swept Yeon's side of the bedding with her hand and bit her lip. *Know that any other thing you do for me will only harm me . . .* These were his last words to her.

A realization come too late is bound to strike the heart.

It took four days for Jin to learn that Yeon did not go to China. Jin had gathered the orphans on the porch to tell them the story of *The Hunchback of Notre Dame*, which she had first read in Paris. The children forgot the heat as they listened to Quasimodo's story. Jin was too bereft by Yeon's departure to teach the children how to read. But even the children who were bored with learning were excited by the story. The children, despite the heat, sat close to Jin and clung to her skirt with their little hands, their eyes shining. *The Hunchback of Notre Dame* was not only a story for children. Yeon had also listened with so much concentration when she told the story of the hunchback to him that she could not stop telling it. When she told it, she felt she was herself sinking deeper and deeper into the narrative. Jin and Yeon were both angry at the cruel archdeacon. They wanted so much for the hideous but pure Quasimodo and the beautiful dancer Esmeralda to love each other that Jin briefly considered changing the ending of their story from Victor Hugo's. There had been such days.

Jin tried to stop the story, but the children refused to be dismissed, so she ended up finishing the story in the dark. Almost hoarse, Jin was about to go back home to Banchon, when the woman Suh called her into her room. When had Suh's back become so bent? Suh took out a linen package and put it before Jin on the room floor, knocking her lower back with a fist to alleviate some pain there.

—What's this?

Suh didn't answer, prompting Jin to unwrap the package. Jin watched Suh's eyes as she undid the knot, uncertain of Suh's thoughts. A dread overcame her, rushing her fingers to reveal what was inside. It was Yeon's *daegeum*.

—Sometimes, I think about what will happen after I die. Do not be alarmed. It's just my time to think about such things. I feel weaker by the day. After the children are bathed and fed, I close my eyes and hope I never have to open them again, but it isn't my choice to die when I want to. I don't want to have kept anything when I die. The only thing I shall have when I go will be these clothes, washed clean.

Suh had already sold, upon Blanc's recommendation, anything she had of any value when she moved from Banchon and donated the proceeds to the orphanage. Everything she owned was in this small room.

—This is yours.

—Why is this here? If he doesn't have his *daegeum* . . . How will he survive in that faraway place without it? Why did he leave it behind?

—He can't play it anyway.

—He can't play it?

Suh's tired eyes looked into Jin's.

—Didn't you know?

—Know what? He's not in China?

—China?

—China . . . That's what he told me.

—I tried to make him stay until his severed fingers healed, at least, but he wouldn't listen to me.

Jin gripped the *daegeum*, her face turning into a grimace. Then she turned pale.

—Severed fingers?

She remembered him asking her not to do anything for him. Was his punishment not exile but the loss of his fingers? Was that why he left behind his notebook and fountain pen? And his *daegeum* . . .

—What else do I not know!

Jin grabbed Suh's hands and shook them. *They severed the fingers of a man who couldn't speak*. How could she have been so oblivious? How could she not suspect he was lying about going to China? How could she have accepted his explanation about buying Chinese instruments? *No matter what you hear, do not look for me*. That was what he said. Jin felt she was suffocating. She couldn't scream. She struck her chest with her fist and buried her face in the woman Suh's knees, writhing in pain. Then she abruptly took to her feet.

—I will find him.

The woman Suh closed her eyes.

—I will find him and . . . and live with him.

Jin, holding the *daegeum*, rushed out of Suh's room, hastily shoved her feet into her shoes, and walked out to the orphanage courtyard. There, her knees gave way.

6
On the Edge

The October darkness descended over the ancient pine of the palace.

The chill dark fell on the main gate, on the Gate of Rising Spring where a dragon was said to live, upon the Hall of Diligent Governance nestled in the Baekaksan and Inwangsan Mountains, over the waters of the Pavilion of Festivities, on Amisan Hill, the dowager's residences, the Pagoda of Far-reaching Fragrance, and the eastern watchtower. Jin was waiting for the Queen's summons in the library at Geoncheonggung, and only when it became too dark to read did she reluctantly go to Lady Suh's quarters. Lady Suh, who was just on her way to the Queen's bedchamber, was wide-eyed with surprise at the sight of Jin.

—Are you still at court!

—I was told to wait in the library, but I was never summoned.

—And no word for you to return home?

—No.

—There is a meeting with the French, German, and Russian legates. It's running late. China losing the war with Japan is making things difficult for us. They're working day and night to defend our country against Japan. The Queen hasn't slept in days. But how strange. She asked me to tell her the minute you arrived at court. I thought she would call for you as soon as I announced you.

Lady Suh's face, younger than the woman Suh of the orphanage but still far from young, grimaced as she looked her up and down.

—I told you to come to court observing proper form . . .

She remained disapproving of Jin's Western attire. Jin said nothing and lowered her head. Her dresses did seem to feel awkward as of late.

—But where were you before today? The Queen asked for you several times.

— . . .

—Is it true you cut your hair and dressed as a man, looking for the musician Kang of Jangakwon?

— . . .

—What foolishness is this? Don't you know what would happen if you saw him again? So, did you find him?

—He is gone.

A look of relief crossed Lady Suh's tense expression.

—Don't look for him. That's the only way for both of you to survive. And do not resent Her Majesty. She was anguished when she learned too late of the musician's fate. She had Hong Jong-u sent to China over this affair, albeit there was also pressure from the new Japanese legate. She had trusted him, but she didn't even give him an audience when he was sent away. The musician Kang gave his hands to save your life. But your ridiculous clothes! And your hair! Is this how you repay him?

—I would rather my own fingers be cut off. You know his story as well as I do! They silenced the music of a mute man. What was his crime that he should deserve such punishment?

—His crime was in knowing you.

Jin's dress, the color of water, was looser in fit than it had been, and fluttered with her every movement. Like the time she would wander the streets every night, the dress, designed to showcase her décolletage and her legs, looked as if it had been tailored for a different person.

—Things are not well at court. Not well at all. Her Majesty was going to call for you immediately, I do not know why she hasn't. They say France may establish a school here, and if that's the reason, I hope it becomes a lifeline for you. Spend the night at my quarters tonight, Soa is on the night watch at the Hall of Precious Rest. I shall see what is going on and send word.

Lady Suh left her quarters, and Jin sat alone, staring at the intricate wooden frame of the window. Jin had not been able to sleep lying down since learning that Yeon had lost his fingers for her. She had hacked off the long black hair that Victor had loved so much, dressed as a man like in the old days when she and Victor accompanied Hwang Cheol and his camera around the city, and spent the past three months searching for Yeon over land and stream.

Waves of anguish came over her whenever she thought of Yeon being unable to hold out his hands or grasp someone else's.

She started at Subunli, the village nestled inside the split between the Sobaek and Noryoung Mountains, and walked through the markets, to the ocean, and to the marshes where he was said to go every May to hunt for the best reeds for instrument-making. He was nowhere to be found. Every step of the way she thought she saw severed fingers. What could a man without fingers do? Thinking about it made her wonder if the human form was mostly made of hands, for nothing could be done easily without them. Above all, he could not write letters. Jin had found more than a thousand letters in the closet in Yeon's room. He must have written her incessantly since her departure from France. The only one that had made it to Jin was the single missive delivered by Sister Jacqueline. She couldn't read through them in one sitting, so she took them with her while she searched. Reading his unsent letters made everything around her seem like traces of him. She thought of Vincent, the son of the cheesemonger in Victor's childhood village, so happy to have realized his modest dream. Why couldn't Yeon have such happiness? Three months after embarking on her search, Jin returned to the city fortress. She had once felt enraged enough to cut off Hong Jong-u's fingers herself. But now, she only wanted to show him Yeon's letters. In fact, she wanted to go to Hong and show him the letters herself. But Hong was not in the city. The Japanese had ignored Kim Okgyun when he was alive, but a mania for mourning him had arisen among them since his assassination, threatening Hong and forcing him to flee to China.

During her search, Jin came across countless children who had been abandoned like Yeon as a boy. She also encountered many ugly rumors about the Queen. She heard that an attempt on the Queen's life by a diplomatic official named Park Younghyo had been unmasked. The Japanese legate Inoue was replaced by Miura to better fight the Queen's Russia policy, and Miura was said to be no different from the loitering *rōnin* brandishing their swords around Jaemulpo Harbor. While her eyes searched for Yeon and her ears listened for rumors of the Queen, Jin continued to come across orphans who suffered from disease. They were bullied by other children and scolded away by women and lived near chimneys for their bit of warmth or in pens or by dung piles. On her way back to the city, Jin carried a filthy little girl on her back and left her to the care of the Gondangol orphanage. There were countless orphans, but Blanc's Gondangol orphanage with its one building for boys and the other for girls was the only facility that could take them in. She remembered Blanc's constant requests to the Paris Foreign Missions Society for more nuns and funding to help with the children. As she wandered through the country, searching for Yeon, Jin thought she could understand why Blanc had been so intent on helping them. She could overlook the gazes of everyone else, but the stares of the children pierced her heart. Blanc would have felt the same. She was determined to speak for the children if she ever met with the Queen again. Which was why she complied with Lady Suh's request to come to the palace immediately for an audience with the Queen. She did think there would be a bit of a wait, having been told to meet in the library at Geoncheonggung. She had understood that this was a considerate gesture, that she was meant to read during what might become a long wait. But no word came for her despite the lengthening shadows.

Jin woke from her sleep, leaning against a wall, and heard someone calling her name. She came out of Lady Suh's quarters to find a young lady attendant she had never seen before.

—Lady Suh says you must flee the palace at once.

—What happened?

—I don't know. She only said that you must not hesitate, and you must flee the palace at once.

Jin noticed that the young girl's shoulders were trembling. So was her voice.

—Tell me everything you saw. Is something happening at court?

—I do not know, only there is a great commotion . . .

—A commotion?

—Men brandishing swords . . . they're all over the palace. I think . . . they're Japanese.

Men with swords? Jin put on her shoes and ran toward Geoncheonggung.

At that exact hour, Miura had received official sanction from the Regent and gathered Japanese *rōnin* and troops to join the new Korean army at Seoul's Western Gate to make a push into the main gate of Gyeongbokgung Palace. Miura, judging that a purely Japanese army would compromise the legitimacy of their invasion, cunningly sought the support of the Regent and the new Korean army that had been trained by the Japanese. The new army had it out for the Queen, who had ordered their disbandment for the reason that these troops, commanded by Wu Beomseon, was created through Japanese pressure against Korea. She intended to weaken Japan's political influence by ridding them of an army that was loyal to the Japanese.

The Japanese forces roared as they charged at the gate, guns blazing, and Hong Gyehoon, before he could even finish asking whether there was an order to assemble the Japanese troops, was slashed by the sword of a *rōnin*. The Japanese fired eight bullets at his bleeding body. Jin heard the sound of gunfire as she ran toward Geoncheonggung. The palace defense fought the Japanese forces but were quickly defeated, having lost their commander so early.

Geoncheonggung was soon overrun with *rōnin*, their fiery torches lighting up the sanctum like the sun. The *rōnin*'s swords flashed in the torchlight as they swarmed from room to room. They were searching for the Queen. They grabbed any council member or lady attendant who got in their way and held their swords to their throats, demanding to be told where the Queen was. The young lady attendants, too afraid to say a word, would faint and be tossed aside, their clothes torn. Jin saw the Russian electrical engineer Sabatin shaking his head, the point of a sword poised at his throat. Geoncheonggung was unfamiliar to Jin. Trembling, she ran past Sabatin and the *rōnin*. She came across the King, who was surrounded by even more long-haired *rōnin*.

—Where is the Queen!

The King said he knew nothing. The Crown Prince ran up to the *rōnin* and stood before the King, facing the *rōnin*.

—What's the meaning of this!

His voice could barely be heard in the chaos.

—Tell us where the Queen is.

—We don't know!

The veins in the Crown Prince's neck stood out. A Japanese officer gestured with his chin, and a *rōnin* brought a sword to the Crown Prince's throat.

—Tell us where that bitch is!

The King closed his eyes. He bit his lip and lowered his hands. He intuited that the Japanese had invaded the palace to murder the Queen. But the King believed in her. If she could escape this chaos, just as she did in the Year of the Black Horse, she would survive. He needed to buy her time.

—We'll tell you where she is.

The King firmly pointed in the opposite direction of her bedchamber. The *rōnin* immediately flocked toward where he pointed.

—Sign this.

The Japanese officer shoved an expulsion order before the King.

—What's this?

The King knew very well that it was an expulsion order for the Queen, but he pretended to puzzle over it. The Japanese officer kept insisting he sign it. When he hesitated, a *rōnin* pressed down on the King's shoulder with the blunt back-edge of his sword. The King still refused, and another *rōnin* went behind him and grabbed the back of his robe.

The King was too overwhelmed to feel humiliated.

Even as his dragon robes were grabbed and his crown fell to the ground, he thought of only one thing. As the *rōnin* pressed him down to the ground with the blunt side of his sword, all he hoped for was that the Queen had somehow safely escaped the palace.

—Over there!

The *rōnin* surrounding the King began to rush toward the Queen's chamber. *No.* The King tried to move, but two *rōnin* restrained him. The King's face twisted in anguish. The Crown Prince blocked them, but they roughly pushed past him, stepping on his body in their hurry. The Crown Prince, his clothes torn, got up and ran after them. The crazed *rōnin* tossed or kicked aside the court ladies guarding the Hall of Precious Rest. A sword point found its way before Soa's throat.

—Tell us where the bitch is!

Soa was shaking so hard she could barely open her mouth to reply, so a *rōnin* struck her on the back, felling her. The court ladies being dragged out by their hair to the courtyard of the Hall of Precious Rest were too terrified to make a sound. All that could be heard were the heavy footsteps of the *rōnin* and their incessant shouting for the Queen. Jin found Soa and was helping her to her feet when Soa suddenly shot her arm out, shielding Jin. A *rōnin*'s swinging blade cut into Soa's arm. Jin could barely give voice to the scream that exploded inside her. She frantically shook Soa, trying to keep her conscious, and the *rōnin* stared at Jin's short hair and Western dress before giving her a dismissive kick and running off.

—The Queen will be with her senior lady attendants!

Jin, her arms around her friend, looked up at the sound of this voice. A woman in a kimono was pointing the *rōnin* to the bedchamber. It was So Chonsil's daughter, who had smiled beside the Queen during the throwing game. She handed out pictures of the Queen to the *rōnin*. The scores of *rōnin* rushed toward the direction she had pointed to. Just as Jin was about to lower Soa and run to the bedchamber herself, she felt the finger of So Chonsil's daughter tilt her chin up toward her.

—It's you. Look at yourself. I can't tell if you're a man or a woman.

Jin slapped away her hand and roughly grabbed a handful of her kimono. So Chonsil's daughter cackled, her narrow eyes full of mirth.

—When this is over, why don't we play a throwing game near the Pagoda of Far-reaching Fragrance?

Jin shoved her hard. So Chonsil's daughter stumbled like a marionette, but quickly righted herself and stood before Jin face-to-face. Jin pushed her again, but So Chonsil's daughter only tilted a little before shoving her face back in front of Jin's. She was like a tumbling doll, righting herself no matter how hard Jin pushed her, blocking her way.

—I'll kill you!

Jin threw a handful of Soa's blood into the eyes of So Chonsil's daughter. So Chonsil's daughter brought her hands to her face, smearing the portraits of the Queen in her hands and scattering them on the ground. Her strange laugh haunted Jin's ears as Jin raced into the inner chambers in search of the Queen.

The *rōnin* were throwing open every door.

Their faces were red and quaking with fury.

Every woman in the chambers had the same braided hair tied up, the same indigo skirt, jade-green tunic, and green jacket, the uniform of the senior court ladies. They even had identical large hairpins inserted into the back of their hair, their eyes full of fear and hatred. In the moment the *rōnin* briefly paused before this phalanx, the Crown Prince ran through them to stand before the door of the innermost chamber, blocking it. The *rōnin* pushed him aside and charged into the chamber. Despite the portraits, all the women sitting inside looked the same in their eyes. They had no way of telling which was the Queen. Jin, who had made it to the doorway, locked her bloodshot eyes with Lady Suh, sitting in the back row.

—Which one of you is the Queen!

The *rōnin* held the point of his cobalt blade before the court lady who sat in front.

—Speak! Which one of you is the Queen!

When the court lady before him closed her eyes, he thrust his sword into her throat. Jin fell to her knees. She crawled through the *rōnin* toward the slumped court lady, whose blood had sprayed all over the floor. Was this barbarity a nightmare or was it really happening? Was it possible that the chambers of a queen could be desecrated like this? "Stand back, stand back, stand back!" The shouts exploded from deep within Jin. On her knees, she commanded them, then implored, but the *rōnin* kicked her aside. The only woman in the chambers who clearly was not the Queen was Jin, as she had short hair and was in Western dress, the dress that was blue as water. The *rōnin* brandished their swords at the court ladies who sat the closest to them.

—You!

Her throat was cut.

—You!

Her throat was cut.

—That one will know!

This was shouted by So Chonsil's daughter, who had just entered the chamber, her face thickly smeared with Soa's blood, her finger pointing to Jin. One side of the treacherous girl's face was twisted in pain from having to betray the Queen who had so loved her. The eyes of the court ladies turned in unison to Jin. The bloodshot eyes of the Queen wavered in Jin's dark pupils.

—Which one is the Queen! Point to her!

A *rōnin* held his sword to Jin's throat. The Prince, who had been knocked to the floor, stood up and blocked one of the *rōnin*. The Minister of Palace Affairs Lee Kyung Jik interposed himself between the Prince and the *rōnin*. Without hesitation, the *rōnin* pierced Lee Kyung Jik's belly with his sword, twisting left to right, right to left. Blood poured onto the floor. Lee Kyung Jik's body was kicked aside, as the *rōnin* raised the blunt side of the sword above the Prince's head. The women clung to each other in terror.

—Desist, you filth!

Just as one of the court ladies stood up, another ran toward the Prince. It was Lady Suh. The sword that had been pointed at Jin now swung toward Lady Suh. The other *rōnin*'s sword struck the prince's head, knocking him unconscious, his crown rolling on the floor. "This cannot . . . this cannot be!" It was the cry of the woman who had stood up when the Prince was being threatened. She turned and ran out of the chambers through the back. So Chonsil's daughter pointed at the woman. The *rōnin* who had trained their weapons at Lady Suh shouted, "That's the Queen!" And followed suit. The court ladies crowded after them. An elderly court lady blocked the *rōnin* and shouted, "I am the Queen!" Her throat was cut. Jin was now among the court ladies, getting hit by the sword blades, kicked, and pushed aside with the others, but she still managed to run with the crowd. *Please be safe, please be safe* . . . Her consciousness was slipping, but she willed herself alert, opening her eyes wide. The *rōnin*, who had pursued the Queen to the lawn of an adjacent wing, grabbed her and threw her to the ground. Jin felt her knees give way, her body falling forward. One of the *rōnin* kicked her roughly as he rushed past. Jin tried to crawl toward the Queen, but her arms were seized and held together behind her back. It was So Chonsil's daughter, snickering, but with a dazed expression. Jin's dress was torn from behind, revealing her bare back. In the midst of her struggle to break free, she glanced up and what she saw made her blood turn to ice. Lady Suh, who had followed the Queen to the last, was impaled in the back with a sword. And in the next moment, that same sword was lifted again and plunged into the Queen's heart. Movement in Jin's eyes stopped, and crimson blood flowed from them.

7

A Bird with No Feet

The woman Suh paused before she stepped into the Banchon house. A house falls quickly into disrepair without a constant human presence. The house had looked abandoned ever since Jin began locking herself up in it. The courtyard was overrun with weeds, and dead leaves from the year before tumbled about with no one to sweep them. The vegetable patch, once the first thing to be turned and cared for in the spring, lay neglected off to the side.

Only the flowering apricot tree looked as it always had, standing alone in the courtyard. The woman Suh pushed open the low gate, which hadn't been opened since she last closed it ten days ago. She knew there would be no response, but she called out anyway. She knocked the dust off her shoes. Her voice echoed through the emptiness. Suh went into the kitchen first. Just as she suspected, the furnace showed no sign of having been lit. Suh poured water into the cauldron above it, lit a fire, and rubbed her eyes. She stared at the red flames. Her hair had gone completely white. It had happened when she heard news of the Queen's death, along with that of her younger sister, Lady Suh. Days after the incident, the woman Suh had found Jin lying unconscious in the quarters of Lady Lee, who used to take Jin to and from the palace every day when Jin was a child in service of the Dowager Consort Cheolin. Suh's back had bowed permanently after carrying the bloodied Jin back home. The knuckles of Suh's fingers as they grazed the cauldron were thick and calloused. When she discerned that the cauldron was hot enough, she pushed more kindling into the furnace and closed the furnace gate. She stretched her back and opened the door to Jin's room. Just as she had for the past few days, Jin ignored everything that was going on around her, remaining in the fetal position underneath her blanket. Had she written a letter? A letter lay near her pillow. Suh entered the room and slid her hand underneath the bedding. Jin was in what would be the warmest position in the room, but the fire had not taken effect yet. She picked up the letter. Victor's name was written on it. Jin opened her eyes. She blinked as if the sunlight coming through the paper screen doors was too much for her. Suh spoke.

—The apricot tree bloomed. Did you see it?

Jin hadn't eaten for days, and her eyes were sunken. Not a trace of pink could be seen on her haggard cheeks. Her hair was a mess of tangles. Jin tried to get up, and Suh helped her lean against a wall. The once firm nape of her neck was listlessly leaning to one side as well as peeping out of the lowered shoulder of her dress. Suh stared at her, then removed the patchwork covering of the bowl of congee she had left before. It was uneaten. Suh got up and fetched the congee she had made in the orphanage before coming to Jin. It was thick, having been properly cooked for a long time. Jin did not take it. Suh tried to coax her but then put the bowl back on the table.

—Is it death you want?

—. . .

—Is it?

—. . .

—If you do this, I shall stop eating as well.

—. . .

—I shall.

Tears flowed down Jin's dry face.

—There was nothing you could have done. Everyone thought the Queen had fled somewhere by then. Who would have known she'd be killed in such a manner? The King sought refuge in the Russian legation.

Suh brought another spoonful of congee to Jin's lips.

—Just a little. If you don't eat, I will not eat either, from this day forward.

—. . .

—Just a little . . . just one spoonful . . .

As soon as the morsel made its way into Jin's mouth, she retched.

Jin's body, so tormented, was refusing even congee.

Suh consoled Jin, who managed to down a few spoonfuls before she started retching again. Suh fed, and Jin retched. Eventually, Suh gave up. The hand that wiped Jin's mouth with a piece of folded linen was trembling, and the wrinkles of concern on her forehead were deep. A strange smell floated in the room.

—Open the door.

Suh opened the door. There was still a chill, but the clear, transparent spring sun shone upon the porch. A spring breeze entered the room. Jin gazed at the apricot blossoms for a while, and then pulled at Suh's hand.

—Mother . . .

Suh looked in Jin's eyes.

—Take me . . . take me to the palace.

Suh was silent. Jin seemed to be looking at the blossoms, but Suh realized there was nothing in Jin's eyes. Those eyes would have seen the Queen being stabbed three times by the *rōnin*'s sword, her body trampled beneath their feet.

—There is nothing . . . There is nothing in the palace.

Suh's throat constricted. Not only was there no Queen, but no Lady Suh, not even Soa. Even the King had abandoned the place.

—Take me there.

Suh brought a bowl of lukewarm water to Jin's lips. Jin grasped it with both hands and drank it all down. She handed it to Suh and tried to smile.

—Must you go there?

Jin nodded.

—We have to call a palanquin. You can't walk there in this state. I shall put a word in to Lady Lee and see if she'll grant you entrance.

—Now.

"Now?" Suh repeated the word, and Jin nodded again.

—Would you like me to comb your hair?

Jin nodded. Suh opened a low dresser with a peony engraved on it. She was about to take out a comb, but Jin pointed to the brush. The brush with a rose on it, a gift from Victor. How he had loved to brush her hair with it. Suh gently sat Jin in front of her and handled this strange foreign thing through Jin's dry hair.

—Mother.

Suh stopped brushing and tilted sideways to catch Jin's face.

—Please give that letter to Paul Choi at the French legation.

—. . .

—He said Victor was coming back to Korea in a few days. You must give it to him before then.

Suh's eyes grew wide.

—But why would he ever come back?

—He's been reappointed as the legate to Korea.

—Will you see him again?

—No . . . I can't.

—. . .

—You must give Paul Choi that letter.

Suh was about to say something but thought better of it and left to call a palanquin. Jin sat alone and opened one of the dresser drawers to take out a linen package. She unwrapped it. Inside was a jade-green jacket and indigo skirt, and the red ribbon for her hair. The court lady uniform she wore when she left the palace to visit the legation. She had walked out of the palace in this, not knowing she would never return to live there. On top of it was the yellowing, handwritten French-Korean dictionary that Blanc had used to teach Jin French. She remembered how Victor had silently watched her packing it, the first thing she packed for her return to Korea. Jin had followed his stare and gazed at it herself before putting it away in another package. She examined her old court lady clothes. If she had worn these, she would be with the Queen now. The *rōnin* had pushed Jin aside, but they did not dare kill her. She couldn't bear the guilt of having survived when Lady Suh and Soa had been killed. Jin took off her dress and put on the court lady attire, beginning with the inner garment. She braided her lusterless hair and secured it into knots with the red ribbon, the hairstyle she and Soa did for each other every morning during their days at the Embroidery Chamber. No matter how she tried now, her brittle hair refused to stay neat, with strands that persisted in poking out of the knots.

Suh, who had come back from calling a palanquin, regarded Jin with worried eyes.

Having lost the Queen, the King spent his nights in terror and anxiety before abandoning the palace in February. Sneaking past the Japanese forces training in front of the main gate, the King rode in a palanquin reserved for court ladies into the Russian legation. The Crown Prince escaped with him. The palace, having lost its owner, was a hollow shell of its former glory. Where had all the courtiers gone? Japan declared the Regent responsible for the events of that night, claiming he had conspired with the disgruntled new army to drive out the King and Queen. They spread a rumor that the Queen had fled the palace. They made the King sign an expulsion order for the Queen and made him decree that men's hair was to be cut short. When the King became the first to cut his hair, people on the streets wept in humiliation. The Russian electrical engineer Sabatin and America's General Dye, who was staying at the palace, bore witness to what had really happened there, but Japan continued to deny the Queen's death. The palace could not even hold her funeral. Aside from a few scholars silently protesting with their heads shorn before the Gate of Greeting Autumn, demanding the King's return and an end to the haircutting decree, the environs of the palace were silent. Jin saw one of the Japanese soldiers give something to the woman Suh. The soldiers did not closely question their business. It was like entering an empty house.

Suh wandered through the palace, looking for Jin.

Even with the King gone, Suh had dared not enter the palace as she pleased. She thought she could at least get some form of permission from Lady Lee at her quarters, so she left Jin in a sunny spot to wait. But when she came back, Jin was gone. It was sunset by the time Suh and Lady Lee found Jin, on the hill behind Geoncheonggung. Months ago, So Chonsil's daughter, who held on to Jin as the Queen was being murdered, let her go only when they wrapped the Queen's body in a quilt and moved her to this hill. When Jin saw them throw the Queen's body on top of a stack of kindling and pour fuel over the pile before setting fire to it, she lapsed into unconsciousness. The next thing she could remember was waking in Lady Lee's quarters. They could not find Soa's body, who had fallen near the Hall of Precious Rest, or the remains of the valiant Lady Suh. If Lady Lee had not found Jin lying half-conscious on the hill and spirited her away on her back, there was no telling what would have become of her as well. The *rōnin* wanted to throw the Queen's charred bones into a pond, but Jin heard that someone got to the remains first and buried them somewhere in the palace, prompting her to go digging for the Queen's bones.

Lady Lee tried to help Jin stand up. They were beside that very spot where the Queen had been burned on that terrible night. Jin asked in a whisper to be taken to the Queen's Chambers. Lady Lee told her that there was no one in the Queen's Chambers. Jin insisted. In the end, just as she had done countless times twenty years ago when Jin was in service to the Dowager Consort Cheolin, Lady Lee carried Jin on her back down the hill and into the main court and set her down at the Queen's Chambers. That was four days ago.

Lady Lee came up to the woman Suh, who sat before the Gate of Dualities.

The Queen's Chambers had stood empty for some time. Ever since the Queen moved her sleeping quarters to Geoncheonggung, the Queen's Chambers had lost its vitality, and a chill had descended upon the building. Once, the Gate of Dualities had been practically worn down from all the visitors passing through it, but now there were weeds sprouting everywhere. There the Queen's Chambers sat, neglected, in the early spring sunshine.

—Is she still . . .?

Suh nodded her head. Jin had refused to leave the Queen's Chambers since entering them four days ago.

—What is she doing in there?

—She's touching the things that are still in there.

—They say the soul of the Queen is haunting the Queen's Chambers. But it's just us court ladies at the palace now . . .

Such rumors were only natural, seeing how someone had entered the Queen's Chambers and refused to leave.

The lonely wind swirled around the Queen's Chambers.

Suh and Lady Lee entered the compound to look for Jin. For four days, Jin had passed her hands over every surface of the Queen's Chambers as if to memorize the space, but today she sat across from where the Queen would have normally sat. Her head was bowed as if she were listening to someone, and her lips would move on occasion as if to speak. She had shrunken so much that she looked like a child.

Lady Lee teared up.

—How could she go on like this? Does she eat anything?

—Only water.

They saw Jin slump forward onto her elbows. Lady Lee pulled Suh away.

—Go to my quarters and eat something and rest. Nothing can be done for her now.

Jin felt through her very bones the sound of the two women opening the door of the Queen's Chambers and closing it behind them. Just as she had wished, her body was weakening. The eyes that had watched the Queen being killed were getting weaker, but strangely enough, her hearing was finer than ever before. She could hear everything, from the sound of birds landing on the ancient pine of the empty palace to the rocks being idly thrown against the stonework of the King's well by the patrolling Japanese soldiers.

—I cannot live.

Jin, unmoving, murmured toward where the Queen would have sat.

—I cannot die.

Jin's face twisted in pain.

—I cannot live, or die . . . What must I do?

Her strength had left her, and she could barely see, but she clearly remembered the night she spent in the Queen's Chambers after returning from Paris, when the Queen woke up and lit her own cigarette and whispered the deepest worries of her soul.

—Do you sleep?

Jin lifted her head at the sound of the Queen's voice. The voice sounded like it came from nearby, but she saw only the chilly dimness of the Queen's Chambers about her. Jin realized that the voice had been the Queen's from that night she had slept by her side. She regretted having pretended to sleep that night. Why had she allowed the Queen to become so lonely?

—My poor lady . . .

Tears moistened her dry eyes.

—My poor lady . . .

The tears welled up from inside her. Was it spring, or autumn, when the Queen brought a young Jin, lost and wandering through the palace, to this very room? Memories of time and the seasons were fading. The hands that lifted the fruit knife and cut a circle along the top of the pear . . . She had scraped the moist flesh of the pear with a spoon and fed it to her. *Is it good? Do you like it?* The Queen, taking no heed of the juice dripping on her silk sleeves, filling the spoon again and again, the mouthfuls of sweetness.

—Your Majesty. My poor lady.

Jin swallowed as if she had a mouthful of sweet pear. The moment she had seen the queen felled by the sword, she had realized that she saw the Queen as her true mother. That the Queen was not someone who was difficult to look in the eye, but a mother, kind and strong and powerful. Which was why, despite Jin's disappointment and resentment, she could not help but love her.

Jin managed to stand up and do a deep bow before the seat of the Queen.

Uncertain on her feet, she started to step slowly about the floor.

The final part of the Dance of the Spring Oriole. When she spread her arms, she could see the banquet before her like in years past. The years when she knew without looking that the sound of the *daegeum*, melting into the spreading of her sleeves like wings or her serene and contemplative look as if to a beautiful flower, was Yeon's. In her years as a court lady where she lived day to day in fear of what would happen to the palace and the country, she managed to be truly free only while dancing. She could feel love, or the breeze on her skin, joyful praise, the falling flower, the flowing water. How could she have known that the last time she properly performed this dance was for the Queen, the night before she left for Paris? Where did she find the strength? Jin could barely stand at first, but now she finished the dance in careful form, gathered her breath and her hands, and stepped away from the stage.

The cold spring sunlight prickled her eyes as she left the Queen's Chambers. She held in her arms the linen parcel she had brought with her four days ago and gazed past the roof of the Queen's Chambers to the Dowagers' Chambers in the north. It was where Dowager Consort Cheolin had taught the young Jin about the *chun, gwi, man, su, nak* characters engraved on the patterned wall. She recalled the sadness and patience in the young dowager consort's face as she voiced the characters for her.

Jin walked toward the back gardens of the Queen's Chambers where the Queen would often stroll with her court lady attendants. The once-beautiful Amisan Hill, made from the earth dug up during the construction of the pond surrounding the Pavilion of Festivities, was overrun with weeds. The balance of various trees and flowers that had created a lush tableau was no more. Only faraway Baekaksan Mountain looked gloomily down at the hill where no one dared tread. Dead leaves from the year before tumbled into the Pond of Sunset and the Moon-Bearing Pond. A white and yellow cat, once taken care of perhaps by a court lady, sunned itself on the hill, and sprinted away at the sound of Jin's footsteps. Having listlessly wandered through the palace, Jin sat down on a white rock surrounded by overgrown weeds and leaned her back against a stone lantern. The cat stopped underneath the ancient pine near the Queen's Chambers and looked back at Jin. The former court dancer unwrapped the linen package to reveal the French-Korean dictionary transcribed in Blanc's hand. She placed it on her knees.

—Forgive me.

Tears flowed from her eyes.

—Forgive me.

She repeated these words, not knowing to whom they were addressed. She began tearing off the yellowed pages of the dictionary and putting them, one by one, into her mouth. The Queen's death, brought upon by the *rōnin*'s blade, her body wrapped in a blanket and burned on a pyre in secret—to the world, it was only rumor. Despite having seen, with their own eyes, the *rōnin* ripping open the Queen's inner garment and the sword plunging into her heart three times, they all spoke of the Queen as if she were still alive. No funeral was held. The King was forced to divest her of her title. As rumors of the circumstances surrounding the Queen's death were being whispered throughout the country, Jin obtained arsenic from the palace apothecary, and in her Banchon room, wearing her Western dresses one over another, she had smeared the arsenic on the yellowed pages of her dictionary. Her shivers refused to cease. Between the French words that she had studied as a little girl, her cheeks flush with youth as she bent over the pages, now lay the poison that would soon stop her breathing forever.

—This is the only way.

As Jin tore the pages out one by one and stuffed them in her mouth, she grimaced at first but was soon firm in her task. She almost smiled. Somewhere from the other side of her wavering thoughts came her memories of the streets of Paris. She remembered Yeon's face as he listened, completely absorbed, to her telling of the tale of *The Hunchback of Notre Dame.* In one of his final letters to her, found inside the Banchon house, he had written that he had tried to find something to compare his love for her, but his world was too narrow, and he never could find anything that would suffice.

A little while later, the woman Suh entered through the Gate of Dualities and went into the Queen's Chambers. She searched frantically for Jin. She found her leaning against a stone lantern in the back gardens of the Queen's Chambers, a spot overlooking Baekaksan Mountain. The cat that had run away from Jin toward the ancient pine had returned and was curled up at her feet. A tiny drop of blood trailed thread-like from her mouth, and her hands clutched fistfuls of torn paper. The early spring sunlight shone on the nape of her neck, and the torn pieces of paper scattered into the spring breeze, fluttering away.

They looked like golden butterflies, spreading their wings to the sun.

Epilogue

One winter evening in 1914, Paris . . .

Victor Collin de Plancy lit the fireplace. Back when he lived in this townhouse, he would begin his winter mornings before a fire drinking milk tea and reading the papers. When would he ever have such leisure again? He was ready to leave once he had burned the stack of things before the fireplace. The townhouse was one of the many that surrounded the square with the beech grove, houses built for the upper classes. The house didn't look so big from the outside, but Victor was overwhelmed by its four stories. He sometimes felt like the custodian of his dead father's foolish dreams. His mother had managed the house during the twenty years he lived in the East, and even when they could barely afford a housekeeper, his mother had refused to sell the place. Victor tossed some useless books and documents into the fire and sighed. He had lived frugally and worked hard but the house was exhausting his resources. As a young man, he had chosen a life that had taken him away from the burdens placed on him by his father, but now he found himself looking after his father's legacy, even after his mother passed away.

Victor was seized with melancholy as he tossed the useless things. Was it our fate to resemble the very things we hated? He had resented his father's ambition, but perhaps his life ended up being a continuation of it.

Europe, which extended its reach all the way to the Far East, was at war. A young Serb had sparked it by assassinating the Austrian archduke and his wife in Sarajevo. When it was discovered that this man was a Serbian agent, Austria declared war on Serbia. Russia, Serbia's Slavic ally, mobilized its troops against Austria in support, which led Europe into war. The world was a tangled mess of interests and allegiances. Germany joined Russia and Austria against France and Britain. The stoic Germans in their gray uniforms were pit against the boisterous French, singing their military songs, and the oddly gloomy British. The battle between them was destroying the continent's achievements in modern civilization. The war that began in the summer and produced hundreds of thousands of victims showed no signs of abating in the winter. With rumors flying that the Germans would march into Paris, all hopes ended for the war to be a short one. The killing continued without much awareness of what they were fighting for. Youth gathered at Les Invalides and paraded along the Seine, urging its citizens to take up arms. Parisians made themselves ready to evacuate at a moment's notice.

Victor was burning whatever he could not take with him, but something made him pause. Among his things was one of the Eastern books published by the Guimet Museum. The translation in Hong Jong-u's name. He turned to a page in the introduction. "Korea is situated between two of the most sailed oceans in the world and its shores are glimpsed by countless sailors, but it is also one of the least explored countries." Victor closed the book. He also found an old edition of *Le Figaro*. He looked at the date on the front page. 1910? Four years ago. Why had he saved that edition? Victor, his sideburns almost gray now, spread open the old newspaper. There was an article on the Japanese annexation of the Korean Empire. Victor stared at the words, *Korean Empire*. He remembered the morning he had read this paper. The "Korean Empire" moniker still sounded strange to him. This new incarnation had lasted no longer than the snow that falls in the evening and disappears before the sun rises the next day. He would always remember Korea by the name of its centuries-old reigning dynasty, Joseon. Four years ago, the headline had made him drop his teacup when he turned the newspaper page. He read the article three times. *So that's where I put this newspaper.* Victor frowned and threw it into the fire. The news that once made him break a teacup now fed the flames, which soon settled down again. Britain had welcomed the annexation, given how they disapproved of Russia's ambitions toward its southern neighbors. They thought it would stymie Russia's territorial expansion. Even America, which had just dynamited the last phase of the Panama Canal and opened it for business to steamships, welcomed the annexation, saying that it was for the good of the people of the Korean Empire. Russia, which once provided the Korean king with shelter in its legation, signaled its de facto approval of the annexation through the signing of the Treaty of Portsmouth. China was almost the only country that expressly disapproved, conscious of its sharing a direct border with Korea. As China predicted, Japan was petitioning Germany for the Shandong concession, using the unrest in Europe as an opportunity. With Korea established as its colony, Japan focused on obtaining the English and French rail and mining developments in China. Victor tossed the book Hong Jong-u had translated into the fire as well. As if to rid his mind of something, he hurriedly threw more documents and books into the fire, these objects that seemed so reluctant to depart.

—It snows.

Victor's wife entered, bringing him a teacup filled with milk tea.

—You still have so much left. This could take all night.

She placed the teacup and saucer on a table next to the fireplace and shook a box full of torn-up letters into the fire. A photograph that must have been wedged between the pages of one of the books fluttered to her feet. She picked it up.

—Who is this Oriental woman, Victor?

Victor gave a start. It was Jin. How could he have missed the photo? He had used one of his breaks during his later Korea posting to clean out the Oriental Room and donate the objects to the Guimet Museum. Anything else he found of Jin's, he sent to the woman Suh. This was at Suh's request. Then one day, he had plucked every single one of her photos from his albums and burned them. He thought he had burned them all.

—Who is she?

His wife asked again, as Victor seemed to have fallen into a trance. Her voice sounded as if it were coming from far away. Victor remembered carrying a concealed camera in his first audience with the King. He remembered meeting her for the first time on a bridge over the Silk Stream. *She followed the senior lady attendant with the blue shoes, and her dark eyes looked back at me.*

Victor fell into a rocking chair by the fireplace.

The memories overwhelmed him, of his pulling the camera string the moment his eyes met hers for the first time. Of his saying, in the heat of the moment, "Bonjour!" And her utterly natural reply: "Bonjour!" The friendliness of her regard, as if they were old friends. The official had urged him to keep walking, and when he looked back, he pulled the camera string once more as she also looked back, with those dark eyes that he thought he would never forget for the rest of his life.

—Are you crying, dear?

His wife was alarmed as she looked into his eyes.

Victor had written a final letter to Jin when he had been posted again to Korea from Morocco. He wrote that he was returning to Korea, but they could never return to the past. That he'd had time to think about them while he was in Morocco. That it wasn't just because of his mother's objections that he never married her, nor was it because he was afraid of rejecting his father's ambitions for becoming a nobleman. He wrote, honestly, that it was because of himself. As a diplomat, he lacked the will to defend his love for her. He was returning to Korea, but he could not return to their life together. *I love you, Yi Jin, but I must bury that love in my heart and return to Korea only as a diplomat.* He sent his letter, and after his difficult voyage back to Korea, the interpreter Paul Choi was waiting for him at Jaemulpo Harbor, waiting to tell him of Jin's fate. She had died only five days before he reached Korea. The letter she left him was a detailed testimony of what happened on the night of the assassination of the Queen, or Empress Min as she was later named. That was all. Victor had been too shocked to think about why Jin had chosen to die at the palace, or why she had smeared poison on the pages of her beloved dictionary to do it.

Regret shadowed the creases by Victor's eyes as he rocked in his chair.

Had Jin's dying wish been for Victor to let the world know exactly how Empress Min had died? Was that it? Was that why she wrote him a detailed account of the Empress's assassination and chose the palace, rife with weeds, to be the place where she took her own life? He had written that they could never go back to what they were, but he was devastated nonetheless when she didn't leave a single word for him in her final letter. That devastation made him tear it up without showing her words to anyone.

—You must have loved her.

His wife looked disappointed as she left the hearth.

Was he responsible for making her death meaningless? Aside from a few close friends, no one knew of her death, and she was soon forgotten. Once the King returned to the palace from the Russian legation, the country was renamed the Korean Empire. The Queen was posthumously given the title of Empress, with proper funeral rites observed. Victor heard a rumor of a man with no fingers who was found frozen to death before Jin's grave that winter, but he never visited her gravesite. Hong Jong-u, having returned from China, was said to have had the man with no fingers buried next to Jin. Victor tried to forget the woman who had refused to think of him in her hour of death. He had tried not to think of her for the ten years he'd lived in the land once called the Korean Empire, where he helped build a French school and cathedral.

He brought the photo of Jin to his cheek, warm from the light of the fire.

His memories of holding this photo to his heart, longing to see her again, came rushing up to him like the rough waves of the ocean. The days of standing underneath the phoenix tree and staring at the light coming from her room's window. Jin in the photograph was as beautiful as a butterfly that had briefly alighted on a trumpet creeper and was poised to fly off into the sky. But now he thought she was trying to tell him something through her dark eyes. She hadn't left him without a word; he realized with anguish that she had left him with countless words, but all this time it was he who had failed to understand them. He threw the photo from his cheek into the fire. As the red flames touched it, he thought he could hear her glad voice call out, *Gillin!* He looked back at the fire once more. There she was, standing on the Silk Stream bridge, turning back toward him, her eyes meeting his, the darkness in hers staring into the years of regret in his.

Victor stood up and went to the window. He swung open the windowpanes to the beech tree grove, and the cold, snow-flecked air rushed into the room.